To Love A Highlander

by

Donna Fletcher

Copyright

To Love A Highlander
All rights reserved.
Copyright © July 2017 by Donna Fletcher

No part of this publication may be used or reproduced in any manner whatsoever, including but not limited to being stored in a retrieval system or transmitted in any form or by any means, electronic, mechanical, photocopying, recording or otherwise without permission of the author.

This is a book of fiction. Names, characters, places, and incidents are either the product of the author's imagination or are used fictitiously, and any resemblance to actual persons, living or dead, business establishments, events or locales is entirely coincidental.

Cover art
Kim Killion Group

Chapter One

Scotland, the Highlands, late 15th c.

Espy stared at the blood that soaked her hands. This was not right. This should not have happened. Things had been going well... she shook her head. Something was wrong. She had fought to save the woman and the bairn. Her grandmother had told her once that sometimes you had no choice, death came for everyone. Espy did not like to surrender and she fought death at every turn. After all, that was what a healer, a wise woman, did—she battled death. And Espy did not like to lose.

"You must leave. There is no more you can do for her and Lord Craven will blame you for his wife and child's death. Hurry, please," the woman begged. "He will show no mercy."

"I cannot leave her like this, Britt. She must be cleaned and—"

"No," Britt said. "He will see you punished in the most horrible ways, then see you suffer a slow death. You have to leave."

Espy's grandmother had warned her about Craven, Chieftain of the Clan MacCara. He was a beast of a warrior, large and powerful, and he ruled with a mighty fist. Everyone had been surprised when the gentle Aubrey, from the bordering Clan MacVarish became his bride. Some believed the loving and kind young woman tamed the mighty beast. Others believed the beast could never be tamed and waited in fear of his escape.

Lord Craven had left this morning on a hunt with his friend Dylan and Edward MacPeters, the physician he had brought from Edinburgh to tend his wife when her time came. His wife Aubrey had not been due for another month, but the bairn had thought differently. A messenger had arrived at Espy's grandmother's cottage insisting that Espy, a healer schooled in more than the wise ways, hurry to the keep. That Lady Aubrey needed her. She had been concerned that the bairn was arriving early, but she had managed such births before with much success. Yet all of her learned skills had not helped her to save Aubrey and her bairn. And now Lord Craven would return soon to find his wife and unborn bairn dead. It was not right. It should not have been.

Espy's eyes turned wide when she saw a slight movement in Aubrey's rounded stomach. The bairn was still alive. There was a chance to save it.

"I need a knife," Espy cried out.

Britt's eyes rounded with shock and fear.

"The bairn still lives. I need to deliver him," Espy explained.

"Lord Craven will see you drawn and quartered if you split his wife open," Britt warned.

Espy cared nothing for what might happen to her. She had to save the bairn. She rushed and got a knife from her healing basket and hurried to expose Aubrey's stomach. She had to be careful, if she cut too deep she could harm the bairn. Her hand was steady when she placed the knife to Aubrey's naked stomach, though she trembled inwardly, and she said a silent prayer to please let the bairn live.

Her wrist was suddenly grabbed and she was viciously torn away from her task. "What are you doing, woman?"

Espy fought the short slim man. "The bairn lives. I need to deliver him."

"Have you not done enough?" the man screamed at her.

She fisted her free hand and punched the man in the nose. He yelled, grabbed his face, and stumbled back. She hurried toward the bed, but before she could reach Aubrey another man grabbed her from behind.

"You have killed Lady Aubrey, is that not enough?" the tall man yelled.

Espy pushed at the strong arm around her waist. "Please, please let me free the bairn from her. There is a chance he could live."

With blood spewing from his nose, the man she had hit spoke up with difficulty. "She is a mad woman. Just look at what she has done. Look at the blood on her hands! I am a physician. I know of what I speak."

Espy turned wide eyes on the man and pleaded, "If you are a physician, then you know there is a chance that the bairn could survive. Please! Please! We waste time. Please cut her open and take the bairn."

A vicious roar reverberated through the room and the man holding Espy suddenly shoved her behind him. A man of towering height and thick with muscles consumed the doorway. His dark eyes raged with fury and pain, and he descended on the room and on those within like a beast of prey ready to devour everything in his path. He went directly to the bed and stared down at Aubrey who looked as if she slept, but the blood-stained bedding spoke the truth.

Lord Craven turned to the man who claimed himself a physician. "I brought you here so that nothing would happen to her. Do something."

"There is nothing I can do. She is gone, my lord."

"But not the bairn," Espy called out. "Please, let me save the bairn."

"She butchered your wife," the physician accused, swiping the only clean cloth left in the room off the chest beside him to stifle the blood running from his nose. "She will do the same to your bairn if you let her. The bairn is dead. It cannot live once the mother dies."

"It can for a short time and you are wasting that precious time."

"She speaks nonsense," the physician said. "Look at what she has done to your precious wife. She has made her suffer the torments of hell."

"And if it is not nonsense, you do nothing as the bairn dies," Espy pleaded and watched how gently the large man cradled his wife against his chest, his eyes squeezing tight, the pain too much for him to bear.

"Do not listen to her. She butchered your wife while she lived and now she wants to butcher her in death."

Lord Craven's large hand moved down along his wife to rest on her rounded stomach, and Espy prayed he would feel his bairn move. His silence was louder than any words he could speak as was his hand that remained still.

They had wasted precious time. The bairn was dead. Espy silently cursed the physician. She wanted to rage with anger at his ignorance, but it would do no good. The man who held her, who had pulled her out of the path of Lord Craven, tugged at her now. When she turned her head to look at him, he nodded toward the door and urged her along.

"Do not dare take her from this room, Dylan!"

Espy felt her skin prickle with fear as the deep bellowing voice roared through the room, and the man holding her released her quickly and surprisingly stepped in front of her.

"Step away from her," Lord Craven ordered so sharply that it sent a shiver through the room.

The man went to speak.

"I will not tell you again, Dylan," Lord Craven warned.

Dylan stepped aside reluctantly.

Lord Craven held his wife close against him, pressed his cheek, stained red with heated anger, to her cold one, then gently kissed her lips. "My love, my heart, and my life go with you, Aubrey."

He laid her head tenderly on the pillow, brushing a strand of her dark hair off her face to tuck behind her ear, an intimate gesture shared between husband and wife. He stared at her as though he waited for her to move, to speak, to open her eyes... to breathe.

He turned his head slowly toward Espy, then he flew across the room as if he had wings. His large hand grabbed her around the throat and with brutal force he slammed her high enough against the wall for them to be face to face, leaving her feet dangling several inches above the floor.

Pain shot through her back and head and for a moment her vision blurred and she thought he had knocked the breath out of her. Then she realized it was his hand squeezing at her throat that left her unable to breathe. Her hand shot to his, ripping at his fingers that were choking the life from her, but it did little good. The thick muscles along his arm were taut with such strength that she would never be able to budge him.

"I will have your life for what you did!"

His voice was a roar in her ears as she felt her life draining away. She heard voices yelling at him over and over. She could not understand what they shouted, but they did not stop.

Suddenly, she dropped to the floor and gasped loudly when breath was finally restored to her. She took great gulps like one so parched she could not get enough to drink. She winced, her breath barely recovered when she was abruptly hoisted off the floor, the grip on her arm feeling like an iron shackle pinching painfully at her skin.

"Leave my land and all the lands that surround me or I will see you tortured unmercifully before I make you suffer an unspeakable death." He shoved her so hard that she fell to the floor. "Get out of my sight before I do what Aubrey would not want."

Espy stumbled to her feet and went to speak.

"Say a word and I will cut out your tongue and eat it in front of you."

Espy turned and hurried out the door and out of the keep, the frightening glare in Lord Craven's dark eyes and his barbaric threat, proving he was more beast than man.

Chapter Two

One year later...

Cyra sat at a bench by the fireplace warming her hands. They had ached more than usual today, which meant only one thing, a storm was brewing. A crack of thunder had her jumping and confirming what her aching hands had already told her. But there was something else troubling her, though she could not understand what. More than a rainstorm was brewing and she worried what that might mean.

Another crack of thunder and wind rapping at the door had her getting to her feet and reaching for the crock of chamomile leaves. She would brew herself a cup of chamomile tea and crawl into bed early tonight. Her tired bones could use a rest. Besides, two women were soon to give birth and she would need her strength for both deliveries.

Espy.

Her granddaughter's name whispered like a soft wind around her. She missed her terribly. It had been a lonely year without her and Cyra worried how Espy had survived. She had had no one to turn to when lord Craven ordered her gone from his land and the surrounding land. Espy had come to stay a few short months prior to last year. Cyra still recalled the day Espy had shown up at her doorstep, exhausted and suffering from the loss of her parents. She had often spent time, through the years, with Cyra when her had parents traveled. Her father had been a physician who traveled in an effort to gain as much knowledge as he could and bring the most current medical practices to the people, even if it had meant going against the current acceptable practices and the physicians who extolled them.

In so doing, William of Inuerwyc had indulged his never-ending, curious daughter, Espy, with what he had learned. Inquisitive and as stubborn in nature as Espy was, she had combined her da's acquired knowledge with Cyra's knowledge, that had been handed down from all those before her, to form a vast wisdom of healing. Something that should have served her well, but had managed to cause her more harm than good.

Cyra wondered everyday over her granddaughter's whereabouts and safety, and she wished there was a way that Espy would be allowed to return home and remain here where Cyra could keep watch over her.

A soft smile surfaced on her face that had not aged as rapidly as most. She had some lines and wrinkles, but not many for her five decades, though her hair had turned completely white. She wore it in a single braid that more often than not rested on her chest. Her hands, gratefully, had not gnarled with age, though they ached with it. And she had maintained a fine posture, though of late she felt her shoulders more heavily burdened as did so many.

It seemed that when lord Craven's wife, Aubrey, died, life diminished for the clan. Life had become more burdensome, smiles were rarely seen and, worse, hope had all but vanished. Most believed with Aubrey gone that the beast of MacCara castle had once again been released, and Cyra was beginning to believe it was true.

Cyra winced when a sharp pain struck her hands and winced again when another crack of thunder sounded as if it split the earth in two.

A strange noise that followed the thunder had Cyra stilling to listen. Had she heard a horse approach? Who

would be foolish enough to ride in such a terrible storm?
Someone who needed help.

Cyra left the chamomile leaves to steep in the tankard while she went to the door. She was a healer and no matter the weather or how late the hour, she was available to all those who needed her. She opened the door, prepared to offer help and comfort. Her breath caught as her mouth dropped open and fear froze her in the open doorway.

A *kelpie* had come for her.

The large black horse's backward hoof pawed the ground impatiently as if demanding she step forward, and though the rain had yet to start, he was drenched from the river he had risen from. A demon sent to collect her.

It took a moment for Cyra to see that someone sat atop the beast. Had the *kelpie* brought her someone? Who could a demon horse have delivered to her door and why?

The person on the horse seemed unable to keep himself upright and he toppled to the side, falling to the ground. The beast of a horse grew angry and stomped the earth near the fallen body as if demanding Cyra see to his care.

Fearful the *kelpie* would do her harm if she did not bend to his command, she hurried to the crumpled body on the ground. It took a moment to untangle the cloak around the fallen figure and when Cyra was finally able to reveal a face, she gasped loudly and her heart slammed against her chest.

It was her granddaughter Espy.

"Horse. Shelter. Horse shelter," Espy muttered as Cyra fought to get Espy to her feet.

"After I get you inside, I will see to your horse."

"No. Now. A rainstorm follows. Needs shelter." Espy fought to raise her voice. "Go, Trumble, go with *Seanmhair*. She will not harm you."

It had been too long since Cyra had heard Gaelic roll off her granddaughter's tongue so easily and so lovingly. Though, the large beast of an animal frightened her, Cyra did as her granddaughter asked. She took hold of the reins and the beast snorted, but followed her as she guided him to the small barn that sheltered the cow and her mare. Both animals seemed none too pleased at the large animal's presence.

With trembling hands, she freed the horse of his saddle and blanket, realizing it had been a rainstorm that had drenched the horse and Espy, and no doubt would arrive here soon. She secured him in the only stall available, though she did not think that the rope she hooked across the front would stop him from going where he pleased. She grabbed the sack that had been attached to the saddle and hurried to her granddaughter.

Cyra struggled to get her granddaughter to her feet and inside the cottage, the rain having started to fall, dropping like sharp arrows from the sky. Once inside, Cyra hurried Espy to the fireplace to get her warm and out of her wet garments.

She could not stop her sudden cry of anguish when the fire's light fully exposed Espy's face. A scar ran down her right cheek. It was not a fresh scar, though it was recent, for it was still red and angry, still healing.

"Do not ask me now, *Seanmhair*, or ever," Espy whispered.

Cyra placed a gentle hand to Espy's scarred cheek. "You are home, Espy. I will let no one harm you." She would keep her word. Espy had exhausted herself to return home to her. But why when she knew what awaited her here? She did not know, but whatever it was, Cyra would keep her safe no matter the consequences.

It took time to get Espy out of her wet garments and into Cyra's soft white wool nightdress. Tears touched her eyes when she saw not only how slim she had gotten, but the bruises on various parts of her granddaughter's body. She had suffered a beating of some sort and Cyra wondered what else Espy had suffered, though she did not ask. That was better left for another time.

Espy almost collapsed when she tried to walk to the bed, and Cyra was quick to slip a strong arm around her and take all her weight upon herself as her granddaughter grew heavier against her. She eased Espy down to sit on the bed, then helped lift her legs so that she could stretch out.

"You will stay in bed and rest and heal," Cyra ordered, tucking the blanket around Espy as she had done so often when she had been a wee bairn. "While you do, I will prepare a brew to warm you."

Espy reached up, and gripped her grandmother's wrist. "He will come for me."

Cyra leaned down as she rested her hand over her granddaughter's. "I will let no harm come to you, Espy."

Espy gave a weak smile and shivered.

"You need to get warm." Cyra quickly got another blanket from the chest at the end of the bed and after she made certain it was tucked tight around Espy, she went and got the chamomile brew she had left steeping. She quickly discarded the crushed leaves and went and sat on the bed alongside, Espy. She placed the tankard to her granddaughter's lips and helped her to sip some of the brew. Espy drank eagerly and Cyra sat patiently, feeding her the brew until none was left and Espy's eyes had closed.

Rain pounded the cottage and thunder continued to roll over the land. It was when a crack of thunder sounded as if it had hit the cottage and sent a shiver so strong through Cyra that she collapsed to the chair growing ever fearful.

He knew. Somehow he knew.

The beast of MacCara castle knew that Espy had returned.

~~~

The morning woke without the sun. Grey clouds

lingered in the sky, though the rain had stopped. Cyra would have preferred the rain to continue, the downpour keeping people in their cottages and the beast confined to the keep. It would give her time to think of a way to convince Lord Craven that Espy should be allowed to remain with her. Though, the idea seemed senseless, Cyra had to try.

"*Seanmhair.*"

Cyra's worried thoughts evaporated upon hearing her granddaughter call out softly to her, and she hurried out of the chair by the fireplace and over to the bed. Espy looked much too pale or perhaps it was the fresh scar that forced such a ghostly color.

Espy slipped a weak hand from under the blanket and reached out to her grandmother as she approached. "I do not want to put you in harm's way."

"Worry not about me. It is you that concerns me," Cyra said and taking her granddaughter's hand and keeping tight hold of it, she sat on the bed.

"I had no place to go," Espy said a croak in her gentle voice as she tried to hold back her tears.

Cyra pressed Espy's hand to her chest. "You do have a place. It is here with me. It is your home."

They both heard the noise at the same time... the pounding of several hooves growing ever closer.

Espy's hand tightened around her grandmother's.

"Lord Craven will not take you from me again," Cyra said and eased her granddaughter's hand beneath the blanket. "You stay here and worry not." Espy went to speak, but Cyra placed her fingers gently to her lips, stopping her. "Not a word and stay where you are."

Cyra left her granddaughter's side and grabbing her worn wool shawl from the back of the chair, she went to the door, squared her shoulders, lifted her chin, then opened the door and stepped out, closing it behind her.

The sight that met her had her heart thumping madly

against her chest and fear rushing through her, quivering her limbs until she thought for sure her legs would crumble from under her.

Lord Craven could put fear in the devil himself. He had always been a large man, though he seemed to have grown larger since his wife had died, his muscles straining against the black shirt beneath his plaid. But then it was whispered that he worked his warriors senseless on the practice field each day and that he could often be found chopping down trees in the woods and hoisting the felled tree on his shoulder and carrying it without help. Cyra believed some of what she had heard was possibly true while others mere tales. Seeing lord Craven now, she wondered if perhaps it was more truth than tale.

"Is your granddaughter here, Cyra?" Craven demanded.

Cyra kept her courage strong, though it was not easy in the fierce warrior's presence. While he had the finest features she had ever seen on a man, there was a fiery anger in his dark eyes that made one want to step back and keep his distance from him. He wore his dark hair shorter than most men, it faintly brushing the tops of his shoulders, and pulled back tightly and secured with a pewter clasp, at the nape of his neck, that everyone knew had been a gift from Aubrey.

"Answer me!"

Cyra jumped at his snarling bark and her fear grew. He had six warriors with him. His intentions were obvious and Cyra worried that she would not be able to stop him from taking Espy from her.

"Espy is here and she is ill and needs tending," Cyra said, keeping her voice steady and clear, fighting down the tremble that threatened to break free.

"Tending is not necessary for the punishment she faces for returning here when I ordered her to stay off my land," Craven said and dismounted swiftly.

Instinctively, Cyra took a step back. She had forgotten how tall he was and with the added muscles, he appeared even more intimidating than usual.

"Did you think to keep her presence from me? Do you think I am ignorant of what goes on around me? I was alerted to her arrival as soon as she appeared on my land. Turn her over to me now or suffer the consequences," Craven commanded, his last few words a near roar.

Cyra knew she was sealing her own fate as she shook her head and said, "I cannot do that, my lord."

"Your granddaughter killed my wife and child. She deserves to suffer and suffer endlessly before she meets her death." Craven took a quick step toward Cyra. "And I will see that she does."

Cyra stood firm, fear quivering her limbs, but the need to protect her granddaughter keeping her strong. "Espy did all she could to save your wife and child. It was not her fault they died."

"The physician said otherwise and I will not stand here and argue with you. Get your granddaughter out here— NOW!"

Cyra gave a slight turn of her head as his warm breath struck her face, his words having been delivered with such force. She did the only thing she could think of... she pleaded for her granddaughter to be spared.

"Please, Lord Craven, have mercy on an old woman. Espy is all the family I have left. Please, I beg you, do not take her from me."

"Aubrey and our unborn bairn were all the family I had and your granddaughter took them from me. I will spare her not an ounce of mercy for what she took from me." Craven turned and signaled to his warriors and the six men dismounted and stepped forward. He raised his voice again. "I will not tell you again to bring her out here to me."

The door suddenly opened. "I am here."

Cyra turned to see Espy leaning heavily on the door and went to take a step toward her.

"No, *Seanmhair*, this is my fate to face," she said softly.

Cyra reached for her arm when Espy stumbled slightly as she took a weak step forward. Tears rushed to fill Cyra's eyes. She never felt so helpless in her life. Instinct had her stepping forward and wrapping her granddaughter in her arms. They would have to pry Espy away from her. She would not let go.

"Let her go, Cyra or I will rip her from your arms and care not what happens to you," Craven ordered.

Espy eased away from her grandmother, though not before pressing her cheek to hers and whispering, "I love you, *Seanmhair*."

Tears slipped down Cyra's cheeks as she watched her granddaughter approach Lord Craven.

Espy struggled to take each step and when she stopped in front of Craven, his face blurred, her legs lost what little strength was left in them, and only one word past her lips before her head fell on his shoulder and her body collapsed against him.

"Help."

Chapter Three

Craven's one arm caught Espy around the waist. She lay limp against him, her body feeling so frail in his arm that he thought his strength would snap her in two. Her nightdress had fallen off her one shoulder and he caught a glimpse of a bruise that extended part way down her upper arm. It appeared as if someone had taken hold of her there with a brutal grip. He also wondered about the scar on her face. With questions turning him curious, he yanked her limp body up as his other arm reached to slip beneath her legs.

"Please. Please, my lord, bring her inside," Cyra begged, fearful he would cart his granddaughter away to suffer and die.

Craven gave her words no heed. It was his curiosity that had him entering the cottage with a twist of his body and a dip of his head to fit through the doorway. Seeing the bed, he went to it and dropped Espy down on it. He wanted her out of his arms, away from him. Her warmth and vulnerability reminded him too much of how Aubrey had first felt in his arms, and he would not betray his deceased wife's memory by having such disloyal thoughts about the woman who had killed her.

He stared down at her body, appearing as lifeless as Aubrey's body once did. She seemed slimmer than he had remembered her, having barely felt the weight of her in his arms. She was deathly pale, leaving him to realize that Cyra had not been lying about her being ill. Her face had been seared in his memory. He would never forget it. He had not wanted to, since he had always regretted letting her live. He had hoped one day to meet her again and see that she got what she deserved for what she had done to the woman he loved beyond measure.

Seeing her face again and the scar she carried upon it, he wondered what evil she had brought upon another to have suffered such a wound. "What happened to her face?"

"I do not know. She has not spoken of it to me," Cyra said, wishing Craven would move away from the bed so she could tend her granddaughter. Espy's nightdress had slipped off her shoulder, exposing the top of her one breast and her one leg lay bare nearly to her thigh from being dropped carelessly on the bed.

Craven's glance drifted to Espy's bare shoulder and the bruise there that showed no signs of fading which meant she had gotten it recently. His eyes followed down the length of her to her exposed leg where he spotted two more bruises, neither of them showing signs of fading.

"She suffered a recent beating," Craven said.

"It appears that way, though she has spoken little since her arrival here last night."

"Get her well," Craven ordered as he turned away from Espy. "I want her to feel, down to her soul, everything I do to her."

Cyra hurried to close the door behind him after he stormed out of the cottage. She returned to her granddaughter's side and pulled the blankets over her. She needed to get Espy well and send her away before Craven could harm her.

The door flew open as she was tucking the blanket tightly around Epsy and Cyra turned, taking a protective stance in front of the bed when she saw the fury on Craven's face, not that shielding Espy would do much good, but instinct had insisted upon it.

"One of my warriors will remain here to see that Espy goes from your cottage to my dungeon."

Cyra jumped when he pulled the door shut with such

force that it shuddered the planks, and helplessness once again, descended on Cyra.

~~~

Craven barely brought his horse to a stop when he flew off him and up the steps to the keep, leaving a young lad, he did not even acknowledge, to tend the animal. The Great Hall was empty when he strode in and went to the table nearest the large hearth and filled a tankard with ale from the pitcher. He swallowed nearly all of it, then slammed the tankard down on the table to stand and stare at the flames.

When he took a step around the table toward the hearth, the flames seemed to retreat in fright just as most everyone did. He did not care. He had not cared since Aubrey died. Life was meaningless without her. Light and goodness had left him the day she had taken her last breath. And it was all Cyra's granddaughter's fault.

It continued to trouble him that Aubrey had preferred Espy to attend her at birth than the physician he had brought from Edinburgh. She had told him repeatedly that she had more faith in Espy's skills than the physician's. Aubrey had not known Espy long, Cyra's granddaughter having only arrived here a few months before Aubrey was to give birth. He had known of Espy, having seen her on occasion when she had stayed with her grandmother. But he had not known her well.

Craven turned and swallowed down the rest of the ale, then filled the tankard again. The image of his wife soaked in blood, her body limp in his arms, forever haunted his thoughts and produced nightmares that woke him until he hated the thought of going to sleep.

Help.

It was the very word that Aubrey would call out to him in his nightmares and he could do nothing to help her. Blood was everywhere and she would reach out to him, begging him to help her.

Craven turned away from the flames, grabbed the tankard, and threw it with such force into the fireplace that it bounced off the stones of the back wall, landing near Craven's feet.

"That one almost got you this time."

Craven did not turn around. He did not need to. He was aware of who had spoken to him... Dylan. They had been close friends since they had been wee bairns and they had fought together in many battles, though their friendship had suffered since Aubrey's death. Dylan's wife, Britt, had been a good friend of Aubrey's. She had also been the one to help Espy kill his wife and Craven could not forgive her.

Where once Dylan and he had spent much time together, they now kept a distance and only spoke when necessary.

"What brings you here Dylan?" Craven asked in no mood to speak with his onetime friend.

"I heard that Espy has returned and wondered over your plans for her."

"And if they included your wife?" Craven asked, turning a heated glare on him.

"Aye, since I have told you often enough that you will need to take my life before I will let you take hers."

"I ache to make all those suffer who made my Aubrey suffer so horribly, including that fool of a physician who did not remain close to my wife with her time being so near. But I will settle for the one person who was most at fault."

"You brought Espy here to the dungeon below?"

Craven shook his head. "Not yet. She has fallen ill and I want her well so her torture lasts longer before I finally see her blood drained from her as she did to Aubrey."

"Will torturing Espy and taking her life ease the pain of Aubrey's loss?"

"Nothing will ever ease that pain. It is mine to bear forever for failing to keep my wife safe," Craven said with a bitterness he could taste. "I have questions for Britt of that day and I will ask them in front of Espy."

"What good will it do for you to relive it? Punish the one responsible and be done with it, and let yourself live again."

Craven leaned down and scooped up the tankard and flung it at the fireplace again. "My heart died with Aubrey." He snatched the tankard up again where it had fallen near his feet and flung it into the fireplace again and when it flew back out, he threw it in again and again and again.

It was not until Craven had finished two pitchers of ale that he realized he had burned the palm of his hand. He did not care. He was glad for the physical pain. He preferred it to the endless pain of losing Aubrey. He wrapped the burn with a cloth and took himself off to the practice field.

~~~

Two days of bed rest and her grandmother's skilled care and Espy was feeling better, not completely but enough to venture out of bed.

"It will not be long before I am well," Espy said, having joined her grandmother at the table for a hot brew and porridge.

"Do not say that," Cyra warned, her voice low and her eyes darting to the door. "Lord Craven will come for you."

Espy sighed and cupped her chilled hands around the heated tankard to warm them. "It is time for me to face my fate, whatever it may be."

Cyra tried to make her granddaughter see reason.

Espy shook her head, stopping her. "I have no place to go."

"Higher in the Highlands where even the king will not

go—"

"No!" Espy shivered. "I have been there and I will not go back."

Cyra reached out, resting her hand on Espy's arm. "What happened to you?"

Espy shook her head again. "Do not ask me—ever."

Cyra nodded and patted her granddaughter's arm before removing her hand. In time, if by some miracle they should have it, Espy would confide in her just as she had done when she was young. When something happened, Espy would refuse to speak of it until she had time to think about it and reach her own conclusions, learn her own lessons. By the time Espy did speak with Cyra, she usually had the problem worked out and all she needed was to talk with someone about it. Unfortunately, Craven may rob them of that time.

"Cyra!"

Her name shouted in such distress had Cyra hurrying outside.

The warrior who Craven had left to stand watch was blocking a man from getting any closer to the cottage.

"Let him pass!" Cyra ordered sharply upon seeing it was Finley, the farmer whose wife was due to deliver their first bairn any day.

The warrior turned a glare on Cyra.

"You are here to prevent my granddaughter from leaving, not to stop those seeking my care."

Before the warrior could argue with her, Finley spoke up. "It is time. You must hurry. Eira is in great pain."

"I will get my things and be right with you." Cyra hurried inside and cast a worried look upon her granddaughter.

"Go. You are needed. I will be fine." Espy smiled, the first time since being home. "I only wish I was going with you."

Cyra wished the same, though she did not voice her

thought. She gathered her things, reminded Espy that she had seen to Trumble, her stallion, earlier and though she did not say it, she hoped she would return soon. Births, however, were unpredictable and it could take much longer than expected.

"Hopefully this wee one will deliver fast," Cyra said, after giving her granddaughter a hug.

"That will be up to the wee one. Keep your thoughts on the birth, not me. I will do fine."

Leave it to her granddaughter to do what she always did… think of others before herself.

Espy felt restless after her grandmother left. Not one to sit idle, especially feeling some of her strength returning, she got her sack, placed it on the table, and sat.

The sack actually was an old worn cloak that she used to carry her few meager belongings. One of her most cherished possessions was her da's drawings and writings. Her father had studied medicine at Queen Mary Barts and the London School of Medicine. He had followed his studies with extensive travel in search of various ways to better treat illnesses not normally ascribed to by current physicians. He was often ridiculed, his theories ignored, but Espy had seen proof of his work and frequently used his findings in treating the ill, which sometimes got her in trouble.

She unwrapped the ties that bound the piece of folded leather and felt a twinge of sadness upon seeing her father's precise handwriting. She missed her da and mum terribly, having lost them in a few months of each other. She had only her grandmother left and she wished with all her heart she could remain with her. This last year had been horrible, more horrible than she could have ever imagined. She wanted nothing more than to remain here and do what she loved… help heal people.

The crudely made book was a treasure trove of knowledge that she read again and again and one she added to whenever possible, which was not as near as often as she would have liked. She particularly loved her father's drawings of plants. He was meticulous in his detail so that there could be no mistake in the plant he was referring to and properties of the plant were specifically described.

She had read over her da's writings so much that she knew them by heart, but reading them again and again gave her insight to what else her father's findings might be able to help.

Her reading was disturbed by voices outside. Her grandmother could not have returned from a birth that fast. She listened and fear prickled her skin when she heard only male voices. She hurried to her feet and looked around for something to defend herself with when the door suddenly burst open.

Her breath caught, the gasp that rose up in her throat lodging there unable to escape. She had forgotten how large Craven was or was it that he had gotten even larger, his chest broader and his muscles thicker, since last she had seen him? He turned slightly to the side to enter, his shoulders too wide to fit through the door and he bowed his head, too tall to clear the opening. He was much handsomer than she remembered, but then he had been filled with fury when she had last seen him and squeezing the life from her. With him devoid of a fiery rage, she could see why the beautiful, petite Aubrey had fallen in love with the handsome Chieftain of Clan MacCara.

"Will Cyra return today?" he asked abruptly.

Espy noticed his wrapped hand. "You suffered a wound." Her instincts as a healer took over and she stepped forward. "I can see to it for you."

"You think I would let you touch me," he spat.

Espy kept her voice strong, refusing to show him any fear. "If it is a fresh wound you can wait for Cyra to return, though it may be a day or two since she is attending a birth.

But if you suffered the wound a day or so ago, I would advise you to wait no longer to have it tended."

The wound did not look good to him or to Dylan when he had seen it on the practice field earlier this morning. Dylan had urged him to see the healer and while he thought to let it go and let death take him, his responsibility to his clan and all his ancestors before him who fought to keep their land had him make the wiser choice.

"See to it," he ordered, sticking out his wrapped hand. "But know this, if you kill me, as you did my wife, this time you will suffer endlessly for it."

"I am sorry—"

"Do not waste your meaningless apology on me."

He stepped forward rapidly and was surprised she did not even flinch. "Never dare speak her name to me. Now see to my hand and be done with it before I use it to do what I should have done that day."

"Please sit," she said, keeping the fear that lingered near the surface at bay. She would not let it take hold of her. Clear thought and her healing skills would see her through this. She placed the pages of her da's crude book in the piece of leather and moved it to the bed. She then grabbed a bucket and went to the door.

"Where are you going?" Craven demanded.

"I need water from the rain barrel."

Craven stood and snatched the bucket from her hand. He opened the door and called out to the warrior. "Fill the bucket, Tass."

The young warrior hurried to obey Craven's command.

"You will not leave this place until I come to collect you," Craven ordered.

Espy nodded, having no trouble with his command since she had no place to go and besides, she was so very tired of running.

Craven returned to his seat and Espy took the bucket

from Tass and poured half the water into an empty bucket. She went to the narrow work table under the window to scoop up the lavender soap sitting in a broken piece of crockery and washed her hands in the one bucket, the lovely scent bringing back fond memories of time spent with her grandmother.

After drying her hands, she reached out for Craven's bandaged hand and he lifted it up to her. She was relieved to feel that his large hand was warm, but not heated, so there was no worry of fever being present. She tenderly unwrapped the cloth and almost winced when she saw the raw, red skin.

"You burned yourself."

"What does that matter, tend it."

She rested his hand on the table and went to gather what herbs she needed. She quickly cut up some chickweed and coltsfoot, took some animal lard from the crock her grandmother kept it in and added it all to the cauldron in the fireplace. While it simmered, she returned to tend to his hand.

Craven watched with interest as Espy worked. She appeared skillful in her task, not hesitating in any of her preparations and she remained focused like a warrior who went into battle with only one thing in mind... victory.

He also noticed that the nightdress she wore hung like a sack on her and when she stood in front of the fireplace, the flames highlighted her naked body beneath. She might be slimmer than he recalled but she was shapely, her hips curving nicely and her full breasts sizeable enough to spill over in his hands.

What the bloody hell was he thinking?

He had not thought that way of a woman since he wed Aubrey. She had been the only woman he wanted. The only woman he loved. The only woman he wanted to make love to. He wanted no other woman and no woman wanted him.

He was called the beast for a good reason and women ran from him in fright since Aubrey had died, and he did not care.

However, he did care that he had briefly felt a stirring for Espy as he had once felt for Aubrey, and anger bubbled inside him.

"Hurry and be done," he snapped.

"The burn would have healed with a smear of honey if you had sought the healer as soon as you suffered the burn. Now it will take more than a bit of honey to heal it. I need to cleanse your hand and the ointment I make will need to cool before I can apply it. The task cannot be rushed if you wish the wound to heal," Espy said.

"Then since we have time… tell me why you killed my wife."

Chapter Four

Espy felt his words strike her like an arrow to her heart. There was not a day that went by that she did not think of Aubrey and how she had failed to help her. No matter how many times she went over what had happened that day, it still made no sense to her. She was missing something, and she feared if she did not come to understand it, she would never be able to help another woman if it should ever happen again.

"I take responsibility for your wife's death, for I failed to help her, but I do not know what killed her and that troubles me." She reached for his hand and he pulled it away from her.

Craven hated that her voice was soft, thoughtful, and touched with sorrow, sounding as if she truly regretted what had happened to his wife. Then he remembered the physician's words. "When the physician learned who your father was, he claimed that you followed his irrational practices. He also informed me that many pure physicians believed your father was insane."

Espy did not hesitate to defend her father. "If by insane you mean that my father embraced all knowledge, all possibilities, all thought whether foreign or senseless so that he could help heal those who suffered, those in need of healing, then indeed my father was insane. He was the *wisest* of insane men."

Craven's temper flared. "So you did as your father did? Practiced your insane beliefs on my Aubrey?"

"I treated your wife no differently than the many other births I tended."

Craven stood and brought his face so close to hers that it looked as if he was about to kiss her. "So you have taken a knife to other women's bellies as your father had done?"

Espy could almost feel the intense hate and hurt wash over her that she saw in his eyes and no words of regret or sorrow she offered would make a difference. His hate for her ran far too deep. And with the way he loomed over her, his large body feeling as if it wrapped around her, ready to squeeze the life from her, put a rare fright in her more than she wanted to admit. She had learned to fight her fears and keep them at bay or she would have never survived this past year.

"Perhaps you should wait for my grandmother to return to tend your hand," she said, taking a step back, not that she got far. His arm snapped out, hooking her around her waist and yanking her against him. His body was taut with restraint even though he held her tight and though a twinge of fear rose up to poke at her, she kept it at bay. She held her tongue, knowing silence was best at times, but when she saw the sorrowful ache in his eyes, instinct as a healer had her laying her hand gently on his arm. "I meant no harm to your wife and I would have given my own life to have saved hers and your bairn."

Craven released her with a slight shove. "Such an apology is easy now since the deed is done." He sat and stretched out his hand. "Hurry and be done with it."

Espy did as he said, it best that she finishes quickly. She kept her thoughts on her task, cleansing his hand. When she was done, she got busy preparing the salve.

Craven stood. "I will wait outside. Fetch me when it is ready."

Espy nodded and when the door closed behind him, she released a heavy sigh. She had hoped—she shook her head. Hopes, dreams, wishes, she was never granted any. So why had she even dared to hope that Craven would look upon her with mercy? Nothing she said, no apology she offered, not even the truth made a difference to him. Her fate was sealed. He would see her dead.

~~~

Craven took a deep breath and released it, trying to gain control of all he was feeling. Espy sounded as if she was filled with sorrow over Aubrey's death, but then she would want it to seem that way. She would want him to believe she felt regret and had grieved for what had happened to Aubrey. It would make her seem less the monster that she was and perhaps save her from awful suffering and death.

He had held a deep hatred for Espy this past year, thinking of how he should have drained the life out of her that day as she had done to his wife. When his sentinels had informed him of her return, he knew he had been given another chance to take his revenge.

He could not recall how the physician had learned that Espy's father was the physician William of Inuerwyc, but he had made it known what he thought of the man. He felt the man had no right to have the honored distinction of being called a physician. Many believed that William followed too many healing ways of his peasant wife and held far too many ridiculous, foreign opinions, and unsupported theories on how to treat illnesses.

The physician's rant on William of Inuerwyc had fueled Craven's anger and desire for revenge. He should have never allowed Aubrey to befriend Espy let alone treat her. But Aubrey had believed in her skills and had been impressed with her knowledge and as usual she had talked him into getting her way, since it had been difficult to refuse her anything. Though, he had made it known that the physician would also be there if need be.

He should have never allowed the physician to go

hunting with him and Dylan that day, but Aubrey had insisted she was fine and the physician had even concurred that delivery was a week or more away.

Craven rubbed his brow, wishing for this nightmare to end. He turned and looked at the cottage. Once he got his revenge, Aubrey would be at peace, though he doubted he ever would be. He began to pace in front of the cottage, his disturbing thoughts churning his anger and pain.

"Lord Craven!"

Craven stopped, his hand going to the hilt of his sword upon hearing Tass shout at him.

"The woman has called to you thrice now," Tass said with a nod toward the cottage door.

Craven turned to see Espy's head peeking around the wood door.

He had been so lost in his thoughts he had not heard her and that annoyed him. He took hasty steps to the cottage.

Espy was at the table when he entered and once again he caught the silhouette of her body beneath the oversized garment. He was caught off guard when his loins tightened, something that had eluded him since Aubrey's death.

Espy remained still, seeing how his eyes roamed intimately over her and she never felt so exposed while clothed. It was as if he saw her naked and she felt a sudden need to cover herself, though she was already covered. She was relieved when he quickly averted his glance and sat on the chair.

Craven held his hand out to her, keeping his head turned away from her. It did not help. Her touch was so soft and gentle, like a feather brushing across his palm as she applied the salve, and it only served to arouse him more. He forced his thoughts on his hatred for her, but with each tender stroke of her fingers across his palm his hate seemed to lessen, almost fade away as fast as the morning mist did.

"Hurry and be done," he said, turning a snarl on her.

She jumped and though her fingers worked faster, her touch was still so tender, so tempting, that his body betrayed him and his manhood sparked to life, something he had not felt since he had lost Aubrey.

Her fingers suddenly left him and instead of being relieved, a strange ache settled over him and he found himself wishing for her gentle touch to return, which annoyed him all the more. Her hand returned and a rush of pleasure hit his manhood with such sudden force he hardened and continued to do so as she took great care in wrapping his hand in a clean cloth.

"The cloth must be changed daily and fresh salve applied if you are to heal, and do not get it wet or take your sword in hand unless necessary until it is well healed," Espy explained, concentrating on her words. She could not help but think of the strength in his hand and how he had lifted her clear off the ground that fateful day and had proceeded to squeeze the life from her. His immense strength trembled her insides. "My grandmother can see to it for you."

Do not take your sword in your hand unless necessary. Her words resonated in his head, for he had not been the least tempted to do so until now... until Espy had touched him.

He stood as soon as she finished tying the bandage at the back of his hand. He needed to get out of there, get control of himself.

"Have her come to the keep tomorrow to tend it," Craven ordered and walked to the door.

"Lord Craven."

He turned to see that her chin had gone up and there was a sharpness to her soft blue eyes he had not taken note of before.

"My father was a far more knowledgeable physician than the one you brought to look after your wife."

Craven looked ready to spew several oaths at her, but he

remained silent and walked out of the cottage. Espy quivered as the door closed behind him, perhaps she had been wrong about returning home. She shook her head. Here there might be a slim chance to save herself. Where she had come from there had been no chance. Death would have been her only escape.

~~~

When Craven returned to the keep, he handed his horse off to the lad he usually paid no heed to. This time, however, he stopped and gave the lad a look when he took the reins from him. He was thin, his garments worn beyond repair and covered with far too much grime.

"Have you eaten today, lad?" Craven asked.

The lad paled as he shook his head.

"Go to the kitchen and tell the cook I said to feed you," Craven ordered.

The lad's head dropped a notch as he nodded.

"What is wrong, lad?" Craven demanded.

He lifted his head and his voice quivered as he spoke. "The cook takes a strong hand to anyone who comes begging for food."

"Why should anyone beg food from him? There is plenty to be had for all." Craven asked, then realized that he was asking the young lad to tell him something he should know himself.

Had he been that removed from the daily happenings of the clan that he knew so little of what was going on around him? But then Aubrey had seen to the old cook, Alfen, who she had adored, and his wife had also been familiar with all that went on around them, often telling him what needed his attention. Dylan had warned him this past year that he was not leading the clan as he should, reminding him frequently that he had not given his people time to hear their complaints and requests, his main focus having been keeping his warriors' skills sharp. Or had the strenuous activity been more to help him keep memories at bay?

"The cook demands more than his share of the crops," the lad said.

"His share of crops? He is assigned sufficient crops. Why is he demanding more?" Craven shook his head. He should not be asking this lad such questions. He should be aware of this problem, but then if he had not neglected his duties the problem would have never existed. "What is your name lad?"

"Leith, my lord."

"Come with me, Leith," Craven ordered.

"Your horse, my lord," Leith reminded.

Craven was impressed that the lad thought of his task before seeing to his own hunger. He summoned one of his warriors standing nearby and ordered him to tend the horse. Leith followed beside him, his scrawny legs pumping hard to keep up with Craven's mighty strides. Raised voices greeted Craven as he rounded the corner of the keep to where the kitchen sat. Everyone there stilled immediately upon seeing him.

Craven had not expected to see Dylan's wife Britt there or to see her arguing with a man, average in height and slim in form and wearing a filthy apron. A young lad stood off to the side, his cheek swollen red.

"What goes on here?" Craven demanded with harsh authority and caught Leith backing away as if ready to run. "Stay as you are, Leith."

The lad froze, not moving a single limb.

"This woman thinks she can tell me how to tend to my workers, my lord," the man said with the importance of a man far above his station.

"You are?" Craven asked and all eyes widened.

"I am Todd, the cook," he said as if insulted. "I took the

position after Alfen died about six months ago."

"Who appointed you cook?' Craven asked annoyed that he had forgotten Alfen had passed.

Todd shrugged. "No one else stepped forward to take it after Alfen died."

Britt spoke up. "That is not true. Aggie should have been appointed. You forced your way into the position and the whole staff has suffered for it as well as the clan." She reached out and gently took hold of the young lad, easing him to her side. "How many times a day does Sayer here suffer your brutal hand or others suffer because they displease you."

"It is my kitchen and I make the rules," Todd sneered, "so mind your business, woman."

"Everything here belongs to me and I alone make the rules," Craven said his deep voice booming with such command that everyone took a step away from him, except Leith. The lad was too frightened to move. "And you, Todd, are no longer the cook. Someone fetch me, Aggie."

That got Leith and Sayer moving along with several other kitchen helpers that had been watching.

Todd took a step toward Craven.

"One word, and you will find yourself on your arse on the ground," Craven warned, his hand fisting at his side, ready and eager to keep his word.

Todd paled, knowing one blow from Craven's powerful fist could break his jaw.

A short woman with gray hair and a round, full face stepped out of the cookhouse, wiping her chunky hands on her apron.

Craven looked to her, recalling the woman and how good she had been to Aubrey while she had been with child. "Aggie."

"Aye, my lord," she said, cautiously.

"You are the new cook."

"I am?" Aggie asked, her eyes widening in surprise.

"You are as long as you treat your staff well," Craven said and everyone around her nodded along with her, as if assuring him she would.

"Thank you, my lord, I will serve you well," Aggie said with a respectful nod of her head.

Craven pointed to Leith. "See that he is kept well fed." He turned to Todd. "You will go to the keep and wait for me in the Great Hall. You have much to answer for, starting with why you have demanded a share of the crops from the people."

Todd wisely remained silent, bowed his head, and did as he was told.

"Aggie, if there is anything you need, come see me," Craven said. "Now all of you get back to work." He waved his hand, dismissing everyone and walked over to Britt.

He had not seen her in some time. Her belly was quite swollen with child and he tried to remember when Dylan told him the bairn was expected, two or three months or was it less? He remembered the jealousy he felt instead of happiness for his friend when he had learned the news. But then he had still blamed Britt for not seeking help when Aubrey's delivery had turned bad.

"You are well, Britt?" Craven asked.

"I am, my lord," she said, placing her hand on her stomach. "We both are."

"That is good. I want to speak with you."

"Then you should have come to me and asked permission first." Dylan stepped around Craven and went to his wife's side, his arm going protectively around her shoulders.

Craven had, at first, thought them an odd couple, Dylan tall and slim and Britt, short and petite. Where he was quiet and thoughtful of his words, except when it came to defending his wife, she spoke up in defense of others. She had tried to tell him that Espy had done everything she could to save Aubrey, but the physician had disagreed with her, calling her an ignorant peasant.

Dylan had wisely removed Britt from the keep and she had kept her distance from Craven from that day on.

"I do not need your permission to speak to anyone, including your wife," Craven reminded him, his annoyance flaring.

Dylan reminded him of something himself, his tongue sharp. "We are friends or, at least, I thought we were."

Britt broke in as if stepping between the two, her heart aching that their longtime friendship had suffered because of her. "Is this about Espy?"

Craven glared at Dylan, though kept his response to Britt tempered. "It is."

"Ask what you will, but I will reiterate what I said that day. Espy did all she could and more to save Aubrey and your bairn."

"You saw her do nothing strange, nothing out of the ordinary of other healers?" Craven asked, needing desperately to make sense of his wife's death.

"The only thing she did was insist on keeping things clean around Aubrey and our hands as well. We washed them often and the water in the buckets was kept fresh. She kept Aubrey comfortable, talked soothingly to her, and encouraged her to stay calm when the pain turned harsh. When the bleeding started, I froze, frightened for Aubrey. Not so Espy, she was right there to try and see to the cause of it and what she could do." Britt shook her head, tears filling her eyes. "There was no stopping the bleeding, no matter what Espy did. And now that she has returned, I will have Espy and no other tend me when I am ready to give birth."

"No!" Craven and Dylan said in unison.

Britt glared at her husband as if he were a traitor.

"You will go nowhere near that woman. I will not take a chance with your life no matter how much you trust Espy," Dylan warned.

"Dylan is right," Craven said glad his friend agreed with him on this.

Britt shot each man a stinging glare. "I do not care what either of you say. Espy will deliver my bairn."

"She will not," Craven said as if he had just declared an edict. "You will do as your husband commands, and as for Espy? She will suffer her fate long before your birthing time arrives."

Chapter Five

Espy had grown strong over the past two weeks and her grandmother had grown more worried that any day now Craven would come for her. Cyra had suggested several escape possibilities, but Espy had been adamant. She would not leave. If she dared sneak off, her grandmother would suffer for it and that she could not bear. Besides, she had no other recourse. Wise or foolish, her return home was all that was left to her.

"I fear every time I leave you that I will return and Craven will have taken you away," Cyra said as she packed the last few items in her healing basket.

"Do not think on that now. You must go and tend those in the outlying crofts. You have delayed your visits because of me and someone may need care," Espy said, snatching her grandmother's cloak off the back of the chair and draping it over her shoulders.

Cyra hugged Espy. "I do love you."

Her words touched Espy's heart, but it pained her to see the worry in her grandmother's eyes. "Something I never doubted and return tenfold. Worry not, I will be here when you return."

Espy saw her grandmother off, waving to her, then watching until she disappeared in the distance. It would be two or three days before she returned and while she hoped she would be here when her grandmother came back, she could not be sure.

Craven's hand had healed nicely and Cyra no longer had to go to the keep. Tass was replaced by other warriors, who took turns making certain Espy remained at the cottage.

But each day that passed no summons came from the keep and since that day she had tended Craven's hand, Espy had not seen him.

She delayed going inside the cottage, the sun bright, and there was an unusual warmth to the air for the middle of spring. Of course, it probably would not last, which was why she wanted to take advantage of the sun while she could.

She wished she could take Trumble for a ride, but that would not be allowed. Once she had felt well enough, she had seen to his care herself and had assured him all was fine, hoping her words would hold true.

The sun started to fade after an hour and a chill blew in with a sudden wind. She was about to enter the cottage and make herself a hot brew when she caught the approach of someone in the distance. The person staggered rather than walked, then suddenly dropped to the ground.

Espy did not hesitate, she ran to help the obvious ill or injured person.

Tass was guarding her today and yelled after her to stop as he fumbled to get up from where he sat as she sped past him. She paid him no heed. He would catch up with her soon enough and could help get the person to the cottage.

Espy saw that it was a woman. She lay curled on her side, her hood partially covering her face, and Espy dropped down beside her and reached out a tender hand to offer help.

"Please do not hurt me," the woman whimpered, drawing back away as if Espy might strike her.

"I will not hurt you. I am a healer and can help you." Cautiously and gently, Espy drew the woman's hood fully away from her face and almost gasped at what she saw.

The woman had been beaten unmercifully in the face and God only knew where else. Her one eye was swollen completely shut. The large bruise on her jaw was as deep a purple as her closed eye and blood was caked under her nose and in the corner of her mouth. Espy did not need to ask if she had suffered a beaten to other parts of her body. She could tell by the way she lay curled up that she was accustomed to feigning off blows that way.

"Please do not let him take me…" the woman's strength failed her. She could get no more words out. She stretched a bruised, bare arm out to Espy, the sleeve of her blouse hanging tattered from her shoulder.

"You are safe here," Espy said and looked to Tass as he came to an abrupt stop in front of her, causing the woman to flinch. "Help me get her to the cottage."

Tass' face betrayed his shock when he reached down for the battered woman, and Espy was glad to see him handle her gently. Once inside the cottage, Tass helped get the woman to the bed and her cloak off before taking his leave.

The woman could not keep her uninjured eye open after her head touched the pillow. She was exhausted and Espy wondered how long she had been walking or perhaps she had run all the way out of fear.

Glad that the woman was getting the rest she needed to help heal, Espy got a bucket of water from the rain barrel, grabbed a fresh cloth from the ones folded neatly in a chest, placed a chair by the bed, and got busy cleaning the woman's face. The sleeping woman winced now and again but she did not wake. A once pretty face was revealed after Espy cleaned away the grime and blood, and it would be so again once she healed.

With the woman's odor potent, Espy washed her arms as she took a closer look at the bruises there. It was obvious they had been caused by being grabbed by a strong hand and squeezed so tightly it left its mark. There was also a bruise by her ribs, but it was already fading in color which meant she had suffered a previous beating to this one.

Her father had often reminded her that it was what you could not see that often caused the most trouble. She hoped the woman's eye had not suffered any serious damage. There was little she could do for the bruises, but let them heal. She did, however, plan to wash her thoroughly and get her out of her filthy garments when she woke. Clean garments and a good meal with a hot brew would help heal her in more ways than one.

"Be gone!"

Espy jumped, hearing Tass shout, and she hurried to the door to open it a crack and see who Tass had ordered away. It was a large man, with a hooked nose, full beard, and long brown hair. He did not wear the MacCara plaid and the one he did wear was so filthy that it was difficult to distinguish any colors.

"Bring my wife to me and I will leave. I know Bonnie is here. She seeks the aid of the healer after she gets the beatings she deserves," the large man said, raising a threatening fist at Tass. "You have no right to keep my wife from me."

"This is MacCara land and Lord Craven will be the judge of that. Go take your complaint to him," Tass ordered, his hand going to rest on the hilt of his sword in warning.

The large man looked ready to spew fire and, with warning, he lunged at Tass, locking his meaty arms around the young warrior, squeezing him tight, then hoisting him in the air over his head and slamming him to the ground and kicking him even though Tass lay motionless.

Instinct had Espy running to help the young warrior. She grabbed a split log from the stack near the door and charged at the man. He was so intent on beating Tass senseless that he did not see her coming. She whacked him in the back of the head and he stumbled. He shook his head and turned to glare at her, his eyes growing wide with rage.

"No woman hits me," he snarled and dove at her.

Espy was fast on her feet, having learned to be so out of necessity and she moved out of his path with ease, slamming the log down on his shoulder as she did. He cried out, more in anger than pain, and before he could turn around, she slammed her foot into the back of his leg, sending him tumbling to the ground and whacked him again in the head with the log.

Though stunned, his hand shot out to grab her ankle, and she jumped out of his way and brought the log down on his wrist with such force that he let loose a guttural scream.

His intense anger had him surging to his feet, his face so red he looked as if he would burst into flames and his eyes so wide she feared they would pop from his head. He roared and dove for her once again and this time he was able to swat the log out of her hand with his arm as she swung it at him. His hand swung back at her with tremendous force, catching her scarred cheek so hard that her head snapped back and she fell to the ground.

He straddled her before she could gather her senses and get to her feet, his legs locking her arms to her sides, and he raised his hand ready to batter her face.

Espy struggled against him. She would not give up. She would never give up as long as she had a breath left in her.

A furious roar like that of a mighty animal tore through the air, halting the man's hand as his head snapped up. Fright turned him pale and in the next instant he was ripped off her.

Espy hurried to her feet and was stunned to see that Craven had the man by the throat, his powerful hand squeezing tightly.

"You dare come on my land, attack one of my warriors and clanswoman," Craven growled, his fingers digging tighter into the man's fleshy throat.

Cyra had repeatedly warned her that Craven had gotten even stronger since his wife's death and even his warriors feared facing him on the practice field and neighboring clans made sure to remain in his favor. She had felt his strength once, but her size was nothing to this large man's size and yet Craven contained him with one hand, choking the life from him as he did.

The man clawed at Craven's fingers and wrist, struggling to break free. He even swung at his arm, but it did little good, Craven held him firm.

Without any warning, Craven threw the man to the ground and called out, "Take him to the keep and put him in the stocks."

Espy had not realized that six warriors had arrive with him and not a one had stepped forward to help him. They all understood he needed no help.

"My wife," the large man spat as he struggled for breath.

Craven turned to Espy and she was quick to explain. "He beat her unmercifully. She came here for help and begged that we not return her to him." She turned to glance at Tass who was just coming to. "He needs care, the man kicked him brutally after he was on the ground unconscious."

Craven could not take his eyes off her scarred cheek. It was flaming red. "You came to Tass' rescue?" He knew the answer. He had seen it for himself, though had not believed his eyes as he had approached the cottage with his warriors. She had battled that large man with nothing more than a split log and courage.

"Why would I not?' Espy asked and she did not wait for a response, she hurried over to Tass.

Craven stared after her, shocked that she had walked away from him without asking permission to take her leave. He followed after her, annoyed.

"Do not move until I see to your injures," Espy ordered, bending down beside Tass.

"I am good. I need no help," Tass insisted though groaned when he went to sit up.

Espy laid a firm hand on his chest to keep him from

moving. "It will only take a moment." She ran a gentle hand around his head, feeling for any bumps, but there were none, a good sign. But it was his side that concerned her since the large man had kicked him several times there. She pressed her hand a partial way between his waist and chest, feeling for his ribs, and he winced loudly.

She kept her hand there. "Take a deep breath."

Tass tried, but he cringed in pain.

"Your ribs are bruised or could possibly be broken. To have them heal properly, you need to rest, no swinging your sword, no practice field, no work that is strenuous for three to four weeks." Espy explained.

Tass shook his head and he let loose a sharp groan when he went to sit up. "I have my duties."

"Which will be difficult for you to perform if you do not let your ribs heal and then it will be much longer before you can lift a sword without pain." Espy stood. "The choice is yours."

"You will do as she says until Cyra returns and can look at you," Craven ordered, having listened to the exchange, and Tass gave a reluctant nod.

That Craven knew Cyra was not there was not a surprise to Espy. His warriors who stood guard no doubt reported everything they heard to him and he would know that Cyra had left today. It was also not a surprise to her that he continued to doubt her ability as a healer. She did wonder, though, if Craven had planned to wait until Cyra was absent from the cottage to come fetch her. Why else would he be here with six of his warriors?

"I will speak with the man's wife," Craven said.

"She rests," Espy said.

"Wake her," he ordered.

"I do not think that will be necessary once you see her. Besides, she needs all the rest she can get to heal."

"I will not repeat my command," Craven said and

walked toward the cottage.

Espy followed and hurried around him as they got to the door to open it.

Craven stopped inside the door, his nose wrinkling. "What is that odor?"

Espy pointed to the woman on the bed.

Craven walked over to her and anger twisted in his gut. He turned and took two quick steps to Espy. "You saw what he did to his wife and still you went after him with nothing more than a split log?"

"I could not let him take her. He would have killed her," Espy argued.

"He would have done the same to you."

"Then you would have gotten what you wanted."

Craven lowered his face close to hers. "I want the pleasure of doing it myself."

Espy reached for his hand and placed it at her throat. "Then be done with it, for I am tired of the wait." She dropped her hand away, but his remained at her throat.

Craven gave her smooth flesh a gentle squeeze. His manhood had jumped to life when she had taken a gentle hold of his hand and had stirred even more when she placed it against her throat. It was not choking her that had entered his head when his hand closed around her neck. It was how much he wanted to caress her smooth skin before his lips settled there to taste her.

The thought jolted him and he shoved her away.

"I will come for you when Cyra returns," he said and went to the door. "Remember a warrior stands guard."

"It matters not," Espy said. "I will not run." Again she was reminded that she had no place to go, but then she was finally home and there was no place else she would want to be.

Craven did not look back. He walked out and barked orders for one of his warriors to remain and for Tass to ride back with them. Two warriors had already left with their prisoner in tow and Craven wanted to be gone from there as well.

He did not like that Espy stirred him to life with a simple touch, even Aubrey had not done that to him. It was because he had gone without coupling for far too long that this was happening. He needed a woman, but he did not want just any woman. He wanted Aubrey. He missed her tender touch, her sweet voice. The way she would slowly melt in his arms when he touched or kissed her.

Why, though, had it been Espy who he responded to after all this time?

~~~

Espy sat at the table, locking her hands together to keep them from shaking. It was not her words to Craven that had her trembling, it was the look in his eyes she had seen when his hand rested at her throat. She was familiar with that look, had seen it on men's faces, and had guarded against it, for not all men asked permission of a woman. She did not understand why it had sparked in Craven's eyes. He hated her, wanted nothing to do with her except to see her suffer. So why had she seen passion flare in Craven's eyes when she touched him?

Worse though… why had she felt the same herself?

Chapter Six

"Howe will come for me when he is freed from the stocks and this time he will kill me. I will never be free of him."

Espy sat at the table across from Bonnie and watched her take a quick, nervous glance at the door, as if expecting her husband to burst through it. It had been two days since the incident and Bonnie was healing well, though fear had her jumping at every sound. She was looking much better as well, having washed up nicely and the swelling having gone down a little in her eye while the bruise at her jaw had turned a paler purple.

"From what the guard told me, Howe is to remain in the stocks until Lord Craven says otherwise, so you have nothing to fear right now," Espy said.

"Like a condemned prisoner, I have a short reprieve before death takes me."

Espy had treated battered wives before and there was not much recourse left to them. Some ran away, most had no choice and continued to suffer the beatings, and then there had been one she met who made sure her husband never beat her again and made his death appear natural.

"I am sure Lord Craven will offer you safe haven with the clan," Espy said in hopes of reassuring her.

"Lord Craven is as much a beast as Howe," Bonnie said, tears gathering in her eyes. "I remember when I first saw him. I had never seen a man the size of him. He towered over every man there and he was covered with sweat, blood, and grime, returning home from battle. He and his warriors had stopped at Clan MacVarish to let our old laird know that there was nothing for him to fear that Clan MacFillan would not encroach on MacVarish land any longer. No one would go near Lord Craven, no one but Aubrey. She brought him food and drink and most believe that it was her kind heart and beauty that tamed the beast." Bonnie wiped a tear away. "Aubrey had the gentlest soul and with her gone, the beast has returned and soon will lay claim to our clan."

"What do you mean?" Espy asked surprised and curious over her remark.

"Clan MacVarish's old laird lies at death's door and Aubrey was his only heir, a niece, I believe. She had come to live there about a year before she met Lord Craven. The land and clan now goes to Lord Craven once the laird dies, greatly enlarging his holdings since MacVarish land borders MacCara land. The beast will rule us and he does not care about his own people since Aubrey's death, why should he care about the Clan MacVarish or me. He put Howe in the stocks because he attacked one of his warriors, not because Howe beat me. He will release my husband and he will come for me, and there will be no one to stop him."

Espy felt helpless as she so often did when there had been no recourse to help people. Her hand went to her cheek, reminding her differently.

Bonnie stood, wincing as she did. "If I leave now, I may get far enough away that Howe will not be able to find me."

Espy stood and with gentle hands on Bonnie's shoulders eased her back down in the chair. "Do not let fear make you do something foolish. You are not well enough to walk a distance and besides, it is not safe for a woman to travel alone. Believe me, I know. You could find yourself in a worse situation than you are already in. Right now, you are safe here. We will think of something to continue to keep you safe."

Bonnie took hold of Espy's hand. "I wish I had your courage. I heard the two guards talking about how you beat

Howe with a split log. I wish I was that brave."

"You left him to seek help for yourself and that takes courage. You are braver than you know," Espy said with a smile and a reassuring squeeze of Bonnie's hand.

The door suddenly opened and Cyra walked in with a smile, about to speak when she caught site of Bonnie.

"Cyra," Bonnie cried and went to the older woman, her arms going around her.

Espy smiled, seeing the two women hug. Bonnie had talked about how Cyra had helped her more than once after Howe had beaten her, the MacVarish healer too frightened of Howe to offer any help. It would take Bonnie hours to walk here and Cyra would tend her, then take her home on her horse. Once Howe had caught her and threatened Cyra. Cyra had returned the threat, letting Howe know that Lord Craven protected his own.

"I have not seen you in some time, Bonnie," Cyra said. "I feared that I made things worse for you when I returned Howe's threat."

"He warned me against seeking your help, but this beating was too much. I feared I would not survive it." Bonnie turned to Espy. "Your granddaughter helped me and did more than threaten Howe, she beat him."

Cyra grinned. "You must tell me all about it."

The three women sat at the table and talked and after about an hour Bonnie began to yawn. Cyra insisted she needed to sleep and helped her into bed. Wanting Bonnie to have quiet and wanting to talk privately with her granddaughter, Cyra handed Espy her cloak after grabbing her own and the two stepped outside.

They walked a short distance from the cottage and glancing around, Cyra asked, "Now I know why Craven left two guards to watch over you, though I see only one now."

Espy's skin prickled, feeling like a hundred tiny bugs crawled along it. It could mean only one thing if one of the guards had left. He went to take word to Craven that Cyra was home, which meant... Craven would be coming to get her.

She no soon had given it thought, then she saw riders approaching in the distance.

Cyra gasped and reached out for Espy's hand.

Espy took tight hold. "You must promise me, *Seanmhair*, that you will do nothing. I will not see you harmed."

"How can I stand by and do nothing while my granddaughter is carted off to..." Cyra shook her head, tears filling her eyes.

"You must promise me. It is time I face this. I cannot run any longer. I do not want to. God willing, all will go as it should."

"You have a brave soul, Espy," her grandmother said and hugged her tight.

Espy choked back her tears. She was not as brave as her grandmother thought, but she did not want her to know it. She wanted only to make sure no harm came to her grandmother.

Espy took a quick step away from her grandmother. "I must see Trumble before I go. Please promise me that you will see to his care and keep him safe. He has saved me on many an occasion."

"Trumble will be safe with me," Cyra promised.

Espy hurried to say her good-byes to the horse that had been her companion and friend for almost the whole year she had been gone. She pressed her cheek to his face and he pawed the ground, sensing something was wrong.

"I will come for you if at all possible. Otherwise Cyra will take good care of you, my friend." She gave him one last hug and hurried away, her heart breaking at leaving him.

Craven was just pulling his horse to a stop when she reached the front of the cottage. He stared at her, not saying a word and dismounted. She understood his silent command. She was to go to him and surrender. She went to her grandmother, gave her a hug and told her not to worry, and with an even stride and her chin up, walked over to Craven.

He placed his hands at her waist and lifted her onto the horse, then he mounted behind her, his arms circling her as he reached to take the reins in his hands. He turned his horse and his six warriors followed, and they rode off.

"You will not harm my grandmother?" Espy asked when the cottage was far behind them.

"Cyra did nothing and you came without protest. She is safe," Craven said, trying to ignore the ease in which Espy had settled against him and how she seemed to fit so comfortably in his arms.

"I have a favor to ask," Espy said, glancing up at him. His dark eyes showed not a hint of caring and yet she felt something different in his body. It seemed to wrap comfortably around her as if—she almost shook her head at the insane thought—she belonged there in his arms.

"A last request?"

"If it must be so," she said, a chill racing through her that death waited close by for her.

"Tell me," Craven said curious as to what it might be.

"Please do not return Bonnie to her husband. If you do, he will kill her. Please invite her to join the Clan MacCara and keep her safe."

Craven had had all intentions of doing just that before she asked, having had Dylan find out what he could about the couple. That Espy asked protection for another when she could have begged for her own life gave him pause.

"Bonnie will be kept safe within the Clan MacCara," he said and was again surprised when he felt her body sigh against him in relief.

Silence followed them for a while until Craven asked, "How did you get that scar?"

"It matters not," Espy said.

For some reason, the shudder he felt run through her told him differently and it also disturbed him. "That is for me to decide, though I suppose you deserved it."

"There would be some who would agree with you." Espy turned her head when she saw Craven's head lift a bit and his glance move beyond her.

The sight of a rider fast approaching diverted Craven's attention and when he saw the fast pace Dylan rode, he knew something was wrong.

Dylan brought his horse to an abrupt stop. "Britt has been in labor for a full day and the baby will not deliver and the women who help do not know what to do. She has begged me to bring Espy to her."

"Cyra has returned, she can help," Craven said.

Dylan shook his head. "No, she pleaded with me to bring Espy to her and now I plead with you to allow Espy to tend her."

Espy turned to Craven. "Please let me help her—"

"You mean kill her," he accused, his words sounding harsh to his own ears.

"I cannot change the past as much as I wish I could, but please do not let the past hurt Britt and her bairn. You will still be able to have your revenge on me once I am done helping Britt."

"We are wasting precious time," Dylan argued.

"Be warned, Espy. If anything happens to Britt or the bairn—"

"I will kill her myself," Dylan said.

His remark stabbed at Craven's gut. It was something he should have done himself a year ago and the thought sparked anger him, he shouted sharply for his men to follow.

Dylan and Britt's cottage did not sit far from the keep. Several women lingered outside as they came to a stop in the front. They all stared wide-eyed at seeing Espy on the horse with Craven. They quickly blessed themselves, though Espy was not sure if it was protection against her that they sought or if it was for her for what she would face at Craven's hands.

Craven dismounted and reached up to take her by the waist and lift her off the horse. His strength was hard to ignore and so was the growing flutter in her stomach that she got every time he touched her. It was odd and she wished she could make sense of how the man who wanted her to suffer and die stirred something in her, but at the moment she had no time to dwell on it, Britt came first.

She went to walk away from Craven, when he took hold of her arm, stopping her. "I will be waiting right here."

"I remind you again, I have no place to go." With that, she pulled her arm lose and hurried into the cottage, Dylan following behind her.

"I brought her," Dylan said and wanted to scream with rage, seeing his wife near to the point of collapsing from exhaustion as she was helped by two women to walk back and forth.

"Espy!" Britt cried, tears springing from her eyes to roll down her flushed cheeks.

Dylan went to go to her, but Espy slipped around him and hurried Britt into her arms.

"Time to rest, Britt," Espy said and looked to Dylan. "Please help her get in bed."

The two women hurried out of Dylan's way and he lifted his wife gently in his arms and carried her to the bed.

"I need you all to wait outside for a moment," Espy said.

"No," Dylan said, though it sounded more like a shout and it sent the two women scurrying out of the cottage.

"Please, Dylan, do as she says," Britt said with what strength she had left. "I am safe with her."

"I will not leave you alone in her care," Dylan insisted.

"I have no time to argue with you. Stay if you want, but keep out of the way," Espy said and bent over Britt to feel her stomach.

"The bairn refuses to be born, though he does come earlier than I expected," Britt said, fear in her every word.

"He or she is stubborn and will have it his way," Espy said with a smile as she continued to press on Britt's rounded stomach.

"Like his father," Britt said, smiling for the first time in hours.

"I need to feel inside you, Britt," Espy said and Britt's smile faded.

"You will not," Dylan said, stepping forward.

Espy ignored him. "I believe the bairn's head has not turned and I need to make sure."

Britt began to cry.

"What is wrong?" Dylan demanded.

"Go wait outside, Dylan," Britt said softly and when he went to argue, she reached out to him and he grabbed her hand tightly in his, as if he intended never to let go. "Please, do this for me, Dylan. We have nothing to fear with Espy here to help."

Dylan did not agree with his wife but one thing he and Britt had done since falling in love was to trust each other. He had to trust her instinct now even though memories of what had happened to Aubrey flashed through his mind. He bent down and kissed his wife's brow. "I will be right outside the door." He looked to Espy, a warning ready to spring from his lips, and before he could say a word she spoke up.

"I have delivered stubborn bairns before."

Dylan felt a twinge of relief and hoped it was so as he said, "Please keep them both safe."

Espy looked to Britt as soon as the door closed. "This is not going to be easy, Britt."

"I know," Britt said, "but promise me you will keep my bairn safe no matter what you have to do."

Espy took her hand. "It will take some doing, but I will keep both of you safe."

Britt smiled through her tears. "I have so wanted to come see you and ask you to tend my birth, but Dylan forbid it and I did not have the strength to walk out to Cyra's place. I am so relieved you are here now."

"We better get to work. With the way the bairn is positioned and possibly arriving sooner than he should, there is much care to be taken."

"Tell me what I must do and I will do it," Britt said with a determined yet tired voice.

"Rest a moment while I prepare things and worry not, we will get through this," Espy said. She turned, then turned back again. "The two women who helped you?"

"Elva and Mina. They have helped with many births."

Espy went to the door and summoned the two women. When she explained what was amiss with the bairn, both women turned worried glances to Britt.

"I have seen this before," Mina whispered, "and it does not bode well for mother and bairn."

"Because the delivery was not done properly. All will go well with us working together," Espy said, reassuring them with a confident smile.

The two women did not appear as confident, but they both were quick to do as Espy instructed.

~~~

"I should go in there," Dylan said, having paced in front of the tree Craven leaned against for the last hour.

"You should have let me send for Cyra," Craven argued.

Dylan shook his head. "She wanted Espy."

"As did my Aubrey, and look what happened to her."

Dylan stopped pacing. "Britt has told me over and over again that Espy fought like no other she had ever seen to save Aubrey and your child. She says she is skilled in ways other healers and physicians are not."

"Heathen ways from what that useless physician I brought from Edinburgh to tend Aubrey told me. It seems Espy's father traveled extensively to heathen lands and returned with barbaric treatments that had his colleagues thinking him insane."

Dylan snapped his head toward the cottage.

Concerned for his friend and family, Craven urged, "Go and make sure she is not harming your wife."

Dylan was about to step forward when an agonizing scream rang out from the cottage. He did not hesitate and either did Craven. They ran.

Elva stepped out the door just as they were a few steps from it. She held her hand up to stop them. "Britt does well. It will not be long now."

Dylan reluctantly backed away, Craven did not.

"Dylan will see for himself," Craven ordered.

Elva stepped aside, fearing the mighty Craven.

Dylan stepped forward and the door opened.

Espy looked to Elva. "Hurry and get those blankets." She looked to Dylan. "Make sure there is enough firewood. If the bairn is small, he will need to be kept extra warm." She turned to go inside and her eyes caught with Craven's. She had expected to be met with hostility, but there was concern and sadly there was sorrow there. He was thinking of his wife and bairn, and her heart hurt for him.

Craven watched the door close behind Espy. There had been no blood on her, which was a good sign and she spoke with confidence as if all was well. He hoped it was so. He did not want his friend to go through the horror and misery that he had suffered.

Craven placed a strong hand on Dylan's shoulder.

"Come, I will help you with the wood."

Dylan nodded, staring at the closed door and Craven gave him a slight shove to get him moving, but once they started swinging the axes there was no stopping Dylan. Craven could not help but wonder if the wood was needed or if Espy had given Dylan a task to keep him too busy to worry.

~~~

Espy attempted what her father had learned from the old healers, to try turning the bairn. It had taken some coaxing and manipulating, and at first Espy thought the bairn would not turn, but he began to move and to Espy's relief he turned completely. It was not long after that ordeal that the bairn slipped out of Britt more easily than expected and let loose with a loud wail as if he was relieved to finally be free.

"You were right, Britt. He is a fine stubborn lad just like his da," Espy said with a soft laugh as she held him up for Britt to see.

Britt grinned as happy tears rolled down her cheeks. "He is a good size."

Elva and Mina agreed, smiles and a few tears on their faces as well.

"Let us hurry and finish so that the new da can meet his son and see that his wife did a fine job," Espy said with a smile of her own. A good, safe birth never failed to bring happiness to all. It was one of the joys she loved about being a healer.

Elva saw to getting the bairn cleaned and swaddled while Mina helped Espy tend Britt, change the bedding, and get Britt into a fresh nightdress. When all was done, Britt was sitting up in bed, beaming at her wee son sleeping comfortably in her arms.

Britt looked to Espy. "Please, get Dylan, I am impatient

for him to meet his son."

Espy removed her apron, Elva taking it from her and adding it to the soiled beddings she and Mina would take with them to wash for Britt, and opened the door. The cool air kissed her warm skin and she took a deep breath enjoying the refreshing feel of it.

When her eyes met Dylan's, full of worry and fear, she smiled broadly and he dropped his axe and ran for the cottage.

"You have a fine, fit son and Britt is eager for you to meet him," Espy said as he came to an abrupt stop in front of her.

"Britt is well?" Dylan asked anxiously.

"More than well." She stepped aside, turning to the open door. "See for yourself."

Mina and Elva hurried out after Dylan entered and before he closed the door, Espy heard Britt say joyously, "Come and meet your son."

Elva and Mina stopped briefly in front of Espy and before hurrying off they whispered, "Bless you and may God keep you safe."

Espy wondered over their words and when she turned around, she understood. Craven approached. He must have been helping Dylan cut wood, his naked chest glistening with sweat as well as the taut muscles along his arms. She shivered at the strength in every step and movement he took and knew he would soon use that strength to make her suffer.

The door flew open and Dylan stepped out, bursting with pride. "Come, Craven, and see my son."

Craven gave a nod and quickly snatched his shirt off the bench and slipped it on before reaching her. She hastily stepped aside, but he caught her by the arm and forced her into the cottage before him.

Espy's heart once again went out to Craven as he

looked upon the wee bairn sleeping peacefully in Britt's arms. Though there was happiness there, there was also pain.

Craven praised the wee lad. "He will be as strong as his da."

Dylan grinned, besotted by his wee son.

A knock sounded at the door and Espy opened it to see Elva there.

"I mistakenly gathered this pouch up with the soiled linens," she said and handed it to Espy.

Espy took it and thanked the woman.

"Who is it?" Britt asked.

"Elva took this by mistake," Espy said, holding the pouch for Britt to see.

She turned an accusing eye on her husband. "I told you to get rid of that."

"I put it aside, thinking you might change your mind," Dylan said.

"I did fine without it," Britt quipped.

"That you did, wife," Dylan said and gave her a kiss.

Curious, Espy opened the pouch and poured some of the dried, crushed leaves in her cupped hand. "What is this?"

Dylan and Britt remained silent and kept their glances away from Craven.

"It belonged to my wife," Craven said and held his hand out to Espy for her to give it to him.

Espy ignored him, pushing the leaves around in the palm of her hand, then held them up to her nose to sniff them. "Aubrey took these when she was with child?"

"That does not concern you," Craven snapped.

"Who gave these to her?" Espy demanded.

Craven stepped toward her, ready to grab the pouch from her hand. "What does it matter?"

"It matters greatly," Espy said. "One of these herbs taken by itself would have done little to harm Aubrey, but mixed together they cause bleeding."

"Would the physician have known this?" Craven asked, his stomach clenching at what it might mean.

"The physician gave this to her? How long did she take this and how often?" Espy asked, clearly upset.

"The physician had it sent three months before his arrival and had her take it twice a day." Craven's heart began to pound against his chest. He had made sure that she followed the physician's directions, even bringing her the brew at times.

Espy shook her head as if trying to make sense of it. "A knowledgeable physician would have never blended these herbs together."

"Are you saying that whoever mixed the contents of that pouch knew what he was doing?" Craven asked anxiously, his mind reeling with the implication.

"Whoever mixed this pouch was either beyond ignorant of the property of herbs or did so with the intent of causing extreme bleeding," Espy said.

There was complete silence in the room for a moment as everyone gave thought to Espy's remark.

Craven finally spoke. "Are you saying that someone intentionally killed my wife?"

Chapter Seven

Espy raised her arm, the pouch dangling between her fingers. "I am telling you this mixture is meant to harm not heal."

Craven reached out and grabbed Espy's wrist, forcing the dried leaves in her hand to spill to the timber floor. With a glance to Dylan, he said, "Enjoy time with your newly born son and we will speak in the morning." He hastened Espy out the door, keeping a firm hold on her and once outside and a few steps from the cottage, he swung her around to face him. "You expect me to believe this tale?"

"It is no tale. It is the truth," Espy insisted.

"You sniff some dried leaves and I am supposed to believe that you were not at fault for my wife's death? That you are an innocent in this all? Here you are about to be punished when suddenly a pouch of herbs is presented to you and you ask if my wife took the herbs and how often, and then you claim they harmed her. How convenient for you."

"I tell you what I know," Espy said frustrated that he did not believe her, yet understanding his skepticism. She would think the same if she were him.

Craven let go of her wrist and took a step away from her, his brow wrinkling in thought.

Espy remained silent, wondering how she could make him understand that she spoke the truth. Besides, he needed to realize that someone had wanted Aubrey dead. But why?

Craven turned suddenly. "I will take this pouch to Cyra and see what she says about it."

Espy shook her head. "Some of the herbs in that

mixture are foreign to this soil. My grandmother would not be familiar with them."

"Again, how convenient."

Annoyed that he would not even consider the possibility, Espy said, "Should you not be asking yourself who would want your wife dead?"

"I am asking myself if I should be so foolish as to believe your tale and delay your punishment and death."

"Or would you be more foolish to ignore the truth and take the life of one who is innocent while the true culprit goes free?" she challenged.

"You are far from innocent in my wife's death," Craven accused.

Espy's heart twisted in pain as it had done this past year whenever she thought of Aubrey, which had been daily. "Aye, I failed your wife and bairn that day." She raised the pouch. "I will not fail them again. What will it hurt to find out who mixed the herbs in this pouch? If in the end you still blame me, you can take your revenge."

Anger jabbed at him, annoyed she was right. He needed to know the truth, know the one guilty of Aubrey's death. Revenge would not taste sweet if he took it against one who was innocent.

"You will remain at the keep until this is settled." He reached out as he stepped toward her, his hand closing around her neck. "And make no mistake, I will be a shadow that haunts your every step. You will do nothing, go nowhere without my permission, and if I find you lied to me... you will beg for death."

His hand was not tight at her neck, it more rested there, reminding her of what he was capable of... *tenderness*. The unsolicited thought startled her eyes wide and no doubt he believed it was fear she displayed when it was more confusion she felt. It continued to trouble her that she could think of his touch as tender when he did nothing but threaten her.

Craven leaned his head down so close to hers that their brows almost touched. "It is good you fear me. You would be foolish not to."

She gasped when his hands went to her waist and took hold, his fingers digging in tight as he lifted her, walked over to his horse, her feet never touching the ground, and placed her on it. He mounted behind her and they took off, the short ride to the keep a silent one.

Clansmen stopped and stared when they rode through the village. There were no smiles to be had or sounds of children's laughter, a far different scene than Espy had remembered. The people as well as the village appeared neglected and lifeless, much like Craven himself.

It saddened her to see what had become of the clan in her absence. She had not known Aubrey long, but she knew that it would not please her to see what had happened to the people and especially to Craven. Aubrey would also be terribly upset to know that Espy had never gotten to tell Craven her last words to him. Espy wished so badly to tell him, but Craven had given her no chance that day to speak and she did not feel the time was right to tell him now or that he would even believe her. One day perhaps, at least she hoped and she hoped Aubrey's last words would be a tonic that would help heal his heart

A young lad waited by the keep steps, wearing the only smile she had seen since arriving here.

Craven dismounted quickly after stopping in front of the lad and hurried her off the horse as well.

"You are well fed, Leith?" Craven asked, though it was easy to see how the lad had improved. There was good color to his now nearly full cheeks and while he was still slim, it was not a gaunt slenderness. His garments had improved as well, being much cleaner than before.

"Aye, my lord, and I am grateful."

"You deserve it, Leith. You do your task well and without complaint." Craven wanted the lad to know he should be proud of doing such fine work.

Espy watched their exchange and saw what Aubrey must have seen in Craven, a beast with a heart.

His hand took hold of her arm and he did not let go until they entered the Great Hall. It was gloomy and untended, the timber floors in need of a good sweeping and the tables a good cleaning. The hearth was overflowing with ashes and a stale odor permeated the whole room.

"Wait here," Craven ordered and disappeared through an archway.

Espy saw bunches of dried lavender along the top of the mantle and walked over to see they had crumbled, their scent long gone. She brushed some into her hand and tossed them into the flames.

A hand suddenly closed around her neck and she found herself shoved against a wall. "You touch nothing here," Craven ordered his face a mask of anger, then he quickly released her.

Espy's hand rubbed at her throat, not that he had hurt her, though he had frightened her, coming up behind her so silently that she had heard nothing. She had only felt his hand close around her neck.

She could not help but ask, "Your hand is forever at my throat. Do you ache so badly to finish what you did not that day?"

"You deserve it," he spat.

"Prove it," she challenged for a second time that day.

"Be very careful, Espy, I am called a beast for a good reason," Craven warned. "Come with me."

She walked behind him, having to keep her steps quick to keep up with him. They climbed the stairs and he led her to a door. She followed him in after he opened it and she realized he had brought her to a servant's chamber. The small, cold hearth would have no difficulty warming the pint-sized room when lit. A narrow bed, a chest at the foot of it, and a table, one small candle atop it struggling to light the room, and bench barely big enough for one gave the chamber a confined feeling.

"I am across the hall and I barely sleep, remember that if you decide to take your leave in the middle of the night," Craven warned. "I will remind you again that you go nowhere without my permission."

Only too familiar with how fast gossip spreads in villages, she said, "Tongues will wag that I occupy the same floor as you."

"I care not for your reputation or what people think of me, but I could move you to the dungeon if you have fear of your reputation being soiled."

The threat sent a shiver through her and she hugged herself tightly as if shielding herself. This confined room would be difficult enough to bear, never mind a dark, locked cell.

"You will take your meals here alone, unless I say otherwise."

There were things she wanted to ask for but she feared he would deny her, visits with her grandmother being one of them and to have her meager belongings brought to her, especially her father's journal. It might help her to confirm what she believed about the herbs in the pouch.

"May I have a place to study the herbs in the pouch and see what more I can learn?" Espy asked hopefully.

He looked ready to deny her, but for some reason he held his tongue for a moment. "We shall see." He held his hand out.

Espy scrunched her brow in question.

"The pouch," he said.

"You will keep its contents safe?" she asked, reluctant to hand it to him.

"Do not question me," he cautioned and she wisely handed him the pouch.

"Supper will be brought to you. I will see you in the morning." He turned to go.

"You mean I must stay here until morning?" she asked anxiously, the thought of being confined to this room until the morn sending a fright through her.

"Aye, you are confined to this room until I come for you," he confirmed.

Espy followed him to the door, reaching out and grabbing his arm. She had never before felt a man's arm as large or rock hard as his. No wonder he had the skill to lift a man off his feet with one hand.

Craven stared at her hand grasping his arm. Her touch was strong, as if she did not intend to let him go and for some strange reason he did not want her to let him go. At that moment, he realized how very much he missed his wife's touch and why Espy's touch should remind him of that was beyond annoying… it was maddening.

Espy did not beg, even at the worst of times this past year she had not begged and she would not beg the beast now, but she also knew this confined space would be a challenge. "Please, I give you my word I will not run away. I will remain in the keep."

"Why should I trust you?" he asked.

"Why should I lie? You would just come after me and I am tired of running. I am here to stay whether it is to live out my days with my grandmother or be buried beside her cottage."

His dark eyes seemed to soften, but only for a moment. "I will think on it." He was out the door in two quick steps, the door closing behind him.

She was suddenly engulfed in complete darkness, the lone candle's flame flickering out as the door closed and she felt her heart pound against her chest in a wild rhythm and roar in her ears until she thought herself deaf, and her breath quickened, making it difficult for her to breathe. She reached for the door, frantically searching for the handle, her fear escalating as her fingers fumbled to find it.

Espy almost screamed with relief when her hand fell upon it and she threw it open and rushed out, taking deep breathes.

"I knew you would try and—" Craven rushed over to her when he saw her fighting to breathe. "Slow breathes," he ordered firmly, his one hand hurrying to rest low at her back and his other hand, pressed just beneath her breasts. "Easy, one breath at a time."

Espy focused on his voice, strong, confident, and soothing to her fears.

"Slow and easy."

His voice chased her fright, it scurrying away to hide, but not to leave her entirely, never to leave her entirely. It would return again. It always returned. She had not realized that she had placed her hand on his arm. She had more than placed it there, she was gripping his arm so tight, she wondered if her hand would leave a mark.

"What happened?" he asked when her breath turned slow and even.

"I fear I am a coward when I am confined to a small space," she admitted truthfully and without shame. It was a fear that too often she failed to combat.

He did not believe her a coward. To return here of her own volition took courage, and she had to have had a great deal of strength to have survived whatever had caused her to get that scar on her face. No, she was far from a coward. Something had to have happened for her to fear small spaces and he was curious to know what, just as his curiosity was growing about her scar, though he would not ask her now.

"As I said, it is either that room or a cell," he reminded.

"The room will suffice," she assured him quickly. "I

only ask that I not be confined to it all day and that I may leave the door open at night."

Her quiver ran through his hands that still rested on her and it sent a shiver of his own racing through him, stirring his loins to his annoyance. He took a hasty step away from her. "You have no right to ask anything, and I certainly have no wont to grant it."

Espy looked to the dark room, fear strangling almost as hard as Craven's hand when at her neck.

Craven knew fear when he saw it. There was not a Highlander alive, except for one he knew of, that did not taste fear one time or another. He had tasted it the day he had entered the birthing room and had seen his wife's lifeless body on the bed. He had known the depths of true fear that day.

Why then should Espy not suffer the same?

Aubrey would not want it.

The thought hit him like a punch to the face and he turned to go. "I will send a servant to set the fire." He walked off, calling back to her after a few steps, "Leave your door open."

~~~

Espy had eaten little of what was sent her for supper, having no appetite. The servant lass who had set the fire and brought her food had said not a word to her. She had kept her eyes averted as well, as though she feared punishment if she engaged with Espy in anyway.

She hoped and prayed that her stay here, while no doubt difficult, would eventually prove beneficial and in the end the truth about Aubrey's death would be discovered. She wanted that more than anything.

Though the fire burned brightly, a slight chill lingered and Espy tucked the blanket up around her. She was not able to sleep or was it that she feared sleep and the nightmares that followed. They had not been as frequent since returning home, but then her grandmother's cottage had always been a safe haven for her, at least once it had been. Still, she had felt safe upon arriving there, knowing her grandmother would care for her, heal her, and love her.

She let her thoughts wander to happier times when her da and mum were still alive. Her da and mum both had had adventurous souls, that and along with their thirst for knowledge, had had them carting their young daughter off on endless adventures. She had visited and lived in foreign lands, something that was inconceivable to most, and she cherished the memories.

It was what, she believed, made her da an outsider to the physicians in Glasgow and Edinburgh. They were stubborn and steadfast when it came to their beliefs and practices and ignored or ridiculed the knowledge her da had gained in foreign lands, calling his different approaches ridiculous and barbaric.

A yawn rose up, her eyes widening along with her mouth. She did not want to sleep. She did not want the nightmares. She fought against sleep as long as she could and it was not long after that the nightmare began.

Chapter Eight

The agonizing screams echoed off the stone walls of the cell and the odor of burnt flesh permeated the dank air. She had to get away. She had to escape, but what of the other innocents? She could not leave them there to suffer endless torture until finally they had no recourse but to beg for death.

She stared down at the heavy, iron keys in her hand. She only had so much time. If she hesitated a moment longer, all would be lost. She hurried along the narrow corridor, slipping now and again on the slimy stone floor. Three cells. Three women were all she needed to free. The others were beyond help and would not make it through the night.

"Go! Hurry!" she whispered to the first one after freeing her.

The second one she had to revive and get to her feet. "Hurry!" she urged once the woman gained her footing.

The stench from the third cell had her gagging and she was afraid of what she would find… death. She was too late and her heart ached. She said a quick prayer over the woman and cautiously left the cell, closing it behind her as she had done with the others. She took careful steps along the barely lit corridor, her heart pounding with fear. A few more steps, just a few and she would be free of this nightmare.

An arm suddenly coiled around her waist and dragged her back. Down. Down. Down. She felt herself being pulled farther and farther into the depths of hell, the flames burning at her flesh. She struggled to break free, but his arm was like an iron shackle around her waist. Still, she fought.

Even when she was slammed down on the cold slab she fought, the odor of sickness, torture and death nearly suffocating her. When she looked upon the face of her captor, she screamed, for there was no face just darkness.

She felt the tip of a blade catch high on her cheek and she screamed as the sharp blade was dragged slowly along her flesh. Her hand suddenly connected with a broken piece of slab and she grabbed it tight and swung with force at the blackness hovering over her, and she gave it a hard shove. It stumbled back and she rushed off the slab and ran, her feet pounding the slimy stones, but try as she might she could not escape the narrow corridor or the flames that rose up around her. She kept running and running, getting nowhere and behind her the pounding of footfalls grew ever closer, resonating in her head.

~~~

Craven climbed the stairs, slipping his shirt off as he went and though he yawned, he had no desire to seek sleep. He hated climbing into bed without Aubrey there. He had slept well with her beside him, the nightmare of battles, death and destruction having faded with her presence beside him. Now a different nightmare plagued him, his wife calling out to him for help, over and over and over.

Please help me. Please.

He had promised he would let nothing happen to her, that he would always protect her. He had failed her and for that he would never forgive himself.

He gazed down the short corridor to the servant's chamber he had secured Espy in as a temporary cell. He thought to go and see if she was still there, but where else would she be. The word had spread that she was his prisoner and was forbidden to venture anywhere without his permission. All would keep watch and none would dare go near her.

His thoughts were mixed when it came to the pouch of herbs. Had it been a tale to prevent her torture and death? Or could there be truth to it? It was that question that haunted him and he wanted it answered.

After entering his bedchamber, he tossed his shirt on a chair and was about to slip out of his plaid when he heard a noise that had him turning abruptly.

"Let me go!"

He hurried to the servant's chamber, his anger mounting that anyone would dare come to his private floor and attack his prisoner. He stopped abruptly in the open doorway. Espy was struggling frantically against the blanket that had wrapped itself tightly around her.

"Let me go! Let me go!"

Her cries grew louder as did her struggles and he went to her, wondering who she was battling in her nightmare. With her struggling, it was not easy to free her and when he finally caught the corner of the blanket, he yanked it hard, flipping her over as it unraveled.

He dropped the blanket and hurried to catch her before she rolled off the bed and once he did, her arms clamped around him, clinging to him tightly.

"Do not let him get me. Please, I beg you, do not let him get me."

Her eyes were wide as full moons, yet it was obvious she had yet to wake from her nightmare, and he sat on the bed, keeping tight hold of her.

She pressed her cheek to his and her cries turned to a soft whimper. "Please help me."

Hearing the words his wife cried out to him nightly, he instinctively wrapped his arms around Espy, trying to shield her, keep her safe, though he had no idea who from.

She raised her head and brought her mouth near his, her warm, whispered breath brushing his lips as she said, "Keep me safe. Please keep me safe."

All rationale thought left him or was it that he missed his wife's lips so badly that he foolishly…

His lips came down on hers in a hungry kiss and Espy responded with the same hunger. Craven's hand went to the back of her head, holding it firm, keeping it from moving, from freeing herself of his kiss. But it mattered little since Espy's arms shot up and around his neck, locking around him as if she had no intentions of ever letting him go.

The more he tasted her, the more familiar she tasted, and the more he wanted to linger in the delicious kiss. His body felt the same, growing more aroused as the kiss deepened. With his hand to the back of her head and his other arm going around to rest at her back, he eased her down on the bed, following to stretch over her.

He fed off the kiss, as if he had been starved for so long that he could not get enough. She responded in kind, her body pressing up against his in wont of more.

Her firm breasts dug into his bare chest, her hard nipples stabbing at him and growing him hard. A hard that he had not felt since he had last made love with Aubrey.

The sudden thought of his wife and who he was kissing shocked him so much that he tore his lips away from Espy and jumped up off her so roughly that she rolled off the bed onto the floor. This time he did not catch her.

She got to her feet, shaking her head.

"You had a nightmare," he said as if that was explanation enough.

She stared at him, nodding.

Craven returned her stare, though his eyes rested on her plumped lips and her heated cheeks, and the way her chest heaved from her heavy breathes. He hated her at that moment more than ever, for she had made him forget—for a short while—his wife. Who was it his thoughts and desires had focused on? The woman who he blamed for his wife's death.

Craven's anger spoke. "Keep your door shut and your nightmares to yourself." He stormed out of the room, the door slamming with a thud behind him.

Espy hurried to the bed, bracing herself in the corner and bringing her knees nearly up to her chin to circle her arms around them. Her nightmare had returned stronger than ever, only this time someone had rescued her from it, and she remembered clinging to him. His warmth had seeped into her chilled flesh along with the strength of his hard muscles. He would protect her, keep her safe, she could feel it. He had also kissed her with strength and that made her feel safer than ever.

What had startled her though was when she had awakened to find Craven kissing her and she willingly returning his kiss and realizing that she did not want to stop kissing him. As maddeningly as it seemed, she had enjoyed his kiss.

How could she even think that? He was out for revenge against her. He hated her. Why than had he kissed her?

She had no answer and it would be wise of her not to question it any further, but it continued to haunt her even when her head fell to rest on her knees as sleep claimed her.

~~~

Espy sat in the Great Hall, having finished the morning repast and eager to be about doing something, anything. She could not continue to sit idle. She would go insane and yet she had little choice, Craven having left her there with orders she was not to move. With the stares she got from the few warriors who lingered and the servants who tended the room, Craven would be alerted to any move she made.

It was foolish of him not to take advantage of her skills while she was here. She was certain there were those in the clan that could use a healer. No doubt, though, Craven did not trust her to treat any in his clan.

She sighed, her impatience growing at being idle and also at not being able to see what she could find out about Aubrey and who might want her dead.

A young servant lass kept glancing her way as she cleaned off the tables from the morning meal. She looked as if she wanted to approach Espy, but seemed reluctant. Espy encouraged her with a smile and the young lass quickly turned her head away.

It was when the lass got to the table next to her that Espy noticed the dirty cloth wrapped around her hand. She immediately got to her feet and went to her.

"You injured your hand?" Espy asked softly.

The lass backed away from her, a look of fright in her large round eyes.

"I am a healer. I help, I do not cause harm," Espy said and before the lass could run away in fright, she reached her hand out to her. "May I have a look?"

The lass hesitated, glancing around the room, looking to see who watched them.

Those in the hall were engaged in conversation, though glances strayed their way.

Espy kept her voice low. "It will not take long."

The lass leaned in close to Espy. "My hand hurts."

"What are you called?" Espy asked with a soft smile.

"Tula," the lass said, a hesitant smile at her lips.

"Let me tend the wound, Tula, so it no longer pains you," Espy offered.

Tula gave another glance around the room, then nodded.

In no time, Espy had Tula's hand cleaned and a fresh cloth wrapped around the minor abrasion.

Espy barely finished knotting the cloth on the back of Tula's hand to keep it in place when one of the warriors in the hall approached her, sticking his finger in her face and causing Tula to scurry around the table away from the large man.

"Can you heal it?" the warrior asked gruffly.

Espy took a close look at the red and swollen tip of his finger. "A splinter you have yet to remove?"

He nodded. "I cannot find it, no matter how much I dig."

"Sit," Espy said, seeing he had dug far too deeply. She turned to Tula and nodded at the two buckets of water on the table she had had the lass fetch. "I need these two filled with fresh water and I also need some wine."

"Thirsty are you?" the warrior asked with a laugh.

"What shall I call you?" Espy asked, smiling at his teasing words.

"Morta," he said, his wide shoulders going back and his sharp chin rising a bit. His long beard and moustache were as red as his long hair.

"This may hurt, Morta," she said, holding up a slim bone needle she had retrieved from her healing pouch that she kept tied to a loop she had sown to her waistband.

"I have suffered worse," he said with a shrug.

Tula returned and filled a goblet of wine for Espy while another servant placed two buckets of water on the table.

Espy washed her hands in one, then took the goblet of wine and poured some on Morta's swollen finger.

"What are you doing wasting good wine, woman?" Morta protested and grabbed the goblet and tilted his head back, downing what was left.

Espy did not wait for him to finish. She went to work on his finger. She found the splinter right where she suspected it to be from the swelling, embedded in the side of his finger right near the nail. A bit of probing with her needle and a quick pinch of the skin and she was able to snatch the long sliver out.

She poured more wine in the goblet and went to pour it on his finger again.

He snatched the goblet from her hand. "You will not waste good wine." He stuck his finger in the goblet, left it there until Espy nodded, then downed the remainder of it.

"Do that a few times a day until the swelling is no more," Espy advised him.

Morta grinned. "Best healing I ever had."

Tula tapped Espy on the shoulder as Morta walked off, giving a nod in his direction.

Espy turned to see a line of about five people waiting to approach her. She smiled, pleased to be doing what she loved and waved the first person on line toward her. She asked each one their names, committing them to memory, and spoke with them as if she were their friend and knew them well. Her smile never tired and her pleasant nature soon had smiles surfacing not only on the person she was tending, but those waiting, and even those working in the Great Hall.

The line began to grow and Espy cheerfully tended everyone who sought her help, her smile never wavering nor her gentleness.

Espy was surprised to see that the next person who stepped forward was a woman heavy with child. She helped her to sit on the bench.

Tears pooled in her eyes as she spoke. "I have lost two bairns at birth. Please help me. Please do not let me lose this one."

"What are you doing?"

The mighty roar had everyone cowering, too fearful to move as Craven came barreling down on them in rapid strides. Espy almost backed away herself, seeing his threatening scowl, but held her ground. When she saw the pregnant woman struggle to stand, she reached out to help her.

"Stay as you are, Doria!" Craven ordered, pointing his finger at her.

Doria obeyed and with Espy's help lowered her back down on the bench.

Craven stepped in front of Espy and brought his face close to hers. "What are you doing?"

She stared at his lips, moist and full, and the memory of his powerful kiss came flooding back, fluttering her stomach, quickening her heart, and had her struggling to find her voice.

It was not anger that had Craven glaring at her, it was the reminder of how sweet and luscious her lips had tasted last night when he had kissed her. Damn if he did not want to kiss her again. Annoyed at himself, he barked at her more roughly than he intended. "Answer me now."

His terse tone so startled her that she snapped back. "Your people came to me for help. They need a healer."

"And they should trust you?"

"I trust her."

Craven and Espy both turned to look at Doria.

"Forgive me, my lord, but I have lost two bairns. They did not even take a breath at birth. I do not want to lose another. The women talk about how Espy turned the bairn in Britt's stomach and delivered him safely. Not many healers can do that. I want a healer who will fight to deliver my child alive. Please, my lord, I beg you, let her tend me."

Craven heard his wife's words in Doria's and how she had begged him to let Espy tend her at delivery. He had agreed and looked what had happened. He turned away and was met with expectant faces, all waiting to see what his word would bring.

He saw then what he had not noticed before... clansmen who needed help. One person's eye was swollen so badly he could not see out of it and it was not bruised. Another had his arm wrapped with a blood-stained cloth. There was a child with red blotches covering the whole side of his face and a pale, wee lass, her head resting on her mother's shoulder, and the worried mother looking at him with pleading eyes.

Craven turned to Espy, though spoke loud enough for all to hear. "You might as well make yourself useful while you are my prisoner. Tend the ill." He brought his face close to hers once again. "Save Doria's bairn and I might let you live."

He turned and walked away, not understanding why he was offering her a reprieve when he had yet to determine if she was guilty of his wife's death. Or was he realizing that all signs pointed to her not being responsible? If so, who was responsible? Who could he blame? Or was there no one to blame but himself?

"Most grateful, Lord Craven."

"Bless you, Lord Craven."

Craven barely heard the words of gratitude that followed him through the hall from those waiting patiently to see Espy. He was too lost in his dark thoughts.

Espy watched Craven walk away, his powerful gait having lost its anger. She turned her head sharply when she felt a hand grasp her arm and she looked to see Doria, tears running down her cheeks.

"You will deliver my bairn safely and deliver your own salvation."

Chapter Nine

"That is the third practice pole you have felled in two days," Dylan said, shaking his head.

Craven drew his forearm across his brow, wiping the sweat away and looked down at the felled pole he had toppled with a battle axe. "Did you send that message?"

"I did, and it should not take long to hear that Edward MacPeters is now physician to Laird Eason."

"The Clan MacLagan?" Craven asked and Dylan nodded. "When did that come about?"

"I do not know, but we can ask him when he arrives in about two weeks as long as Eason doesn't object to your request that the physician be sent here. Though, I see no reason why he would."

"I wonder why MacPeters did not return to Edinburgh," Craven said, resting the battle axe against the bench and snatching his shirt off it, though he did not slip it on. "He had come highly recommended, though I was warned that he would not journey to the Highlands."

"You can be persuasive," Dylan said.

"When necessary. How are your son and Britt?" Craven asked, leaving the practice field with Dylan walking alongside him. They had been talking more since the birth of his son, discussing clan matters daily as they once did, and Craven was pleased. They had grown up more like brothers than friends and he had not realized how much he had missed that strong bond. Or how much he had allowed grief to steal it from him.

Dylan beamed with pride. "He is good and has a strong cry and stronger appetite. Britt is good as well. There is no keeping that woman down."

Craven stopped suddenly and Dylan looked to see why.

There was a line of people waiting to enter the keep.

"I heard Espy was tending the ill and those in need," Dylan said.

Craven turned to him, openly admitting what had just dawned on him. "I have allowed my grief to steal far too much from me and the clan."

"It has been a difficult time for you, but your grief is finally passing and you have begun to embrace your duties once more."

"Like this one I am about to tend to," he said as he took powerful strides toward the line of people, and Dylan followed behind him, shaking his head.

Faces paled as those on line moved to the side to let Lord Craven pass and whispers started to travel up and down the line, many worried that the beast's sharp tongue would strike and stop the gentle healer from helping them.

Craven stopped a short distance from where Espy stood by a table in the Great Hall. Her long, dark hair was braided, though falling loose, several strands having already fallen free, looking as if it was about to come completely undone. Her cheeks were flushed red, her smile gentle, and her soft blue eyes were filled with just as much tenderness as her voice when she spoke. But what caught his attention the most was the caring and loving way Espy held the wee lass in her arms, swaying as if to a soft melody and rubbing her little back as she did.

Espy not only had a loving heart but a tender soul. So how could such a woman have killed his wife? The more and more he saw of Espy and her kind ways, the more he believed her innocent in the death of his wife. His troubled thoughts slowed his gait, though the strength of them remained. He no longer appeared like a man charging into battle, though his lack of a smile gave one pause.

It did not take the tiny lass long once she caught sight of him to begin crying and instead of reaching out for her mum, the little lass threw her arms around Espy's neck and clung to her.

Craven silently cursed himself for frightening the wee bairn and he attempted a smile and kept his tone gentle as he came to a stop in front of them. "It is a brave little lass we have here."

The lass peeked out at him and he titled his head, narrowing his brow for a moment. She looked familiar and he looked to the lass's mum. He realized then that he had seen them both. They had been on line the first day Espy had started tending people.

"Espy has helped you feel better?" he asked, his smile growing without difficulty.

The little lass raised her head and smiled with delight. "My tummy does not hurt anymore."

Craven's smile spread as the little lass' smile stretched from ear to ear, highlighting the sprinkle of freckles across her nose and cheeks as her bright red hair sprung in curls around her head. That she was happy and well, pleased Craven.

"We are all so grateful, my lord, that we now have a healer here at the keep to tend us," the lass' mum said.

Craven looked to Espy and his smile faded some as he saw that her smile could not hide the fatigue in her lovely eyes, and the thought that she had tired herself looking after his clan that he had neglected disturbed him. She was giving all she could to his clan without thought to herself. She truly was selfless.

"I am pleased to know that Amber does well, Ellen, "Craven said with a gentle tap of his finger to Amber's tiny nose, making the lass giggle.

Espy was surprised that Craven knew not only the mum's name, but the little lass' one as well. And from the look on Ellen's face, she was also surprised. She handed Amber to her mum. "She does well, Ellen. There is no need for more of the brew."

"Thank you. Thank you so much, Espy," Ellen said and with a nod to Craven, the woman hurried off.

"You know Ellen and Amber," Espy said.

"These are my people, my family. I know many of them since I was young."

Espy nodded, her hand going to her mouth to stifle a yawn.

"Have you eaten or rested at all today?" he asked.

She shook her head, he surprising her again with the concern in his voice.

Craven caught other signs of her fatigue in the slight slump of her shoulders and the way her eyes had lost some of their usual shine. They were minor changes, but noticeable, to him at least, and he wondered why he could spot them.

"You cannot keep tending people," —he rushed his finger to press at her lips when she went to speak— "here in the keep. I will see that you have a cottage to use." He lowered his voice. "You will see that you get rest and that you eat. You will also continue to sleep in the keep."

Her warm, moist lips tingled the tip of his finger and sent his lips aching and tingles shooting down to tease his manhood unmercifully.

Damn, but he wanted to kiss her. Instead, he wisely turned and walked away without a word, his desire to kiss her much too strong for him to remain there and ignore it. What was it about the woman that made him want to kiss her, touch her, and aroused him much too fast? He had hated her this past year more than he had ever hated in his life. Yet now he found himself... he shook his head. How was it that he was feeling such desire for this woman? It had been too long for him, too long without a woman, though not any woman—his wife. After Aubrey, the thought of a fast poke with a woman did little for him. He wanted to feel, feel deep when he buried his manhood in a woman. He had known when he lost Aubrey he would never know that depth of love again. Would never want a woman with the hungry passion that he had wanted Aubrey... until Espy.

When he passed Dylan, he said, "Find her a cottage she can use for her healing. Make sure it is close to the keep."

He was keeping her close. Lord help him, he was keeping her much too close.

~~~

Espy sat on the edge of the bed, fighting sleep. Her head bobbed with it and her body ached for it, and she needed it. Tomorrow would be a busy day. Dylan had taken her to a cottage that would be perfect for her. It needed cleaning, but she planned on rising early and seeing to it. She also was hoping that her grandmother would be permitted to visit. She had heard that Howe would be released from the stocks soon and she feared him going after her grandmother since as far as she knew Bonnie was still there with her. Then there was the help she would need. These were things she wanted to discuss with Craven and so she fought sleep, waiting for him to seek his bedchambers so she could speak to him.

It grew ever later and ever more difficult to keep her head up and her eyes open.

"Do you fight the nightmares?"

Espy jumped up off the bed, her hand going to her chest, her heart beating so madly she thought it would break free.

"I frightened you," Craven said from the open doorway.

"I have waited for you," she said, not bothering to answer his question since he did frighten her but not in the way he thought.

"Why?" he asked, stepping into the room and filling it with his massive presence.

"There were some things I wished to ask you," she said, feeling the coward for drawing back away from him, his looming presence much too intimidating in this confined space. Or was he much too inviting?

He folded his arms across his naked chest, the muscles there and in his arms sprinkled with what Espy thought were dewdrops, the fire's light making them glisten. His dark hair barely brushed his shoulders and was wet. Had he just bathed? When a fresh scent tickled her nose, she knew the answer and she envied him. She wished she could bathe, instead of using a washing jug to see to keeping clean.

"I am waiting."

He startled her out of her musings and she silently chided herself for letting her thoughts drift off. She dared not step closer to him since she had the overpowering urge to lick the dewdrops off him and that was such a foreign thought to her that she wondered where it had come from.

"With so many needy people to look after, I was hoping it would be permissible to have someone help me," she said glad she was able to speak without her voice quivering. "If it is permissible, I was hoping I could request Tula. Also, I would so appreciate it if my grandmother would be allowed to visit with me. I worry with Howe being released from the stocks soon that he will go after her and harm her." She rushed her hand to her mouth to cover the yawn that unexpectedly crept up on her.

He did not answer her. He stood there and stared in thought, annoyance, disinterest? Or had his dark eyes softened? A strange thought that left her wondering.

"You are tired. You need sleep."

That may be so, but sleep was not her friend and after what happened with Craven the other night, she feared even more going to sleep only to wake clinging to him. Not that she had not found it pleasant, it had been more than pleasant and that was the problem.

"Do you fight the nightmares?"

Espy had not answered him when last he asked and she would not answer him now. "You are right. I am tired and need sleep."

That she would not even acknowledge his question told him that she was keeping something from him, and he did not like secrets. Secrets never failed to cause problems. He would find out sooner or later.

"Good-night then," Craven said and turned.

"Will you grant my requests," she asked, but her question followed him out the door unanswered. He did to her what she had done to him, ignored the question.

~~~

Espy was surprised to not only see Tula but three other women already at work cleaning the cottage when she arrived. She was also surprised to see that the cottage was larger than she had expected and it had two windows. What she liked most though was the large garden on the side that ran the length of the cottage and had good width to it. She could grow many of the plants and herbs she needed there.

Tula waved from the door, a broad smile on her face, and hurried toward her. "Lord Craven instructed me to serve you. That is my daily chore now to help you and I am thrilled to do so."

Espy's smile showed how pleased she was as well that Craven had granted her request. "You will make an excellent helper."

Tula nodded vigorously. "I will work hard, for I enjoy helping you much more than working in the kitchen." She turned to the three women who had stepped out of the cottage and waited behind her.

"This is Faye and you know Elva and Mina. They have come to help prepare the cottage. More women will be joining us as well and some of their husbands will arrive to make some needed repairs."

"How generous of all of you," Espy said, looking to each woman. "I appreciate the help."

"When word spread that you were to get a cottage where you would tend the ill, everyone rejoiced. It has been difficult for many of us to visit Cyra," —Tula lowered her voice— "and many were fearful that Lord Craven would grow angry if they did."

"You have brought good changes in such a short time," Faye said, her cheeks growing fuller with her wide smile and highlighting her pretty features.

"I have brought no change," Espy said, wondering what the woman meant.

"You have," Mina said with a firm nod. "Everyone has seen it. Even before Lord Craven brought you to the keep things had begun to change for the better."

"You have quieted the beast and we are grateful," Elva said a tear in her eye.

"We must get to work," Tula ordered, a tear in her eye as well as she shooed the women into the cottage.

Espy stared after them, too shocked by their words to move. She had done no such thing, had she?

Tula turned in the doorway, waving at Espy to join them. "Come and see. It will make a good healing cottage."

Espy hurried forward, chasing the ridiculous thought from her head.

~~~

While work went on around her, Espy saw to tending those who sought her healing skills. She also shared a brief repast with the women who came to help, enjoying the talk and laughter. She had forgotten the camaraderie a clan, a village, a family provided, and she realized how very much she had missed it.

The women drifted off when it drew nearer the evening meal and shortly after the last woman left, Tula told her it was time for them to return to the keep.

"Go on ahead, I will be there shortly," Espy said. She wanted a moment alone in the cottage to gather her thoughts.

Tula seemed reluctant to leave her. "Lord Craven will expect you."

"I will not be long. I just want a moment," Espy assured her.

Tula smiled, nodded, and took her leave.

Aubrey had been mentioned now and again when the women had talked and not a bad word had been spoken about her. She had been admired and respected, which was what Espy had seen for herself for the brief time she knew Aubrey. That would rule out anyone hating Aubrey enough to want her dead. So why would someone want her dead?

Through the years, Espy had seen the greed and heartlessness in people and more than once she had seen a life taken for the purpose of gaining wealth, for power or simply for revenge.

So the question begged, what benefit had served Aubrey's death?

Craven would inherit MacVarish land because of his marriage to Aubrey, but he would inherit whether Aubrey was alive or dead. So there would be no reason for him to want his wife dead. Besides, everyone knew how much he loved her.

She wondered if Craven knew anything of Aubrey's life before she came to live with her uncle. Could there be something in Aubrey's past that could be the reason for someone wanting her dead? Or could someone have wanted revenge against Craven and took it by killing Aubrey?

"Were you not told to go to the keep?"

Espy jumped and turned away from the small fire burning in the hearth to see Craven standing a short distance from her, the door to the cottage closed behind him. Espy's heart began to quicken in her chest as the once good-sized cottage suddenly began to close in around her.

"Time slipped away from me," she said, clenching her skirt as she fought to remain calm.

"Is it only me or all men you fear?" he asked, all too familiar with fear when he saw it in another. It was almost tangible the way it rose up to grab at someone and squeeze tighter and tighter until it felt like a shackle had clamped around one's entire body.

"I do not fear men... I fear what they are capable of. I am not so foolish to think I can defend myself against a man of your size and strength, or against men of power."

"You have come up against such men?" he asked, his brow tightening. Any man who forced himself on a woman was no man... he was a coward.

"The evening meal awaits," she said.

"Let it," he said, realizing that she did as before and did not answer him, though it was not so much that as he wanted some time alone with her. As much as he tried to ignore it, he found that his time spent with her brought him an ease he had not felt in some time. And he ached for that as much as he ached to kiss her.

"I am most grateful that you have granted Tula permission to help me and for this cottage. It will work well." She stepped to the side, hoping he would see she was ready to leave.

"Do you always avoid a subject when you do not want to answer a question?"

"Some things are better left unspoken," she said.

He took another step toward her and the room suddenly shrunk around her, imprisoning her, locking her away. Her chest tightened and fear pierced her as sharply as a blade, and she went to run past him, needing to break free.

Craven's hand shot out, capturing her arm and bringing her to an abrupt halt. "Espy?" he questioned with concern, seeing her eyes awash with fear.

She did not hear his concern. Her only thought was escape. She tried to pull her arm free of his ironclad grip as she demanded, "Let me go!"

His took hold of her other arm, though not tightly just enough to keep her from running off. "You are safe. I will not hurt you."

Espy could not stop her panic from rising. It threatened her limbs and clenched at her stomach. She fought against it, told herself she was in no danger here, but the more she tried to reason with herself, the worse her panic grew. The next thing she knew, she felt as though a hand had clamped around her throat, squeezing ever tighter.

She gasped repeatedly, fighting for breath.

Craven watched the fear begin to consume her. It had crept up on him a time or two, but he had always managed to contain it, stomp it down, bury it. Had he caused such fear in Espy? Or had a memory reared its head to torment her?

"No one is going to harm you, Espy. You are safe here with me. I will protect you."

He loosened his hold, hoping it would help her realize she was not being held prisoner, and her hands quickly latched onto his arms, her soft blue eyes wide and full of fright, and the urge to kill whoever had put such fear in her jabbed at him repeatedly.

Craven eased his one arm to lie around her waist gently, while his hand went to caress her scarred cheek. "Easy, Espy, slow breaths. You have nothing to fear. You are safe. I will let no harm come to you." He kept reassuring her and encouraging her to take slow breaths until finally her breathing slowed, and her head fell to rest on his shoulder.

His other arm went around her, his hand caressing her back. Not a thought entered his head to push her away or to let her go. As much as he wanted to fight against it, make endless excuses of why he should not enjoy having her there in his arms, this time he let it be.

Espy had never felt so safe, never felt her fear fade away so fast, but then she had never been held so gently, so protectively by a man. Aubrey had been lucky to have Craven love her as much as he did. The thought of his deceased wife had Espy shifting to step out of his arms as she raised her head to thank him.

Her eyes met his and held for a moment and an ember of passion flickered in his dark eyes, waiting to be ignited. Espy's stomach churned and fluttered uncontrollably and her mouth fell open, the soft gasp that fell from it too silent to hear and too much for Craven to ignore.

His lips came down on hers in a kiss that neither of them could deny.

Chapter Ten

Something sparked to life inside Craven, heating him, and chasing away the cold emptiness that had consumed him for far too long. Her kiss was like a healing tonic to his heart, the hurt and pain fading as she responded generously, eagerly, freely, as if she needed healing as much as he did.

He let himself get lost, he let himself feel, he let himself enjoy the kiss.

Her lips were strong against his demanding ones, her tongue eager to spare with his, and his body growing with a desire he had not felt in a long time. He could easily couple with this woman, feel her flesh, taste every bit of her, sink deep inside her, and get lost in pleasure.

The tempting thoughts grew him hard as did her taut nipples poking at him through his shirt. She was as aroused as he was. His hand slipped down along her skirt, between her legs and caressed the delicate spot and her soft gasp against his mouth confirmed his thought. She was as needy as he was.

Take her. Surrender your pain.

The thought of surrendering to her had him ending the kiss to his disappointment and guilt. "I want you. I should not want you, but God help me I ache for you."

Espy pulled herself out of his arms, a task that would have proved difficult if he had not willingly let her go. "You are right. You should not want me. I failed you, Aubrey, and your bairn."

She ran past him and this time he did not stop her. He stared after her, watching her disappear into the dusk that was rapidly fading to night. He could not believe what he had seen in her soft blue eyes as she had spoken.

Pain so strong that he had felt it himself.

She blamed herself as much as he blamed himself for Aubrey's death. But if not her, then who was at fault?

~~~

Espy went straight to her bedchamber, her food waiting there for her. There were nights she wished she could eat with others, join in their conversation. Tonight was not such a night. She had lost her appetite and she did not want to see anyone. She preferred to be alone.

It troubled her that she felt such an attraction to Craven. She told herself that it was because of those moments when fear had managed to break through her resolve and he had shown her kindness that she felt that way. There been no one there to help her this past year when fear had conquered her. She had not always been that way and she hated that she was now. She had always been strong, her da and mum had seen to that. It had taken only one incident to change everything.

Helplessness.

She had never known true helplessness until that day and she never wanted to experience it again. It was one of the reasons she had returned home. She had to face Craven willingly and be done with it but most of all, she had wanted to feel her grandmother's arms around her and know that she was loved.

She sat huddled in the corner of her bed, braced against the wall, her cloak pulled tightly around her. She did not want to sleep. She did not want the nightmares to return. But she was exhausted, mostly of fighting, always fighting. That was all she had done this past year to stay alive. Though there had been times she had thought death would be preferable, but her healing ways would not allow her to betray her beliefs. There had been many who had been grateful to her for her skills and she herself had been grateful that she had been able to help them, in more ways than just healing.

If only she had not... but what choice had she?

She shook her head. It did no good to dwell on it. It was done. At least, she hoped it was.

She yawned and rested her head against the wall, closing her eyes. She would rest, not sleep, but rest as she had taught herself to do. To always be alert. To always be ready to flee.

That was how Craven found her hours later. He had told himself not to look in on her that he had been informed that she had retired to her room upon entering the keep, but he had to make sure. To his annoyance it was not to make sure she was there, but to see how she fared after the incident in the healing cottage.

Seeing her huddled against the wall, still wearing her cloak and boots was a familiar scene to him. It was the way warriors slept when in battle, ready to fight or flee at any given moment.

The question was... who was she fleeing from? Him or herself?

He told himself to leave her be, but something about her tucked away in the corner full of fright, tugged at his heart and he went over to her. He reached out to gently lift her in his arms to lay her on the bed so that she would not find her limbs aching in the morning. As soon as he did, her arms latched around his neck, clinging to him, and she buried her face in the crook of his neck.

He went down with her on the narrow bed, intending to lay there with her until the stiffness lift her rigid body and he could unlock her arms from around his neck without waking her.

It was his body that surrendered first, resting more comfortably on the narrow bed with her tucked against him than he did in the large bed he slept in alone. When his yawns became more frequent, he knew it was time for him to take his leave.

He reached up to pry her hands loose from the back of his neck, but her fingers dug in tighter each time he did and she snuggled closer against him. But it was her whisper that had stopped his hand from trying again.

"Please, I beg you. Do not let him get me."

Someone was after her? Who had frightened her so much that it had sent her home to face him... the beast who wanted her dead?

His arm draped protectively over her once again. It was one thing for him to order her punishment, she belonged to his clan. That another should attempt to harm her was something else. Something completely unacceptable, but then he had sent her away, had banned her from the clan, from the only family she knew.

He thought of Cyra and decided it would be good for her to visit with Espy and for him to speak with her and see if she could shed some light on what had happened to Espy this past year. With his thoughts busy, he did not realize that sleep was sneaking up on him and drifting him into a deep, peaceful slumber.

~~~

The soft hair tickled at his nose and he did not want to wake and find it was only a dream. That Aubrey was gone forever and these special moments would only come in dreams. He sniffed, wanting to inhale deeply of the familiar scent and his brow furrowed. It was not Aubrey's scent, a light, fresh sweetness. This was bolder, more potent, and tempting.

The sound of rushing footfalls disturbed the pleasant moment and had him opening his eyes to stare into Espy's blue ones wide with surprise.

A loud gasp from the open doorway had them both sitting up quickly, Craven's arm going around Espy to catch her before she toppled off the edge of the narrow bed.

"I see you had a pleasant night," Dylan said while Tula stood in front of him, mouth wide, blinking several times, not believing what she saw as she stared directly at Craven and Espy in bed together.

Espy went to hurry out of Craven's arms, but his strong order stopped her.

"Stay as you are, and as for you two," he said with a nod to Tula and Dylan, "leave us."

Tula turned, bumping into Dylan in her haste to obey and squeezed herself past him to rush off.

Dylan smiled as he gave Craven a nod and turned to leave, his steps not rushed. "Do not waste your breath in telling me to hold my tongue about this," he called back. "Tula will have the word spread before I reach the last step."

Craven kept his arm around Espy's waist as he eased her as well as himself off the bed. He let go of her once she was on her feet, though he remained standing in front of her.

Espy waited for him to speak, too befuddled over waking up to find him in her bed and in his arms. What surprised her even more though was that she had slept well. No nightmares had disturbed her sleep. She actually felt well-rested.

Craven's words caught in his throat. He intended to tell her that she was to sleep in the cottage from this day on, yet he could not bring himself to say it. He also could not bring himself to admit that he had slept soundly in the narrow bed with her cuddled close against him. It was not something he should be thinking and certainly not something he should think of doing again. Why then was that his thought?

"Go, eat, and tend to those in need," he said and walked out of the room without glancing back, though he wanted to.

He wanted another look at her face, flushed from her surprise at finding him in bed with her and, lord help him, he wanted to kiss her moist lips.

"Damn. Damn. Damn," he muttered as he walked to his bedchamber and closed the door behind him.

As soon as Espy heard the door to his bedchamber close, she hurried out of the room, working the braid out of her hair as she went past it and braiding it again as she went down the stairs. She did not bother to stop in the Great Hall and inform anyone that she would eat elsewhere today. She walked straight through without a word or nod to anyone and once outside, she went directly to the cottage.

She should be hungry after not eating last night, but this morning's surprise had stolen her appetite. What would happen once word spread that Craven had been found in her bed this morning? Fully clothed or not made no difference, tongues would wag. It was not a place he should be found.

What had he been doing there? She remembered nothing of last night and how could that be when she usually slept light, listening for every sound, making sure to keep herself safe.

His arms had kept her safe.

That had been one of the thoughts that had raced through her mind when she had woken and found herself nestled tightly against him, his arms snug around her. She was safe, but how could that be when he had other plans for her?

A tap at the door had her shaking the multitude of thoughts away as she went to see who was there.

A young lad, about ten years, frowned as he raised a red, swollen arm to her. "My name is Reed and I got bit."

She smiled softly and ushered him in. "Let me have a look, Reed."

Tula arrived with food shortly after the lad and seeing the lad's eyes turn wide at the generous plate of bread, cheese, and meats—far too much for her alone—placed on the table, she offered him some. The lad ate with gusto as he regaled Espy and Tula with his tale of how he went after the bug that bit him and killed him dead.

Espy instructed Reed to return tomorrow so she could see how his arm was healing and the lad nodded with enthusiasm, no doubt looking forward to another hardy meal.

By mid-day it had quieted and Espy took time to give herself a quick wash from the bucket she brought into the cottage, while Tula stood guard outside to stop anyone from entering. Espy slipped off her blouse and twisted her hair up to secure with two bone combs, a few teeth missing from both, to the top of her head.

She lathered a clean cloth with lavender scented soap and got busy scrubbing herself, starting with her face and working her way down. It felt so refreshing that she quickly stepped out of her skirt and boots and went to work on her lower half, where she was reminded of how slender she had gotten, her stomach flat and her hips having lost their fullness. The warmth from the hearth caressed her backside, less rounded than it once had been and as she gave her legs a scrub, she realized how slender and taut they had grown. Her body had changed along with everything else in her life.

She stood, dropping the wet cloth in the bucket, and stepped to the side of the table to reach for a towel on the stool to dry herself. She did not want to chance anyone seeing her naked.

The door swung open before her hand could grab the towel and Espy froze as Craven entered.

He froze as well, his dark eyes on her... all of her.

Espy was relieved when Tula closed the door on them, though that turned quickly to concern. Not only had they been found in bed together this morning, but he was now alone with her while naked. She grabbed for the towel, this time his words stopping her.

"I have need of you."

The way he looked at her, his eyes full of passion, his voice husky and wanting, had her rushing to grab the towel and hold it in front of her like a shield.

"Get dressed. I have need of you," he ordered and turned to leave, but stopped and turned around and took quick strides toward her.

Espy instinctively went to step back, but his hand shot out and took hold of her arm, stopping her.

"That towel is a flimsy shield against me and against your own desires." He turned. "Hurry, as I said, I have need of you and bring your healing pouch."

Espy stared at the closed door. Her own desires? He thought she desired him? Why not? He had not forced her to return his kiss. She had done so willingly, though she continued to ask herself why. Had it been desire? She shook her head. It was madness to think that she could care for a man who blamed her for his wife's death. Complete and utter madness. Now if only she could make her heart understand that. She needed to settle the mystery surrounding Aubrey's death, proving her innocence and free herself of Craven. She would return home to her grandmother and finally live a peaceful life. Unless her past deeds returned to haunt her

Craven will keep you safe.

If only, she thought and rushed to don her garments, braid her hair, and gather her cloak and pouch. She stepped outside to see Craven standing by his horse with at least a dozen of his warriors mounted on horses, waiting for his command.

Craven held his hand out to her and she went to him. "Who needs a healer?" she asked as his hands settled at her waist and he lifted her onto his horse.

He did not speak until he mounted the horse, his arms closing around her as he took hold of the reins. "The laird of

Clan MacVarish."

Espy recalled Bonnie telling her that the old laird was near death and when he died, Craven would inherit the clan and all its holdings. Bonnie had not seemed too happy about that and it made Espy wonder how the rest of the Clan MacVarish felt about having Craven as their new laird.

An awkward silence fell between them on the short ride there, Espy feeling comfortable in his arms, yet knowing it was foolish. Sound reason or perhaps it was an attempt to control desires that would not serve her well that had her trying not to lean against him, to keep a space, if a narrow one, between them.

Fate seemed to be against her, since she found herself jostled against him as they rode until finally Craven hooked his arm tighter around her, settling her more firmly against him. As foolish as it was, she let it be. She enjoyed how his strength embraced her, coiled around her, comforted her. She would allow herself this brief time of feeling protected, of feeling that no one could hurt her while she was wrapped in his arms.

Craven wished the ride would take longer. He favored having her in his arms, the fresh scent of lavender filling his nostrils and stirring his senses. Then there was the fit of her against him, like two pieces of a puzzle or mystery coming together and fitting perfectly. Like a mystery, he wondered about the why of it. Why did they fit so well? Why did she feel so right in his arms?

They passed through the MacVarish village, all eyes on them and Espy wondered what they had heard about her and Craven. She had brought enough misery to her grandmother, she did not need to bring disgrace as well.

She kept herself erect, showing no shame, for she had done nothing wrong. She did not shy away when people glanced her way. She smiled and nodded and all returned her acknowledgement in kind, as if they admired her, and she wondered if it had anything to do with the women believing she had quieted the beast.

As they passed the stocks, she saw that they were empty. Howe had been released. She turned her head, their faces so close that she could see his fine looks appeared even finer when having the chance to look upon him without haste. She noticed for the first time, the tiny scar that sat at the right corner of his mouth and was barely noticeable unless up close and in good light. She felt it an intimate discovery as if no one knew about it but her.

"You wish to say something?" he asked, looking into her upturned face and thinking how tempting her lips looked.

Hs words caught her unaware and she nodded, trying not to look at his lips that had kissed her nearly senseless. She mentally shook her head and silently admonished herself. His kiss had meant nothing and she almost laughed at the foolishness of her own thought. A kiss always meant something, though not always what we wanted it to mean.

"Howe has been freed?" she asked.

"He has and he has been warned to stay away from Bonnie and Cyra."

"But she is his wife. He will want her back. Have you at least sent warriors to ensure their safety?"

"Howe will not be foolish enough to disobey me."

"You cannot be sure of that. He is unpredictable," she argued worried for her grandmother and Bonnie.

"You question my authority?" he asked, finding it difficult to believe that while men would dare not attempt to challenge him, this woman had the courage to speak her mind to him, and he admired her boldness.

"I would not do that, my lord, however, I do question Howe's anger and his temper that he cannot control." She rested her hand on his arm, giving it a gentle squeeze. "Please, I worry what he might do."

Her delicate features were marred by her heavy frown,

but somehow a spark of beauty escaped, her scar even unable to diminish it. She was brave enough to question him, yet wise enough to placate him as well.

"They are safe. Worry not," Craven assured her.

"My grandmother is all the family I have left. I have no clan. I have no one but her."

It had been difficult enough when he had lost Aubrey, but he still had his clan and a good friend in Dylan. He had been foolish not to realize it and turn to them in his time of grief as he had done once before. Espy had had no one but Cyra, and he had banished her from the only person who loved her.

"I have sent warriors to watch over Cyra and Bonnie," he said, not wanting her to worry needlessly. He felt her body jump and turn a bit as if she intended to hug him, then stopped, and he wished she had not stopped. He would have loved to feel her arms around his neck again and he would love to feel her cheek, tinged pink from the ride, pressed to his.

Thrilled that he had been so considerate of her grandmother, Espy almost went to hug him, but caught herself. Instead, she said, "I am most grateful, Lord Craven."

The sun disappeared behind clouds and the air had chilled considerably when they passed through the MacVarish village, on their way to the keep. Somber and worried faces greeted them and as they dismounted and were directed to the old laird's bedchamber Espy sensed one thing.

Death waited for someone here today.

Chapter Eleven

A healer often acquired a sense of death after battling it so often. Espy had fought death on many occasions and had been victorious, but there were those times death lingered near, waiting impatiently. That was the sense Espy got now. Death waited. He was here to collect a soul and she was here to battle him.

Espy stepped into a barely lit room, the odor so pungent she raised her hand to cover her nose.

Craven stepped around her and went to the lone window to swiftly draw back the tapestry covering it. Light blasted through the window, filling the room and Craven's jaw tightened and he clenched his hands when he looked upon the withered man in the bed.

"You leave your laird uncared for?" he roared at the servant who immediately cowered. "Why was I not summoned sooner?"

The lass trembled as she raised her head. "We sent a message before this recent one, but you never came."

Craven clenched his hands tighter, his knuckles turning white as his anger mounted, though not at the lass, at himself. He was reminded once again how others had suffered while he had buried himself in his grief.

Espy stepped forward, smiled, and calmly said, "Lord Craven is here now and will see to what must be done."

Espy's sincere smile and reassuring words had the lass' eyes brighten with relief.

"I will need several servants, some to help me with the laird, and others to clean this room," Espy said, slipping her cloak off and draping it over the back of a dusty chair and wasting no time in rolling up her sleeves, showing the young lass she was here to work along with them. "I will also need plenty of water, soap, and clean cloths. Fresh bed linens as well."

"Do as the healer instructs," Craven said, his anger subsiding with how gently and encouragingly Espy handled the situation.

The lass bobbed her head, turned a smile on Espy, and rushed out of the room.

Espy went to the frail man in the bed who appeared to be barely breathing.

"Owen, his name is Owen and he was a brave warrior in his day," Craven said with respect for the old man.

"Owen, I am here to help you," Espy said softly, placing her hand on the man's brow.

"Au—" A cough racked his body, shaking the whole of him.

Espy slipped her hand beneath his head, lifting it and looked to Craven, then to the pillow.

Craven cringed in disgust at the soiled pillow as he placed it beneath Owen's head.

The old man stopped coughing and breathed a bit easier. He managed to reach up and place his weak hand on Espy's arm as he struggled to speak. "Do not leave me, Aubrey." He gasped for breath, fighting to continue. "I do not want to die alone."

"I will not leave you, Owen," Espy assured him, "and while death may knock, we do not have to answer."

Servants entered the room and a flurry of activity began under Espy's direction.

Craven looked to Espy. "I will speak to you."

She nodded and followed him out of the room.

"Tell me," Craven said, fearing the worst.

"I cannot say since I do not know enough of what he has suffered."

"He looks close to death."

"I have seen men in worse shape who have recovered, so I cannot say for sure," Espy said.

"You cannot perform miracles. If you could, my wife would still be alive."

The barb stung Espy until he continued speaking.

"You would have saved Aubrey from whatever evil was after her."

Was he admitting she was not at fault? That he had wrongly blamed her? Did he now think that Aubrey's death was no accident, but intentional? Hope soared in her heart along with sorrow for him.

Instinct to help and to heal had her reaching out to rest a gentle hand on his arm. "Knowledge can be as powerful as miracles. We must find out what happened to Aubrey and let her finally rest in peace."

A hacking cough from Owen had Espy giving Craven's arm a squeeze before hurrying into the room.

Craven turned and took the stairs slowly, wondering how after all Espy had been through because of him, she would want to help him. The answer came easily.

She continued to fight for Aubrey.

While he had wallowed in sorrow, she had fought to survive and questioned what had happened, the intense bleeding not having made sense to her. Where he blamed, she searched for answers. Where he let guilt nearly destroy him, guilt grew Espy more determined. She was more a warrior than he was… but no more would he languish in grief.

He had unknowingly helped the culprit, forcing Aubrey to take the mixture the physician had insisted upon, making him culpable in her death. If it was not Espy's fault, then someone had used him to help murder his wife and, if that was so, he intended to find out who, and when he did… he would let the beast loose.

Carven hoped Owen would survive at least the night, though he had his doubts. There was much he wanted to ask the man about Aubrey, things he should have asked long before this, but at the time he cared nothing about. He had fallen in love with Aubrey and nothing could have stopped him from marrying her. But what if there had been something in her past he should have known about? What if there was a reason someone wished Aubrey harm? The more important question that nagged at him was that if there was something in Aubrey's past she ran from, why had she not shared it with him?

Please, I beg you, do not let him get me.

He heard Espy's words as clearly as she had spoken them to him. Was Espy running from something as well? His stomach clenched tight. He would let nothing happen to her. He would keep her safe, unlike his wife. He would find out what happened to Aubrey and, if it proved so, free Espy of the guilt and place it where it belonged... on himself.

~~~

Craven climbed the stairs to Owen's bedchamber after several hours of seeing how the Clan MacVarish fared. It did not take long to see how the clan had suffered this past year with their laird taking ill. Much work would be required to rebuild the clan and have it prosper once again. The clan was an aged one, not enough young hardy men to share in the work or young enough women to bear more children to strengthen and grow the clan.

Owen had realized it and it was why he had been so pleased when Aubrey had joined with Craven in marriage. With Craven as heir, the Clan MacVarish was safe when Owen died.

Craven stopped upon entering Owen's bedchamber, the difference from only a few hours ago was remarkable.

Daylight not only shined in through the lone window, but light also filtered through the room from a fire blazing in the hearth and several candles. The odor was gone, the air now having a pleasant scent of lavender about it and there was not a spot of dust or dirt anywhere. But the most remarkable change of all was Owen.

He was sitting up in bed, braced against pillows that were covered in clean linens and he wore a clean nightshirt. He appeared freshly scrubbed, his face having a pink hue to it, and his long gray hair had been combed and tied back away from his thin face. He also wore a smile.

Craven could not believe the difference. It was as if Espy had performed a miracle, but then what was it she had said... *knowledge can be as powerful as miracles*. Obviously Espy was an extremely knowledgeable woman.

"Craven my dear friend, you brought me an angel," Owen said and turned teary eyes on Espy.

"I brought you a skilled healer," Craven said, walking over to the bed and Espy stepped aside as he did.

"She cleaned me up and forced a potion on me that has me feeling better than I have in some time," Owen said, extending his hand out to Craven. "It is good to see you, Craven, and I am grateful for your help."

Craven took his frail hand and squeezed gently. "You have only to call on me, Owen."

"You have proven that to me many times and I believe it is time, and also a wise decision, for me to formally yield the Clan MacVarish to you. I want my clan not only protected but to prosper and grow and it can do that by being part of Clan MacCara."

"We had agreed for that to take place once you past, but seeing that your clan is in dire need of help, I agree with your wise decision. I will have the documents drawn and the word spread, and I will begin to move some of my clan here to help rebuild."

"I wish I could live to see that," Owen said, fighting the tears in his eyes.

"You will, if you do as I say," Espy said.

Craven turned, arching his brow.

"He is weak from an illness that took a toll on him, but with proper care, he will grow strong again," Espy explained. "He will need to be looked after and made to do as told, since I believe he is a stubborn man, which is why he probably survived the illness. He was simply too tenacious to die."

Craven turned a smile on Owen.

Owen returned it as his tears continued to fall. "Aubrey always said the same thing about me... I was too stubborn to die." Owen's smile faded as soon as Craven's smile vanished. "I am sorry. I should not have mentioned my niece."

"Of course, you should," Craven said. "Aubrey was a good and loving woman and should always be remembered."

Owen smiled. "I am glad you feel that way. I miss her. She would sit and listen to me ramble on for hours without complaint. I thought she would forget about me once she wed you, but she visited me weekly and I looked forward to seeing her smiling face."

Memories stirred in Craven, the all too familiar pain of losing her returning and though he would have much preferred for talk of her to end, he needed to know more about her.

"Aubrey rarely talked about her life before she came to live with you. Tell me about it," Craven said.

"I know little myself," Owen admitted. "Aubrey arrived on my doorstep one cold winter day, shivering and nearly frozen, telling me that my sister Faline and her husband Gregory were dead and she had no place to go. I had not seen her since she was a wee bairn, but there was some slight resemblance of my sister in her and she was as kind as her as well. I could tell the memory of losing her parents was a painful one, so I did not ask her more."

"Where was that?"

"High in the Highlands where old ways and beliefs still exist. Where most fear to travel, even the King himself." Owen shook his head slowly. "I warned my sister against going where no Godly man would go. I even begged her to leave her wee daughter with me and come for her when she was sure all was safe. But there was no stopping her and off she went, taking Aubrey with her, and I never saw her again until Aubrey landed on my doorstep."

"Do you know exactly where in the Highlands?' Craven asked.

Owen lowered his voice as if fearful of being heard. "Where evil lives."

A loud sound had Owen's body jolting in fright and Craven spinning around to see that Espy had dropped a bucket on the floor, what little water was left spilling out.

"Forgive me, it slipped from my hands," she said, stooping down to pick it up.

Craven did not believe her. He had caught the flash of terror in her eyes and the gasp she tried to hide. Was that where she had been this past year... where evil lives?

"I must get more water," she said and hurried out of the room.

Craven wanted to follow after her, but Owen said something that stopped him.

"Espy looked as terrified as Aubrey did when she told me that evil had claimed their clan. I should not have spoken of such horror in front of her." Owen tilted his head, his brow scrunching. "But then she must be a brave one to return and face you, for is she not the one you blamed for Aubrey's death? Cyra's granddaughter, if I remember correctly."

"She is on both accounts," Craven confirmed, "though I

no longer believe she is responsible for Aubrey's death."

"I am glad to hear that. Aubrey trusted her and Aubrey was good at knowing the good and bad of people. Look how she saw the good in you." Owen yawned and his eyes began to droop with fatigue. "I recall her saying that if anyone could save her the young healer could."

"Save her?" Why would she think the healer could save her and not him? He voiced his other thought. "Save her from what?"

"Evil," Owen whispered as his eyes closed in sleep.

Craven sat there staring at the old warrior, wondering what he meant, what Aubrey could have meant. And why had she spoken of this with Owen and not him? He had thought they shared everything. Now he wondered how much Aubrey had kept from him and why?

He stood, disgusted with himself. If he had not been so consumed by anger and sorrow, he may have seen the truth in his wife's death and had found the one responsible for it by now. Instead, he had turned all his anger toward Espy. The one person his wife believed could save her.

Questions he should have asked back then needed to be asked now, and he did not care what it would take to find the answers.

~~~

Patience was not one of Craven's virtues, but he found it forced upon him. Every time he found Espy to speak with her, she was engaged in conversation with those who looked after Owen or she was teaching the MacVarish healer, who did not have near the skill that Espy did, how to prepare the potion Owen required.

When he finally found her alone, later that night, her head was nodding with fatigue, and her eyes fighting to remain open as she sat in a chair beside Owen's bed.

He dropped down on his haunches in front of her and

placed his hand gently on her knee so not to frighten her.

Her eyes shot open as her head shot up.

"You are no good to him exhausted," Craven whispered.

"Death often stalks the ill at night. I will not chance letting him creep in and carry Owen off."

"I will sit with Owen while you get some sleep. Death has no wont to battle me." Craven almost lost his balance and tumbled when Espy turned a smile on him. It was a soft, natural smile that lit her face with a beauty that her scar could not even diminish and it gave a slight punch to his heart.

"That is not—"

"A request," Craven said. "You are to get some sleep. I will summon you if you are needed. Take the stairs to the room below. A bedchamber has been prepared for you." He stood and extended his hand to help her stand.

Espy kept herself from looking upon his face as she reached out to place her hand in his. Her stomach already fluttered madly just from opening her eyes and having seen his dark eyes caress her face and a foolish thought had rushed in, wishing it had been his hands that stroked her face.

His fingers closed around her hand with such strength and warmth that her legs turned weak and his arm coiled quickly around her waist and held her firm. She wanted so badly to rest her head on his chest and linger there for a few moments, let his strong and tempting scent settle around her as naturally as his arms did. She wanted to believe that fatigue caused these foolish thoughts and feelings, but she knew better. Though if she truly knew better, she would not linger in his arms.

Espy went to step away and found herself locked in his embrace. He would not let her go.

"What are you doing to me?" Craven whispered,

bringing his brow down to rest on hers. "Every time I touch you—" He ached to keep her in his arms and kiss her until they were both beyond caring about consequences. Instead, he eased her slowly away from him, his brow the last to part from her as he whispered, "Go before it is too late."

Espy forced her weak legs to move and her feet to hurry her out the door away from Craven, though she worried the distance would not matter. Her thoughts would continue to linger on him, her stomach would continue to flutter when around him, and she would continue to want him to kiss her again.

Before it is too late.

Her hand went to her churning stomach. It was already too late.

A servant stopped her on her way down the stairs.

"Please, Phedra's bairn comes. She needs you."

"Your healer—"

"Is not as wise as you and this is Phedra's first."

Espy nodded, glad her healing pouch remained at her waist. It was not until she was outside the keep that she realized she should have told Craven where she was going.

Once at the cottage, Espy said to the servant, "You must tell Lord Craven where I am."

The young lass nodded and hurried Espy inside just as a loud wail broke loose.

~~~

Espy felt her exhaustion in every aching limb as she walked slowly back to the keep. She was even too tired to smile, recalling the beautiful round, chubby face of the tiny lass with a thatch of dark hair who gave her mum endless hours of agony, then slipped with ease into the world. Mum and daughter were now sound asleep with a proud da watching over them.

The servant lass who had brought her to the cottage had left shortly afterwards and a friend of Phedra's who had been there helping took her leave just before Espy, leaving Espy to return to the keep alone.

Espy glanced up at the night sky. Clouds hugged the partial moon, allowing for barely any light and there was a chill in the air that shivered her. It was also quiet, not a sound to be heard and she suddenly felt the need to hurry and see how Owen fared. Or was it that Craven was there and with him she would feel safe?

Her heart began to pound in her chest and she broke into a slight run, telling herself she had nothing to fear, yet she could not help but think that the silent darkness was warning her somehow. Instinct had served her well, especially this last year, and she would be wise to pay heed. When her foot touched the bottom step of the keep, a sense of relief washed over her.

Her foot never touched the second step. She was grabbed from behind, a smelly hand clamped over her mouth and nose, while the point of a blade pricked her neck.

Chapter Twelve

Sleep had eluded Craven more often than not since Aubrey's death. The only time he had slept soundly through the night had been when he had accidentally fallen asleep in Espy's bed. He had had no nightmares of Aubrey calling out to him. It had been the first time in a long time that he had felt rested.

Sitting here now in a chair that was far from comfortable, keeping watch over the slumbering Owen, sleep once again eluded him. He was as alert as when he had first sat down and his mind as active as ever. He could not get Espy out of his thoughts, she lingered there tormenting his every waking hour as she had done since he had brought her to his keep, though it was a different torment she brought upon him now. Where before it was revenge that drove thoughts of her, now it was his need that drove thoughts of her, lips that plumped so easily when he kissed her or how her skin was as soft and smooth as fine wool cloth, and her scent was... he shook his head. He was growing aroused just thinking about her.

Go join her in bed.

He shook his head, warning himself against it.

She needs you.

He looked around, the voice so clear he thought someone had entered the room. No one was there and why would there be, the voice had been his own.

He went and stood before the hearth, a sudden chill invading his bones as it was wont to do when he sensed something amiss. He glanced at the open door. Could something be wrong with Espy? Was she suffering from nightmares like he so often did?

A servant entered the room unexpectedly and Craven did not wait, he ordered her to remain with Owen.

She went to speak, but Craven was already out the door.

His steps were anxious as he sped down them to the room below and when he found it empty, fear rather than anger flared in him. Where had she gone? Had someone harmed her? She would have never left the keep without his permission. Or would she? Had she made him believe she was trustworthy while waiting for an opportunity to escape him? Had she played him for a fool all along? Had she lied about everything?

He shook his head. No, that was not Espy. She had told him time and again that she had no place to go and he believed her. So where was she?

He turned and hurried off in search of her. The Great Hall was empty, not a person in sight, only lingering shadows that rushed back into corners and crevices when he strode through the room, and the only sound was the crackle of the fire in the large fireplace.

His worry mounted, though he tried to ignore it. Someone probably needed the healer, most likely it had been a birth that had her leaving the keep. He was about to open the front door when a terrifying scream rang out from beyond the door and his heart hammered against his chest when he realized it was Espy shouting his name.

~~~

The stench of her attacker had Espy's stomach roiling and alerted her to his identity. It was Howe.

"I am going to give you a good poke before I take my knife to you."

His breath was so rancid that Espy gagged against his hand that covered her mouth. His threat fired her anger and instinct had her trying to pull away from him. She stilled instantly when the sharp point of the blade stung her neck and she felt blood trickle down from the wound.

"Good, lass," he said, with a sneering laugh. "You do not want another ugly scar to match the one you already have." He laughed again. "Though, it will make no difference by the time I get done with you."

Espy had to break free of him and seek the safety of the keep. Surely, he would not chance entering after her. First, she had to get him to move the knife away from her neck. She did something she did not want to do, she leaned back against him as if in surrender, and then she did something that disgusted her, she rubbed her backside against him.

"Much better lass," he said and dropped his hand, holding the knife down to rest against her leg as he pushed her back hard against him.

She grinded her backside harder into him and felt him bulge against her and when he moaned, she wiggled against him as hard as she could.

His moan grew and his hand fell away from her mouth to grip her breast and that's when she drove her backside into him with force, sending him stumbling, and she ran up the steps to the keep, screaming as loud as she could, though not realizing she was screaming out for Craven.

Craven flung open the door to see Howe, a knife in his hand, about to grab Espy as she clambered up the steps. He launched himself off the top step, flinging his arm out to push Espy out of the way and dove on Howe.

MacCara warriors were suddenly pouring out of the darkness and villagers hurried out of their cottages. They watched in awe as Craven threw Howe around like a powerful prey tormenting his catch before tearing it apart. Several gasps echoed through the crowd when Howe scrambled along the ground frantically searching for his knife that Craven had knocked from his hand, found it, and charged at Craven.

Loud gasps rang out again when Craven, with little effort, got hold of Howe's wrist and turned the man's knife on him, jamming it through his throat. Blood spurted on Craven's neck and shirt and he shoved Howe away from him. The man fell to the ground, gagging on his own blood as his life drained away.

Craven turned and faced the gathered crowd. He looked a sight, more beast than man, his eyes still raging with fury and his voice so strong it carried throughout the village. "Hear me! No one. No one, is to touch *my* healer… or they will *die*." He gave a nod to his warriors and they got busy dispersing the crowd and disposing of the body.

Espy was shocked not only at what had happened, but what he had announced. She was under his protection and woe to anyone who dare hurt her. The thought that she was not alone, that there was a man who cared enough, even if it was because she was his healer, to protect her brought a tear to her eye.

She wiped it away and was struggling to get to her feet when Craven reached her and took hold of her arm to gently ease her to her feet. She stumbled and let out a small wince when he loosened his hold on her.

Craven's arm went around her. "You are hurt?" He swore and not low. "I pushed you too hard down the stairs."

"For my own safety," she reminded, not wanting him to blame himself for something that could not be avoided. "It was not a bad tumble, but my ankle suffered in the fall. No more than a sprain from what I can surmise, but enough to make it a bit painful to walk."

She could try to make light of it all if she wanted to, but it was still his fault. He nodded, as if agreeing, and scooped her up so fast in his arms that her breath caught and he carried her into the keep. He yelled to a lone servant to bring a bucket of water and towels and took the stairs easily, as if she was no added burden to him.

After entering the bedchamber that had been prepared for her, he placed her gently on her feet, slipped her cloak off to toss aside, then lifted her once again in his arms to carry her to the chair by the bed. He astonished her once more when he lifted the chair with her in it, without any difficulty, and carried it over to rest near the warmth of the hearth.

He hunched down in front of her, the muscles in his legs thickening as he did and his hands slipped beneath the hem of her skirt to run them tenderly along her legs and over her ankles.

He nodded when he found the one he was looking for and lifted the leg and, as careful as possible, worked her boot off her foot, trying not to disturb her slightly swollen ankle.

To look at the size of him, one would never expect him to have a gentle touch. He appeared more a fierce warrior who could easily take a life with his bare hands and yet at the moment his hands were anything but deadly.

Once her boot was off, he ran his hand faintly over the swollen area. "It swells only slightly and has not discolored."

"A small twist of my ankle that is all. It will improve in no time," she assured him, the tenderness of his touch doing more to ease the constant throb in her ankle, than anything could.

"You will stay off it until the swelling goes down," he ordered.

That was exactly what she would advise, but then he was a warrior and would have some knowledge of injuries.

"You disobeyed me," he said, raising his head and settling his dark eyes on hers. "You left the keep without permission." How could he keep her safe if he did not know what she was about?

"I was needed to deliver a bairn and I instructed the servant to tell you my whereabouts."

"I received no such message."

"It was my fault, Lord Craven."

He and Espy turned to see a young servant lass, standing in the open doorway.

"Espy asked me to tell you where she had gone and when I returned to the keep, I was called to the kitchen and forgot. When I remembered, I came directly to you, but before I could tell you, you ordered me to watch over Owen and fled the room. It is my fault, not Espy's."

Craven stood and summoned the lass in with a sharp snap of his hand, and she hurried to obey. "It is both your faults. Espy for not coming directly to me and yours for forgetting."

Espy's heart went out to the lass. That she was frightened was obvious, her body visibly trembling. It was difficult not to when standing in front of Craven, his size alone intimidating.

"Put the bucket and towels on the table and go," Craven ordered and the lass hurried to obey. "Do not let it happen again."

His sharp command had the lass nodding vigorously as she backed out of the room.

Craven went to the door and shut it. He slipped the swath of plaid that crossed his chest over his head to hang at his side and yanked his shirt off to toss on the chest next to the door. He dunked a cloth in the bucket and rinsed it.

"May I have a wet cloth?" Espy asked. In all that had happened, she had forgotten about the wound at her neck and while she felt no recent bleeding or pain, she needed to cleanse the wound. She also needed to concentrate on anything but his naked back and chest, broad and thick with muscles and that tempted her senses.

Craven stepped over to her and held out the wet cloth. "Why do you have need of it?"

Espy pushed back the strands of hair that had fallen loose and turned her head to show him her neck as her hand reached for the cloth.

An angry scowl sprang to his face and he yanked the cloth away from her. "What did he do?"

"He held a knife to my neck and when I tried to free myself, he nicked me with it. At least I assume it was a nick, since the blood felt as if it only trickled from the wound."

Craven mumbled beneath his breath as he leaned over her and carefully pushed her hair off her neck to gently wipe at the solid stream of dried blood that had run down her neck and crusted. He admonished himself for only providing protection to Cyra and Bonnie and not realizing that Espy needed it as well, and he wished he could kill Howe all over again.

Espy closed her eyes as he tended her, his face much too close to hers for her not to. His fine features always seemed to send her stomach fluttering and with how near he was to her, his male scent seemed to intoxicate. She fought to retain her senses, but they had other ideas. His gentle touch, his warm breath fanning her face, his fine features, the scent that was his alone when combined made her want to... do more than kiss him.

She fought the foolish urge and squeezed her eyes closed even tighter and her lips as well.

"Am I hurting you?"

His sincere concern caressed her as gently as his hand. She shook her head, fearing if she opened her eyes he would see her desire burning brightly in them. If she released her lips, she feared she would surrender to her foolish desire and kiss him.

Craven did not believe her. He feared he was causing her pain since he hurried his touch, her neck, faintly pink from his scrubbing, far too tempting for his lips to ignore. He did not know what it was about this woman that tempted him so. How was it his hatred for her was fading, replaced by... desire? That could not be possible. It made no sense, but nothing had made sense once he had brought Espy to the keep.

He stepped away from her as soon as he finished and returned to the table. "It is as you thought, a minor wound and should not even leave a scar."

"That is good," she said softly, staring at the flames, not trusting herself to look his way. How was it that he tempted her with a simple glance or touch? It was complete madness and she could not succumb to it. She fought the growing urge to glance at him. He would be done soon and leave and she would seek the comfort of the bed and sleep, and pray that no nightmares would torment her.

She yawned, her hand going to her mouth.

"You need sleep," Craven said.

She unwisely looked his way and thousands of flutters let loose in her stomach. Whatever was the matter with her? She was not a young lass besotted with a handsome lad. She was a woman full grown who had learned more about men than she cared to know. Yet all she had learned had not prepared her for how she felt when she looked upon this man.

Craven walked over to her, intending to lift her in his arms and carry her to the bed for her to rest, but something stopped him. He stared down at her and she stared up at him. No words were exchanged and yet somehow he knew how she felt… she wanted him to kiss her. And he wanted to kiss her.

It was not right. He should not feel this way. His heart had died with Aubrey. He had no feelings to share, to give to another. Nothing. He was empty.

He scooped her up fast, her arms going around his neck to stop herself from tumbling out of them, though with the strength he held her that was not likely.

He carried her to the bed and she kept her head turned away from his. A few steps and he would put her down and it would be over.

"Espy."

He whispered her name, his breath warm against her cheek, and she unwisely turned and looked at him. Their eyes locked and she foolishly murmured his name. "Craven."

He captured her lips in a kiss before his name completely slipped from her mouth. It was a hungry kiss, one he had ached for, one that would give him the sustenance he needed, if only briefly, for he could not trust himself to take more. She returned it in kind, her need as great as his and her passion fueled his.

He went down with her on the bed, stretching out partially over her and his hand ran down the side of her, enjoying how his hand drifted along her valleys and curves and wishing it was flesh he was touching rather than her garments.

All thought and sound reason fled Espy as his powerful kiss took command, his tongue slipping into her mouth, urging her, teasing her to respond. When his hand drifted to cup her breast, his thumb grazing her nipple, she responded instinctively, pressing her body against his.

Her eyes flew open when he broke the kiss so suddenly that a chill sent her body quivering. He stared at her and she was not quite sure what she saw in his eyes... regret, hate? No, there was no mistaking it. That was passion that flared so brightly.

He shook his head, almost as if he was trying to shake his feelings away and failing to do so. His whisper seemed to direct his words more at himself than her. "This cannot be."

He turned and fled the room, his words making Espy see reason. He was right. This could not be. He did not love her or even care for her. She was no more than his healer and she would be a fool to believe there could be any more than that between them.

The problem was that his kisses, his touch, had stirred something inside her that she feared would not settle so easily. It would demand more and she worried she would surrender to it. More than that, she worried that her heart, she had guarded so closely, had opened to this man she had once feared.

Chapter Thirteen

Espy sat at the table in the healing cottage, taking stock of what herbs and plants she had. She needed to forage in the woods to replenish her dwindling supply and also get started on her garden soon. Thankfully her ankle had healed remarkably well, but then it had been a minor sprain, since the incident at the MacVarish keep a week ago. She had applied a fresh comfrey wrap repeatedly to her ankle and had kept off it as much as possible. The swelling was completely gone and the pain was minimal.

Not so for the pain that her heart had sustained that day. Craven had kept his distance from her, including having her ride alone on their return journey. She had admonished herself over and over again for being so foolish and losing her senses. There could be nothing between them not now, not ever.

Espy continued her task. thankful for the light that poured through the open doorway and through the window. It was a beautiful day, the sun strong, though it could be gone soon enough, the weather always unpredictable. She continued making mental notes of what she would need to collect when the light from the open door suddenly vanished and she shook her head, disappointed that clouds had arrived early, until she saw sunlight still flooded through the window.

Only one man was large enough to block the sunlight from entering the cottage—Craven.

Espy raised her head to see the breadth of him filling the open doorway and cradling his left hand against his chest, a blood-soaked cloth wrapped around it. She hurried to her feet and over to him, her hand gently going to rest at his bent elbow and with a gentle tug eased him into the cottage.

"What happened?" she asked, directing him to a chair at the table.

"An accident."

He offered no more and she asked for no further detail at the moment. She carefully unwound the bloody cloth from his hand and saw that it was a minor puncture wound to the palm that had caused all the bleeding.

"The tip of a knife?" she asked.

Craven nodded.

"Clean or dirty?"

Craven scrunched his brow.

"Was the blade clean or dirty?" she clarified.

"I was too busy keeping it from stabbing at my face to notice."

"Who would dare take a blade to you?" she asked not able to keep concern from her voice.

"Morta, who will be shocked to find out the problems he caused and who he injured while in a drunken stupor."

Espy nodded, having seen her share of injuries caused by drunkenness. It was odd that the brew that caused such injuries also helped heal some of them. She snatched an empty bucket off the floor and had Craven hold his hand over it, then grabbed a small cask from the ones lined up beneath the window and poured some of the contents over the wound.

Most people howled or at least flinched when *usige beata* was used on an open wound, Craven did not budge or make a sound. She set to cleaning his hand, gently washing the blood off each of his fingers. She worked gently and slowly so as not to cause him pain. Or was it because she enjoyed touching him, seeing up close the fine lines and tiny scars that marked his long fingers? Fingers that had almost squeezed the life from her, fingers that had touched her with tenderness, and fingers that had touched her with the briefest of intimacy and stirred her heart.

Her delicate caresses aroused Craven and he almost yanked his hand away from her... almost. His wound needed tending or so he told himself. He had wanted Dylan to tend it, but he had refused, telling him that was why the clan had a healer, and it was Espy he needed to see. He did need to see her, but not as a healer.

Since that night at the MacVarish keep, Espy had haunted his every waking moment and had even managed to chase his nightmares away. Now he dreamed of Espy, kissing her, touching her, stripping her naked and...

"Are you almost done?" he asked, thinking it would be wise of him to get out of there as fast as possible before he did something foolish, something he should not do.

"I need only to wrap it," she said and dropped the soiled cloth into the bucket of water and placed it beside the door. She grabbed a clean cloth from the stack on the chest and began to wrap his hand. "This cloth will need to be changed every few days."

He stood abruptly when she finished tying the bandage, his chair almost tumbling over.

Espy stayed as she was, no fear running through her as it once did in his presence. Now it was desire that plagued her when near him and though she fought against it, it was useless to deny it. However, it was wise to remind herself that there could never be anything between them.

He warned himself not to do it, but how did he ignore her soft touch even when it was only meant to heal. Or was she healing more than his wound... was she healing his heart? The next thing he knew he had her in his arms and his lips were on hers.

His kiss was filled with such a powerful passion that Espy quivered straight down to her toes. As much as she wanted to throw her arms around him, lose herself in his kiss, she warned herself against it. He did not care for her, he never would.

She let herself enjoy the taste of him, let passion tease her senses, let the kiss burn in her memory, for it would be the last of his kisses she would ever know. With a heavy heart, she pulled her lips away from his and pushed at his chest.

Craven stepped back, disbelief evident in his wide, dark eyes along with desire, burning so hot that she almost felt scorched by it.

Espy gripped the sides of her skirt, fearful her hands would reach out and take hold of him. "Why do you kiss me?"

"I want to," he said, surprised that he admitted it so easily. "Why do you kiss me?"

Espy spoke honestly as well. "My heart tells me to."

"How can your heart tell you such nonsense when I have shown you nothing but hatred?"

She shook her head. "I have seen no hatred from you. Anger yes, at losing Aubrey, at thinking me responsible, but I wonder with what you have learned if you still think that about me. Do you? Do you believe it was my fault your wife died that day?"

"I do not know, but I want the truth." He should speak the truth himself, for he was thinking less and less that she was responsible, yet something in him needed to prove it, perhaps more so that others did not question it. Or was it to free him to do more than just kiss her?

"What do you want from me, Craven?" she asked softly.

At one time he would have told her that he wished he had never laid eyes on her, but that was no longer true. He wished things were different. He wished Aubrey did not stand between them.

"I want the truth," he said, wanting to free not only her but himself.

"Once you have it you will let me return to my grandmother so I may live out my days peacefully?" she asked, her own words upsetting her and bringing an ache to her heart.

"You are the clan healer now, you will remain here," he said, giving her no choice since the thought of not seeing her each day, surprisingly twisted at his heart.

That he intended for her to remain with the clan without even asking if that was what she wished to do angered her. Anger was something Espy always tried to avoid. She had learned through the years that it rarely benefitted anyone and usually made matters worse.

Yet anger sparked in her and surprisingly she gave it rein. "Then be warned, I am your healer, no more than that. You are never to kiss or touch me again."

"You dare dictate to me?" Craven asked with a surprising laugh.

"I dare to protect myself."

He shook his head at her absurd response. "From me?" He laughed again, though wore no smile. "I have never forced a woman and never will. You responded willingly to me as you no doubt have done with other men."

If he had slapped her in the face, he could not have hurt her more. She raised her chin along with her pride. "You are right. I decide who will touch me and you are not one of them."

Craven's temper soared like a fast rising sun, heating every part of him and he barely held it back as he spoke. "You have reminded me why I hesitate in going any further than a kiss with you. I do not care to rut with a woman who has entertained countless men." He turned and stormed out of the cottage.

Espy dropped down on a chair, her legs too weak to

hold her, and her stomach churning.

"Espy?"

She raised her head to see Britt peeking in from around the side of the open door, then casting a cautious glance at Craven's retreating back a distance away.

"Please, come in, Britt," Espy offered.

Britt turned to Espy, then turned her head away again to see that Craven was no longer in sight before finally entering the cottage, her sleeping bairn cradled in her arms. "He is gone. Are you all right?"

"I am well," Espy said or so she told herself as she had done time and time again when hurt had been difficult to bear. "Please, sit." She hurried to clean off the table.

"That was not fair of him," Britt said.

"You heard? Did others?' she asked and went to rush to the door to see for herself.

Britt reached out and grabbed her hand. "No one else is about. I was the only one who heard."

Espy sat, fighting the urge to cry.

"Why ever did you return here?"

"I know how foolish it must seem to most, but what I faced here was far less dangerous than what I faced out there." Espy stared at the table a moment, then shook her head slowly. "Aubrey's death plagued me. She had been doing fine and to all of a sudden bleed as profusely as she did—" She shook her head again. "It was as if something burst inside her and all her blood spilled out."

Britt nodded. "I thought the same myself. I had never seen anything like it. Even where there is bleeding during a birth, it was nothing to what I saw happen to Aubrey. Do you think those herbs she took caused her death?"

"I believe there is a good chance they did."

"Dylan received word today that Laird Eason of the Clan MacLagan has granted permission for his physician Edward MacPeters, the one who tended Aubrey, to journey here and speak with Craven. He should arrive any day."

Espy smiled, though it faded quickly. "I do hope Craven will allow me to speak with him."

"Craven wants the truth as much as you do. It has been a difficult year not only for him, but for the whole clan."

"You have been in my thoughts often this past year. I feared that you would suffer for having helped me," Espy said.

"If I had not been Dylan's wife, I may have suffered, but he protected me from Craven's wrath. He even threatened to leave the clan if Craven intended to punish me."

"If I remember correctly, Craven and Dylan have been longtime friends," Espy said.

"They are, though their friendship has suffered some over the past year and it is a shame, since they are more like brothers. It was Craven losing his brother that brought Dylan and him closer together."

"Craven had a brother?' Espy asked.

Britt nodded. "And a sister."

The news surprised Espy. "I do not recall him having siblings."

"Craven was about eight years when his brother was born and his sister followed less than two years later. He was protective of them both, always watching out for them. A fever hit the clan one winter. It took both children. Four years later his mother succumbed from injuries she suffered in a riding accident. After that there was unrest amongst some of the clans and Craven's da sent him off to fight and keep the clan safe. When he returned the clan and his da barely recognized him. He had gone from a young man to a fierce warrior. His da died soon after he returned home... peaceful in his sleep. Many in the clan believe that when his da laid eyes upon him, he knew his son was ready to lead the clan."

"I did not realize that he had lost his whole family," Espy said. "I do recall my grandmother mentioning the fever striking the clan and that far too many children and old ones were lost. Craven has known deep sorrow. No wonder he grieved so hard when Aubrey died. It must have been like losing his family all over again."

"I never thought of it like that," Britt said.

"It was good he had Dylan's friendship… a brother of sorts to standby him." Espy shook her head, feeling the guilt. "Not so when Aubrey died."

"True, but their friendship has begun to heal. I see they are returning to their old ways, spending more time together, talking more, and I think Craven being there when Andrew was born made a difference as well. And it's all due to your return." Britt shook her finger, stopping Espy from speaking. "It is true. Much has changed since Craven brought you to the keep. You must see it yourself; people smiling, laughter returning, children running in play, repairs—long needed—being made, thanks to Craven finally emerging from his grief and beginning to live once again. That is all thanks to you."

Espy sighed. "It is not my doing. He hates me."

Britt's son began to stir in her arms and she rocked him gently. "Perhaps or perhaps your return has given him a reason to live once again."

"Aye, to finally seek his revenge," Espy said with a heavy sadness falling over her heart.

The wee bairn began to cry.

Espy held her arms out to Britt to free the woman so she could adjust her blouse to feed him. There was nothing that could bring a smile to one's face like that of a newborn held in one's arms.

"Andrew, meet Auntie Espy," Britt said.

Espy's smile grew. Having no siblings and believing she would never find a man to love and wed her, especially now with the scar, she never thought she would be anyone's auntie, let alone a mum.

"It is kind of you to have Andrew know me as his auntie," she said in appreciation.

"He would not be here if it were not for you and either would I," Britt said.

Espy handed the squirming Andrew to Britt and he latched onto her nipple as soon as she placed his tiny mouth at it.

"Believe me when I tell you how very grateful not only my son and I are, but not a day has gone by that Dylan has not been thankful and praises your skills. I have meant to come and see you before this, but Dylan advised me to wait. He told me how busy you have been tending to the ill and needy. Mina told me how you asked her to look after me and let you know that all was well with me. It is good to know we have such a kind and generous healer among us, and I pray you did not suffer much yourself this past year you have been gone, but your scar tells me differently," Britt said.

"It is the past and that is where it shall remain. Now I will fix us a brew of chamomile and we will talk of more pleasant things," Espy said, though it was difficult for her to keep her thoughts from straying to Craven and all that he had lost. No wonder he had grieved so long and hard for Aubrey. He had been about to have a family again and once again it had been snatched away from him.

~~~

"Why do you hide and sulk?" Dylan asked, joining Craven at the table buried in the shadows in the far corner of the Great Hall.

"I do neither," Craven said and picked up the pitcher of ale to refill his tankard and discovered it empty. He tossed it across the room.

"Do you not get tired of throwing those pitchers?" Dylan asked.

"It is better than throwing a punch and leaving a friend with a broken jaw or black eye that would remain closed for several days."

"On that we agree, but why are you angry?" Dylan answered for him. "You are angry because you find Espy appealing."

"I hate her more than I have ever hated," Craven said annoyed that his friend had seen what he hoped others had not. He did not hate her. Hate was far from what he was feeling for Espy.

Dylan rested his hand on his back. "No, my friend, you do not, for we both have seen what deep hatred can do to a man, to a friend, and it is not something either of us want. Besides, what happened to Aubrey may not be Espy's fault, and I know you well enough to know you want the one responsible to suffer not an innocent person."

"It is time for all this to end, to finally lay everything to rest along with Aubrey."

"It will be soon enough... the physician is on his way. When Espy's innocence is proven, then take her to your bed and be done with it. Surely, she expects no more from you. After all, she is well-traveled for a woman, from what I hear, and has been on her own even before this year. No doubt she has more experience than most women when it comes to bedding a man, which should prove satisfying for you. Unless you are looking for something else."

"I can never love another woman like I loved Aubrey," Craven said once the thought unthinkable, but now he wondered.

"Then there you have it, bed Espy and enjoy her and stop hiding and torturing yourself because your manhood has let you know it is not dead."

Craven glared at him.

"You have poked many women, we both have. Then we found love or it found us, for I remember the day well that you met Aubrey. I could see when you first laid eyes on her that you lost your heart to her."

Craven nodded his head at the vivid memory. "She was brave. She did not fear me like most, though what she saw in such a beast, I will never know."

"Live, my friend, it is what Aubrey would want you to do and it is a way to honor her memory."

Craven sat for some time, after Dylan took his leave, staring at the empty pitcher lying at the edge of the hearth, the fire having dwindled down. He should seek his bed, morning would come soon enough, but then so would the dreams that had replaced the nightmares.

They were so real that he could almost feel Espy's flesh as his hands roamed over her naked body. He would writhe with intense pleasure when she took hold of his manhood and pleasured him until he felt himself ready to come. Then she would climb on top of him and slip his rigid manhood into her and he would groan deep and hard as he felt her close tight around it.

What troubled him about it is that Aubrey had never done that with him. She had been a virgin, though knew what had been expected of her as a wife and she certainly had not disappointed him. Her touch had been hesitant and uncertain at first, but he had encouraged her to explore and little by little, she had. She had been learning and he had enjoyed teaching her. He only wished they had had more time.

A noise caught his attention and he watched as Tula hurried into the Great Hall and up the stairs. Not long after, she returned and Espy was with her. She wore her cloak and her hands were busy hurrying her hair into a loose braid.

She stopped suddenly and Tula followed suit. "As soon

as Lord Carven wakes, you must make sure to tell him that I have gone to deliver Doria's bairn. You must not forget."

Tula nodded. "I will make certain."

It pleased Craven that Espy remembered to keep him apprised of her whereabouts and he stood, the noise of the bench scraping along the wooden floor drawing the two women's attention. He was surprised to see Espy step in front of Tula as if ready to shield her. It was an instinctive reaction, learned from frequent use, as men often did in battle, and it made him wonder what had been the cause.

Espy's shoulders sighed with relief when Craven stepped out of the shadows.

"I heard and I will go with you," Craven said, walking toward her.

"That is not necessary," Espy said, preferring they kept their distance.

"It was not a request," Craven said, the timbre of his voice leaving no room to doubt it was a command.

"As you say, my lord," Espy said with a bow of her head and turned away and hurried to keep several steps ahead of him.

That she rushed away did not sit well with him. That it was to keep distance between them did not sit well with him. That she forbade him to ever touch or kiss her again did not sit well with him. But then she would learn fast enough that a beast could never be tamed.

Chapter Fourteen

The sun was well up and still Craven waited along with James, who grew ever more fearful with the passing hours and his wife's increasingly painful cries. It made Craven wonder if Aubrey had cried out in pain, though he would not have waited as James did now, casting worried eyes at the cottage. He would never have let Aubrey suffer alone. He would have remained by her side through the whole ordeal. If he had, she may not have died.

He cursed himself every day for going on that hunt. He had not wanted to go, but Aubrey had insisted that he needed to go and take the physician as well, who had seemed only too pleased to be invited along.

Craven looked away from the cottage to the flames in the fire pit and gave thought to that day. Aubrey had been adamant about him going on the hunt, so much so that he had teased her about her wanting him gone. Had she known she was in labor before he left? Had she wanted him gone? She had scolded him enough for worrying so much over her. Did she think to ease his concern by delivering their bairn before he returned home?

An agonizing cry broke through his musing. It was not like the other cries… it was one of sorrow.

James ran for the cottage and Craven followed close behind him.

James reached for the door latch and opened it to his wife's mournful cries.

"No! No! Please not again."

James looked to Espy holding the lifeless bairn in her hands. He paled and the stab to his heart was more painful than if a knife had pierced it. He went to his wife to comfort her as he had done when the other bairns had been born lifeless.

Craven closed the door behind him after he quietly entered the cottage. His heart hurt for the couple, though he was relieved that at least James had not lost both his wife and bairn. There was still someone there to love him.

He watched as Espy seemed to ignore all those in the room as she placed the child on a blanket on the table, one that probably was intended to swaddle the wailing newborn, but now would be a shroud for the lifeless bairn.

Craven was surprised when Espy turned the bairn over to rest in her one hand while her end finger seemed to probe the bairn's mouth. It looked as if something spilled out and she turned the bairn over and began to gently rub the tiny chest.

When she leaned down, placing her mouth close to the tiny bairn's lips, James pushed away from his wife to stop her, but it was Doria's hand on his arm that stopped him as did the soft plea in her eyes to let Espy be. He sat back down beside her on the bed, resting his brow to hers.

James wanted to hope as much as his wife did that Espy could perform some miracle, but he knew better... another bairn was lost to them.

The loud wail had everyone turning to Espy with disbelief in their wide eyes. The continuous, loud wail brought smiles to everyone and tears of joy to Doria.

Espy wrapped the tiny bairn in a fresh cloth and carried the wailing bundle to his parents. "You have a fine son." She handed the lad to his mum.

Doria took her son and cradled him against her chest, tears streaming down her cheeks. She did not try to stop his crying. His strong cries were the loveliest melody she had ever heard. She looked at her husband. "He is handsome like you."

James wiped at the tears in his eyes before they could fall. "Handsome I am not. His fine looks he gets from his beautiful mum."

The little lad's wailing stopped and feared gripped Doria as she saw that her son was choking.

Espy quickly took the wee bairn and held him up against her shoulder and gently caressed his back. After only a moment, he was wailing again and she handed him back to his mum. "That is all you need to do when that happens. Keep his head up more when you hold him and feed him, and that should help. He is still clearing out his breathing. It will pass."

Doria nodded, though worry marred her face and she raised her son's head to rest against her breast. He quieted, yawned and promptly fell asleep.

"He will do well, Doria, as will you as soon as I finish seeing to you," Espy said. She looked to James. "Give us a few minutes and you can return to your wife and son."

James nodded, kissed Doria's cheek, and stood. He stopped beside Espy. "There are no words to express how grateful I am."

Espy smiled. "Your son's strong wail expressed it for you."

James grinned and nodded. "Still, if there is ever anything I can do for you, please know I am at your service."

Once outside, James turned to Craven. "If I speak out of term, my lord, please forgive me, but I must say that Espy has brought much healing to the clan and I do hope you will allow her to remain our healer."

Tula shouting out the open door for James to fetch her a bucket of water, kept Craven from responding, not that he intended to respond. The clan had made it clear that they favored Espy and hoped she remained with them. He favored her himself and was one of the reasons he decided Espy would remain the Clan MacCara's healer.

Espy stepped outside shortly after James was called into the cottage. She stretched her arms up and out to her sides and rolled her head. Craven watched her every move from beneath the oak tree he leaned against. Strands of her dark hair fell loose from her braid and her cheeks were flushed, making the scar on her cheek appear more prominent.

He had been amazed when the lifeless bairn had released a hardy wail. It was as if she had breathed life into the child. At that moment, he could not help but think of his own bairn and how Espy wanted to cut him out of Aubrey and he had stopped her. He had never even considered the possibility that perhaps she could have saved the child, but now he wondered. He had thought it a barbaric act as did the physician, but had Espy known something they had not?

He pushed away from the tree and walked over to her. Her face lit with a smile at his approach and it felt as if it devoured him and squeezed at his heart. A slight scowl surfaced at the unexpected reaction as he stopped in front of her. "Are you finished?"

Her smile did not waver and her tone was soft and pleasant. "It will not be long now, though there is no reason for you to remain here. I will go to the healing cottage when I am done."

"You have had little sleep and no food since last night. You need both," he reminded.

"As do you, so do not let me keep you," she said and turned to enter the cottage.

His hand reached out and took hold of her wrist.

She turned and cast her eyes on his hand that held her before she raised them to look upon him. "You need not touch me to speak to me. I answer to my name."

That she reprimanded him for his actions and also reminded him that he was not to touch her, fired his ire and as he released her, he ordered, "I will speak to you when you are done."

Espy gave a respectful nod. "As you wish, my lord."

It was not long before she emerged from the cottage again, her cloak draped over her shoulders. She spoke before he could. "I was hoping to see my grandmother soon."

He shook his head.

"Please, I know she must be worried about me as I am about her." Espy did not care that she begged. Her grandmother needed to know that she was well and she needed to know all was well with her grandmother.

"I do not deny you that. I forgot to tell you that I sent Dylan to speak with your grandmother and let her know that you were fine and would remain so for now. I also asked that she come visit you. She was relieved and extremely pleased to hear the news. She had to decline a visit at the moment and told Dylan you would understand. It seems that a young lass arrived at her doorstep needing help and until she has healed, your grandmother cannot leave her. She also told Dylan to tell you that your horse is doing fine."

"I am grateful to you for that," Espy said and followed alongside Craven as he began to walk. "Is Bonnie still with my grandmother?"

"No, as soon as she learned of Howe's death, which did not upset her in the least, she returned home."

They walked in silence for a few steps.

"What you did to save James and Doria's son, did your father, the physician, teach you that?"

"No, I learned it from an old Highland healer who delivered bairns since she was ten and two years." Espy smiled, recalling the old healer, much like her grandmother, who had shared her years of healing knowledge with her. She had learned so much from her. Her father would have been thrilled to meet her and learn her ways. He never judged healers he met. He would listen and learn and study different techniques endlessly before applying what he thought appropriate.

"Did this healer teach you to cut a woman's belly open and take the bairn after a mum dies and before she has a chance to deliver it?"

Espy kept her words honest, though measured, not wanting to cause him anymore pain than he had already suffered, especially after learning he had lost other loved ones. "No, my father learned the procedure during his stay in a foreign country."

"No doubt a barbaric one," Craven said his accusation met with silence. "Did your father ever do such a hideous thing to a dead woman?"

"No, but he had seen it done twice."

He remained silent, fearful of asking, yet wanting to know, though more needing to know if he had done the right thing by his bairn. He spoke before he could stop himself. "The bairns were dead, of course."

Espy understood why he asked and her heart once again hurt for him, for her answer would no doubt bring him more pain. "No, both bairns lived."

Craven fell silent, his thoughts in turmoil. He had not only failed to keep his wife safe, he had failed his unborn child. His head snapped to the side when he felt Espy's hand rest on his arm.

"The circumstances were far different with those two bairns than with your child and the people who performed the procedure more knowledgeable."

"Still, you wanted to take the chance and try to save my child's life."

"I hate losing to death so I sometimes take chances that are better left alone. I rushed in judgment, wanting to beat death when death had already laid claim."

Craven stepped back, her hand falling off his arm. "I do not need you to take the blame for what I did wrong."

"We will never know who was wrong in that circumstance. The only thing we can do is find out who caused it and see that the person is punished for his foul deed." She tilted her head to the side to peer past his shoulder and without a word, she hurried around him.

Craven turned to see what caught her attention and he saw an old man, leaning heavily upon a staff, trying to make his way toward the healing cottage. He quickly caught up with Espy who already had her arm around the man, helping him.

The old man raised his stooped head to look up at Craven. "You are very large. You must be the beast I heard about." He turned to Espy. "And you the healer I have come to see."

Craven's arm replaced Espy's in supporting the old man as he took slow steps to the cottage.

"I am Ober and I have walked a distance to see you," he said, looking to Espy.

"I am pleased to meet you, Ober. I am Espy and I will do my best to help you."

Once Craven assisted Ober inside the cottage and saw him seated at the table, he left without a word to Espy. She wished the past did not hang over them so heavily and she wished she could ignore her feelings for him. But they simply would not go away. Actually, it seemed hers soared a little more each time she saw him and forget the tingles in her stomach that seemed continuous when he stood near her. She wished she could make sense of it, but that was not to be and either were her and Craven.

There was only one thing that could save her from this madness and that was her healing work. She turned to see that Ober was sitting with his eyes closed, his legs stretched out to the hearth and his hands folded over his mid-section. He seemed a frail man when she first glanced him in the distance, hunched over and leaning heavily on his staff. But looking over him now, his shoulders did not appear that stooped or his chest as sunken. His long hair was pure white and braided on either side, some strands having broken loose. His face was spattered with wrinkles and his skin touched by considerable time spent outdoors, though neither hindered his fine features. His fingers were long and lean, not a gnarl or twist to one of them.

She looked upon his face again and smiled when she saw that his eyes were open. They were plain brown in color like many eyes and yet she thought there was something familiar about them.

She wrinkled her brow and asked, "You seem familiar to me."

"I cannot say the same of you," he said and groaned as he drew his legs back away from the warmth of the hearth. "These old bones are letting me know that it is going to rain today."

Espy rested her hand on his shoulder. "You will have shelter from it. Now tell me what ails you."

Ober patted his stomach. "Too much pain. I fear death stalks me."

"Do you mind if I press against your stomach?" she asked.

"It is what I am here for, to see if you can help me." He rested his arms to his sides.

Espy hunched down beside his chair and gently probed his stomach and the areas around it. The aged man was more muscle than softness, to her surprise, and her curiosity about him grew. It continued to grow when he groaned every now and then, though not always in the same spot.

She stood when she was finished. "How long have you had the pains?"

"For some time now," he said, bobbing his head.

"Does the pain come and go or is it a steady pain?"

"Comes and goes and then sometimes it lingers."

"Have you had any trouble eating or keeping food inside you when you do eat?

His brow creased for a moment before he answered quickly, "A little of both."

"Do you pish clear?"

His eyes popped wide at her query and he stumbled over his words before he finally said, "Not always."

Espy nodded and purposely narrowed her brow as if troubled.

"Does death stalk me?" he asked anxiously.

"I cannot be sure," she said, though she was sure about one thing. This man was not being truthful with her. He had not been able to give her a direct answer on anything she had asked him. A person who was truly ailing always gave direct answers, especially when it came to pain.

"Can you help me?"

"There is a brew we can try. It may help your pain and you should do nothing but rest at least until we see if the brew works."

"Will Lord Craven allow me to stay here since I am unable to contribute in any way to the clan?"

"I will speak to him," she said as she got busy preparing the brew. "I am sure he will allow it. Besides, when you get well, you can share in the chores. What is it you do, Ober?"

"I once was a fine smithy, but," —he held up his hands— "I have lost my strength and can no longer ply my trade."

Now she knew for sure he was lying to her. His hands bore no scars one usually got when doing the chore of a smithy. So who was he and what was his true reason for being here?

Chapter Fifteen

Espy climbed the stairs, longing for bed. She did not care how small her bedchamber was tonight it would make no difference. She was too exhausted to care. It had been a busy day and she had been up since before dawn. It seemed as if everyone in the village needed a healer today. They were all minor ailments and three women who would deliver bairns in the next few months had come to her, asking that she tend them when their time came. Word had spread of how she had saved Doria's son and now more women were trusting her to birth their bairns.

James had rushed his son, Finnan, to her twice during the day, fearing something was wrong with him. Espy had patiently explained both times what he was to do and assured him again and again that the bairn would do well, especially hearing how clearer and louder his wails had become.

She had made a point of stopping at James and Doria's cottage when she finished at the healing cottage and was pleased to see that Doria appeared more confident while holding Finnan.

"I am getting used to his ways," Doria had said proudly and James had agreed with relief.

Now all Espy wanted was her bed, but there was one more thing she needed to see to before she collapsed for the night. She had to tell Craven about Ober. She had had no chance before now and she thought it important he know. She had left Ober to sleep in the healing cottage at the end of the day until a place could be found for him.

She had hoped to find Craven in the Great Hall, but the hall had been near empty. She had spotted Tula talking with

Tass, the warrior who had helped defend her against Howe and had suffered for it, though his ribs were healing nicely. She had found out from him that Craven had recently retired to his bedchamber.

Espy raised her hand to knock, but stilled it before it touched the wood. What if he had already fallen asleep? Tass did say he had retired to his bedchamber. Before she could talk herself out of it, she rapped at the door.

"This better be important!" he shouted and the door flew open.

Espy took an abrupt step back. He stood completely naked before her. She could not stop herself from taking a quick glance down the length of him, before her eyes hurried up to his face and there is where she kept them.

That he was large all over was now confirmed.

Craven had to admire her. She did not blush, turn her head away, or run off in fright, and she even gave him a hasty all over glance. Having come to know her some, he realized she would not dare knock on his door unless it was important.

"What is wrong?" he asked, reaching out, snatching hold of her arm, yanking her into his bedchamber, and shutting the door.

"I thought it important to tell you about Ober," she said, keeping her eyes fixed on his face, which was not an easy task since his handsome features sent her senses stirring. Or had it been his sizeable feature that did that?

Craven kept his smile from surfacing. She was fighting so hard not to look anywhere but his face. He found his own eyes remaining on hers. They held fatigue and she was not wearing her usual pleasant smile. Her braid had come almost completely undone, dark strands falling around her face and he almost reached out to push one errant strand behind her ear. Oddly enough he was growing accustomed to seeing her hair disheveled. It suited her. He could not understand why he found her so appealing when she was so unlike Aubrey. Yet he obviously did, his manhood stirring to life with a will of its own.

He released her and turned away from her to sit on the bed in a way that his shaft would not be so visible. He would not let her see how she affected him, but he also would not cover himself, for then she would think the same.

"Tell me," he said.

Espy hurried to speak, wanting to be done and away from him, the more her eyes rested upon him, the more her desire grew. "I do not believe Ober is who he pretends to be."

His brow shot up. "What do you mean?"

"He is not a feeble and fragile old man nor is he ailing. His answers to my questions concerning his ailment were vague and he told me he was a smithy but could no longer do the work, his hands having lost their strength. Yet he has no burn scars that a smithy often gets from working with the forge and hot iron. His eyes are sharp, always watching all that goes on around him."

"That makes no sense. Why come here under false pretenses?"

"I wondered the same myself."

It struck Craven then. "He sought you out, the healer. Is there something in your past that follows you here?"

God, she hoped not, though kept the thought to herself. She did however admit, "He looks familiar somehow, but I cannot place where I may have seen him. I tended many people in the past year. I cannot remember them all."

"Are there any who may wish you harm?" he asked, the ramifications of his own question disturbing him.

She answered the best way she could. "I did not stay long in one place until I reached the old healer I told you about. I spent much time with her."

"Why did you not stay with her?"

Espy hesitated, turning her head away for a moment and decided to tell him a partial truth. "She died and I realized that my grandmother was growing old and I might never see her again. It was time for me to come home and be with her."

"And chance what I might do to you?"

"I told you that I do not like losing to death."

"So you took the chance and faced it... faced me," he said, not letting her know how much he admired her courage.

"What other choice did I have?"

"You tell me, since I do not think you are telling me the whole of it, and your scar proves it. How did you get it?" Her scar was like a thorn in his side. He wanted to know what had happened to her. Who had taken a blade to her and why?

"That is not important."

"Too you perhaps, but I want an answer," he demanded.

"I will not speak of it."

Her sharp tone had him getting to his feet and walking toward her as he spoke. "It was not a request."

Espy backed away until the door hit her back and she could go no farther.

Craven came to a stop in front of her and planted his hands against the door at either side of her head. "You will answer me."

Espy tossed her chin up. "I will not. It is none of your concern."

Craven laughed, though it was not a joyous one. "You dare defy me?"

Espy felt as if he was devouring her, he loomed so large over her. She shut her eyes and spoke. "Please, Craven, it is a memory I cannot relive again, not even in words. It is too painful."

"Or is it a tale you wish to keep a secret?" he

whispered.

She felt his warm breath fan her lips and she opened her eyes as his mouth came down on hers. His kiss was bold and commanding, daring her to deny him, deny them both. She had to fight her passion that raced like a mighty fire through her, turning her nipples so hard she thought they would poke through her blouse, and turning her skin so sensitive, she feared if he touched her that she would submit to him without protest. But it was the wicked tingle that he had flared to life that settled and grew between her legs that tempted her the most.

Espy gripped the sides of her skirt, her hands itching to touch him, feel his warm, naked flesh and explore every intimate part of him. But she had warned him not to kiss her again and the only way she could make him realize that she meant it was not to respond.

He pressed in close against her, his stiff manhood poking between her legs and her passion soared beyond measure. Never had she felt this way before. Never had there been a man she ached to join with.

When his manhood probed harder against her, common sense poked along with it. He wanted her, that did not mean he cared for her. Many men had wanted only to poke her and be done with her and she had kept them all at bay. She needed to do the same with Craven even though with him she felt different. He wanted a poke, no more, and she wanted more, so much more. Something she could never have with him.

What was it the old healer had said?

Guard your heart and body well, for once you give it away, it belongs to another and there is no taking it back.

She let the taste and warmth of him settle in and around her, holding it tight in her memory and she struggled to break the kiss, a heavy sadness squeezing at her heart.

Craven stepped back, shaking his head as if breaking

himself out of a daze, trying to ignore the passion he felt for her, trying to ignore how she refused to respond to him while her body sent a different message. He slowly backed away from her, his eyes locking with hers before turning his back to her, "Go. Now."

He heard the door open and close quietly and he stood as he was, staring at the empty bed. Espy would be there now with him on top of her, inside her, pounding against her until he released this aching need, this endless desire, this tormenting hell he was going through.

How could he even think of coupling with her in the same bed where he had made such precious love to his wife? And how was it that he only thought of that now?

Craven dropped down on the bed, stretching out and staring up at the ceiling. The truth was that since he had brought Espy to the keep, Aubrey occupied his thoughts less and less while Espy filled them more and more. As much as he wanted to deny it and fight it, he felt himself feeling for the healer and it annoyed him to admit to himself that a fast poke would not satisfy the ache he had for her.

He admired her strength and bravery and the way she gave so unselfishly of herself to help those ailing and in need. She thought of others before she thought of herself. He wondered how often she had done that this past year and if it could be the reason she had gotten the scar on her face. Or had she been fighting off the unwanted demands of a man? His nostrils flared at the thought.

If a quick poke would not do, what was it that he truly wanted from Espy?

Everything.

~~~

Craven went to Espy's room when he woke. She was sitting on the edge of the bed, braiding her hair. He did not need to see the bucket of water and cloth to know she had given herself a fresh scrubbing. Her face glowed and the scent of lavender drifted around her, and it was not surprising to him that his loins tightened.

"You will not be going to the healing cottage today. I have other plans for you," he said.

A servant appeared at the open door with a tray of food for Espy.

"Espy will take her meal in the Great Hall this morning," Craven ordered and the lass bobbed her head and hurried off.

Espy sat stunned when he turned and left without saying another word. She wondered what plans he could have for her. Her hand went to her stomach as a nervous flutter settled there. Did he intend to punish her for denying him last night?

She shook her head. No, he had thought she had bewitched him and wanted nothing to do with her. And that was for the better, though it had pained her some to hear him accuse her of such.

With a sigh, she stood. There was no point in dallying. She would enjoy a good meal in the Great Hall for a change and face whatever fate he intended for her, for there was little else she could do.

Espy took a seat by the hearth, seeing Craven in deep conversation with Dylan at the long table on the dais.

Tula soon joined her. "Lord Craven ordered Ober moved to a cottage near the entrance to the village. I will see him settled there."

"It is good that he will have shelter," Espy said, thinking that Craven had put quite a distance between Ober and the healing cottage.

"He tells me he does not have long," Tula said sadly.

"He has longer than he thinks," Espy assured her.

A soft smile lit Tula's face. "You are a skilled healer and I am so glad to be helping you."

"May I join you, ladies."

Espy and Tula looked up to see Tass standing near and Tula blushed, while Espy smiled at the obvious... the two were enamored with each other.

"Aye, do join us, Tass," Espy offered, pointing for him to sit beside Tula, her blush deepening. "How are your ribs feeling?"

"Much better, only a little pain lingers," Tass informed her while his eyes rested on Tula.

Seeing the attraction, the two had for each other Espy decided something needed to be done about it. "Tula, I will not be tending the healing cottage today. Lord Craven has some things I must attend to. I would be grateful if you would see to whoever comes in need of help. You know how to tend minor wounds and such. Anything more, send word to me." She glanced to Tass. "Please have a look at Tass and see that his injured ribs are improving as he claims."

Tass went to object, then stopped and turned to Tula. "I believe I am healing well, but it would be good to have someone knowledgeable confirm it for me."

Tula cheeks remained pink. "I will be only too glad to tend you."

"Espy!'

The three of them jumped at Craven's loud command of her name.

"I leave you in capable hands, Tass," Espy said with a smile as she stood, slipping her wool cloak off the bench to drape over her shoulders and walked around the table to meet with Craven as he came to a stop beside it.

When he saw that she was ready, he walked off without a word and she followed, wondering what he had planned for her.

His horse was outside the keep waiting for him along with six of his warriors. Espy grew nervous when he grabbed her around the waist and hoisted her onto the horse, then mounted behind her. He said not a word as he directed the animal away from the village.

She could not hold her tongue once the village and keep disappeared behind them. "Do we return to the Clan MacVarish to see how Owen fares?"

"No," he said and offered no more.

After more silence, Espy thought to ask again, but decided it would do little good. He obviously intended to keep her ignorant of their destination and perhaps it was wiser she did not know. She had faced the unknown before and survived. She would do so again.

Tired of the lingering silence, she said, "We have something in common."

"What is that?" he asked, his tone curious.

"We both lost our parents." She waited and when he said nothing, she continued. "My heart ached when my mum died and I was ever so grateful to still have my da, but when he died… my heart broke." She swallowed the lump that rose in her throat to choke her. "I thought it would never heal."

"It finally healed?" he asked, settling his arm a bit more snugly around her.

"I do not believe it ever did. I believe I learned to live with the loss of my mum and da. I think of them often and keep them close to my heart, though I know I will never stop missing them."

"I buried my grief in battles only to see endless suffering and sorrow on the battlefield. In a strange way those battles numbed me to my own sorrow. I had no time for suffering, hurt, or pain, I was too busy trying to stay alive to care about much else."

Espy waited when he grew silent and was glad she did since he resumed talking.

"Aubrey changed all that by coming up to me when I was covered in grime and blood from a battle and offering me a drink, and she smiled at me." He smiled himself at the memory. "It was like an angel had touched the beast in me and calmed him. She opened my heart that had been closed far too long."

"You are lucky to have known such a strong love. My da once told me that I should always remember that death was part of life, but not part of living. That living was what life was truly about and I should grasp it tight and embrace it so that when death did strike those I cared about, it did not rob me of living."

Craven gave thought to her words. He had stopped living after Aubrey died, surrendering part of himself to death whereas Espy continued living and selflessly, helping others, facing danger, and battling death.

Espy suddenly recognized the path they took and her stomach turned with excitement. She smiled at Craven. "You take me to see my grandmother."

"Aye, I do," he said.

She almost asked why when she bit her lip to stop the question from spilling out. She did not care. All that mattered was that she was going to see her grandmother. He surprised her again when next he spoke.

"You can ride your horse when we return and stable him with the other animals," Craven said.

Espy almost hugged him. "I will be so pleased to see Trumble again and have him with me. I miss him terribly. He is a wonderful horse." She did not say that they had been through much together, that she kept to herself.

"I hear that you ride a *kelpie*," Craven said.

Espy satisfied his curiosity. "Trumble is no kelpie. He was born with a backward hoof and has suffered for it ever since. Anyone who sees him claims him a demon when he is no more a demon than you are."

Craven's brow went up. "A beast. A demon. What is the difference?"

"A beast can be tamed, not so a demon."

"A beast may appear tamed, but his brutish instincts lurk beneath the surface ready to strike at any moment," he said.

He was warning her and Espy would be foolish not to pay heed to it. Yet, she did not think of him as a beast. He was a warrior who had bravely faced death each time he stepped onto the battlefield and survived. He was a man who suffered and continued to mourn the loss of the woman he loved. What beast would do that?

Espy was ready to slide off the horse when Craven brought it to a stop in front of her grandmother's cottage, but his arm tightened around her middle.

"Do not move," he ordered.

The strength of his arm and the heat of his body against hers had her recalling last night and how he had trapped her against the door with his body. The spark of passion that had flared in her then, flared to life once again. She warned herself to look away, but her eyes betrayed her and hurried to his eyes to see... passion there as well.

"I am curious. Is it that you have been too long without a man that you look at me with such hunger?"

Unlike her father who ignored the never-ending barbs to his character and beliefs, she was growing tired and angry at the endless insults and falsehoods she had been accused of.

Espy kept her voice to a whisper. "Did you ever think that I look at you that way because I have never been with a man and I wonder what it would be like to be intimately touched, for the first time, by you?"

Craven hooked his arm tighter around her waist as he lowered his mouth near hers to murmur, "Be careful, I just may settle your wonder and my curiosity."

"Espy!" her grandmother called out.

Craven quickly dismounted and with a strong tug had Espy off the horse shortly after him.

Espy ran to her grandmother's outstretched arms and when they closed around her, she almost burst into tears. They held on to each other, hugging as if they feared someone would tear them apart.

Finally, her teary-eyed grandmother spoke, though not to Espy. "I am grateful you have returned my granddaughter to me, Lord Craven."

"Only for a visit," Craven said.

"I am still grateful, for I have sorely missed her."

"Two of my warriors will remain here while my other warriors and I hunt," Craven said and mounted his horse and looked to Espy. "Be prepared to leave when I return."

She nodded and watched him ride off, feeling a strange tug at her heart, which she told herself to wisely ignore. She had seen how women suffered for making unwise choices when it came to men and love, and she did not want to be counted among them.

Upon entering the cottage and seeing it empty, Espy asked, "Where is the woman you were tending?"

"She is well and has returned home only yesterday," her grandmother said and pointed at the table. "Sit and I will fix a brew and you can tell me why you look at Lord Craven with such longing."

Chapter Sixteen

Espy could never keep anything from her grandmother. She only hoped no one else saw what was so obvious to the observant old woman.

"I see the same in his eyes," her grandmother said as she busily prepared a hot brew.

Espy's head went up a notch upon hearing that.

Her grandmother laughed softly. "It is always good to hear someone say what you have seen for yourself, but are not quite sure if you are seeing it correctly. Let me assure you that you have seen it as clearly as I have."

Espy went to speak, to let her grandmother know that nothing would ever come of her and Craven, but the old woman provided some wise words.

"Let it be, Espy. Let it find its way on its own." Her grandmother patted her hand. "Now tell me all that has happened since last I saw you."

Before she could share, curiosity had Espy asking, "What ailment had the woman, who kept you from visiting with me?"

"Actually, it was rather odd. She believed herself quite ill and complained of pain, but the more I tended her the more I believed there was nothing wrong with her. Then she suddenly proclaimed herself well and took her leave."

Espy was reminded of Ober and his similar complaints. She tucked the thought away to discuss later with Craven. Now all she wanted was to talk with her grandmother and gather her few personal items to take to the keep with her.

Grandmother and granddaughter talked and talked and talked until a comfortable silence finally settled between them as they finished their brew.

"I have missed you so much," Cyra said, reaching out to place her hand over Espy's and give it a firm squeeze.

"And I you, *Seanmhair*," Espy said, her heart already aching that she would be leaving her grandmother again, then a thought came to her. "I have been given a cottage where I tend the ill. You should come stay there until this is settled. Then we can return home together."

"I am pleased to know that Craven allows you to provide healing to his clan just as I provide healing to the surrounding area. Besides, home is where your heart is and my heart claimed this place before your mum was born. I cannot leave it."

"I understand," Espy said. "When all is done, I will return home."

"To where your heart is," Cyra reminded. "We should gather your few things so that you may take them with you."

It was when Espy held her father's journal filled with knowledge that she shared her intentions with her grandmother. "I am going to go through every page that da painstakingly recorded in hopes of identifying all the leaves in the pouch of deadly herbs that had been given to Aubrey and see what it may reveal."

"That was horrible of someone to do." Cyra shook her head. "Greed, jealousy, revenge are just a few of the things that can cause people to do harm to others." She shivered as if a sudden chill had taken hold of her. "Then there is pure evil, which causes harm without provocation or consideration."

"I find it difficult to believe someone would want to harm Aubrey. She was a lovely, sweet woman and liked by all."

"Perhaps it was not Aubrey they wanted to hurt," Cyra suggested. "There is good reason Craven is referred to as the beast. He slaughtered many in battle, perhaps someone wants revenge."

"I will find out the truth," Espy declared as if it was already done.

"You always were a determined one, but you must be careful," Cyra cautioned. "If you pose a threat to someone who seeks revenge against Craven, you could be harmed."

Sound of approaching horses caught their attention and the two women hurried and hugged each other.

"I will be taking Trumble with me," Espy said, swinging her cloak over her shoulders.

"Is that wise?" Cyra asked. "Many will think him a *kelpie* and may try to harm him. He is safe here tucked away from everyone."

"He cannot stay locked away. It is not fair to him and it is what his previous owner did to him. I will not see him become a prisoner once again. I will watch over him just as he has watched over me."

"You and Trumble are perfectly matched. You are both strong-willed," Cyra said with a gentle laugh.

Espy stepped out of the cottage, a wrapped bundle in hand to see one of Craven's warriors headed to where Trumble was lodged. She hurried over to Craven. "He does not go for my horse, does he?"

"He does," Craven confirmed. "He will bring—"

Espy did not wait for Craven to finish speaking, she took off after the warrior. The loud sounds and beating of hooves on the ground warned Espy she was too late, Trumble was warning the warrior to stay away and if he did not pay heed, Trumble would do him harm.

Trumble's legs were raised and looked ready to come down on the warrior who had tumbled to the ground when Espy entered the small barn.

"Trumble! It is all right. You are safe," she called out and the horse snorted and moved back as he brought his hooves down away from the warrior. She took a step toward

Trumble when a powerful hand gripped her arm, stopping her.

"Stay away from the beast," Craven ordered.

"He is not a beast. He is my friend and I will not let you hurt him," Espy challenged.

Craven's commanding tone and that he had grabbed Espy did not sit well with Trumble and he pawed the ground, snorted, and paced in agitation.

If Espy did not let Trumble know she was all right, there could be a serious problem. "I am fine, Trumble. No one wishes me harm." She raised her free arm, swinging the bundle in her hand for him to see. "You are coming with me, my friend."

He stopped pacing and acknowledged her with several nods.

"Let me go. He thinks you mean me harm. He will not hurt me," she whispered softly to Craven, though never took her eyes off Trumble.

Craven was not sure about that, but he recalled how she had spoken with affection about her horse on their ride here and so he trusted that she knew what she was doing. He let her go.

Espy walked at an even pace to Trumble, so that he would see that there was no reason to think they needed to hurry and escape as she and the horse had done on other occasions. She reached up and he brought his face down to her hand. She rubbed him gently, then placed her face against his and whispered softly to him.

Craven grew annoyed watching her and his annoyance mounted as she lingered and lovingly rubbed the stallion's long, slender neck.

"We need to be on our way," he snapped.

The horse raised his head, nodding, and gave a snort as if he agreed with Craven.

"I would ask if you could manage to ready the horse,

but I see that you can. Hurry and be done with it. I received word that the physician will arrive soon at the keep and I wish to be there," Craven said and took his leave.

"As do I," Espy said to Trumble. "It has been too long since we raced across the land. Today we fly like the wind."

Espy took hold of Trumble's reins and escorted him out of the barn to see one of Craven's warriors presenting her grandmother with a rabbit ready to put on a spit. That Craven had shared the hunt with her grandmother warmed her heart.

Craven watched as the large horse looked around and tugged Espy toward a large rock. She climbed up on it and mounted the stallion with ease. She and the horse certainly seemed compatible and why that should annoy him frustrated him even more.

His frustration turned to concern when it seemed that the horse appeared anxious and he feared the large animal would take off, leaving Espy unable to control him. She also appeared anxious and he would be concerned that she was planning to flee if he was not confident that that was not her intention. He no soon as approached Espy then the large horse took off. Instinct, born from years of riding into battle, had him following after her and it was a good thing he did. His horse struggled to catch up with her. Never had he seen such speed in a horse and never had he seen a woman ride a horse with such confidence. Bent low, it appeared as if Espy was whispering encouragement to the stallion. The pair were quite a sight, though it did not sit well with Craven that his horse could not match the stallion's speed. His mare was fast, often leaving his warriors to follow in his wake as they did now.

His stomach began to twist in a knot and as she grew smaller in the distance the tighter the knot got. She was much too far from him. If something happened, he could not get to her fast enough.

Helpless.

He would be helpless to save her, keep her from harm.

A bend in the path was coming up and she soon would be out of sight. His heart pounded against his chest like the force of the mighty sticks that pounded unmercifully on the battle drums when warfare was imminent. He would never let her ride that beast of a horse again.

He thought his heart would burst from his chest when she suddenly disappeared from sight and when he finally reached the bend, his anger erupted and he spewed several oaths. She was even further away from him than before. Her horse was flying across the land and there appeared to be no stopping him.

Craven was never so relieved to see the village and keep come into sight and to see Espy slow the horse down and enter the village in an easy trot.

Espy's heart raced madly, her cheeks stung from the wind that had whipped at her face, and she could not, nor did she want to, keep a broad smile from surfacing. It had been far too long since she and Trumble got to ride without caution or care, and she was so pleased that they finally had been able to do so.

She paid no mind to the stares and mouths that dropped opened as she rode through the village. Trumble often caused a stir, though he held his head erect proudly, almost daring anyone to say something.

Espy rode Trumble straight to the barn and the young lad Leith, who mostly tended Craven's horse was there. He backed away, stumbling over his own feet as he did, while keeping wide eyes on Trumble.

One thing Espy was sure of was that Trumble favored children. He calmed around them and behaved well.

"Trumble will not hurt you, Leith," she said after dismounting. "He will be your friend if you let him."

"Truly?" Leith asked, taking a cautious and curious step

forward.

"He lets only those he likes touch him," she said and patted Trumble's neck. "Trumble this is Leith and he is going to look after you. He is a friend."

The lad bravely stepped forward and stretched his hand out and Trumble nodded his head as if to give the lad permission to touch him, and Leith smiled.

Craven watched from a distance and could not believe when Leith took the reins from Espy and led the horse into the barn without incident.

His warriors came up behind him and stopped and when Craven directed his horse forward, his warriors followed.

Craven was off his horse and in front of Espy so suddenly that Espy almost stumbled back if it were not for his hand taking hold of her arm and steadying her. Keeping his hold firm on her, he hurried her away from the barn.

"Never do that again," he ordered sternly.

Her eyes narrowed in question. "Do what?"

"Ride a distance from me," he said and tugged her along, forcing her to walk faster.

"It was not intentional." She tried to explain while taking two steps to his one stride to keep up with him.

"So your horse was in command, not you," he accused.

"I am always in command when I ride," she assured him proud of the riding skills she had acquired, though more out of necessity than want.

He stopped so abruptly that she nearly fell against him and once again his powerful grip steadied her.

"Shall we test that assumption?" he challenged.

One look at the passion swirling, like a storm about to break, in his eyes and it was obvious it was not the horse he was talking about her riding.

He lowered his head until their brows almost touched. "I am in command—always—and you will obey me."

"Is it obedience you want or surrender to your

command?" she dared to whisper to him.

His lips nearly settled on hers when he said, "Both!"

Espy was glad when he released her.

"Go. I will let you know when the physician arrives, for I have questions for you both." Craven watched her take eager steps away from him. A wise choice, since if she had stayed… he chased the troubling thought away. He still could not fathom what made him want Espy so much. A single word, an innocent look, a simple touch from her… any or all aroused him.

He shook his head and continued up the steps to the keep. He called out for a drink upon entering the Great Hall and downed a tankard of ale as soon as one was placed in front of him. Watching Espy today and the strength it took to ride the stallion with such skill had fired his desire for her, but then his desire had been growing steadily for her and trying to deny it was useless. But what to do about it was another question, a question that continued to haunt him.

"You need a good poke."

Craven raised his head and brow at Dylan.

Dylan threw his leg over the bench and joined Craven at the table. "Though you never were one for picking up a stray woman. You were always particular with the women you took to your bed." He shook his head. "I could never understand why you denied some of the women who made it clear they wanted you to poke them."

"My father once told me that a good poke would satisfy a man for a while, but to couple with a woman you loved was beyond satisfying. I realized the truth of his words when I wed Aubrey."

Dylan filled a tankard for himself. "I may have disagreed with you if I had not wed Britt. It does make a difference when you lose your heart to a woman."

"Not for all men," Craven said.

A quiet settled over the table for a few moments until

Dylan finally spoke, though kept his voice low. "Have you heard anything from him lately?"

Craven shook his head. "No and I do not want to hear anything from him."

"What of the other one?"

"He keeps himself locked away in that decrepit castle, the nearby villagers far too fearful to go anywhere near it."

"How does he survive?"

"You are talking about Slain. He always survives."

Quiet settled over them again while they each downed what was left in their tankards, then Dylan filled them once again.

"I never saw such fierce and mighty fighters like you, Slain, and—" Dylan stopped as if he feared saying the name. "Is it true he killed an entire camp of warriors by himself?"

Craven turned his head away, memories better left forgotten stirring in his mind. "Every last one of them."

"No wonder people call him a demon."

Craven looked once again to Dylan. "Endless battles and loss can steal the heart and soul out of a once good man. I was lucky. I found Aubrey just at the right time."

"I did not fight as many fierce battles as you and your two friends, but the ones that I did, linger forever in my mind." He raised his tankard. "To the brave ones who did not return home."

Craven raised his tankard and thought about the two men who were once as close as brothers to him. He wished there was something he could do to help Slain and as far as the other one—*Warrick*—there was no help for him.

A warrior entered the hall and approached Craven. "The physician has arrived, my lord."

Chapter Seventeen

Edward MacPeters downed his wine with trembling hands as he sat fidgeting nervously on the edge of the chair in Craven's solar. "I do not know how I can help you, Lord Craven. I did all I could at the time. It is that barbaric healer who is responsible and should be punished."

Seeing the frail looking man now, Craven wondered how he had ever had such confidence in him. His beady eyes and sharp-hooked nose reminded him more of a bird of prey rather than a man who was supposed to heal.

"She is the reason your wife and bairn died," MacPeters added with a firm nod as if his remark confirmed it as truth.

Craven nodded at the empty chair beside MacPeters. "The healer will be joining us shortly."

Edward turned and cast an anxious eye at the closed door. "She is here? That is good. She deserves to be punished harshly for what she did to your poor wife."

The door opened then and Espy entered, Dylan following her into the room and shutting the door behind him.

Craven saw that her cheeks were still tinged with color from her spirited ride, though she had taken the time to re-braid her hair that the wind at torn at. He almost smiled seeing the dark strands that stubbornly refused to stay tucked away, much like Espy herself.

"Lord Craven," she said and gave a respectful nod.

"Sit, Espy," he said, pointing to the chair beside MacPeters.

Espy walked over to the empty chair, MacPeters tilting to the side as if he feared being too close to her, though it could have been her scar, either way she paid his reaction no mind.

Craven signaled Dylan and he walked over to him and handed him the pouch of herbs.

Craven waved the pouch at the physician. "Where did you get this?"

MacPeters squinted his eyes as if having trouble seeing it. "I have no idea what that is."

"It is the pouch of herbs you gave my wife and insisted be made into a brew for her to take daily," Craven reminded with a hardened tone that had MacPeters twitching nervously in his chair.

"I did give her a pouch of herbs," he said with a nod, then quickly shook his head. "But I have no idea if that is the pouch."

"You are a skillful physician," Espy said. "You should recognize if the mixture of herbs is yours."

"Of course I can," MacPeters snapped, "and I do not need a daughter of an irrational physician, who thinks she knows better than learned men who treat people wisely, advising me." He stuck his hand out to Craven.

"You knew my father?" Espy asked curious.

"Every physician knew of your father whether they had ever met him or not, and they not only laughed at his ridiculous ideas, but warned of them as well. But then what could one expect when he wed a woman who claimed herself a healer and who was from the godforsaken Highlands."

Before Craven could chide the man for disparaging his home, Espy spoke up.

"If you find the Highlands so distasteful why did you remain here? Why not return to Edinburgh?"

MacPeters's chin went up. "I do not need to explain myself to you."

"But you do need to explain yourself to me," Craven

said. "So tell me what kept you here in my home… the beautiful Highlands."

MacPeters stumbled over his words as he attempted to offer a suitable explanation in a way of an apology until he finally cleared his throat and gained control of his words. "Laird Eason inquired if I would be interested in being his personal physician since he suffers from several lingering ailments. I chose to stay and help the man as best I could. It is by his kind graces that I have come here, though I do not know why since I had nothing to do with poor Aubrey's death. Unless, of course, you want me to confirm that it was the healer who killed your wife."

Craven dropped the bag of herbs in MacPeters's hand. "Right now, I want you to confirm if that pouch is yours and what herbs it contains."

MacPeters opened the pouch, gave it a sniff, then grabbed some of the mixture with the tips of his fingers and gave it a look. "I do believe this is the pouch I gave your wife. It contains basic herbs that would help ease her worries, since many women get hysterical when giving birth and make their delivery that much more difficult."

"What herbs would that be?" Espy asked.

"I should share with you—a Highland healer who knows nothing—the skills of a learned physician. I think not," MacPeters said resentfully.

"You may not tell her, but you will tell me," Craven ordered, the deep scowl on his face warning MacPeters that he had no choice.

"As you wish, Lord Craven, though I request that this woman—this charlatan—be removed from the room first," MacPeters said.

"Espy remains and I strongly advise you to do as I say without question or Laird Eason will be told of your failure to cooperate with me," Craven warned.

"I meant no disrespect, Lord Craven, it is just that this

woman—"

Craven brought his fist down on the arm of the chair so hard that it sounded as if it splintered. "You will answer me now, MacPeters."

MacPeters's face drained of all color until he looked as pale as freshly fallen snow and he stumbled over his words once again before finally gaining some control of them. "Chamomile, wild mint, St. John's Wort. Nothing that would harm your wife."

Espy could not hold her tongue. "Not one of those herbs you mentioned is in that pouch."

MacPeters snickered. "You know nothing. I am a physician and know of what I speak."

"Espy yanked the pouch out of his hand and dipped her hand inside, extracting a small amount. She stood and walked over to Craven. "Wild mint has a distinct scent even when dried and crushed. Do you smell any mint?" She stuck her hand under Craven's nose.

He sniffed and looked to MacPeters. "Not a scent of it."

Espy turned around and shook the pouch at MacPeters. "Did you blend these herbs yourself?"

MacPeters's eyes went from Espy to Craven several times, stumbling in search of an explanation. Until he finally spits out an excuse. "A physician offered to blend me a mixture that he had had good results with."

Craven did not care for the way MacPeters hesitated. He was purposely lying to protect himself. If the pouch of herbs turned out to have harmed Aubrey, then the physician was making certain he would not be blamed for it.

"What physician?" Craven demanded.

MacPeters eyes turned wide with panic and he blurted out, "MacBarnes, Samuel Mac Barnes."

"That is not possible," Espy said, looking directly at MacPeters. "Samuel MacBarnes died two years before I returned home."

"You are lying!" MacPeters accused. "I have visited with MacBarnes several times in Edinburgh."

"Samuel MacBarnes resided in Fifeshire not far from St, Andrew's University."

"He was visiting Edinburgh," MacPeters said quickly.

Espy shook her head. "Impossible. He did not leave Fifeshire due to a lingering illness."

"You knew him?" Craven asked.

"I had the honor of meeting him on several occasions and the honor of attending his funeral," Espy said a sadness in her voice. "He was a wise and kind man."

"She is lying," MacPeters said. "Send a missive to MacBarnes and you will see for yourself that he is well. He will also confirm the mixture in the pouch."

"You will wait here until Lord Craven receives his response?" Espy asked with a slight smile that MacPeters did not return.

"Laird Eason needs me to tend him. I cannot linger here and it will take far too long for a letter to reach MacBarnes and for his reply to reach here."

"Or to have your lies discovered?" Espy asked, though it was more of an accusation.

MacPeters jumped up. "I will not sit here and have this common woman demean my integrity."

Craven rose slowly out of his chair and as he did the breadth of him overpowered the room, causing MacPeters to sink down on his chair.

Not so Espy, she remained where she was, the side of Craven's arm brushing against hers and it pleased her to feel his strength and warmth.

"Until I can ascertain who speaks the truth to me, neither of you will be going anywhere," Craven ordered.

Espy was not going anywhere anyway, so his response was meant more for MacPeters than her, and she did not think it sat well with the man.

"Laird Eason will not be pleased with you keeping me prisoner," MacPeters complained.

"Laird Eason will be more than pleased to know if his physician is a liar," Craven said and when MacPeters went to speak, Craven raised his hand. "Not another word. This is done until I hear from MacBarnes."

"I have done nothing wrong," MacPeters pleaded.

Craven glared at him. "You just spoke when I told you I did not want to hear anymore."

MacPeters wisely looked contrite and lowered his head.

"Quarters have been prepared for you. Dylan will escort you there. Rest after your journey and I will see you at supper."

MacPeters bobbed his head and followed Dylan out of the room.

Espy turned to Craven as soon as the door closed and he waited to hear her complain as MacPeters had done.

"I need to change the bandage on your hand and make sure it is healing properly. Will you walk with me to the healing cottage?"

Her words surprised him and stole his tongue, for she was placing his well-being before anything else.

"It will not take long, I promise," she said.

He extended his hand toward the door for her to lead the way, and she did. His hand itched to reach out and take hers, lock fingers, and hold firmly. He also ached to kiss her, the thought having lingered in his mind since seeing her looking as wild and excited as the horse she had ridden. He had not been able to stop thinking that she would have ridden him with the same wildness.

Once. He should mount her once and be done with it.

"Why does he lie?"

"What?" Craven snapped, for a moment thinking her question was directed to his thought that had been anything but honest, and that troubled him even more. Once, he feared, would not be enough.

"MacPeters. Why does he lie?"

Craven shook off his lingering thoughts of coupling with Espy and considered what she had said. "I was told MacPeters was a highly regarded physician, well-learned and well-respected by his peers. If you met MacBarnes, how is it you never met MacPeters before coming here?"

"MacBarnes was a good friend to my father and the only physician who would even speak with him. He enjoyed hearing about my father's adventures in foreign lands and was sincerely interested in the knowledge he had gained there. He envied my father's courage to be different, to question current healing beliefs and be brave enough to try new ones that others scoffed at.

"Though, he did caution my father in teaching me the things he knew. MacBarnes warned him that a woman would never be accepted as a physician. But my hunger to learn was far too great to ignore. Besides, my da was aware that I wanted to learn all I could and return with that knowledge and, together with all my mum and grandmother had taught me, help the people of the Highlands. It is why I helped Arran."

"Who is Arran and how did you help him?" Craven asked, wondering what this man meant to her.

Espy could have bit her tongue for letting it slip. She had been enjoying her conversation with Craven so much that she had not given careful thought to her words. Now how did she explain what she should have never said?

She decided on telling a partial truth. "He was an innocent man accused of a crime and I helped him escape torture and death."

Her words paused him in the open doorway of the healing cottage and he was glad it was empty, for he would not have wanted anyone else to hear what she had said. "You helped a man accused of a crime escape?"

She pointed to the chair at the table for Craven to sit. "An innocent man."

"How do you know he was innocent?" he asked as he sat.

"Innocent or not, his crime did not match the punishment."

He shook his head, finding it difficult to comprehend what she was telling him. "That is not for you to decide."

"It is healing well," she said, after removing the cloth and glancing over the wound. She reached for the small crock of salve. "I suppose it was not, but how could I let a man die because he stole a cabbage, a single cabbage?"

"What of you? You placed your life in danger because of a cabbage," he argued, trying to ignore the intimate sensation of her fingers rubbing the salve ever so lightly in circles on the palm of his hand.

"Not a cabbage... people in need."

"There are people in need everywhere. You cannot save them all," he continued to argue, having seen the truth of that in battle over and over again. "You would have suffered far worse if you had been caught."

"My suffering would have been just as bad if I had done nothing. To turn away when I knew I could help someone, would have been unthinkable to me. I would have disappointed my da and mum, but worst of all I would have disappointed myself."

Craven did not think he had ever met anyone as selfless as Espy or as more determined to do what was right even if it caused her suffering and harm.

"I had to save Arran. I had no choice," she said.

As she had had no choice with Aubrey and his bairn. She had not known if she could save his child, but she had been willing to take the chance, willing to face the beast's wrath. She had given no thought to herself. Her only thought had been of Aubrey and his bairn.

She wrapped the wound with a clean cloth. "Arran is a good, unselfish man. He did not deserve to die over a stolen cabbage."

Craven did not know why her praise of Arran irritated him, but it did, and he demanded, "You care for this man?"

"He is a good friend," she said, securing a knot to keep the cloth in place.

"He is not more than a friend?" he persisted as did his irritation.

Espy thought she heard a bit of jealousy in his tone, but that made no sense. Why would Craven be jealous? "Arran stole the cabbage to feed his wife and young daughter. What little crop they had, had been taken by the chieftain's warriors."

"Who is this chieftain?" he demanded.

Espy stepped away from him, a glare of determination in her soft blue eyes. "I will not tell you that."

Instead of an angry scowl grabbing hold of Craven, he smiled as he got to his feet. It was with a slight laugh that he asked incredulously, "Why?" His laugh quickly died. "You think I will tell this chieftain that Arran is not dead."

"No, it is that I cannot chance placing Arran and his family's life in danger."

"You do not trust me?"

"It is not that. I gave my word. I should have never let my tongue slip. Please do not ask me to betray my own word and Arran's trust."

Craven wanted to believe her, but that she placed her concern for Arran above him annoyed him. "How did this all come about?"

"I cannot. I have already said too much," she insisted.

"This Arran means that much to you?" he asked with a sharp tongue.

"I did what I felt was right."

"Even though it was wrong," he accused.

She squared her shoulders and lifted her chin. "I do not regret what I did and if you think me wrong then punish me as you see fit, but I will not say another word about it."

Craven could not stop from saying, "To put yourself in danger for a man as you did, then you must have cared for him more than you will admit."

Espy crossed her arms over her chest and purposely clamped her lips tight, letting him know she had no more to say.

He continued anyway. "Was this Arran your first?"

Espy tightened her lips.

"How many more were there?" He met the anger that shot from her eyes with an icy shield that to his surprise failed him when he felt a jab to his heart. "It does not matter," he snapped.

Espy's chin went up a notch when he took a quick step forward to stand in front of her. Her heart slammed with such force against her chest that it felt as if someone punched her.

His hand went to her neck and he saw defiance grow stronger in her eyes. He ran his thumb along her smooth skin. "I will be the next one to bed you."

There was a short rap on the door before it flew open.

Dylan walked in, his eyes wide, and almost out of breath.

"What is it?' Craven demanded.

"The physician was found behind the barn, his throat slashed."

Chapter Eighteen

Craven sat alone in his solar, staring at the fire. Rain pounded at the window along with a chilled wind. It was just passed mid-day, the downpour having started shortly after sunrise. Three days of clouds and gloom had preceded the storm, though he had attributed the gloom more to the physician's brutal murder than the gray skies.

His clansmen knew he would not tolerate any killing among the clan. It was his duty alone to pass judgment and issue punishment. Which meant, it was not a clansman who had committed this grievous act.

He recalled Espy's question when she had looked over MacPeters's body. "Who would do this to him?"

It had not been a thought to leave her in the healing cottage when they had learned the news. He had wanted Espy beside him, where he could keep her safe. It had also not been a thought to have her glance on the gruesome scene, but she had had a different thought.

She had rushed past him before he could reach out and stop her once they had been a short distance from the body. She had squatted down beside MacPeters to study the wound.

One look had told him that the attack had been quick. The ground around him had showed no signs of a struggle and the blood that pooled beneath his neck and head proved he had been killed there. Which had begged the question... what had MacPeters been doing behind the barn?

Espy had shared similar findings with him and the conclusion reached was that MacPeters had met someone familiar to him there.

MacPeters's murder was another piece to a puzzle that Craven had not known existed and it had started with Aubrey's death. A death he had blamed on Espy and was proving not to be her fault.

Though, there had been whispers among some of the clansmen that perhaps Espy had killed the physician since he could prove Aubrey's death was her doing. As soon as it was learned that Espy was with Craven from the time MacPeters had left the solar until the time Dylan had delivered the news, all gossip stopped. Instead, tongues began to speculate that perhaps somehow the physician had been responsible.

Craven had had a missive sent to Samuel MacBarnes, even though he believed what Espy had said, that MacBarnes had died, he wanted proof for all to see. So that no one could ever question her word.

A knock at the door had Craven calling out for the person to enter. Dylan stepped in, Craven had been expecting him.

"What did you find?"

Dylan sat opposite Craven and shook his head. "Too much. It seemed the day MacPeters arrived here several travelers had also stopped here for water and rest before they continued on. Then there were a few from the Clan MacVarish, though mostly women, who came to visit with friends. Also, there were two warriors who stopped briefly, needing only their thirsts quenched. So there were any number of people that MacPeters could have met with."

"But they would have to have known MacPeters was to arrive here that day or that his arrival was imminent. The two warriors, what clan were they from?"

"They did not say and from what I was told, no one recognized their plaids. Their stay was brief, though they certainly could have returned and waited behind the barn to meet with MacPeters."

Craven shook his head. "Why? Why kill Aubrey? That

is the question that haunts me. Did someone want revenge against me? Or did her death have nothing to do with me? Why would a physician from Edinburgh be involved?"

The door flew open and Tula rushed in out of breath.

Craven leaped to his feet, ready to reprimand her when he saw that her eyes were wide with fright.

"What is wrong?" he demanded.

"Leith, the stream, Espy went after—" Tula stopped to steady her rapid breathing.

Craven did not wait, he hurried to the door.

"Trumble." Tula got out as Craven passed her.

He stopped. "She took her horse."

Tula nodded.

Craven rushed through the door, Dylan hurrying along with him.

~~~

Espy reached the bank of the rushing stream where Leith's sister had led her to find Leith clinging to a thick branch, wedged between two rocks, that jutted out into the stream. It was pouring bucketsful as she dismounted and got the little lass off the horse. Espy had to pry loose the rope the lass held in her hands, she clutched it so tightly, before she ordered her to wait under a large pine tree that sat back a distance from the bank.

Espy hurried to knot a wide loop and toss it over Trumble's head. "You know what to do, Trumble," she said to the horse as she fashioned another loop at the other end and dropped it around her waist and pulled it tight. Trumble nodded and snorted.

Espy yanked off her boots and rushed into the turbulent water. It grabbed at her like strong hands, dragging her under, though she surfaced fast and the cold rushed through her, letting her know her limbs would suffer soon enough if she did not hurry. She grabbed onto anything solid that she could manage to reach as she made her way to Leith. He was crying and trembling with fright.

The angry water took her under twice before she reached the lad and she was not surprised to see that he clung as tightly to the broken branch as his sister had to the rope. It took her two attempts to get up on the branch beside Leith, the tumbling water and wet bark, making it difficult to get a good grip.

"Sit up, Leith," she said as she struggled to get the wet rope from around her waist. "I am going to put this around you and Trumble is going to pull you out."

Leith kept shaking his head.

Espy leaned over the young lad. "Trumble is your friend. He will not let anything happen to you. With the rope around you, Trumble will make sure you get to shore. You are a brave lad, so do as I say before this branch cracks and you fall, and then there will be no saving you."

That thought frightened Leith even more and he let Espy secure the rope around him.

"Hold your breath good when you go under. Trumble will have you to the shore in no time," Espy said her lips pressed beside his ear to make sure he heard her. "Throw the rope back to me as soon as you can."

Leith nodded and Espy waved to Trumble as she eased Leith off the branch.

The horse backed up quickly, dragging Leith through the turbulent water.

~~~

Craven swore as his horse made her way through the woods to the stream. He was going to give Espy a good tongue lashing, though she deserved more for doing something so foolish. She should have come and gotten him, not send Tula to tell him while she went off on her own.

He broke past the trees and came into full view of the stream and what he saw made him want to roar with fury. Espy was clinging to a branch caught between two rocks that sat in the raging water while Leith attempted to throw the rope to her from the shore, missing each time.

He urged his mare forward, Dylan and six of his warriors following behind him. He barely brought his horse to a stop when he dismounted and as he did, he watched as the branch Espy clung to crack and she dropped, the angry water swallowing her.

Craven did not stop to think, he ran for the stream, but Trumble got to it before him and the large black horse rushed in after Espy. Craven followed him, snatching the rope from Leith's hand as he went.

Craven had battled turbulent waters before and did not panic as most did when sucked down and tumbled around. He had been a hardy swimmer since he was young and he was familiar with the waterways on his land and beyond. He let the water carry him along as well as Trumble who seemed to understand the flow of the water as well. Craven clung to the rope, keeping his head above water and he turned his head when Trumble did and though it was difficult to see through the pouring rain, he caught sight of Espy not far ahead, fighting to get to shore.

She vanished so suddenly beneath the surface, it was as if a powerful hand had reached up and yanked her down. He cursed the mighty river, silently demanding that it release her and was grateful when she finally surfaced. Her arms flailed above her head, her hands trying to grab at anything that could slow her down.

Craven was suddenly yanked forward and he blessed the huge beast over and over as the animal fought the angry water to get to Espy. When the horse rushed past her, Craven understood it was on purpose, giving him a chance to grab

Espy and he did just before the water had a chance to suck her under again.

His arm went around her waist and held her so tight that he feared he would crack her ribs. He yanked on the rope with his other hand to let Trumble know he had hold of her, then closed that arm around her as well. He rushed to cover her mouth with his when they both were dragged under, hoping to help her breathe since she looked like she did not have a breath left in her.

Once Trumble reached land, Dylan and his men, who had been following along the bank, helped pull the couple to shore.

Craven got to his feet, scooping Espy up. She coughed and spurted and her head fell against his chest.

"I need to get her to the keep and get her dried," he said to Dylan. "See to what needs doing here."

Dylan nodded.

Trumble pawed the ground and snorted when Craven approached his mare.

Craven looked to the beast. "I ride with her or she goes with me."

Trumble gave a nod.

Dylan took Espy from Craven so that he could mount the horse, though he slipped the rope off his neck first. Dylan handed her up to Craven and he tucked her close against him. Without a word, he took off.

The rain began to slow by the time he reached the keep. It was no longer a downpour. One of his warriors waited at the bottom of the steps to the keep, expecting to tend Craven's mare and when he saw the black horse appear, snorting and stamping the ground, he backed away in fright.

"Swallow your fear and take Espy from me," Craven ordered his warrior.

The warrior hurried to obey.

Craven dismounted and spoke to the horse. "I will see

to her care. Let this warrior see to yours."

The horse pawed the ground agitated.

"Do as I say!" he ordered sharply and the horse stilled and stared at him. Craven turned to the warrior. "Take him to the barn and see to his care. He will not harm you." He had turned to Trumble when he said that and the horse hesitated a moment then went with the warrior after he gently placed Espy in Craven's arms.

Craven held Espy close against him as he rushed into the keep and up the stairs. He did not stop and think about it, he took her to his bedchambers. She shivered when he stood her in front of the hearth and he held her there steady until she could stand without support. Then his hands got busy.

He did not ask permission. He began stripping off her drenched garments with some difficulty since her blouse refused to let go of her wet skin. Her arms went around her naked breasts when he finally got it off her, and her eyes glared at him with alarm.

"You need to get dry and warm," he said, trying to ease her discomfort.

He yanked her skirt down and try as he might to keep his eyes from straying over her naked body, he could not help it. Beautiful was not sufficient to describe her; curvy waist, rounded hips, and the loveliest and smoothest pale skin he had ever seen on a woman.

She closed her legs tight, dark curly hair peeking out between them.

Craven reached for a cloth and hurried to dry her, rubbing her wet skin until it turned red with warmth, then he scooped her up and got her into his bed as fast as he could, pulling the blanket over her and tucking it tight around her almost as if he was constructing a shield that would protect her.

Protect her from who? Him?

He would love to strip off his garments and climb in

bed with her and warm her. He could heat her body in no time, a touch, a kiss, and so much more. He shook off the thought. This incident could not be ignored. It had to be dealt with immediately, for if he remained he would join Espy in bed and he would do more than just warm her.

"Take your garments off," she said, her slight tremor in her voice and her lips still tinged blue.

For a moment, he thought she knew his thoughts, then he realized that she was advising him to get out of his wet garments and get warm himself. He turned away from her and shed his garments in front of the fire. With rushed strokes, he dried himself and quickly dressed.

A knock sounded at the door and Craven opened it to find Tula standing there.

"A hot brew," she said, explaining her presence.

"Stay with Espy and keep me informed of how she does," he ordered and walked out of the room.

He went straight to his solar and found what he had expected... Leith and his sister, their hair wet, though otherwise dried and in warm garments and a blanket over them. They sat squeezed in one of the chairs together, their eyes wide with fright that filled with more fear as soon as Craven had entered the room.

Dylan stood near the hearth and gave him a nod, letting him know all had been seen to.

"Our mum is waiting in the Great Hall," Leith's sister said bravely as if somehow that would protect them.

Craven recalled meeting Leith's sister, Haddie, at the healing cottage one morning. She could be no more than six or seven years and skinny, a wee bit of a thing. He was surprised she had spoken up since she had seemed shy the day he had met her, barely looking at him. Not so now. She held his gaze, though there was no mistaken the fright in her pale blue eyes.

He walked over to the pair and looked down at Haddie and she cuddled closer against her brother. "And that is where your mum will wait until I am through with you."

Craven admired Leith's courage as he protectively slipped his arm around his sister.

"Haddie has done nothing wrong. It is my fault," Leith said, holding back his fright, though barely.

Haddie was quick to speak. "He did not know I was following him, but I am glad I did. If I had not…" Haddie sniffled back tears and said no more.

"Tell me what happened, Leith," Craven commanded, his tone not nearly as harsh as when he reprimanded his warriors.

Leith hurried to explain. "The man just wanted a message delivered to the physician. That was all he asked and he promised me a coin in exchange for the task. All I had to do was wait for him near the stream after I delivered the message." Leith shut his eyes and shook his head.

"The stranger threw Leith in the stream and walked away laughing," Haddie said, a tear running down her cheek. "As soon as I saw Leith get snagged by the branch and climb up on it, I ran for help. I knew the healer would help. She always helps."

"Can either of you tell me what this man looks like?" Craven asked, sitting in a chair across from the two, slightly annoyed that the lass had gone to Espy with no thought of coming to him for help.

"He was not as tall as you," Haddie said and wrinkled her nose, "and he had a mean face."

"Neither of you have ever seen him before?" Craven asked.

The two children shook their heads.

"What was the message he asked you to give the physician, Leith?" Craven asked.

"To meet an old friend behind the barn."

"Old friend, not just friend?" Craven asked and Leith confirmed with a nod. "He said nothing more?"

"He told me after I delivered the message to go wait by the stream where the two large pines hugged each other." Leith chewed on his bottom lip briefly as if hesitant to continue, then he finally spoke. "He also told me that if I did not tell anyone, he would give me two coins. I wanted to surprise my mum and give them to her."

"That was good of you to want to give them to your mum," Craven said and stood, looming over the lad. "It was not good that you did not inform me of what this stranger asked of you. You should have come to me with this immediately."

Leith swallowed hard. "Aye, my lord, I am sorry and I am ready for my punishment."

Haddie threw herself over her brother. "No! No! You cannot hurt my brother."

Craven truly admired the little lass. She had courage for one so young. "Leith will be a man one day and he will face his punishment like one. Is that not right, Leith?"

Leith eased his sister off him. "Lord Craven is right, Haddie."

"No! No!" Haddie demanded again and stepped in front of her brother, her little body shielding him and her thin arms spread out from her sides as if sacrificing herself for him.

For some reason the small lass reminded him of Espy, dark hair, soft blue eyes, and protecting another with no care for herself.

Espy and he would have such a strong-willed and brave daughter. The thought came from out of nowhere. He may want to couple with Espy, but have children with her? No, all thought of having children had died with Aubrey. Or had it?

Craven pushed the ridiculous thought away and

snatched Haddie up in his powerful arms. She gasped and her round cheeks that had flushed with anger while defending her brother, lost all color, and she paled.

"You will go and wait with your mum," Craven ordered and lowered her to her feet.

Haddie turned and went to her brother's side, taking his hand. "I wait with him."

"Haddie! Do as Lord Craven commands," Leith scolded.

"I will not leave you. He cannot make me."

Craven saw that Dylan was trying to hide a smile and so was he. He did not hesitate, he snatched Haddie up in his arms again and marched out of the room and to the Great Hall, depositing her in front of her mother.

"See that she waits here with you," he ordered the woman, her eyes red from crying. He looked down at Haddie, her mother's hands gripping the top of the little lass' shoulders. "You will obey me when I speak, Haddie, or face punishment yourself."

"I am so sorry, my lord, she is a stubborn one," Haddie's mum apologized.

"Your son will join you soon," Craven said and saw the relief on the woman's face.

"Thank you, my lord, thank you."

Craven returned to his solar, Leith looking to him anxiously, though he held his tongue.

"Your sister waits with your mum," Craven said and saw the same relief on his face that had been on his mum's. "As for your punishment, besides seeing to the horses, you will do extra chores in the kitchen for the next two weeks."

Leith looked about to smile, but stopped himself. "Aye, my lord, I will go there right now."

"No, after your ordeal you need to rest and regain your strength. Tomorrow is soon enough. You may take your leave."

Leith bobbed his head and before walking away, asked, "Is Espy all right?" He chewed at his bottom lip again. "She jumped right in and got yanked under the water twice before she reached me, and she struggled to get up on the log, but she did not give up. She saved me and I am so grateful."

"I expect you to tell her that when you see her and she does what you are about to do… rest."

"I will, my lord, I will," Leith said, bobbing his head as he walked backward toward the door and bumped into the wall before turning around, pulling open the door, and running off.

Dylan poured ale for them both and they sat.

"This person who met with MacPeters has to be familiar with the area if he told Leith precisely where to meet him," Craven said.

"Aye, I thought the same myself and he would have to know MacPeters was expected here," Dylan added, shaking his head. "But why would a physician from Edinburgh want to harm Aubrey? And with him now dead, how do we ever find out why?"

~~~

Craven climbed the stairs, intending to sleep in Espy's bedchamber for the night. Tula had kept him informed as to how Espy was doing. She last apprised him that Espy had gone to sleep for the night. He supposed that was what made him enter his bedchamber. He wanted to see for himself that she slept.

Before he reached the bed, he could see it was empty.

Chapter Nineteen

As soon as Espy's bare feet touched the cold stone stairs a chill ran up and through her, feeling as if it reached down into her bones. Unfortunately, having left her boots on the shore and not knowing if anyone had retrieved them had left her barefoot. Tula had been reluctant to tell her that Anwen had started labor and even more reluctant to help her slip into her still wet garments. Tula had insisted that Lord Craven had made it known that Espy was to rest and he had reminded her of that each time she had informed him how Espy was doing.

Tula was too afraid to disobey Craven, and Espy understood. To keep Tula from risking punishment for disobeying him, Espy had taken it upon herself to do what was necessary on her own.

Once at the bottom of the stairs, she hugged the shadows close to the wall. She could hear noise and laughter coming from the Great Hall and though she would come close to entering it, she would not have to walk through it to get outside. She would slip through the narrow passage that connected to the kitchen and make her way from there to Anwen's cottage.

She had told Tula that she was exhausted and wanted to sleep and that Tula was no longer needed. She intended to deliver Anwen's bairn and get back in bed before anyone discovered her gone. This was Anwen's second bairn and with the first one having delivered fast, there was a good chance the second would as well.

She had let her dark hair fall loose down the sides of her face to keep herself from being recognized since everyone was used to seeing her hair braided. She walked with a quick stride through the kitchen, appearing as if she belonged there and no one paid her heed. Once outside she hurried to the healing cottage, grateful the rain had turned to a trickle, and grabbed a cloak that had been left there and the healing basket, and rushed off.

Shivers took hold of her again, the wet, cold mud squishing through her toes and sending more chills through her.

After an hour with Anwen, Espy was glad she was there. It was not going to be as easy a birth as she had believed.

Several hours later, one son lay cradled in Anwen's arm and the other in his da's, and their sister, barely three years looked on with sleepy eyes.

"I cannot thank you enough," Anwen said. "If you had not been here, one of them would have died."

"Aye, we owe you much," Nevin, Anwen's husband, said.

"It is what I am here for," Espy assured them. "I will check in on you and the bairns later in the morning. "Rest, for you will need it with these two strapping lads."

Nevin beamed with pride.

Espy left the cottage relieved the birth was done and all had turned out well. There had been a moment she feared she would lose the one bairn, the cord having wrapped around his neck and looking as if it was choking the life out of him. But she had managed to pry it loose and the bairn cried out loudly. Now if only her body did not ache so badly.

She did not know if she would make it back to the keep and besides, she wanted to desperately clean her feet of the mud. With the healing cottage closer, she decided to go there. Every step hurt more than the last one, but when a hand suddenly grabbed her shoulder form behind, Espy found the strength to swerve around sharply, her arm swinging out at whoever stood behind her.

Her wrist was caught in an ironclad grip and Espy was never so relieved to see Craven. Whether it was relief or instinct—she did not care which—she collapsed against him and sighed with relief, and his powerful arms closed around her.

Craven was ready to turn an angry scowl and angrier words on her. What was she thinking walking the village in the dead of night when the physician had just been murdered, then she fell against him and his anger fled. He lifted her up in his arms, hugging her tight against him, and walked to the keep.

"What are you doing out?" he demanded, though knew it would have something to do with a birth or an illness.

"A bairn that turned into two and a delivery that proved a bit more difficult than expected." Espy smiled. "Anwen and Nevin have fine twin sons."

How could he scold her for seeing that twin bairns were safely delivered and the mum did well? Had she not told him that no man would want her as a wife, for she would be forever seeing to those who needed her help? She was a woman who gave much of herself, but who truly gave to her?

"I am glad to hear all went well, but you should have told me that Anwen needed you."

"Would you have given me permission to tend her?"

Craven smiled. "Probably not, though I have no doubt you would have persuaded me."

"It is your kind heart that would have been persuaded."

He snorted. "You do not know me at all if you think I have a kind heart."

"Perhaps it is you who do not know yourself."

"I know myself all too well," he argued and felt the dampness of her garments seeping through her cloak. One shiver followed by another annoyed him even more and he hurried his steps.

He carried her through the empty Great Hall and up the stairs and, as he had done earlier, he gave no thought to taking her anywhere but to his bedchamber.

"Do not put me in the bed," she said, upon entering and before Craven could argue, she continued. "My bare feet are caked with mud."

Craven halted. "Where are your boots?"

"The last I saw them they were on the bank of the stream."

He lowered her to her feet. "I should give you a good thrashing for not obeying me."

"Can that wait?" she asked softly and unable to hold her head up, she rested it on his chest. "I fear that without some rest, I would never survive such a beating."

He muttered several oaths at himself for threatening something he would never do to her as he stripped off her cloak and tossed it aside. Then he once again proceeded to strip her, though this time her hand stopped him.

"What are you doing?" she asked.

He shoved her hand aside. "You should have never dressed in wet garments and with your feet bare, the cold has seeped deep inside you. You need to get warm."

Espy could not argue with that and for the second time that day she let Craven strip her naked. She had no worries over his touch. The last time his touch had been swift, not at all intimate. It had had her wondering why then his innocent touch had sent a rash of heat running through her and set off a flutter of intimate tingles?

He wrapped a blanket around her, scooped her up, as soon as he had her naked once again, and sat her on the chair close to the hearth. He got the bucket of water that had been left near the door and sat it by her feet. When she leaned down, her hand sneaking out of the blanket, he pushed it away.

"I will see to your muddy feet." She went to speak and Craven pressed his finger against her lips. "Not a word."

Espy was too tired to argue, besides there was no one else to help her and she doubted she could see to it herself.

He took her one foot and stuck it in the bucket and she gasped, the water chilly. He dipped his large hand in and began scrubbing off the mud. He was thorough, rubbing every inch of her foot, his fingers gliding between her toes, rubbing hard along the bottom and around her heel, and Espy never felt anything so wonderful. She leaned back in the chair and closed her eyes.

Her skin was smooth and soft, her toes perfectly shaped with a slight arch along the bottom of her foot. He ran his hand up her leg some and around her slim ankle, making certain he got all the mud. When he finished he dried her foot thoroughly admiring the view of what his hands had only felt. He did the same to her other foot and when he finished drying that one he looked up at her and saw that she was sound asleep.

The blanket had fallen open across her chest, leaving her full breasts to peek out. There was no denying she was a beautiful woman and no denying he wanted her. But not here, not now. He wanted her wide awake and willing. Now she needed to rest and stay warm.

He lifted her gently and placed her on the bed, leaving the blanket tucked around her and pulling another blanket up over her, and still she shivered.

"Cold," she whispered and continued to shiver, turning on her side and drawing her legs up and locking her arms against her chest, looking for warmth.

He stared down at her, fighting the urge to climb in bed with her and chase her chill away. It would not be wise. She would warm up eventually.

Her shivers worsened.

Leave now! His own voice warned in his head.

He groaned, annoyed, and forced himself to turn away and walk toward the door.

"*Craven.*"

It was enough of a pleading whisper for him to hear and for him to return to the bed. Her eyes were closed, she remained sound asleep. She had called out to him in her sleep.

"*Craven.*"

He should turn and walk out of the room and close the door soundly behind him. He should not—

He shed his garments, letting them drop to his feet, and climbed naked into bed, easing his way beneath the blanket to lie beside her. He gently stripped away the blanket that he had wrapped around her and curled his body around hers, slipping his hand to rest over her two that she held tightly clasped together against her chest. He placed his leg over her chilled ones, rubbing it up and down several times to warm them, then pressed himself against her back. Her chill assaulted him, but his warmth overpowered it and he held her tight, letting his heat soak into her, warming her, keeping her safe.

Never in his wildest imaginings would he have ever thought that he would share his bed with the woman he had had so much hatred for, but then he would have never imagined that his hatred had been misplaced. He had wasted a year loathing her when she had never deserved it. He had wrongly accused the one person who had been there to help his wife, to fight for her and his bairn.

Aubrey had recognized Espy's kind nature and having now seen it for himself, he understood why his wife had trusted Espy. She truly cared about helping people, always placing their safety above her own. Aubrey had known that Espy would have done whatever was necessary to save her and the bairn, and she had been right.

Craven was pleased when Espy's shivers finally drifted

off, his heat having warmed her. He could leave her now, but it was not his intention. He would stay wrapped around her. It was where he wanted to be, as strange and unbelievable as that was, and he believed it was where Espy wanted him.

Sleep finally poked at Craven and in a few moments he drifted off to sleep.

~~~

Espy did not want to open her eyes, she felt so warm and comfortable. She wanted to linger there in the peacefulness, something she had not felt since she was a young bairn. She cuddled closer to the heat and its strength and the fresh scent of forest and rain. She breathed deeply, smiled, and pressed her head against… a naked chest.

She sprang up in bed, the blanket falling away from her chest to pool at her waist and she stared at Craven's dark eyes that rested upon her. She grabbed the blanket and pulled it up to cover her bare breasts.

"There is no need to hide your lovely breasts when I have already seen them more than once," he said, raising his arms to stretch above his head.

Espy's eyes fixed on his muscles that bulged and stretched as he did.

"You were cold and I warmed you," he said, bringing his arms down to tuck beneath his head.

"I am cold no more."

"No, you are not. You warmed nicely against me."

She felt heat tinge her cheeks and she turned away just as the door burst open.

Dylan stopped so abruptly he almost tripped over his own feet, and he stared speechless.

Craven pushed himself up to sit and he was surprised when Espy scurried closer to him, dragging the blanket along with her to cover herself some more. He slipped his arm gently around her, offering whatever it was she sought from him. He was pleased when she leaned against him.

"It must be important if you rushed in here as if the devil was after you," Craven said.

"He is," Dylan managed to say.

Craven sat up straighter, seeing not only concern, but a hint of fear in Dylan's eyes, something he rarely saw there, and his arm tightened around Espy.

"Six of Warrick's warriors are in the woods and they are headed this way."

Craven turned to Espy. "You remain in the keep until I tell you otherwise." He hurried out of bed and into his garments and was out the door without another word to Espy.

Espy sat stunned, fear gripping her stomach and churning it so badly that she thought she would retch.

How had he found her? She had been so careful, never mentioning her past, her grandmother, Craven, nothing that would connect her with home. She also had been careful to leave no tracks, no trace of where she had gone.

She pressed her hand against her roiling stomach as she recalled the old healer's words.

You cannot hide from evil.

Craven had enough problems already. He did not need to take her problems on as well. Besides, Craven would have no choice but to bow to Warrick's demand. Everyone bowed to Warrick's demands.

A knock sounded before the door opened and Tula entered with garments and shoes in her hands. "For you," she said, walking over to the bed. "Lord Craven ordered fresh garments brought to you." She placed the garments on the bed and keeping her voice low, she asked, "Is it true? Have Warrick's warriors been spotted in the woods?"

Word always spread fast in a keep and through a village... along with fear.

Tula continued. "At least, Lord Craven is friends with Warrick—" she paused, a tremor rushing through her at the sound of his name. "At least, they were once friends, though more like brothers."

"They were?" A chill settled over Espy. She stood no chance against Warrick if he and Craven were friends, though she could not fathom how Craven would be friends with such an evil man.

Tula nodded. "There were three of them, feared like no other Highland warriors. It is said that an enemy troop had once turned and fled when learned they would face the three fierce warriors. It is believed they each earned the names their enemies bestowed upon them. Craven the beast, Slain the savage," —Tula hugged herself tightly— "and Warrick the demon."

Espy had heard tales of the beast, the savage, and the demon warriors when she was up high in the Highlands, but she had never associated that particular beast with Craven. From what she had heard, the three warriors were heartless men who did whatever was necessary to claim victory.

Craven was not heartless, though she knew Warrick certainly was.

"Lord Craven says you are to stay in the keep until he returns," Tula said, breaking through Espy's thoughts. "I doubt anyone would seek the healer today anyway. Most will stick close to their cottages, waiting to hear what Warrick's warriors want here."

Me.

Espy wished she was wrong, though she doubted she was and she could not wait around to find out. She also had to make sure her grandmother was safe. If Warrick had tracked her here, then he knew about her grandmother. He would use her to make certain Espy was returned to him.

"Tass has been told to stand ready with the other warriors," Tula said. "I worry for his safety. I cannot believe that Lord Craven would even think to fight Warrick."

While Tula talked, Espy slipped into a brown skirt and pale yellow blouse. The shoes were a bit tight, but they would do.

"I am sure Lord Craven will handle it without incident," Espy said, trying to calm the lass, though fearful herself of what was to come.

"I pray he does." Tula nodded and as if just remembering, said, "The morning meal awaits,"

"I will be down shortly."

Tula nodded again and walked to the door and froze when a bell tolled loudly. She turned a deathly pale face on Espy. "Warrick's warriors have arrived."

Chapter Twenty

Espy followed Tula down the stairs and into the Great Hall. That fright had arrived with Warrick's warriors was evident in the way the servants huddled together, whispering among themselves while some visibly trembled. Several of Craven's warriors stood guard at all entrances and exits, keeping watch and keeping everyone confined to the Great Hall.

There was no way Espy would be able to get passed any of them. At that moment, she made a crucial decision and she hoped a wise one. She went to Tass, stationed at one of the closed doors.

"I need to speak with Lord Craven now," she told him and as he shook his head and went to deny her request, she hurried to add, "Warrick's warriors have come for me."

Tass' mouth dropped open and he stared at her as if he was still trying to make sense of her words, then he abruptly came out of his shock, nodded, and signaled another warrior to take his place, and hurried off.

Espy prepared herself to face an angry Craven, but when he entered the Great Hall in powerful strides and approached her, she was surprised to see concern in his narrowed brow and dark eyes. He took hold of her arm and hurried her through the hall and into his solar.

"What do you mean Warrick's warriors are here for you?" he asked, keeping hold of her arm as if worried someone might enter the room and snatch her away from him.

A pang of doubt poked at Espy and her hand went to rest at her stomach. She hoped she was making the right choice in confiding in Craven. "When you ordered me off your land and the surrounding area, I had no choice but to go higher up in the Highlands. I went from village to village, croft to croft, helping the ill in exchange for shelter and food. I stayed off the well-traveled paths for they were dangerous for a woman alone. In one village, a laird had me brought to his dungeon where he ordered me to tend a man who he had had tortured. He wanted me to get him well enough so that he could continue to torture him. There came a time I told him that the man was dead, but he was not dead. I knew no time or effort would be spent in burying the man and when they dumped his body in the woods, I dragged him off and tended him."

"Arran, the man you told me about," Craven said.

Espy nodded "Arran survived and left the area as soon as he was well enough. He found me about a month later and told me about other innocent people like himself who were being tortured, and he asked me to help rescue them."

Craven grabbed her by the shoulders. "Do not tell me you rescued prisoners from Warrick's dungeon."

"I did but," —she hesitated briefly— "in order to do that I first became his healer to gain his trust."

"No one gains Warrick's trust and those who betray him suffer endlessly."

Espy thought Craven shivered, but realized it was she who had quivered. "I tended and saved many of his warriors after battle and him as well, though there seemed to be nothing that could do him harm nor was there anything that could touch his heart," she explained as if still trying to make sense of the fearless warrior. "Unbeknownst to him, I managed to save several lives from horrible deaths. It was when three women were brought to the torture chamber that I knew my time there was done. I could not wait long to rescue them or they would die.

"I freed two, one I was too late to help." Pain filled her eyes as she spoke next. "I was caught leaving the torture chamber. I fought for my life, knowing what awaited me if I was taken prisoner. I would have rather died fighting than allowed that to happen."

"That would explain the bruises you had when you arrived here and how you got the scar?" Craven asked anger at what she had gone through because he had sent her away from the only home she had, twisting his stomach into endless knots.

Espy nodded. "I fought, and the guard who grabbed me lashed out with his dagger." She shuddered, recalling the feel of the knife slice through her flesh.

Craven dropped his hands off her shoulders and rested them at her waist. "How did you manage to escape?"

"Sheer luck. I shoved the guard so hard that he stumbled back and was impaled on one of the torture devices."

"Warrick's castle is like a fortress. How did you avoid his warriors?"

"I was their trusted healer. Why would they stop me? Besides, they were too busy fighting the fire."

"What fire?"

"The fire I set to the dungeon before I left."

Craven rolled his eyes and shook his head. "You set fire to Warrick's dungeon?"

Espy nodded. "I hoped it would delay them in discovering my part in it all, while giving me time to get far away. Since they knew nothing of my past, I had hoped they would not find me. I came here because I knew whatever waited for me here was nothing to what Warrick would do to me. And I wanted to come home to my grandmother and know love once again since I have known none, felt none, since leaving here." She rested her brow to his chest for a moment before glancing up at him. "I am sorry. I did not mean to bring this trouble and danger to you. I will go with Warrick's warriors."

"You will not," Carven ordered sharply.

She raised her head, her eyes wide as she pleaded with him. "Warrick will not only bring harm to you and your clan, but to my grandmother as well if I do not go with his warriors. I must go with them."

Craven brought his face close to hers, her scar a stark reminder of the hell she had been through. "You are not going anywhere, and you will keep silent when I speak with Warrick's warriors. I will have your word on that."

"But—"

"Your word," he ordered sternly.

"What choice do I have," she said, knowing it was useless to argue with him.

"You made your choice when you returned here to me. Now it is mine to handle."

Is that what she had done, brought her problem to him to settle? Could the beast actually defeat the demon?

"Your word," he reminded her.

"I give you my word," Espy said and somehow felt safer for it.

Craven took her arm and hurried her out of the room and into the Great Hall.

Espy's heart lurched in her chest when she caught sight of Warrick's warriors. They wore black robes with hoods that fell low over their faces, making them appear as if they were warriors of death. Swords were strapped at their waists, the metal so sharp it was known to slice those who dare got too near to them. There were six of them, six that could do more damage than sixty.

One stepped forward and drew back his hood. "Warrick has sent us to fetch *his* healer." He nodded at Espy. "That woman."

"Not a word of greeting, Roark, only demands?" Craven asked, keeping a keen eye on the man. He knew Roark though not as well as Warrick. He was a fierce fighter and stronger than most men, though one would not think it to look at him. He was lean, every part of him pure muscle and woe to anyone who thought to prove otherwise. He wore his dark brown hair shorter than most and had fine features women favored, but there was only one woman for Roark, his wife, Callie. He was also Warrick's right hand man.

"I am here for one thing, Craven... to return the healer to Warrick. He means you no harm and I do not believe I need to make you aware of the consequences if the healer does not return with me." Roark's bold blue eyes went to Espy. "No harm will be suffered by any as long as you come with me."

Espy would not let others suffer because of her, but she had given Craven her word to hold her tongue and she would... until there was no other recourse but for her to go with Roark.

"She is not going anywhere," Craven said with such confidence that it had Roark's brow shooting up.

Roark shook his head. "I cannot believe you would be foolish enough to defy Warrick, but then you always had tremendous courage. This time, however, it is misplaced."

"I think not," Craven challenged.

"Do not be a fool—"

"It is Warrick who is the fool if he thinks I will let him take... *my wife*!"

Complete silence filled the Great Hall, not a word was mumbled, not a sound was heard. The crackling fire in the hearth had even quieted.

"Return to Warrick and tell him that the beast does not surrender what is his. If he wants my wife, he will have to fight me," Craven said. "You will be given drink and food, then you will be on your way, for—under the circumstances—you are not welcome here."

"Warrick will want to hear this news right away. We will take our leave now," Roark said and turned, then swerved back around to look at Espy. "My wife believed you her friend."

Espy bravely stepped forward, though Craven caught her hand in his as she did. "Callie knows I am her friend. It is you who doubts it."

Dylan walked over to Craven once the door closed behind the warriors.

"Send a troop to follow them to make certain they leave the surrounding area and are not meeting up with more of Warrick's warriors. Also send the tracker to Clan MacVarish and have him make sure he is not followed. A priest recently arrived there by Owen's request. Have the tracker bring the priest here right away," Craven ordered.

"You are going to wed Espy?" Dylan asked.

"It is the only way to make certain she is not harmed," Craven said.

Espy spoke up. "Sacrificing yourself for me will serve no purpose."

"It will not only save you unspeakable torture and death, but it will also see that my clan is kept safe," Craven said.

"Your clan will be safe if you let me go with them," Espy argued.

"But you will not be." Craven nodded at Dylan. "See it done."

"Why wed me when you had wished the same fate for me as Warrick would deliver?" Espy asked as Dylan took his leave.

He once again took hold of her arm and propelled her toward his solar. "You question me when I am saving your life?"

Espy yanked her arm loose of his grip once in the room. "Saving me from one hell only to have me live in another?"

He stepped in front of her and lowered his head slightly. "You feel it will be hell to be my wife?"

"I have seen enough hate to know that it would be hell to be wed to a man who despises me."

"I do not hate you, not any longer. My hate was misplaced. Besides, you have no choice in the matter. You will be my wife and that is the end of it." Craven's sharp tongue stopped the protest before it reached her lips. "Not one word."

One word? She had a slew full of words to unleash on him, though she wisely let silence reign. He did, after all, admit his hate had been misplaced and at least that was a start. But if he no longer hated her, what did he feel for her? She would do as he ordered and keep hold of her tongue. It would do no good to do otherwise. Nothing she said would change his mind and why would she want it to? She did not want to be returned to Warrick. She wanted to stay here and if that meant wedding Craven then why argue with him?

If truth were told, Craven had stolen her heart bit by bit from the first moment he had kissed her. She could not explain why nor did she understand it herself that she could lose her heart to a man who had once hated her, misplaced as it had been. But there was something there between them, though she would have believed it nothing more than fancy-filled thoughts if her grandmother had not seen it herself and so clearly. So, was there a niggling of hope that part of the reason he decided to wed her was that he possibly cared for her?

A knock had them both looking to the door as it burst open.

Dylan hurried in. "Warrick's warriors are headed to Cyra's and another six of them move in from the west to join them,"

"Roark is no fool. He looks to verify what I told him," Craven said.

Dylan approached Craven. "We cannot reach Cyra before Warrick's warriors do."

"You cannot leave her to face them on her own," Espy insisted, fear for her grandmother's safety rushing over her. She shook her head. "How does Roark know Cyra is my grandmother?"

Craven looked at her oddly. "Warrick knows everything." He turned to Dylan. "Then hurry and get the priest here. I want this done so Roark takes the truth back to Warrick."

Espy looked away from Craven as the two men spoke. A question had lingered in Craven's eyes, and she had seen it clearly. She knew what it was and that he would eventually ask her. How had she been able to keep Warrick from knowing her true identity?

"Do you think he will challenge you?" Dylan asked concern heavy in his tone.

"It is difficult to say. You never know with Warrick. It is how he wins so many battles, he is unpredictable. There were times when it would seem that he was going to walk away from a fight only to turn and with one blow knock a man out."

Craven's words brought back memories that had her instinctively leaning closer to him as she spoke. "I often had to see to the results of his unpredictable nature, and I kept my distance from him as much as possible."

"See to the priest, Dylan," Craven ordered and took hold of Espy's hand. "We will wait for him in the Great Hall together.

~~~

"*Seanmhair!*" Espy cried out upon seeing her grandmother enter the Great Hall with the priest.

Cyra threw her arms wide as her granddaughter ran to her. Her slim arms closed around her to hug her tight. A broad smile lit her face when they parted. "You will wed,

Lord Craven?"

Craven answered for her, having followed behind her when she hurried to her grandmother. "We do not have time to explain, Cyra. After the exchange of vows, Espy will explain everything." He walked away to speak with the priest.

Cyra nodded and gave her granddaughter's hand a squeeze and after kissing her on the cheek, she said, "I am glad I was visiting with Owen or else I would have missed this special day."

Espy went to tell her there was nothing special about it, though she was beyond pleased that her grandmother would share it with her. The delight dancing in Cyra's eyes and her broad smile had Espy holding her tongue.

"Love is afoot. Let it be," her grandmother said with a soft laugh.

"He does not love me." Was that sorrow she heard in her own voice?

"He would not wed you if he did not love you."

"He weds me to save me from harm, to spare his people pain and suffering," Espy corrected.

Cyra shook her head. "He weds you because his heart tells him to and for no other reason." Espy went to argue but her grandmother stopped her. "No one tells the beast what to do, remember that."

"Espy."

She turned with a sudden jerk at Craven's summons.

"Go to him, he worries over you," her grandmother said and gave her a gentle push and walked to take a spot where she would watch her granddaughter exchange her wedding vows with Craven. Her heart filled with joy as she watched them join hands. The way Craven closed his long fingers around Espy's with purpose and strength, how he stepped close beside her, tucking her against him, laying claim to her for all to see, but most of all it was the way his dark eyes settled on her granddaughter that caused her heart to catch. She had seen that look in William's eyes for her daughter Sidra. That looked that said my heart is yours now and forever.

Whether he realized it or not, she did not know, but he would learn soon enough that her granddaughter's love would not tame the beast... but free him.

Chapter Twenty-one

Espy sat talking with her grandmother in the Great Hall while Craven had gone to wait outside for Roark's return. He would not leave without confirming that Craven and Espy were wed, for that would have been Warrick's first question upon Roark's return.

The priest had been only too pleased to present confirmation of the marriage until he heard who he had to face, then he begged to be freed of the duty. Craven had given him no choice, though he had given the man his word that he would keep him safe.

Espy had heard the priest mumble that no man is safe from the demon lord, then he had begun to pray as he followed behind Craven.

"You will stay a day or two, *Seanmhair*?" Espy asked hopefully.

"You do not need me here having just been wed." Cyra patted her granddaughter's hand. "Besides, I have a woman who needs healing that I must see to." She gave her head a brief shake. "Her spirit needs more healing than her body. I know so little about her since she barely speaks, a word or two is all she says and then turns silent on me."

Something poked at Espy to ask, "Have you learned her name?"

"She has not trusted me with it yet. She is small, thin, and frail. Her one hand appears to have suffered an injury, leaving two of her fingers crooked and—"

Espy interrupted her. "Does she stay at your cottage?"

"I wish she would, but she will not tell me where it is she resides. She simply appears at my door every other day and I feed her, tend her, and—"

Again Espy interrupted her grandmother. "Today she will come to you."

Cyra nodded and stood. "Which is why I must be on my way."

"Yes, you must go and tend her. She needs you," Espy said, standing and hugging her grandmother. "I will visit soon."

Cyra smiled. "Remember, let things be. All will go well."

Espy hugged her grandmother again, tighter this time. "I love you, *Seanmhair*."

"And I you," Cyra said.

"I will see you to your horse," Espy said but soon learned that no one was to leave until further word from Lord Craven.

"But there is someone I must tend," Cyra explained.

"Please go explain to Lord Craven and ask his permission for my grandmother to take her leave," Espy said to Tass, and it was not long before he returned to let her know Craven had granted it.

The bell tolled for a second time that day, letting everyone know that Warrick's men were returning. Warriors left the Great Hall to gather outside, not one noticing Espy and Cyra slipping through the passage that connected the castle with the kitchen.

Once Espy saw her grandmother off safely, she hurried to the stable. There was no one around, everyone lingering near the front of the keep to watch Lord Craven defend the clan. She soothed Trumble while she readied him to ride, letting him know that they were sneaking off for a while but would return. In minutes, she led Trumble out of the stable and into the woods.

~~~

Craven stood on the steps of the keep, the priest beside him as Roark entered the castle grounds. This time, however, Roark arrived with more warriors. When he brought his horse to a stop, Craven raised his hand before Roark could speak. "If Warrick has anything to say to me, let him say it himself. Espy and I are wed and nothing is going to change that. The priest here will confirm it."

The priest nodded vigorously while his body trembled.

Warrick ignored the quivering man. "She betrayed Warrick."

"Espy did what she felt was right," Craven corrected.

"That is not for her to decide," Roark argued.

"And this is not for you to decide. It is between Warrick and me. As I said, let Warrick speak for himself. Now be on your way. There is nothing left for either of us to say," Craven ordered.

Roark glared at Craven. "She lies. She is not known as Espy to us. Who truly is she and what else does she lie about?" He turned his horse around and took his leave, his men following suit, and Craven knew it would not be the last of it.

She lies. Who truly is she? His words rang in his ears along with the answer. *A woman who cares deeply and will do anything to protect the innocent and helpless.* A woman he now called *his wife.*

He had never thought to wed again, but this was no true marriage like when he had wed Aubrey. It had been a grand celebration, friends coming from all over and food and drink galore. Music played, songs were sung, tales were told, and the future stretched out brightly in front of them.

What awaited Espy and him? He did not know, but he was eager to find out. Lately he had realized he had grown accustomed to her being in his life and, for reasons he could not fathom, he wanted her to remain in his life.

I care for her.

He almost shook his head. Did he care for her or was it simply that he desired her, and would that be enough to sustain their marriage? Only time would tell.

He entered the Great Hall expecting to see his wife there speaking with her grandmother. Only servants lingered about. He felt his stomach clench. There would be no reason for her to run off now that they were wed, so where had she gone.

Tula entered the hall and he was quick to ask if she had seen Espy.

"No, my lord, not since you wed. I have been busy preparing your bedchambers. She may have gone to the healing cottage to see if anyone was in need."

Craven dismissed her with a wave and turned to see Dylan walking toward him.

"Our warriors follow Roark and his warriors to make sure they do not linger in the area," Dylan said, coming to a stop in front of Craven.

"Roark will send a message to Warrick and linger here until he hears from him. It is what Warrick would expect."

"Warrick will come here?"

Craven nodded. "He will face me himself, though he will not come right away. He will wait and one day he will arrive and make his demand."

"He will want Espy?"

"He will want something. We will see," Craven said, not sounding as if he worried about it. "Have you seen Espy?"

"Tass told me that Cyra had to leave to tend someone and that Espy walked her to her horse."

Leith burst into the Great Hall and spit out in one great breath, "Trumble gone."

Dylan turned a quick glance on Craven. "Why would

Espy go with Cyra?"

Leith shook his head, his hand pressed to his chest.

"Espy did not go with Cyra?" Dylan asked.

Leith faltered once or twice but got his words out. "I saw Cyra ride off alone."

"Get my mare, Leith," Craven said to the lad, and Leith hurried off.

"You will want the tracker and a troop of warriors since Roark and his warriors are still in the area."

Craven nodded. His heart beat so furiously that he thought it would burst from his chest. He did not know why she had taken off as she did and at the moment he did not care. He only wanted to make sure he found her safe and unharmed, then he would see that she got what she deserved for being so foolish.

~~~

Espy made her way as quietly as possible, on foot, through the woods. She had dismounted Trumble once the trees became so dense that it made travel more difficult. The ground was just beginning to sprout with the beautiful violet blue, fairy flowers that carpeted this section of the woods in the spring. When young, she had lingered enjoying their beauty, though she would dare not touch one, her grandmother warning her that they belonged to the fairies and were to be left for their use and pleasure.

Today, however, there was no time for lingering. She had to get to her secret place, the one she went to as a child and had continued to go to as an adult, especially when her heart hurt. She had come to the place after her mum and da had died and though her grandmother knew where it was, she never disturbed her, never intruded on her time there.

She had shared it with only one other person... Adara.

Espy swerved around, having thought she heard a footfall, but with Trumble having remained calm, it was not likely. He usually alerted her when someone was nearby. She continued walking, frightened that Warrick's warriors would find Adara and return her to the dungeon. She could not let that happen. She had not freed Adara only to see her taken prisoner again.

With a watchful eye and cautious steps, she made her way to the place that had consoled her and brought her peace. She smiled when she saw the small cottage that had been abandoned and neglected when she had found it. A tree had grown through the lone window and out through a hole in the thatched roof. The front door hung crooked, though closed well enough and the tiny fireplace inside provided sufficient warmth even though part of it had crumbled. And it sat protected, wrapped in the arms of a plethora of trees and a large boulder to the opposite side.

Espy had always felt that the forest lovingly embraced the tiny dwelling and kept it safe from harm. She had told Adara all about the tiny cottage and she could understand why she had come here... Adara wanted to be safe from harm.

"Adara," Espy called out softly. "It is me, Espy and Trumble. We are alone. No one has come with us and no one will follow."

Once Espy had agreed to help Arran, he had taught her how to hide her tracks so no one could follow her. It had served her well as would it now, since no doubt her husband would follow her.

Husband.

She shook her head. She had no time to dwell on her husband or that she even had a husband. She would face the consequences upon her return. At the moment, all she cared about was seeing that Adara was safe.

"Adara," she called out again. "Roark and Warrick's warriors are in the area."

"I know," came the gentle voice.

Espy watched as Adara stepped out from behind the boulder. A patched brown skirt and faded linen blouse hung loose on her painfully thin body, but how could she be anything but thin after having spent time in Warrick's dungeon. She appeared shorter than Espy remembered her, half a head less than her own height. Her pale complexion added to her look of frailty, though nothing could mar her beauty. Her dark blue eyes added to her lovely features, but it was the color of her hair that caught the eye the most. It was a beautiful blond color tinged with red and while it probably looked stunning when long, it now lay just above her shoulders, having been chopped with a knife when she had been brought to Warrick's dungeon.

She held her right hand, with the two crooked fingers, pressed against her stomach. Espy had wished she could have helped heal her the fingers, but she had arrived at the dungeon too long after the injury and it had been too late to straighten the fingers, the broken bones had already set.

"Warrick's warriors are here for me, not you," she assured Adara, "though you must remain hidden until they are gone."

Adara's eyes turned wide in question.

"Lord Craven would have it no other way," Espy said and heard the pride in her own voice for her *husband*. There it was again… *husband*. She could only imagine how angry he would be when he found her gone, but again she pushed it aside, this matter more important.

"You are safe?" Adara dared to ask as if not quite believing it.

"I am." Espy surprised herself with her quick response. She had not hesitated in the least. She was certain she was safe with Craven.

"I came here…" Adara let her words trail off as if they were not worth speaking.

"To be safe—"

Adara shook her head and waved her hand.

"Not to be safe?"

"Never safe," Adara said, fear rising in her eyes.

Espy stepped closer. "I will make sure you are safe. You will stay here. No one will find you. I will bring you food and my grandmother will tend you. The bruising to your body could not have healed yet."

Adara shuddered from the memories.

"We will talk, but not now. I must return to the keep and you must stay out of sight, at least until we are sure that Warrick's warriors do not linger about."

Adara nodded.

"I wish I could confide in my grandmother—"

Adara shook her head and waved her hand, warning her against it. "Not safe." She shooed her off with her hand. "Go."

Espy went to speak, but Adara shook her head and disappeared behind the boulder.

Espy knew they would be no coaxing her out from her hiding spot. She had suffered too much to fully trust anyone. She knew only a little about Adara, but it was enough to know that anyone who had ever claimed to love her had betrayed her.

She had once told Espy that she could live in Espy's secret place forever, and Espy wondered if that was what she intended.

Darkness would settle over the land before she reached the keep, but it could not be helped. She would face whatever consequences awaited her. She would never have seen Adara returned to Warrick's dungeons. The woman would have never survived another stay there.

She hurried to return to the keep. Craven was probably out searching for her and she hoped to return before he did. She thought about what excuse she could offer and the only viable one was that she felt the need to follow her grandmother, without her knowledge, to make sure she got home safely and unbothered. She did not know if Craven would accept the explanation, though she hoped he would, for she had nothing else to offer him.

Espy entered the stable as quietly as possible, no one being about. All were settled in their cottages for the night and with the roll of thunder overhead and the spattering of rain against the stable, it was where everyone would most likely remain.

She cringed when she saw Craven's mare in her stall as she walked Trumble back to his. Night falling, no doubt, had forced Craven to end his search. Or had it been that he had found no tracks? Whatever the case, she would face an angry husband.

Husband.

She rested her cheek to Trumble's face. "I have a husband, Trumble. One who does not want me, though I sometimes wonder if he knows what he wants, since grief consumes him. I cannot blame him. I saw my da wither away and die when he lost my mum. He simply could not live without her." She patted the horse. "With love comes great joy and great sorrow. Perhaps I am lucky to know no such love."

Trumble shook his head and pawed the ground, then stared off to the left.

Espy froze. She was not alone. Someone was here with her.

Chapter Twenty-two

"But you will know the consequences of disobeying *your husband*."

Espy stepped closer to Trumble as lightning flashed outside the lone window, illuminating Craven as he emerged from the shadows. Or had the shadows parted, wanting to be rid of him. The size of him always amazed her, thick, large, and so powerfully built, and he appeared even more so now, his shoulders seeming to stretch on forever. His fine features were stern, his brow wrinkled with anger, his dark eyes equally so. The intimidating sight of him should frighten her, but it was not what she felt, not when her eyes fell on his chest and a tiny quiver ran through her, recalling how comfortable his chest was to rest her head upon and the strength of his arms when they wrapped around her, holding her, comforting her, protecting her.

My husband.

Craven was her husband. Was it true or would she wake to find this day nothing more than a dream? She felt her heart wither at the thought.

Craven reached out, his hand clamping down on her arm, and he snatched her away from the stallion, who was none too pleased by his presence, pawing the ground in agitation.

"Calm him," Craven ordered when he brought her to stand beside him.

"Easy, Trumble. All is well," Espy said in a voice that held not a hint of fear or worry, and the horse instantly calmed.

Craven did not say a word as he kept a strong hold on

her and walked to the front of the stable, yanking open the door only to be met by rain plummeting the ground. He shut the door against the slashing onslaught and stepped into an empty stall, dragging Espy along with him.

Flashes of lightning were the only light in the stable, arriving unexpectedly and highlighting the anger in Craven's dark eyes and the stiffness in his jaw.

It was time for her to suffer the consequences of her actions.

Craven leaned his head down until their faces nearly touched. "I will hear the truth spill from your lips or else..."

Espy went to speak, to try and explain, when suddenly her heart spoke for her. "I believe I am falling in love with you, Craven. I do not know when I first felt it nor can I explain it. It took root on its own and seems to dig in more deeply by the day. The more time I spend with you, the more time I want to spend with you. It makes no sense and I should not even share this with you, and yet I cannot help myself—" She stopped abruptly as if words suddenly failed her. Or had fear of his response stolen her tongue?

Lightning flashed again and she caught the warning in his dark eyes as he said, "Do not love the beast, he will only bring you pain."

Espy rested her hand to his chest. "Too late. The beast already has my heart."

Craven shook his head as he brought his brow to lie against hers. "I give you this one chance and my word. Run from the beast before it is too late, and he will never touch you."

He dropped his hand off her, raised his head, and glared at her, trying to frighten her or perhaps fighting to contain the beast within him. She did not know and did not care.

"I cannot run from you, Craven. My heart would break if I did, and I would die a little each day until I withered away if I never felt your touch again. I told myself I was foolish. You could never care for me let alone love me, but my heart would not listen. It did as it pleased and I am tired of trying to ignore it and trying to deny it. I most certainly am not going to run from you. I have run enough."

Craven felt the anger, the hate, the pure rage of the animal within him, who had sought revenge without thought or reason, draw back into the darkness where it lurked and waited. "You invade my dreams and my waking thoughts. My body aches for you, even more so when I touch you. I grow hard with just the thought of you, but... love. I do not know if I can promise you that"

She reached out tentatively, hoping he would not back away from her and when her hand touched his cheek he flinched, though he let it remain there. "I have enough love for the both of us."

Craven wanted her, his body on fire for her... but love her?

He took an abrupt step at her, meaning to frighten her off and she stumbled backward, and he had all he could do not to reach out and steady her, but he did not, and she did not run.

Her chin jutted out defiantly. "I am not afraid of the beast."

"Then you are a fool," he spat.

"I have been called worse and survived. You cannot, you will not, frighten me, and you will not stop me from loving you."

The growl started low in his chest and rose up, but before it could break loose, Espy stepped forward and pressed her lips to his.

Craven grabbed a handful of her hair at the back of her head and yanked her head back, forcing her lips off his. "Once I claim you, once I make you mine, you are mine forever." Lord help him, he wanted it that way. He wanted to make her his forever.

A soft smile spread across Espy's face. "I already am yours forever."

He brought his mouth down on hers with a growl rumbling deep inside him. Nothing ever tasted as sweet and delicious to him, and he did not think he would ever get enough of her.

His arm circled her waist and he lifted her off the ground as he continued to kiss her, to be nourished by her. Her kisses were as eager and hungry as his and he hated to break away from her mouth even for a short time, but he did, ordering her to, "Wrap your legs around me."

She did, her legs hugging his waist tight and his lips found hers once again, their kiss even more demanding than before. He walked her to the back of the stall, bracing her back against the wall.

He tore his mouth off her, shaking his head. "I burn for you, have a need for you like no other." He pulled down her blouse and scooped one breast out, dropping his mouth to suckle at her nipple. It had been so long, so terribly long, and she tasted so good, much too good.

His manhood had hardened quickly and was growing ever demanding. He wanted nothing more than to slip inside her and feel her close around him, then spill his seed endlessly in her.

Virgin.

The voice shouted loud and clear in his head, reminding him that she had never known a man. This was her first time, if he was to believe her, and he did

He grabbed her hand and shoved it under his plaid. "Touch me," he said.

Espy did not have to be coaxed. She wanted to touch him, feel the length of him and know he now belonged to her. She gasped when she felt his thickness and the silky hardness of him, and instinct guided her hand as she lovingly stroked it.

"Tighter. Harder," he demanded.

She would have preferred to take her time and enjoy the feel of him, but she did as he demanded and tightened her hold around his shaft and stroked him hard, forming a rhythm of sorts and as he expanded in her hand, her rhythm increased.

"Harder," he ordered and she obeyed

The moistness between her legs grew until she felt a heavy wetness there and a throbbing that she knew only he could satisfy. She tried to draw him nearer to her, rub his wet tip against her wetness that beckoned him, but he kept her at a distance and she grew frustrated.

She slowed her pace and he groaned in her ear. "Do not stop."

She did as he said, her own ache growing and tormenting her.

His head suddenly fell back and he let out a long lingering moan and she felt his seed spew out and spill over her hand. She eased her strokes

"No," he shouted as his brow fell on hers.

She kept stroking him until instinct told her, he needed no more.

Craven kept his one arm tight around Espy's waist, his hand clenching her side just above her hip. His other hand he kept braced on the wall just above her head, helping him to keep steady.

He had come hard, harder than he could ever remember and he would not have been surprised if he had come inside her that he would have planted more than one bairn. But he would not have her first coupling be against the wall of a stable or have it be quick because it had been so long since he had spilled his seed.

He took a deep breath and stepped back slowly so that instinct would have her releasing her legs from around him. When he was sure she was steady on her feet, he stepped away from her to snatch a cloth from the pile kept outside the stall and handed it to her.

Espy took it and wiped her hand. She remained silent, not knowing what to say to him.

Craven opened the stable door and while the rain was heavy, it was not the slashing downpour as before. He grabbed one of the cloaks kept by the door and went to Espy and wrapped it around her.

He scooped her up in his arms and held her close against his body. "Now I will seal our vows and nothing or no one can ever separate us," he said as he walked out of the stable and to the keep.

Chapter Twenty-three

Craven's lips found hers as soon as he placed her on her feet in his bedchambers. He had not gotten enough of her, he wanted more, especially her sweet lips that responded in equal enthusiasm. She did not shy away in fright or uncertainty. Her demanding kisses let him know just how much she wanted him, favored him and it fired his loins once again.

His hands worked her blouse out from the waist of her skirt and she hastily broke off their kiss and raised her arms as he brought it up and over her head, her lips returning to his as he tossed the garment to the floor.

His large hand cupped her one breast and her moan of pleasure reverberated in his mouth, and her body shivered when his thumb grazed her already hard nipple.

Her hands went to his waist to free him of his plaid, but it was tucked tight and her hands fumbled in their effort. He pushed them away and took a quick step away from her to shed his garments and boots and he was pleased to see her do the same with her remaining garments.

Once done, he lifted her up in his arms and carried her to the bed. Her hands reached up to cup his face as he lowered them both down and she once again pressed her lips to his. Her kiss did not only excite, it also soothed something in him, letting him fully enjoy her playful lips that teased and taunted and begged for more from him.

He tore his mouth away from hers and she protested with a sorrowful moan that turned pleasurable when he took her one nipple in his mouth.

Pleasure shot through Espy stinging her senses as his

tongue rolled over her nipple and then teased it with gentle nips. She cried out with delight when he treated her other nipple to the same pleasure.

There was not only strength to this man—her husband—but a gentleness as well. She was safe with him. He would not harm her and while he may not love her, he would always protect her. The knowledge that there was now someone that she could trust and count on made any misgivings she had about this marriage begin to fade, and she let herself surrender to his gentleness and strength.

Craven felt the change in her body, her tenseness faded to a supple, soft surrender and his desire soared that she should trust him so. That she should love him. He would not fail her. He would never fail her.

He trailed kisses down along her and as he kissed her stomach he thought of the bairns he would plant within her in the years to come. They would have many, for he would not be able to keep his hands off her.

There was a sweetness to her skin that he favored and he kissed and licked down along her silky skin until he settled on the tiny nub between her legs. When his tongue touched there, she arched her back and released a moan filled with such desire that it caused his loins to swell.

He let not only his tongue continue to ignite her passion but his fingers as well, slipping them inside her, gently, teasingly, and pleasuring her senseless.

"Craven." His name was a plea on her lips.

He lifted his head to see her head tossed back, the slim column of her neck beckoning him, and her hands clenching at the bedding to each side of her. He moved up over her, stopping at her neck to kiss and nip at the sensitive skin.

"Craven," she pleaded once again, her hands grabbing hold of his steel-hard arms and squeezing tight.

He kissed her lips. "You are mine now, Espy and always will be."

She nodded. "Always."

He placed his hands to either side of her head and raised his body over her, then slipped his shaft between her legs.

Instinctively, or perhaps it was more fear that he would take too long, Espy's one hand moved down to guide him inside her. Her hand returned to his arm when she felt his smooth entrance.

Craven stilled and Espy turned questioning eyes on him.

"Tell me you want this, you accept this, you take me as your husband as long as there is a breath left in you."

"Even when there is no breath left in me, I will always love you and the beast," she said with a soft smile.

Craven did not wait, he slid deeper inside her and when she raised her hips, forcing him even deeper, he could hold back no more… he slipped all the way in her.

Espy gasped, sighed, and cried out.

"I caused you pain?" Craven stilled again.

Espy shook her head. "No. No. Do not stop. It feels wonderful."

A brief smile sneaked across Craven's face at her words and the way she wiggled against him to get him moving. He did move. He started slow, though that did not last long since her hips beat to a faster rhythm and he was soon pounding harder and faster into her.

Espy gripped her husband's arms tighter and tighter as if she needed to anchor herself to him, to keep the passion from carrying her off, though soon, very soon, there would be no containing it. She could not wait, did not want to wait.

"Craven!" she cried out, knowing he could help free her.

Craven felt his own passion near to exploding and he brought their bodies closer as he drove into her again and again and again until…

Espy screamed out his name as a blinding climax gripped her, shooting intense waves of pleasure through every part of her so much so that she thought she would surely die from the intense please.

Craven threw back his head and groaned through gritted teeth as his climax slammed into him with such force that it momentarily weakened him and he thought he would collapse on top of her. But the beast would never allow his strength to fail him, and he remained hovering over her.

Espy released a satisfied sigh when the last of her pleasure faded away.

Only then did Craven lower himself down on her. He slipped one arm around her waist and brought her to rest against his side as he rolled over to lie on his back.

Espy was glad for his support, for all her limbs were far too weak to do anything on her own. Besides, she was where she wanted to be… tucked safely in her husband's powerful arms.

"Our vows are sealed. They can never be broken," Craven reminded her.

"Then you best be sure to keep me satisfied, *husband*," Espy said with a soft laugh, looking up at him. She was pleased to see a smile spread across his face.

"I believe I am up to the challenge."

"We will see about that," she said, with a playful poke to his chest.

His smile faded. "I will be a good husband to you, Espy. I can promise you that."

"I never doubted that," she said and ran her finger faintly over his lips. "I will love you no matter what." Her finger to his lips, stilled whatever he intended to say. "Let it be, for nothing will change how I feel."

He remained silent, wishing he could find it in him to love her, but there was Aubrey. There would always be Aubrey, though he had not thought of her once while coupling with Espy. Still, he had pledged his love to Aubrey and his heart had died with her. He had nothing left to give

Espy. He cared for her and would be a good husband as he told her, but there was no love left in him to give.

Espy stretched against him and gave a small groan.

"You have pain?" Craven asked worried he may have hurt her.

"A bit sore, nothing more," she assured him. "I will see to it on the morrow."

"I will not touch you again until you tell me you have healed."

Espy's brow shot up as she tipped her head back to glare at him. "You mean this one time is all we will make love tonight?"

"You are sore," he said as if it was explanation itself.

"Barely," she countered as though it made no difference.

"We wait," he commanded and snagged the blanket with his foot to yank up so that he could grab it and pull it over them.

Espy told herself he was being considerate of her and that she should be grateful she had a husband who was so thoughtful. She had seen for herself the women who had suffered at the hands of husbands who were not thoughtful of their wives when it came to coupling. She was lucky or perhaps blessed that she found making love with Craven so enjoyable. Even though he claimed he had no love left to give, his gentle and loving touch told her differently.

While there were still problems to face, at least now she had the protection of a husband and that made her feel safer than she had in a long while. She would have never thought of becoming Craven's wife, but then she would have never believed that she could have fallen in love with him either.

Her da often had said that life was strange. You never know what to expect from it. She had to agree. Life was strange, for never had she thought of becoming wife to the man who had nearly choked her to death and now held her lovingly in his arms.

Craven felt when his wife fell asleep. Her body seemed to melt against him and her breathing turned shallow. He lay awake unable to sleep, his thoughts keeping him busy. He had never thought he would bring another woman to his bed.

It disturbed and also relieved him that Aubrey was fading from his memory. Not that she would ever fade completely, but she no longer constantly haunted his thoughts... Espy did. Guilt poked at him and yet he was glad Espy rested beside him, tucked in his arms. He was even more relieved she was his wife. He could protect her that way, though if he was honest it was not the only reason he had wed her.

He could not stand the thought of her being with anyone but him. He could not reason why that had plagued him, but it did, and he could not ignore it. Though, he had given her a chance to remain his wife in name only, especially since she had claimed to love him. It was not fair to her that he could not return that love. Though, she believed her love was strong enough for them both, he believed otherwise. No love was that strong.

She was his now and there would be no changing that. The thought settled him and he soon drifted off to sleep.

~~~

Espy slipped out of the bedchamber, closing the door quietly behind her. Her husband slept soundly and she hoped he would continue to do so for some time yet. The sun had yet to come up, but it would not be long before it did. Her feet flew quickly down the stone stairs and she maneuvered the hall with equal haste, her skirt brushing the stone wall as she rushed through the silent keep straight through to the kitchen. She had to be quick to avoid the workers that would soon arrive to get the hearth fires going for the morning repast. She gathered what food she could find, some bread, though it was not fresh, it could be softened in a brew, a good-size piece of cheese, and what was left of the salted fish. That should keep Adara fed for a day or two.

Once everything was wrapped neatly in a cloth, Espy hurried as quietly as she could to the stable. Trumble pawed the ground and snorted, happy to see her, and the two were soon off, riding with great care through the dark.

Espy squinted her eyes as she drew near the cottage. She had not expected to see Adara standing in front of the crooked front door as if she had been expecting her. A soft smile was the only greeting Espy got from her, but it warmed her heart. Adara rarely smiled and barely spoke. It was as if she feared doing either. That if she did she would somehow suffer for it, so she chose to be silent more often than not.

"I brought you food and leaves to brew," Espy said and Adara nodded her thanks and pointed to the sky. The first ray of dawn was just sparking. Adara realized without being told that Espy had snuck out before the castle grounds stirred to life and had to return before anyone found her gone.

Adara shooed her off with her hand after taking the bundle of food from Espy. She shook her head when Espy went to speak and shooed her once again, this time toward Trumble.

"I will return," Espy assured her and a twinge of regret squeezed at her heart having to leave Adara alone, but she had no choice. She reached out to rest a comforting hand on Adara's shoulder and stopped when she cringed and backed away from her. Espy had forgotten that Adara was not used to a comforting touch, she had known only harshness.

Espy wanted to tell her that she was safe, but she recalled Adara's words.

Never safe.

She said the one thing that Adara could count on. "I will

be back."

Adara clutched the cloth bundle to her chest and nodded.

Espy had always loved sunrises and there had been a time she had taken care to watch the sun unfurl its nourishing light, but this morning she wished the sun would slow its ascent. She did not want anyone up and about to see her return, most of all her husband.

Trumble was quick, having sensed her own urgency and she was soon leading him into the stables, grateful Leith had not arrived to see to the horses yet. However, she took cautious steps upon entering the stable, worried that Craven could once again be lying in wait for her. When she made certain no one was about, she took care of Trumble with haste and settled him comfortably in his stall, the unexpected morning ride having pleased him.

The sun had fully risen, bright and strong, by the time she entered the keep and luckily no servants were in the Great Hall as she hurried through it. If her luck held, her husband would still be asleep and she could simply join him in bed and he would be none the wiser. She shook her head. He would know. He would smell the scents of the forest upon her, pungent pine and earth, and possibly the sharp scent of the stable. She would tell him at least a partial truth… she went for a ride.

With explanation in hand, she grabbed the latch to the bedchamber door just as Craven did the same to the handle on the opposite side and gave the door a powerful yank.

Espy flew in, stumbling as the latch was ripped from her hand, and she fell right into her husband's arms.

"Where were you?" he demanded, his arm closing tightly around her middle to swing her away from the door as he closed it.

"I went for a ride," she said, the excuse sounding paltry to her own ears.

"Without my permission?"

"I did not think I needed it now that I was your wife." That was the truth and she hoped that she was right. She was too accustomed to her freedom to give it up.

"Now more than ever you need it. I will know where my wife is at all times. You will *never* ride off on your own again," he ordered. "Not ever, and certainly not when Warrick's warriors may still be in the area."

"Do not take my freedom from me," Espy said, not having considered the burdens of having a husband.

He brushed a stray lock of hair away from her eyes. "Was freedom so tasty this past year that you would prefer it to a husband?"

"It was survival, not freedom and a bitter taste it was," Espy admitted, her body relaxing against his, letting not only him know but herself that she preferred being there with him.

"You are my wife, not my prisoner—but," Craven said, his voice taking on a commanding tone and his arm around her waist hugging her more tightly, "I will know your whereabouts at all times."

"Why?" Espy asked as if his command made no sense.

"I owe you no reason," he said surprised she would ask.

"We are husband and wife," she said, expecting that to be reason enough.

"Out of necessity," Craven reminded, his tongue sharper than intended.

"I see that the beast rose this morning." She patted his chest, stepped out of his arms, and settled a strong smile on him. "Be careful, my dear husband, for there is a beast in all of us."

Chapter Twenty-four

Craven found Espy seated at the table in the Great Hall, waiting, like a dutiful wife, for him to join her for the morning meal. While he believed she would be a good wife, dutiful was questionable, though she had been more than dutiful in bed last night. She actually seemed to enjoy his every touch, his every kiss. She had not shied away and he had woken this morning with every intention of coupling with her again... but she had been gone.

It had angered him not to find her there and it reminded him that he wanted a better answer than she went for a ride. She went for a ride for a reason and he wanted to know where and why. She had still to explain where she had disappeared to right after they had wed.

She smiled and stood at his approach and he gave her a gentle kiss on the cheek when he stopped beside her.

"I thought now, while we share the morning meal, you could tell me what duties you expect of me as your wife," she said after they sat.

A grin surfaced on its own as he leaned over to whisper, "Keep me pleasured."

Espy leaned closer, the sweet scent of mint brushing his lips as she whispered, "How many times a day? Two, three, or more? Or whenever the feeling strikes us?" Her whisper grew softer. "Like now when I ache to have you—"

Espy gasped as Craven stood so abruptly that his chair tumbled backward, hitting the floor and he snatched her up and threw her over his shoulder. She gasped again when his hand came down on her backside.

"You think to tease me? I will show you what it is to

tease," he said and walked out of the Great Hall, chuckles from the few who were there following after them.

Espy was surprised when he entered his solar and her stomach fluttered when she heard the lock on the door fall in place. When he dropped her to her feet in front of the desk, she turned concerned eyes on him. "Was I wrong in being playful with you? If I overstepped my bounds as your wife, please forgive me. This is so new to me in so many ways and even though our marriage is out of necessity, as you said, I cannot help but love you—foolish as you think that may be—I hoped we could make it a good marriage if not a loving one. And I must be honest and admit that I do enjoy making love with you and—"

Craven cupped her face in his large hands and silenced her nervous chatter with a kiss. He ended the kiss sooner than he would have liked to and touched the tip of his nose to hers. "You have crossed no bounds for there are no bounds between us. I love that you make your desire known to me and I must admit that I love making love with you as well, though I fear I may never get enough of you."

I love making love with you as well. His words had her heart soaring, and she smiled.

He smiled as well, though it turned wicked as he said, "Now as for turning me hard with your teasing taunt…"

He spun her around, bent her over the narrow table, and threw her skirt up, exposing her bare backside.

His hands grabbed her firm cheeks, squeezing them tight, and it elicited a gasp of pleasure from her that soared his own. His manhood swelled along with his need as he slipped his hand between her legs and felt her moist and ready. His fingers eagerly sought to stroke and pleasure the little, sensitive bud and her response was a sharp lift of her head and a deep throaty moan of pleasure.

A rippling tingle rushed down to her toes and up to her nipples pressed against the top of the wood table and she shuddered at its pleasurable intensity.

Another moan suddenly took hold, a stronger more aching one, when his thick manhood poked hard against her backside. Her need to have him inside her overwhelmed her. She wanted him now. She wanted to feel his thick member slip inside her and satisfy this hungry ache that he had brought on her so fast and furiously.

She wiggled her backside hard against him and he leaned down over her, his hand wrapping around her braid and yanking her head back to leave her mouth vulnerable to his lips. With a rumbling growl, his lips settled over hers and his tongue delved hard into her mouth, forcing her to respond, and she gladly did. His demanding kiss, his probing fingers, and his thick shaft rubbing, poking, teasing her was too much to bear.

She tore her mouth away from his to demand, "I want you inside me."

"No," he ordered and ground his lips against hers with such a searing demand, that she felt as if he was branding her for all to know that she belonged to him and a ripple of wicked pleasure raced over her, tingling her flesh until she shuddered so hard that she thought she would come there and then.

She managed to break her lips away from his again. "Please, Craven, I am going to come."

"Aye, and more than once," he said and gave her bare backside a tender smack. "And you will not tease me again, wife."

Espy chuckled. "On that, husband, you are mistaken."

It was no gasp that she let loose next, but a roar of pleasure when Craven entered her. He gripped the sides of her backside, holding firm as he slammed into her over and over and he was true to his word.

Espy cried out in pleasure twice before he exploded in his own climax and then she joined him again in another of her own.

Craven collapsed over her, his hands braced to either side of her head as he let the last of the satisfying pleasure drift away. He stayed as he was, wanting to remain buried inside her, wanting to remain joined with her, wanting that feeling of wholeness to linger as long as possible.

When he heard her sigh softly, he slipped his one arm beneath her breasts and hugged her against him. He felt a strong tug at his heart, fighting feelings that rumbled and churned inside him and he spoke the only words he could bring himself to say at the moment and seemed far too inadequate when he did. "I do enjoy you, wife."

"And I you, husband," she said with joyous enthusiasm that could not be denied.

Craven heard not only the joy but the love in her response. She let her love for him be heard in her words, her touch, and since he was admitting the truth, he had also seen it in her eyes when she looked at him. Aubrey had had a similar look, but it had not been as intense, but then Espy had a passion about her that he had never seen in a woman.

Reluctantly, he released and moved off her, though she followed him up off the table as if she too was reluctant to separate from him.

Craven's arm went around her out of sheer instinct. It belonged there. She belonged there beside him, forever beside him.

Espy rubbed gently at the deep lines that suddenly appeared between his eyes. "Something troubles you?"

"No, I am late for the practice field," he said which was true but that was not what had caused his brow to crease. It was the thought of leaving her, even if only for a while.

"Then go, but first quickly tell me what chores are now mine since I am your wife."

"You have chores enough with being the clan's healer," he said, walking with her to the door.

"I will see to the running of the keep, since I believe that is a wife's duty" she said, scurrying out of his arm and out the door when he opened it and off she ran before he could dictate otherwise.

Craven smiled, hearing her light laughter trickle behind her and fall around him. He closed his eyes and inhaled the scent of her lingering on him. He had not felt such joy, such contentment since Aubrey and guilt rose up to jab at him.

He had thought his heart had died with Aubrey that day. That he would never ever feel joy of loving someone again. He had never thought to find love in the first place, but Aubrey had stolen his heart so quickly, he had not even been sure how it had happened.

She smiled at him. He would never forget Aubrey's smile, soft and timid, or her quietness. She had never once argued with him or dared disobey him, and never had she been untruthful with him. He had known peace with Aubrey.

There would be no peace with Espy. She would do what she saw fit to help others even if he forbids it. She would challenge his sanity at every turn and tempt him with every touch. Why did he find that so appealing?

~~~

Espy went straight to the kitchen and spoke briefly with Aggie, the cook, letting her know that she was going to see to the running the keep now and that Aggie should seek her counsel if she required anything. She had been grateful when Aggie offered her help should there be anything she was unfamiliar with in the keep. She had no experience in running a keep, but she never let lack of knowledge stop her before. Her da had always encouraged her to dive in and explore, ask questions, listen, and learn from those more knowledgeable. She would do the same with the workings of the keep. Besides, it was her responsibility and she had never shied away from responsibility.

She went to the healing cottage after leaving the kitchen and was surprised and a bit uncomfortable when people referred to her as *my lady*. She was Espy, equal to all she tended. She did not want a useless title to interfere with that. She would speak with Craven and hoped he would agree with her.

She spotted Ober sitting on the bench outside the healing cottage as soon as the place came into view. He would come to her for a brew when he was not feeling well, claiming the brew eased his suffering considerably. Espy did not know how that could be possible since the brew she gave him was nothing more than chamomile and mint.

Tula had told her that he was friendly to all and offered his help to many when he felt well enough. Still, there was something about him that made her hesitate in trusting him. There was that nagging thought that he seemed familiar, but she could not recall where she may have seen him before. She had been to far too many places and had far too many people to recall them all, though Ober was one person she wished she could recall.

"Congratulations on your wedding, my lady," Ober said, rising up off the bench to stand on wobbling limbs.

"Sit," Espy urged as she drew near and placed her arm around his shoulder to help lower him to the bench. "Thank you, Ober. I am sure it was a surprise to all."

"A pleasant and delightful surprise to all from what I have heard," he said, his smile quickly fading to a grimace. "My bones are hurting bad, my lady. I could use more of that brew, though I think my time is drawing near."

"Nonsense," Espy said, "you are getting better every day. Sit here and rest while I prepare a brew for you." It did not take long and soon Espy returned, handing Ober a tankard and joining him on the bench. It was time to find out some things about the man and see if she could spark her memory.

"Thank you, my lady, I have been in need of this," Ober said, cupping the tankard in his hands.

"Where is your home Ober?"

"Here, there, everywhere. I have been a wander far too long," he said and sipped at the brew.

"How did you ply your trade as a smithy if you wandered so much?" she asked and caught the slight jerk to his body, as if he realized his mistake.

"There is always work for a smithy somewhere," he said, nodding as if it proved his words.

"It does not seem that you got much work," Espy said and watched the knuckles in his hands turn white as his grip on the tankard tightened.

"Why do you say that?"

"Your hands have no scars and a smithy never escapes scars, so I assume you found little work during your wandering."

He nodded in agreement. "Enough to help me survive."

"I have wandered some myself, perhaps we crossed paths along the way."

He shook his head. "I did not travel far up into the Highlands where the old ways still rule."

"How do you know I traveled far up into the Highlands or that the old ways rule there, if you have never been there?"

He tongue was quick to defend. "I heard tales of those who have been there and everyone is talking about Warrick sending his warriors for you and he resides farther up in the Highlands or so I have heard."

"Gossip spreads like the wind over the land," Espy said and Ober agreed with repeated nods and shortly after that he took his leave, refusing any help from Espy as he slowly shuffled off.

What was it about Ober that made him feel familiar, but

not in a comfortable way? Where had she seen him? Or had she? Could she be mistaken? She shook her head and entered the cottage. One day it would come to her. One day she would remember.

Chapter Twenty-five

Espy had just stepped out of the healing cottage the next morning, basket in hand, planning on collecting some of the fresh nettle growing on the outskirts of the woods when she spotted a young lad running straight toward her. It was Sayer, the young lad who worked in the kitchen and a friend of Leith's, and he was crying.

"Please, my *Seanmhair* needs you," Sayer begged, his breathing haggard.

Espy dropped the basket and rushed off with Sayer. She had been expecting this summons having visited Verna yesterday and seeing that death was not far off.

Sayer ran to his mum and cuddled against her as soon as they entered the cottage, tears continuing to run down his flushed cheeks. His mum's arm curled around him, offering comfort as she sniffed back her own tears.

Espy sat on the chair beside the bed and took the old woman's frail and nearly lifeless hand in hers. Her breathing was so shallow that it barely could be detected and it would not be long before it ceased altogether.

She turned to Sayer's mum. "Your mum does not suffer, Cleva. She will be at peace soon."

Cleva fought back her tears, but a few broke loose and she wiped at them with the back of her hand. "She was the best mum and *Seanmhair*. We will miss her."

The door burst open and Celva's husband, Hamill, a man of good height and width, hurried in and he went to his wife and son and wrapped them in his thick arms as tears filled his eyes.

Espy kept a gentle hold on Verna's hand as she waited

for her to take her last breath.

~~~

Craven was lost in thought as he walked through the village. For some reason, his wife's words of the other day had come back to haunt him.

Be careful, my dear husband, for there is a beast in all of us.

He could not imagine that a beast could reside in Espy. She thought of others before she thought of herself and she was always there to help the ill and the needy... yet? Her words had a ring of truth to them. He had seen quiet men turn into beasts when going into battle. He had seen women rage like beasts when defending loved ones. So had a beast within Espy helped her work with Arran to save the innocent?

The thought, and his curiosity, had him going to find her, not to mention that he was missing her, his arms feeling empty. Dust kicked up around his boots, the thought having stopped him so abruptly. He shook his head at the crazy thought as he continued walking again. How could he miss her when he had only seen her earlier this morning? He had woken before her to find her naked body sprawled half across him and naturally he could not keep his hands off her. His intimate touches and strokes had woken her and they had made love.

Love.

Craven stopped abruptly once more, drawing attention, not that anyone would acknowledge his strange behavior, though this time his clansmen did not stare at him in fright, but with smiles and gentle nods as if they understood his plight.

He glared from one person to another and none turned away, they simply kept smiling and nodding. They thought him besotted… *in love*.

He could not be in love. It was impossible. Any love he had to give had died with Aubrey.

You have a huge heart, share it.

Aubrey had said that often to him, especially when he got upset or angry over something. She always reminded him that it was his heart he needed to listen to and not the beast who rumbled and blustered.

He took off walking again and was about to turn toward the healing cottage when he saw his wife, her head down and her gait rushed as she hurried in the same direction.

His gut clenched, and sensing something was wrong, he called out to her. "Espy." She stopped and looked his way and when he saw tears in her eyes every muscle in his body grew as tight as a bow string. Before he could take a step toward her, she flew at him with rapid steps and he spread his arms out and caught her in them, locking them around her.

Her head dropped to his shoulder and she let her tears fall. He walked her, though more carried her, his arm coiled around her waist, to the healing cottage, and was grateful no one was there or he would have chased them away.

Once inside, the door shut, the two of them alone, he kept silent and held her. He let her cry, soft tears, until she finally raised her head and looked at him. Tears dampened her flushed cheeks and her tear-drenched eyes glistened.

"I hate when death is victorious," she said, anger sparking her words.

"Someone died?" he asked concerned not only for those in his clan, but for his wife.

"Verna. Sayer's grandmother."

"Verna is the oldest member of our clan," Craven said, recalling the old woman's many wrinkles and her slow gait that had everyone stepping around her or assisting her when she seemed unable to take another step. "Verna has outwitted death on many an occasion. It was finally her time."

Espy wiped at her wet cheeks while remaining snug in her husband's arms. "That may be so, but it still does not make it easy for me. I always feel I should have done more to battle death."

"From what you have told me about working with Arran to free the innocent, you have defeated death more often than not."

"Not often enough," she said with a hint of regret.

"Whatever possessed you to join forces with Arran and put yourself in such danger?" Espy eased out of his embrace and he reluctantly let her go, eager to learn more about her.

"I had nightmares after saving Arran, faceless people reaching out to me for help and some begging for death to end their suffering. Though, I was not naïve to the suffering of others, it was nothing compared to the cruelty and heartlessness of torture." Espy shook her head slowly. "I was not foolish enough to think I could save everyone, but if I could at least save a few—"

"Do you know what would have happened if you had gotten caught?" Craven asked, fear prickling his skin, something he had not felt since Aubrey's death.

She nodded knowingly. "I would have suffered the same fate of those I was trying to help."

"How many did you save?"

"Many, yet not enough. I never counted. The number never mattered to me, only the person. Arran mentioned something once about thirty, though there were many more after that." Espy turned away. "And even more I failed to help."

That she was disappointed in those she failed to help rather than take pride in the many she had helped spoke of her selflessness. It also worried him since she would not think twice of helping someone even if it meant possible harm to her. "You cannot save everyone and everyone is not worth saving," he warned.

Espy turned to face him. "That is not for me to judge. My da and mum taught me that a healer was there to heal, to help, to comfort. What is done to people in those torture chambers is beyond cruel. It is complete madness, as was the reason for most being there."

Craven rubbed at the back of his neck, a nagging pain stabbing at him at the thought of what she could have suffered. "How was it that you were not caught before the debacle with Warrick?"

"Luck? Good planning? Fate?" She shrugged. "I do not know. I saved those I could and held the hand of those I failed while they took their last breath, then I moved on."

He tipped his head slightly to the side and his brow wrinkled in question. "Was this comfort you offered the dying before or after you helped others escape?"

"Both."

"You put yourself in danger and remained at these places when there was nothing you could have done for the dying?" he asked, trying to comprehend not only her foolishness but the courage it took to do that.

"Yes there was. I could hold their hand so they were not alone when death came for them," she said, making it sound like the most reasonable thing for her to do. "No one wants to die alone."

Craven did not know where the question came from, it simply slipped from his lips. "Did Aubrey fear that moment when death came for her? That moment she knew she would die." He swallowed hard, the next question difficult for him to ask, but impossible for him not to. "Did Aubrey cry out for me?"

His question did not surprise her. It was inevitable that one day he would ask it. She had wondered why he had not asked it of her sooner, but sometimes people do not ask for fear of the answer. She would tell him. She only hoped he would believe her.

The door flew open preventing her from responding and she could not deny she was grateful for the interruption.

Dylan stood in the open doorway. "Some of Warrick's men have taken up camp just on the outskirts of MacCara land."

"I expected no less," Craven said. "They wait for word from Warrick."

"Also, a traveler has arrived and he claims to know Espy. He says he is a physician," Dylan said, looking to Espy. "His name is Innis Lockerbie."

A sudden smile consumed Espy's entire face and she rushed around the table and out of the cottage before Craven could stop her, though he was quick to follow.

"It seems that she is pleased that Innis Lockerbie is here," Dylan said as he kept even strides with Craven. "Though I cannot say the same for you."

Craven grumbled and scowled, and Dylan laughed. His scowl deepened when he saw his wife rush into Innis Lockerbie's arms and they hugged each other tight.

It was with a stern tongue he shouted out his wife's name. "Espy!"

Her smile never faltered when she turned and waved with enthusiasm at her husband. "Come and meet my best friend from when I was young."

"A wee lass," Innis confirmed, "and a stubborn and inquisitive one at that."

That Innis knew more of Espy than Craven did annoyed him to the point he felt the beast grumble deep inside him. But it did help that Innis was not a young man, though he did have fine features and appeared trim and solid for a man who had to be at least fifty years. He was taller than most men, though not as tall as Craven. His reddish brown hair was shoulder length and sprinkled with gray. He wore a plaid of dark green and brown colors and an equally dark green shirt.

"That has not changed," Craven said, coming to stop by the pair. "And she is no longer a wee lass… Espy is my wife."

"You are wed? How wonderful for you!" Innis hugged her again, then stretched his hand out to Craven. "Congratulation, Lord Craven."

Craven shook the man's hand and was impressed by his strength and his obvious joy for Espy.

"Espy would tell me how the man she would someday wed would be special and she would love him with all her heart. I am glad she found her special man."

The beast grumbled inside him. He was not that special man or was he? Espy made it clear to him that she loved him. He did not understand how she could love him, perhaps she did not understand herself. Perhaps she simply accepted and embraced it. Perhaps it was all fate's doing.

"What brings you here, Innis?" Craven asked and glanced at his wife who remained tucked in the crook of the man's arm and looked much too comfortable there.

"I came in search of Espy," Innis said, his smile widening when he glanced down at her for a moment. "I was always intrigued by her father and mother's stories of the Highlands and especially of Cyra, Espy's grandmother. I recall William telling me how knowledgeable the old woman was about plants. I decided that I wanted to learn about them for myself, having seen the success William had had with his plant concoctions, and since I am not getting any younger, I decided to make the journey." He looked to Craven. "I was hoping I could offer my services to you, Lord Craven, in exchange for a place to reside while here." He turned a smile on Espy. "But you have no need of me, having Espy here."

"Nonsense," Espy was quick to say. "An extra hand is always welcome."

"That is kind of you, Espy, but the decision rests with

Lord Craven," Innis said with a respectful nod toward him.

Espy went to her husband's side and coiled her arm around his, hugging it tight. "My husband is a wise man, and he would not turn such a generous offer away."

"Espy, go see that food and drink is made ready for Innis while I have a word with him," Craven ordered.

Espy's eyes narrowed. "You are not going to frighten him off, are you?"

Craven turned a warning scowl on her, but she ignored it and went right on talking.

"I have not seen him in years, not since—" Her eyes suddenly popped wide and she squeezed her husband's arm. "MacBarnes. Innis was at MacBarnes' funeral."

Innis nodded. "I was and it was the last time I saw you, MacBarnes' having finally succumbed to his lingering illness. Many of his colleagues had not expected MacBarnes to last as long as he did and that was thanks to your father's treatment, not that anyone would admit it."

"You can confirm that Samuel MacBarnes is dead?" Craven asked, glad that there was someone and that he would not have to rely on a missive alone to confirm that his wife had told the truth.

"Aye, I remember that day well." Innis bowed his head a moment and when he raised his eyes to Espy they were pooled with tears. "Your parents succumbed a year later and within four months of each other. I am so sorry I was not there for you. I did not receive the news in time to return home from France and when I finally did arrive home, I learned you had gone home yourself."

"Cyra was all I had left," Espy said.

"No longer," Craven said firmly. "You have me now and the whole MacCara clan."

"I am happy for you, Espy," Innis said, "but, if I may ask, why do you need confirmation of MacBarnes' death?"

"The physician Edward MacPeters claimed that

MacBarnes blended herbs for him and that was impossible with MacBarnes having been dead at the time," Espy explained.

"Edward MacPeters?" Innis asked, his brow scrunching.

"You know MacPeters?" Craven asked, hoping perhaps that Innis could shed more light on the man.

"I know he is dead over a year now."

Chapter Twenty-six

"Do you know what happened to the actual MacPeters?" Espy asked.

"From all accounts he suffered an accident while on a trip to the Highlands. It seems that a Highland chieftain had tempted him with a goodly sum to treat his wife and he simply could not refuse it." Innis looked from Craven to Espy and back to Craven. "You are the chieftain that sent for a physician? But why when your wife is an accomplished healer?"

"MacPeters was meant to tend the birth of my first wife, Aubrey," Craven explained.

"Espy was not here at the time?" Innis asked, though did not give anyone a chance to respond. "That is a shame since she has far more experience with births than MacPeters ever did."

Espy's innocence in his wife's death was being confirmed more and more and it appeared more and more that someone had wanted Aubrey dead.

"Was MacPeters death ever confirmed?" Craven asked.

"That I do not know," Innis said. "I was told the tale after I made it known that I was traveling to the Highlands. I heard countless tales about MacPeters and those tales grew with each telling. Some said that he and those with him were attacked and killed by Highland heathens, their bodies left for the creatures of the forest to enjoy. I was warned that the same fate awaited me if I was foolish enough to go." Innis smiled at Espy. "I paid no heed to their ignorant rhetoric. Espy spoke often of the Highlands and not only of its beauty, but of its dangers as well. I am well aware of both."

"The Highlands and Highlanders themselves are not always hospitable. Since you are a friend of my wife's, you are more than welcome here. And as my wife said, an extra hand is always helpful," Craven said and enjoyed the smile it brought to his wife's face, though it was her hand slipping into his and giving it a squeeze that pleased him the most.

"I am most grateful, Lord Craven, and I will do my best to serve you well," Innis said with a respectful bob of his head.

Espy jumped in. "You could help by looking upon the face of the dead man and seeing if he is familiar to you."

Innis looked to Craven for consent and it made Craven respect the man even more.

"My wife speaks my thoughts before I can," Craven said.

Espy laughed softly. "Is Lord Craven not lucky to have such a wife who knows him so well that he does not have to waste words on her?"

Innis gave a brief laugh. "I have missed your wit and logic, Espy, and I am pleased you have found a man who loves you for who you are."

Loves you.

Espy's smile grew upon hearing those words, thinking that perhaps Innis saw what Craven had yet to admit, but could not help to show.

Craven on the other hand ignored the older man's observation or at least he attempted to since it was difficult to dismiss the swell to his heart upon hearing it.

"I will be only too glad to see if the dead man is familiar to me," Innis said.

The three walked to the shed where the body was being left until burial, Espy much too curious to be left behind.

Innis spoke as soon as he laid eyes on the wrapped, dead body. "That is not MacPeters."

"You have not seen his face," Craven said.

"I do not have to. MacPeters was a short, portly man, and this man is not. Therefore, it cannot be MacPeters," Innis explained.

Craven revealed the dead man's face. "Is he at all familiar to you?"

Innis stared briefly, then shook his head. "I have never seen him before."

Espy stepped forward. "We have asked far too much of you after such a long journey. You need food and rest."

"I would not object to both." Innis scratched his head, his brow scrunching. "I must admit though, I am curious as to why someone would pose as a physician."

Craven wondered the same and he intended to find out.

~~~

"You will remain here until I return for you," Craven ordered, reaching up to take hold of his wife's waist and lifting her off Trumble.

Espy kept her hands on her husband's arms when her feet touched the ground. She loved the feel of his warmth and strength and found any excuse to place her hands on him. Not that she needed an excuse since he had encouraged her touches with his own. "I am eager to have my grandmother meet Innis and to visit with her. You will be safe where you go?"

That she worried over him warmed his heart, though he was also aware that she was curious as to his destination, especially since Dylan rode with him. The matter was more pressing anytime the two of them rode off together.

"I learned early this morning that Warrick's warriors have moved their camp to MacCara land. I go to speak to them. I do not expect any problems. Warrick's warriors will do nothing until they receive word from him."

Espy stretched her head up to press her cheek to his and

whisper, "Keep safe, for I have grown accustomed to having you as my husband, and I do so l love you."

Craven felt the all too familiar tug to his heart that had been growing stronger every day since she had first admitted her love to him. He wondered how long it was going to take him to admit he loved her as well. It was bittersweet to realize he could love again after Aubrey and that was the problem. He felt by loving Espy he was betraying his love for Aubrey. Or was it guilt for failing to keep her safe?

He had no words for Espy. He wished he did, but words failed him. He could not tell her he loved her when he had yet to admit it to himself.

Espy stepped away from him and he reluctantly let her go.

She waved to Craven as he and his warriors rode off and went to join Innis and her grandmother who were already talking. She counted the warriors Craven had left behind as she approached the pair—six—not an overabundance, which proved he was not too worried about their safety.

A smile brightened her face as she heard Innis chatting with her grandmother. It had been two days since his arrival and after a day of rest and settling him into a dwelling of his own, he was eager to meet Cyra, and Espy was just as eager to see her grandmother.

Cyra spread her arms as her granddaughter approached. Hugging her close was something she had done since Espy was born and having her gone this past year, she wanted to get in all the hugs she could.

Her grandmother looked good, but then she always did. Her cheeks had a good tinge of pink to them and her soft blue eyes, so much like her own, were bright and sharp, though she caught a sudden concern in them when Cyra looked to Innis.

"I need a moment with my granddaughter, Innis, if you

would not mind," Cyra said.

"Of course, take all the time you would like," Innis said, stepping aside. "Do you mind if I wander through your garden? Plants fascinate me, especially ones I am not familiar with."

"Be my guest, though they are only seedlings yet. I will explain the properties of the unfamiliar ones to you as soon as I am done," Cyra said.

Innis nodded, smiling brightly as he scurried off like a child who had just received the most cherished gift.

"He seems like a nice man," Cyra said, hooking her arm in her granddaughter's and walking away, distancing them from the Craven's warriors.

"Innis talked with me when no one else would bother with me and he encouraged my endless need to learn, sharing his own knowledge with me, and he remained my friend when others warned him to his distance from me. He is a good man and a good friend. But that is not what you wish to say to me, *Seanmhair*. Something is amiss?"

Cyra kept her voice low. "That woman who claimed to be ill returned and asked for more of my brew, saying it had helped her. I doubted that since what I gave her would do little but warm her insides. I was more concerned with the way she looked around the outside of the cottage, almost as if she was expecting someone to show up. For some reason, I thought of the young woman who had come every other day to me, though I have not seen her lately and I am worried for her."

"I know her, but please do not ask me who she is or where she hides. It is best you do not know and it is best you know nothing about her. I went to her and brought her food, while it might not last someone else, she eats little so I imagine she still has food left. But I thought of going to check on her while I was here."

"Let me help," Cyra said.

"Not this time, *Seanmhair*."

"Then let your husband help you. He is a powerful man with powerful friends. He will see that the woman is kept safe."

"I do not know if that is possible," Espy said with a heavy heart.

"Trust him. He is a far better man than he wants to admit."

"That he is, *Seanmhair*, that he is."

"I will distract the warriors to give you time to sneak off. But do not linger, for they will look for you after a while," Cyra warned.

"First, I must let Trumble know he cannot follow me. With him remaining here, the warriors will not realize I have left."

Cyra nodded and they turned, Epsy going to Trumble and Cyra going to Innis.

Espy pressed her face to Trumble's. "I must go and you must stay here. I will not be gone long. I will call out for you if I need you."

Trumble gave a brief snort and nodded, and Espy walked toward the cottage. As she did, Cyra cried out that she thought she saw someone at the edge of the woods. The warriors took off, though two stopped and looked ready to guard Espy when Cyra yelled out again.

"Two more over there." Cyra pointed in another direction and with the other warriors gone, the two quickly took flight.

Espy wasted no time in hurrying away opposite them.

She stopped after a good distance into the woods and listened. She always listened when she entered the woods. It spoke if one took the time to listen. A flurry of birds flying off warned of someone or thing in the area they wanted no part of. Voices carried in the woods and gave one time to hide. The ground trembled when a troop of warriors drew near and if there was complete silence, it was cause for worry, for it meant all went still out of fear.

The scurry of squirrels at play, the tweeting of birds, and a soft whisper of wind with not a voice being carried on it let her know that she was safe to continue. Just to be sure, she stopped one more time before reaching the cottage and listened. Satisfied she heard nothing unusual, she continued.

"Adara," Espy called out softly when she reached the cottage and the young woman stepped around the side of the cottage the tree was growing out of. "I am sorry I have not been here sooner."

Adara dismissed her apology with a shake of her head. "I am fine."

"I worry that you may not be safe here," Espy said.

"Nowhere is safe."

"She is right about that," a voice called out from the woods.

Espy ran to stand in front of Adara, shielding her with her body and glared at the woman who stepped out of a dense part of the woods. She was of fair age, her features plain, and her long, dark hair braided tightly. Her skirt appeared to have been mended many times as was her blouse, while her body looked in fine shape. She stood a bit taller than Espy and in her hand she held a dagger.

"I knew if I waited hidden in the woods long enough someone would lead me to her," the woman said.

"What do you want?" Espy demanded, the only explanation why she had not heard the woman following her sending a sense of dread through her. It meant she was skilled at tracking someone, but why was she tracking Adara.

The woman laughed. "Is it not obvious? I want her dead and now, unfortunately for you, you will be joining her."

"Why do you want her dead?" Espy asked, attempting to keep the woman distracted from her task while giving herself time to think.

"That does not concern you."

Espy held her one arm behind her, signaling Adara not to step past her, and she was glad she did when she felt Adara slip a large rock in her hand.

"There are two of us and only one of you," Espy said.

The woman laughed again and reached behind her back, bringing out another dagger. "One for each of you. And so you know, I am extremely skilled with a blade."

"My husband is a powerful man—"

"The beast does not frighten me. Besides, he will never know what happened to you. He will mourn you, though not as badly as he did Aubrey since he loved her more than he will ever love you. And—"

The woman stumbled almost falling to her knees, Espy's forceful swing sending the rock slamming into her head

"Run!" Espy yelled to Adara as she ran toward the woman, bending to snatch up another rock as she did and used it to knock one of the daggers out of her hand before the woman could gather her senses and steady herself.

The woman swung the one dagger at Espy as she fought to gain her footing, keeping Espy at bay and as soon as she regained her senses, she charged Espy. It did not take Espy long to realize that though she had fought before, this woman was stronger and far more skilled than any opponent she had ever faced, and she feared that she would not be able to defeat her.

That did not stop her from trying. Even when the blade tore down her forearm Espy kept fighting. Death would not claim her easily. But when the woman pinned her against the boulder, she felt her strength ebb as she gripped the woman's wrist, fighting to keep the dagger from penetrating her chest.

The woman's eyes suddenly bulged wide and she let out a gasp and stumbled back, swerving around. A knife handle protruded from her back, the blade having penetrated deep and she lunged for Adara.

Espy surged forward, slamming into her and sending her tumbling to the ground, the dagger flying out of her hand. She crawled toward it, a pitiful sight, her fingers digging into the dirt as she fought with her last ounce of strength to reach the weapon. Death was quicker, claiming her as her fingers fell short of the dagger.

Espy went to Adara, but she took hasty steps back, waving her away.

"I just want to know you are all right," Espy said sad for the young woman that she could not bear to be touched.

Adara nodded vigorously and pointed to Espy's arm covered in blood.

The ripped sleeve had soaked the blood and she did not want to chance pulling the torn pieces apart to see the wound. It was better if she left it for her grandmother to tend. How she would explain the wound to Craven was another matter and there was no time to think on it now. The body had to be disposed of and she had questions for Adara.

"Do you know this woman?" Espy asked.

Adara shook her head.

"Would there be anyone after you besides Warrick's warriors?" Since Adara talked little and trusted people even less, Espy knew little about her past. She had only known that she had been in Warrick's dungeon being punished for theft.

Adara shook her head again.

Espy wished she could hug Adara and help ease her fright. Her petite body trembled and she hugged her middle tight, and her wide eyes seemed to spread wider as she stared at the dead woman.

"I need to get rid of the body. The forest will consume it, but it must be a distance from here," Espy explained.

Adara nodded and patted her chest, letting Espy know

she would help.

Espy did not refuse her. With her arm injured and time passing much too quickly, she needed the help.

It took some doing for her and Adara to drag the body through the woods and up a steep hill and once at the top, they pushed it off. They stood side by side as they watched it roll down and down and down, until the body was speared through the chest by a protruding branch.

They stared for a moment, Espy hoping it was done, yet fearing trouble had only begun. They turned and took time to cover their tracks as they walked back to the cottage.

"I have to go. I will be missed by now. I will come as soon as I can. If you need anything, go to Cyra, she will help you."

Adara nodded and waved her away.

Espy hurried her steps, hoping and praying she could reach the cottage and tend her wound before Craven returned. A bandaged arm could be explained away more easily than a bloody one. The more she hurried, the more she feared she would not make it on time.

Trumble.

She would call out for Trumble as she kept walking. He would come for her. She let out several bursts of short, sharp whistles, took a breath, then repeated the whistles again. She continued with the whistles as she walked, sure that Trumble would hear her call.

Chapter Twenty-seven

"What do you mean you do not know where Espy is?" Craven demanded of Cyra. He admired the old woman's courage, keeping herself erect, her chin high, not cowering in front of him or showing fear even when he roared at her as he tried to stop himself from doing now. Especially since he saw fear spark in her eyes at the mention of her granddaughter's name.

"She went into the woods but where I do not know," Cyra said, hugging her hands tightly. "She told me she would not be gone long, and I grow concerned for her safety."

"Why did she go into the woods?" Craven asked, fighting to contain the anger churning hot and thick inside him since he had returned and discovered his wife was nowhere to be found.

Cyra decided that half the truth was better than nothing. "A woman, claiming to be ill, though far from it, appears to be stalking the area around my cottage. I believe Espy went to see if she could find the woman and discover her true intentions."

Espy would protect her grandmother without thought to her own safety. Yet Craven got the distinct feeling that Cyra was not telling him everything.

Trumble suddenly snorted, stamped the ground, and went to take off when Craven grabbed his reins, stopping him. The horse fought to free himself and Craven knew why... Espy was in trouble.

"Take me to her, Trumble," Craven ordered firmly and the horse did not hesitate. He stilled, allowing Craven to mount him and as soon as he did, the animal took off, leaving Craven's men struggling to keep up with him.

Once in the woods, Craven heard short, sharp whistles echo off the trees. Fear gripped Craven's heart. If Espy summoned Trumble, she must be hurt.

"Hurry, Trumble," he urged. He would not lose her. He could not lose her. She had somehow worked her way into his heart. It beat stronger because of her and he could not live without her. She was as vital to him as the air he breathed.

He was never so relieved when he saw his wife come into view. Her steps quickened and her eyes widened when she caught sight of him, out of fear of being caught or relief, he could not say. Then he caught sight of her bloody sleeve. He did not have to urge Trumble forward, since as soon as the animal spotted her, he headed for her. He was off the horse in a flash when only a short distance from her.

Espy was amazed at how fast her husband moved for a man his size. He seemed to fly off Trumble. She should be worried by the way his brow creased and his eyes narrowed and how quickly he descended on her, almost as if he was about to devour her and he did… with his arms.

He held her against him gently, shutting his eyes and trying to still the rapid pounding of his heart as his hands squeezed at her shoulders, feeling her warmth through her blouse, confirming for himself that she was alive, and he had not lost her.

After a few moments, he opened his eyes and cupped her face in his large hands and kissed her quick. "You have much to explain, wife, but at the moment all I care about is that you are alive and well." His eyes darted to her bloody sleeve. "Tell me you are well."

That he sounded as if he pleaded with her and the stark anxiousness that glared in his dark eyes not to mention how he had flown off Trumble was evidence enough of his love.

"Answer me, wife." His strong voice boomed with a demand that was more tender than commanding.

"I believe I am fine, but it would be good to have Cyra help me tend the wound."

"What happened?" Craven asked, lifting her gently in his arms and walking over to Trumble. "Did the woman who has been stalking Cyra's place hurt you?" He looked around half expecting to see the deranged women run out of the woods before mounting.

"Can we speak of this later, after my wound is tended?" She placed her head on his shoulder. "I am a bit exhausted from the ordeal."

"Rest," he ordered. "We will talk later."

Espy's excuse did not make her feel less guilty even if it was the truth. She would have to tell him about the woman since she felt that Ober somehow was connected with her. It did not seem logical that two people would seek out healers in the same area with the same tale of an illness that did not exist and with the same curiosity of the surrounding area.

They arrived at Cyra's cottage in no time and as Craven carefully lifted Espy off the horse, he asked, "Where last did you see this woman who wounded you?"

Espy did not hesitate to tell her husband since the body was a safe distance from Adara. "She is dead, impaled on a branch after falling down a hill." She did not mention the stab wound, the impaling, no doubt, eradicating all signs of it. She was not surprised when he asked for specifics of the area or when he sent some of his warriors to go locate it.

"Good lord, you are hurt," Cyra cried out, stepping out of the cottage and seeing Espy's bloody sleeve.

Espy was quick to reassure her grandmother. "A minor wound."

"That is quite a bit of blood for a minor wound," Innis said with as much concern in his voice as she saw in her grandmother's eyes.

Cyra hurried to her granddaughter, slipping her arm around her. "We need to see to your wound right away."

"Espy appears to have gotten into quite a serious altercation," Innis said as Craven stepped forward to follow the women into the cottage.

Craven stopped before entering. "What did Cyra tell Espy about this woman?"

"I do not know," Innis said with a shake of his head. "I was not privy to the conversation, but I do want to be privy in helping Cyra tend Espy's wound."

"I would be grateful for any help you can give in tending my wife," Craven said and extended his arm for the physician to enter the cottage before him.

Craven stood in front of the open door, looking at his wife as her grandmother took a blade to her bloody sleeve.

"You block the light, Lord Craven," Cyra said, without glancing up at him.

Craven ducked his head to enter the cottage and kept his eyes on his wife. It was a small space and with four people filling it, he worried Espy would grow agitated and find it much too confining. She seemed not to notice, too busy talking with her grandmother and Innis about tending the wound. Until they both stepped closer to Espy, confining her.

Her body tensed, her breathing grew faster and as he stepped forward, she turned, her arm shooting up and her hand stretching out in a desperate attempt to grab hold of him.

His hand reached hers, taking tight hold, locking his fingers around hers as his other arm circled her waist. "I am here with you. You are safe. There is nothing to fear."

Cyra and Innis stepped back away from the couple, both seeing the fear in Espy's eyes and how she frantically had turned to her husband for help.

Craven brought her hand to his lips and kissed it. "I will

let nothing happen to you... *ever*." He was relieved when Espy shook her head at him. It meant she was calming, her fear fading, enough to disagree with him, though her breathing had yet to fully ease. He rubbed her back gently, chasing the tenseness from her body. "You do not believe me," he asked, a faint smile surfacing.

Espy shook her head, then switched it to a nod, then dropped her brow to rest on his chest.

He kept slow and steady strokes along her back as he whispered, "I would see my life gone before I would let anyone take yours."

Espy raised her head. Was he telling her in his own way that he loved her, for he would not give his life so easily for her if he did not love her. Would he? The thought that he would die for her disturbed her. "You will never do that," she scolded and with her breath still slightly labored, she continued, "and you will not always be able to prevent things from happening to me."

When she paused for a breath, Craven quickly took charge of their debate. "I can and I will as long as my wife does not go running off without a word to her husband." He kissed her brow gently. "You are not alone anymore. *You have me.* You will always have me. I will always be there to help you, protect you, no matter the situation."

He loved her.

The thought spun in her head. He truly loved her, his caring words confirmed it and her love for him spilled freely from her lips, "I love you, my husband."

Her words hit him like a sharp arrow to his heart, though it was not pain he felt. It was pure joy and contentment that he had never thought he would know again. This woman, this healer, had somehow managed to work her magic and heal his heart, a heart he had thought died with Aubrey.

He loved Espy.

The thought jolted him, the words almost spilling from his lips, but he caught them. He would tell her, but not here, not now.

Craven pressed his cheek to hers and a shout from outside broke them apart and a rap at the door had Craven remaining at her side as he bid the person to enter.

"An accident, my lord, while retrieving the body of the woman. Morta needs a healer," Tass said.

Espy went to stand up and Craven laid a firm hand to her shoulder. "You will stay here and have your grandmother tend you." He looked to Innis. "Innis will see to the Morta."

"I would be honored to tend your warrior, my lord," Innis said.

"I have whatever you need," Cyra offered, "and offer any help you need. Remember, things are different in the Highlands."

"I will seek your counsel with appreciation if necessary," Innis said with a smile and followed Tass.

Craven did not like leaving his wife and he let her know it. "I regret having to take my leave, but I must see to what happened and—"

"Go, "Espy urged, "my grandmother will take good care of me."

"I know or I would not be leaving your side," he said and turned to Cyra. "I am glad it is you whose hands I leave her in."

"Espy will be fine, worry not," Cyra assured him.

Espy sighed after her husband shut the door behind him and pressed her fingers to her lips he had kissed before taking his leave. She missed him already.

"I am pleased to see that he loves you as much as you love him."

Espy turned a huge smile on her grandmother. "He does love me. He tells me in his own way."

"Any fool can see or hear how much he loves you," Cyra confirmed with a broad smile of her own, thrilled that fate had finally smiled kindly on her granddaughter.

"I am so happy, *Seanmhair*. I never thought I would be happy again and would have never believed it would be Craven who brought me so much happiness."

"You have suffered enough. It is time you have some joy and peace in your life," Cyra said as she began to tend Espy's wound.

Espy's smile faltered.

"The woman in the woods," Cyra said, knowing her granddaughter well enough to know what troubled her. "Craven told you he would help you no matter what."

"I gave my word I would not betray her, too many already have and it has left her scarred and broken."

"I am sorry to hear that. It takes time and true kindness and love to help heal as you and Craven have done. It seems this woman who remains hidden needs more help then you alone can give her. Think on it, Espy. You will not tell me about her for what I might suffer and look what you have suffered," she said with a nod to the slash on her granddaughter's forearm. "I assume you kept her safe this time, at your own peril, but what about next time. Someone is searching for her and they will not stop until they find her. You are putting yourself in danger along with her. She needs more help than you can give her and she will never heal if she continues to hide. You are a healer. Do what is best to help heal her."

"I hope I am as wise as you one day," Espy said.

"Wisdom grows along with age. When we are young we feel we can conquer anything. As we age we realize it is the journey, with all its victories and defeats, sorrows and joys, that matter the most. Help your friend to live just as you have helped Craven."

The door opened just as Cyra finished tying a cloth

around Espy's arm.

"She is well?" Craven asked of Cyra as he walked to his wife's side.

"She is and she knows how to tend the wound herself and she has Innis to tend it as well," Cyra said.

"But there is nothing that heals as well as her grandmother's hands and heart," Innis said entering the cottage with a smile. "That is what she used to tell me, and I see that she is right."

Cyra smiled at his compliment. "How is Morta?"

"A gash to the leg that he insists he can tend himself with the help of some water of life. I have come to see if you have some of that."

"I do," Cyra said and grabbed a jug from beneath the bench. "Come, I will show you how to use it and enjoy it."

~~~

When it came time to leave, Espy could not keep a tear from filling her eye as she hugged her grandmother. She had tended more than Espy's arm today. She had tended her heart and taught her more about being a healer. She was a bit worried about leaving her on her own.

"I will see you soon," Cyra said as Craven placed Espy on Trumble.

"I am leaving a warrior here with you, Cyra," Craven said, after mounting his mare. Her perplexed look had him explaining. "Between Warrick's men camping on MacCara land and this deranged woman attacking Espy, I will take no chances with your safety."

Espy wanted to reach out and hug her husband. When her grandmother thanked him instead of protesting, Espy was aware that she was reminding her that the danger had not passed and she would be wise to heed her warning.

They traveled a while in silence before Craven asked,

"Do you trust me, Espy?"

"Aye, without question," she was quick to answer.

"Then tell me what happened in the woods." When she hesitated, he reminded her, "Whatever it is I will help you."

A shout from one of his warriors prevented Espy from responding.

Craven turned to see Roark and one of his warriors riding directly at them. He brought his warriors to a stop and directed his horse in front of Trumble.

Roark rode straight to Craven and extended no greeting. "I have need of a healer. One of my man has taken ill."

Craven called out, "Innis."

The physician rode up beside him.

Craven looked to Roark. "This is Innis, a physician from Edinburgh. He will see to your ill warrior."

Roark shook his head. "I want a Highland healer."

"Cyra will help him," Espy said.

"Your grandmother," Roark said, "but is she as good a healer as you?"

"Better than me," Espy said, a twinge of fear racing through her that he should know Cyra was her grandmother. She had shared no knowledge of herself with anyone but Adara, but then Craven had reminded him that Warrick knew everything.

"I will take you to Cyra and join her in seeing what ails your warrior," Craven said.

Roark did not argue that he would join them, he simply nodded and turned his horse to wait a short distance away.

Craven turned his mare and brought the horse alongside Trumble. "You will return to the keep and wait there. Do not dare leave the village."

Espy was shaking her head harder with each word he spoke. "This could be a trap."

"Warrick will confront me. He will set no trap. I will see to this and return home. You will do as I say and stop shaking your head. I can see the smile on Roark's face, though my back is to him, that my wife argues with me. He will tell me I should turn you over to him so he can save me from a disobedient wife."

Espy stopped shaking her head and launched herself at her husband, almost toppling out of the saddle and into Craven's powerful arms. She threw her arms around his neck and kissed him for all to see.

When Espy ended the kiss, she raised her voice so all could hear her. "I love you."

Craven's heart slammed against his chest and it swelled with pride at his audacious wife. She let all know that she truly loved him.

"I will be waiting at home for you, husband," she said and settled herself back in her saddle with Craven's help.

Craven gave his warriors orders and took Tass with him as he rode off.

Espy worried over her husband the rest of the ride home. Or was it that she was parted from him that had her feeling so unsettled? It continued after arriving at the keep and though she tried to keep herself busy, she could not keep her mind off her husband.

With dusk came more worry that he would not return tonight and when night did fall and he was not home, she began pacing in their bedchamber. If he was with anyone other than Roark she would not worry so much, but he was Warrick's man and that alone was cause for worry.

What of her grandmother? Was she safe? And Adara? With Warrick's men so close, how could she be safe?

I will keep you safe.

His words so clear in her head brought her to an abrupt halt. *But who will keep you safe?*

The door opened and Craven entered.

Espy did not hesitate. She ran and leapt into his arms.

Chapter Twenty-eight

Craven caught her around the waist as her legs wrapped around his waist and when her mouth settled on his in an urgent kiss, he felt at home and at peace once again.

Their lips locked as if they would never part, as if they needed each other's breathes to survive When neither of them could no longer breathe, their lips parted, but they did not. He carried her to the bed and sat down with her legs still wrapped around him. His hands left her waist to yank up her skirt and her hands wasted no time in pushing his plaid out of the way.

He grabbed firm hold of her bottom. "I should take my time with you, tease you wet and—"

"I am already wet with the wont of you," she said and tried to maneuver herself over him. "Later you can tease me wet again."

"Promise?" he whispered near her ear and nipped along it.

Gooseflesh tingled along her neck and down her arm and she feared she would come... she was that much in need of him. "I promise if you do not slip into me now, you will suffer for it."

He nibbled along her ear again. "There is only one way you can make me suffer. Never to hear you tell me you love me again... you would break my heart."

Espy snapped her head back away from him. "I will never stop telling you that I love you, for I will never stop loving you. Even when I pass on, nothing will stop my spirit from whispering in your ear how much I love you."

"Hear me, Espy, for I need to say this. I loved Aubrey

with all my heart. I never thought I could ever love like that again and it amazes me to discover that somehow, someway you have shown me that I can love again and with more depth and joy than I ever thought possible. I will always cherish the memories I made with Aubrey, but it is time to put them to rest and make new ones. I love you, Espy, like I never thought I could. You stole my heart and it is yours to keep."

Tears trickled down Espy's cheeks and with a soft whisper against his lips, she said, "Now, husband, show me how much you love me."

Craven kissed her lips gently. "That, wife, will take the rest of our lives and beyond."

He lifted her and she reached down to guide him into her. He lowered her down slowly on his shaft and she sighed, the pleasure more intense than it had ever been now that he had admitted his love for her.

Once fully inside her, there was no stopping either of them. She gripped his shoulders as his hands gripped her waist and helped her ride him.

While Espy wished it would go on forever, her need was too great, his words of love having excited her to the point of climax. She would not last long, but then they had all night.

"I cannot wait," she said, trying hard to delay her pleasure since she had barely settled around him.

"I want to watch you come," he said and bit playfully at her neck before bringing her up and down on him harder and harder until…

Espy screamed out, her head tilting back and her eyes growing wide as she shattered in climax. It rolled and rippled through her like a wave that had captured her, tumbling her with never ending pleasure.

She gasped in dismay when Craven yanked her off him, though he soon had her bent over the bed, her skirt hoisted up and burying himself inside her once again. His hand sneaked around to settle between her legs and tease her already highly sensitive nub, and she cried out as her desire soared once more.

He pummeled her with his thick shaft and nothing ever felt so wonderful and the intense joy had tears pooling in her eyes.

Craven loved how she met his every thrust, throwing her backside against him, letting him know she wanted more and more, and tightening around him as if she would never let him go. And he did not want her to. He delayed his pleasure as long as he could, letting hers build again until their bodies demanded release, and they both exploded in a blinding climax.

Craven let out a roar and he had to drop over Espy, his climax so powerful that it stole some of his strength. He pressed his hands on the bed to either side of her shoulders and held himself suspended over her. He shuddered against her when the last of his climax rippled away and he felt her do the same.

His breath was just calming when he thought he heard Espy sniffle back tears. "Espy?"

She sniffled again.

He slipped out of her and took her in his arms to settle in his lap as he sat on the edge of the bed. "I hurt you. Why did you not tell me I was hurting you?"

Espy shook her head and wiped at her tears.

He brushed her hand away and wiped at them with his thumb. "You should have stopped me."

She shook her head again. "You did not hurt me. My tears are happy tears. I never knew making love could feel so wonderful."

Craven sighed with relief. "Damn it, wife, you frightened the hell out of me. I thought I hurt you."

"You love me too much to ever hurt me," she said and

kissed his cheek.

"That I do, wife, but you will tell me if ever our lovemaking turns too much for you."

She laughed softly. "You will do the same?"

He laughed along with her. "That will never happen."

"We shall see," she teased.

"I need nourishment since I intend to keep you busy a good portion of the night."

She pointed to the table over near the window. "I thought you might be hungry when it grew later and later and you had yet to return home. We will eat and you can tell me how things went with the ill warrior." She eased off his lap when she saw his dark eyes grow alarmed.

"Your arm bleeds," he said, standing abruptly. "I should have never let you lean on it as you did. It must pain you."

"Not much and I will see to changing the cloth," she said in an attempt to calm him. Truthfully, she had not given thought to her wound. She had been too lost in making love with her husband… a husband who loved her. She felt the pain now, but it was far from unbearable.

"I will summon Innis," he said.

"No," she said, grabbing his arm as he went to walk past her. "We finally have time alone. I can tend the wound. You can help me."

"You will do nothing more to disturb it tonight or until it heals," he ordered.

Her chin slumped along with her shoulders and she said with disappointment, "As you say, husband."

Craven lifted her chin. "I do not want you in pain or your wound not healing."

"I want to make love again tonight," she confessed.

He ran a gentle hand along her cheek. "I promise you we will, though you will not move that injured arm."

Espy smiled, pleased. "As you say, husband."

It did not take long to change the cloth on her arm and

to remind herself to avoid strenuous movement until the wound showed signs of healing. As soon as the task was finished, they ate, enjoyed wine, and talked.

Espy learned that it had taken time to treat the ailing warrior since it was a wound to his side that needed cleaning and tending that had caused him to fall ill. Afterwards Craven had seen Cyra home safely.

They talked of when they were young, Craven telling her of his brother and sister he had lost and how much it had pained him while she spoke of the loss of her parents.

"My da blamed himself for my mum's death. She fell ill after returning from a journey he refused to let me go on and did not want my mother going on. But my mum would not let my da travel alone. She feared something would happen to him and she would never see him again. She knew I would have my grandmother to look after me, but there would be no one with my father to let us know if some harm or illness had befallen him. Oddly enough, it was an illness caught in a foreign land that took her from us and my da blamed himself."

They turned quiet until Craven asked, "Have you always had a fear of confined places?"

"No, it started after being locked in some of the cells with the tortured and dying. It did not bother me at first, but one day the guard forgot to let me out and I had to spend the night, though I was glad I did since the person died holding my hand. For some reason the small cell closed in around me along with the darkness and the stench, and I feared I would never get out that they would forget about me and I would rot away."

The thought of what she must have gone through turned Craven's stomach and like her da blaming himself for her mum's death, he blamed himself for her fear of confined places.

"I called out as soon as the guard made his rounds the

next morning and he apologized and begged me not to tell the lord of the keep or he would suffer for it. He made certain I was never locked in again, but the damage had been done and the many times after that I had to tend those in cells only increased my fear."

"This Arran, he knows you will help him no more?" Craven asked, letting her also know that her days of rescuing the so-called innocent were done.

Espy sucked in her lower lip as if to keep herself from responding and turned her head away from her husband not wanting to look in his eyes.

"Look at me, Espy," Craven ordered with a gentle strength that had Espy relenting. He did not like the worry or the sadness he saw in her eyes. "You can tell me anything. I have told you time and again that no matter what it is I will keep you safe."

But would he keep Adara safe? She recalled her grandmother's words.

You are a healer. Do what is best to help heal her.

Espy took a sip of wine, then began to speak. "Arran almost got caught during one escape. After that, his fear of being caught grew as did what his family would suffer, not to mention me since it would be near impossible not to confess under unbearable torture. He took his family and left, not telling me where he was going so that neither one of us could surrender the other if our past deeds somehow caught up with us."

"This was after what happened at Warrick's keep?" Craven asked, thinking he was not going to like her answer.

"No, Arran and I went separate ways months before."

"You freed those women on your own from Warrick's dungeon?" he asked, shaking his head, finding it difficult to believe.

"I did. I had come across the old woman, Nelia, and was staying with her when a summons came for her to tend one of Warrick's warriors. She was not feeling well enough to go and asked me to go in her place. The warrior recovered so well and so quickly from his wound that I was summoned repeatedly to the keep to tend the ill and after a while I was considered the clan's healer."

"Warrick would treat his healer well, why chance his wrath, his revenge by freeing his prisoners? I know Warrick, he does not imprison the innocent."

"The two women I freed and the one who died were innocent. They were brought to the dungeon in the dead of night, accused of theft, though no one would say what they had stolen. They had already been tortured and I was summoned to see to the wounds. I spent days healing them and talking to them. The one woman had been tortured so badly, I feared she would not make it if I did not get her out of there as soon as I could." Espy turned her head away a moment, wiping away a single tear. "I was too late to help her. She died."

"You saved the other two," Craven said, hating to see the deep sorrow in her soft blue eyes that only a short time ago had been filled with such joy.

"Their crime did not fit their punishment," she said, shaking her head. "I do not care if it is not for me to decide. Besides, both women claimed their innocence over and over even though tortured. I could not stand by and do nothing, especially since the one woman had been battered far more badly than the other and it was not just from torture. I did not know how she was even capable of doing what they accused her of, since she was filled with such fear that she barely spoke."

"You did what you could for her," Craven said.

Espy stood and walked over to her husband to curl up in his lap, his strong arms closing around her.

"What is it? Tell me," he urged, seeing her face crease with worry, though pleased she brought her problem to him… pleased she trusted him.

"The woman's name is Adara and I confided my true identity to her and told her about where I lived and a secret place I would escape to in the woods near my grandmother's home when I needed to be alone. I suppose I shared that with her in case there ever came a time she needed such a place."

"She is there now?" Craven asked, though knew it must be so, for it better explained what may have happened in the woods.

Espy nodded.

"That is where you went the morning after we wed?"

She nodded again.

"It is who you were protecting from the woman who attacked you?"

She spoke as she nodded again. "Adara saved my life. I told her to run, but she did not run far and when I thought I was about to die, Adara returned, jabbing one of the woman's daggers into her back."

"Then I owe Adara for saving your life," Craven said, a horrific chill racing through him at the thought of Espy lying dead in the woods never to be found, taken from him as Aubrey had been.

Espy felt another single tear gather in her eye. "I am grateful you will help Adara. She has been hurt, I sometimes fear, beyond repair. But with a home here with the Clan MacCara and knowing she is safe, I hope she discovers how truly strong she is."

"I will need to speak to Warrick about her," Craven said and felt his wife's body grow rigid in his arms. "I will make it right for her. I will pay the person she stole from, more than she owes if I have to."

Espy shook her head. "Adara swears she stole nothing."

"I will speak with her and clear up the misunderstanding or pay the debt whichever it may turn out to be. You will take me to her in the morning."

Espy scrunched her face as she tilted her head to the side. "That might be a problem. Adara has a great distrust of everyone, particularly men."

"She trusts you does she not?"

"Aye, but one look at you and she may run."

"I am that ugly?" Craven asked, feigning an insult.

Espy laughed and poked him in the chest. "You have more than fine features, but you are also large and your size can intimidate."

"Then you will need to make her understand that I will not hurt her. That I am there to help her. There is no telling what danger she is in if someone is out to find her and if Warrick's men find her, there would be no helping her once they have her. She is far safer here than anywhere else. You need to make her understand that. Does she know of any reason someone would be after her?"

"She is as perplexed as I am, though for some reason I feel the dead woman was in some way connected with Ober. It seems unlikely that two people would have such similar, yet vague complaints of an illness," Espy said, suspicions rolling around in her head.

"Tomorrow the body will be available for all to view. I want to know if anyone recognizes her. We will see what Ober does when he looks upon her," Craven said. "For now, the night is ours."

Espy smiled. "Let us not waste it."

Craven laughed and lifted her along with himself out of the chair and walked to the bed.

Chapter Twenty-nine

The morning dawned gray and somber. Everyone was concerned about viewing the dead woman who had tried to kill Craven's wife. It had everyone talking, speculating, wondering if the beast was cursed and would lose yet another wife.

Espy was more concerned with Adara. As soon as the viewing of the body was done, she would take Craven along with several of his warriors to get Adara and bring her to the keep. She worried that the young woman may have already run away or worse that Warrick's men had captured her, and then there was the chance that whoever looked for her had found her.

The more she had thought on it, the more she worried for Adara's safety and the more she wanted to get her safely to the keep. Espy did not want all that the young woman had suffered to be in vain. It was time for Adara to be free just as she had finally been freed.

She kept hold of Craven's hand as she stood beside him, watching clan members file past the woman lying on a slab of wood, all but her head wrapped in a shroud. Craven squeezed her hand now and then, acknowledging her, but did not look at her. His eyes were focused on each and every person who walked past the woman. He was waiting to see if anyone showed even a brief recognition.

He, like Espy, was waiting for Ober to look upon the woman, but as the line grew shorter and shorter, Craven realized that Ober was nowhere in sight.

Craven turned to Dylan. "See if you can find Ober and bring him here."

Dylan nodded and went off, gathering several warriors with him as he went.

"What are you not telling me?" Espy asked her husband, seeing his brow narrow and feeling his hand close a bit more tightly around hers.

Craven kept his voice low. "The wrappings on the body had been disturbed when the warriors went to get it this morning for viewing."

"Ober?"

"Since he is nowhere to be seen, it is possible, though there may be others involved as well and that troubles me. I am curious about Adara. Why does someone want her dead? Why even think she was here in the first place? There is much we need to ask her."

They both turned silent, watching and waiting and when they saw Dylan hurry toward them with anxious steps, they knew the news would not be good.

"Ober cannot be found and no one has seen him since last night," Dylan said as soon as he stopped in front of Craven. "With him taking flight, I would assume that this woman was known to him."

"But why flee with her dead and unable to identify him? His secret was safe," Espy said, her hand suddenly gripping her husband's. "What if he discovered where Adara hides?"

Craven had shared some of what Espy had told him with Dylan, though not the parts where she helped people escape. He did, however, tell Dylan about Adara.

"Keep watch for Ober in case he returns and secure him if he does," Craven ordered. "I will take Espy with me to get Adara and bring her here."

It was not long before they left, Espy riding Trumble, and Craven on his mare while several warriors followed.

"How is it that you never knew that I fought alongside Warrick?" Craven asked, noticing that her scar was less prominent than usual. It was fading and he wondered if it would fade away all together, not that it mattered. With or without the scar, to him she would always be more beautiful than any other woman.

Espy shrugged, not understanding it herself. "I believe you may not have been home the times I came to stay with my grandmother, and since I never heard her refer to you as the beast or anyone else for that matter, it was something I would not have known."

Craven watched how her eyes remained alert to everything around her and how she would tilt her head every now and then as if she was trying to distinguish a sound she heard. She also kept a good grip on her reins, something he did when in a situation he might have to flee. It was all instinct, learned out of necessity to survive. He was glad for her acquired instincts, in case she should ever need them, though he would see that she never would need them.

"What brought you together with Warrick?" Espy asked.

"Hatred of a common enemy," Craven said. "The Crown is forever changing, rulers being murdered, young lads becoming King, men claiming the crown that have no business to it. England fighting for dominance here. The Highlands is a world of its own and we will not tolerate foreigners and lowlanders infringing on our homes and rights.

"Like Warrick, I did not trust those who rule. Promises are made but never kept, so I fought along with Warrick to keep the Highlands, our homes, free."

"The King—"

"Fears the mighty Highland warriors. Besides, Warrick sees to taking care of things for the King that he does not trust others to do. There are many who fear Warrick and many more who need him."

Espy slowed Trumble. "The cottage is up around the bend and there is an area of woods that is too thick to ride the horses through. We will have to walk."

"You will stay close to me," Craven said.

"You will not take Adara by force. You will let me convince her to trust you," Espy said, worried the frightened young woman would not even show herself let alone agree to go with them.

"Until I have no other choice," Craven warned.

Espy was glad he was honest with her. It made her more determined than ever to convince Adara to go with her. That she would be safe and would need not worry any longer.

"Keep your warriors back, out of sight," Espy pleaded when he reached for her waist to take her off Trumble. His hands fit firm around her and he lifted her with ease to place on the ground in front of him. The breadth of him consumed her. She could not see past his broad shoulders and while she was used to the size of him, Adara was not. "Perhaps you should keep your distance as well until I have a chance to speak with her."

Craven brought his face down for his nose to almost touch hers. "That is not going to happen."

"You will frighten her," Espy cautioned.

"Then she will also know I can easily protect her. Now let us be done with this and get her where she will be safe."

He was right. Adara's safety was why she was here.

They reached the cottage, his warriors remaining a discreet distance behind them where they were not that visible. Craven on the other hand was extremely visible and when Adara did not respond to Espy's call, she feared the young woman would never come out of hiding.

"I brought my husband to help you, Adara. He will keep you safe from whoever is after you and he has given his word that he will see to settling the problem of the theft you were accused of, so please, please trust him and come out and come home with us."

No amount of pleading worked and that was when Espy

realized... "She is not here. Adara is gone."

Craven had his warriors search for the woman but they found nothing, not even a track they could follow.

~~~

That night Espy woke screaming from a dream. She was running, trying desperately to reach Adara only a short distance ahead of her and just as she was about to grab hold of her, a black shadow swooped down and swallowed Adara whole.

Craven jumped out of bed and went for his sword, Espy's scream having been filled with such fright. When he realized a dream had been the cause, he hurried back in bed to take her in his arms and soothe her fears.

"It was a dream, no more, just a dream," he said, hugging her tight against him and caressing her bare back in soothing strokes, trying to rid her of the quiver that ran through her.

"I failed her again," Espy said, her heart pounding in her chest the fear was so real.

"You have not failed her. We will find Adara and keep her safe," Craven assured her, intending to do just that. "What of the other woman you saved?"

"Hannah," Espy whispered softly. "I often wonder what happened to her. I thought she and Adara might remain together, help each other, but Adara has made no mention of her."

"You will ask Adara about Hannah when we find her," Craven said, his confidence that they would find her bringing a gentle smile to Espy's face, though it did not chase her quivers. He knew what would change those quivers to something much more pleasurable and he let his hand drift down over her bare backside to slowly caress it.

It was not long before his hand found its way to more

intimate spots and it took even less time for Espy to respond and her quivers to turn to passion and all thoughts of the dream faded away as her husband made slow and gentle love to her.

~~~

Espy beamed with joy as she placed the newborn lad in his mum's arms, eagerly stretched out to take him.

"John will be thrilled," Cerise said with a huge smile. "With three daughters, he was hoping for a son."

"A fine, strapping lad he is," Espy confirmed.

Cerise laughed. "If he had been my first I may never have let John touch me again, the little bugger was so painful to deliver."

"It is his size," Espy said glad the ordeal was over for Cerise and mum and son were doing splendid.

The door flew open and a large man ducked his head to hurry in. His round, green eyes went to his wife in the bed.

Cerise held the swaddled bairn up with pride. "Come meet your son."

John burst into tears. "A son, finally I have a son." He hurried to Cerise. "You are a good wife, the best wife in all of Scotland." He kissed her brow and his eyes turned wide as he looked upon his son. "He is a big one."

"Like his da," Cerise said.

Tears continued running down his cheeks as he took his son in his arms.

Espy quietly left the cottage, leaving the new parents to enjoy the birth of their first son.

The sun had flickered through the clouds all morning, the clouds finally winning and consuming the sky. Rain would fall as usual, but then it was spring and the land and all its seedlings needed nourishment.

Espy strolled through the village. It had been two days and there had been no success in finding Adara. Espy wondered if the young woman had been so frightened that she left the area. But where could she have possibly gone in such a short time? Craven had his warriors search far and wide to the point that Roark had asked if he needed help in finding whatever he had lost.

Craven had declined and offered no explanation to him.

Espy could not make it through the village without being asked how she fared. The many heartfelt queries made her feel all the more part of the clan… part of family.

With her arm still healing, Innis had pitched in and helped tremendously, though none of the women would let him birth their bairns. He was glad of it since he had little to no experience delivering babies. He also visited with Cyra every day and that pleased Espy, especially when he spoke of her grandmother with such affection. That he admired the woman was obvious, but Espy wondered if there was more to how he felt about her and she was curious as to what her grandmother thought of him.

She shook her head at her foolish thought. It had been only two days since they met, but Espy recalled how her grandmother once told her how she knew upon first meeting her husband that she would wed him. It had been the same for her mum. Her da had visited the Highlands just as Innis was doing and her grandmother had told her that when Espy's mum looked upon Espy's da for the first time, Cyra could see that she lost her heart to him there and then and Cyra saw that Espy's da had done the same.

Not so her.

Hate had been what Craven had felt when he had laid eyes upon her. For her, it had been guilt. So how had love grown when there had been nothing there to nourish it?

"Something troubles you, wife?" Craven asked, reaching out and easing her into his arms.

"For a large man you have a quiet footfall," she said with a soft smile.

"You were deep in thought, you heard nothing, not me and not the children who were calling out to you."

Espy looked around and saw a few girls, giggling to each other and looking her way. She quickly waved to them and they waved back and returned to giggling.

Craven took her hand so they could continue to walk.

"John and Cerise have a son," Espy said.

"He must be thrilled."

"He shed tears of joy."

"That would be John. He gets teary-eyed more than any man I know," Craven said, "but then having a son after three daughters would bring any man to tears."

"You want only sons?" Espy asked.

"Every man wants a son to carry on the family name and honor, but as long as no harm befalls you when you deliver our bairns, it matters not to me whether you give me sons or daughters as long as I do not lose you."

He would worry about that after what had happened to Aubrey and she wanted to reassure him, but the only thing that would truly reassure him was her delivering his child safely. She offered him what she hoped would help ease his concern.

"Cyra will tend my birth and, no doubt, Innis will be here as well since I do not think he plans on leaving for some time."

Craven's face brightened at her words. "He may never leave. I saw the way he looked at your grandmother, like a besotted fool."

Espy laughed. "I was just thinking that he might favor her."

"Favor her?" Craven chuckled. "He fell hard as soon as he looked at her."

"How wonderful, now if only my grandmother felt he same way."

"There was a twinkle in her eye I have never seen

before when she talked with him."

Espy's smile spread and she squeezed her husband's hand. "It would be nice for her to know the love of a good man again."

"Tell me what had you deep in thought," Craven asked, curious over the slight frown that had marred her lovely features and pleased to see the many smiles that had replaced it.

"Love," she said, "I was wondering how your hate and my feeling of guilt could produce love."

"That is easy to answer."

Espy halted her steps, turning a perplexed look on him.

Craven stole a quick kiss, her moist lips too inviting to ignore. "We both were wrong. There was no reason for me to hate you and no reason for you to feel guilty. Once we realized that, it was easy for love to grow between us. Though, you were quicker than me to realize it and you let yourself love me in spite of my pitiful treatment of you."

Espy kissed his lips this time, wishing she could linger there. "None of that matters now. What does matter is our love for each other and mine grows for you more each day."

"I am so glad that you were brave enough not to let the beast frighten you away."

Espy grinned and tapped his chest. "There are times I very much favor the beast… like when I hear that growl rumble low in his chest just before it turns to a roar when he—"

"Tease me, wife, and you know what will happen," Craven warned with a whisper, though it was too late, he was already planning on hurrying her off to their bedchamber.

"Aye, I do," she said with a flare of passion in her soft blue eyes.

He took her hand and tugged her toward the keep, but she tugged him to a stop, nodding at the healing cottage that was only a short distance away. They both grinned and hurried toward it.

A high-pitched scream stopped them and when they turned they saw Tula, her eyes nearly bulging from her head and pointing. They followed her finger.

Ober was staggering out of the woods, a dagger handle sticking out of his chest.

Craven yelled for his warriors as he and Espy ran toward the man.

"The woods, find whoever did this," Craven ordered as several of his warriors rushed over to him as he caught Ober before the man collapsed to the ground.

The warriors took off and Espy dropped to the ground beside Ober. One look told her that he had been lucky he had gotten as far as he did and what he had worried about all that time had finally fallen upon him.... death was near.

He grabbed Espy's arm and fought to speak, his eyes turning wide and with his last breath he spewed out, "*Lies*."

Espy glared at him, for at that moment she realized where she had seen him. He was the man who had brought the three women, one of them Adara, to Warrick's dungeon.

Chapter Thirty

"You are sure of this?' Craven asked, handing her a goblet of wine before sitting in the chair beside her in the solar after hours spent handling the Ober incident.

"It was dark and while I did not get a good look at his face, I did his eyes. They were wide, the white standing out in the darkness and they were filled with a sense of glee as if he was pleased to be delivering the women for torture." She shook her head. "I do not know why I had not seen it before, though maybe my memory was spurred by Adara being here as well. It makes some sense now. He brought her to Warrick's dungeon believing she would die there and he shows up here along with that woman and Adara's life is threatened again."

"Adara must know something very important that someone wants her dead."

"We have to find her," Espy said worry creasing her brow.

"My warriors are trying, though whoever did this to Ober escapes us as well. No tracks could be found anywhere." Craven's brow scrunched for a moment, then turned wide. "Do you think Adara could have done this to Ober?"

Espy was about to shake her head and stopped.

"You are thinking what I thought. She stabbed the woman, why not Ober?"

Espy thought back to the young woman she had tended in the small cell. She had been frightened beyond belief, saying over and over again that she had done nothing wrong. Nothing. She did what she was told. She always did what she was told... or she would suffer for it.

She never confided any more than that to Espy, though she would listen in silence as Espy spoke of her home with her grandmother and her secret cottage. It had been the only thing that had calmed her.

"If Adara is at fault, then she did it to protect herself." Espy shook her head again, refusing to believe it. "I do not think she did this. Besides, what did Ober mean by *lies*? His last word and he says lies? What was he trying to tell us? I also wonder if MacPeters was connected with this in some way."

"MacPeters?" Craven questioned as if it made no sense. "That would mean it has something to do with Aubrey's murder. But how could Adara in anyway be connected with Aubrey's murder?"

Espy shrugged. "I have not a clue, though it seems strange that both MacPeters and Ober both were murdered. Could they both have known something that someone did not want made known?"

Craven grinned at her. "I can just imagine how you must have driven your parents and grandmother mad with endless questions when you were a young lass."

"They encouraged my questions," she said and laughed, "lucky for me."

"At least, I have forewarning before you give me a daughter with your inquisitive nature. I will be prepared to answer all her question and the ones I cannot, I will tell her to take to you." He liked the thought of having a daughter who would resemble her mum in more ways than features. Espy was an intelligent and courageous woman and he would love for his daughter or daughters to be the same.

"What if it is a son who has my traits?" she challenged.

"Then he will lead the Clan MacCara with more wisdom than previous chieftains," Craven said proudly.

Espy bounced forward in her chair. "I think we should

go see about starting our family right now."

"I think we have been doing that since I first made love to you," he said with a chuckle.

"Hmm…" Espy tapped her chin. "If I remember correctly, you had me pleasure you first… in the barn."

Craven stood and leaned over Espy, forcing her back in the chair as he gripped the arms. "Aye, since it had been too long since I had spilled my seed and I did not want to disappoint you, but…" He leaned down in front of her. "I can pleasure *you* now and ignore my own need."

Craven did not wait for her to respond, he slipped his hand under her skirt and along her inner thigh.

Espy shuddered at the feel of his fingers inching their way to between her legs, squeezing and caressing as he went. She did not want him to ignore his own pleasure, but then she did not believe he would be able to, so she let herself get lost in his teasing touch.

She jolted a bit when he slipped his finger inside her and again when his thumb grazed her sensitive nub.

"You like that, wife?" he asked on a whisper and slipped another finger inside her, and she gasped. He slipped his arm around her waist to yank her forward and she gasped again, though his mouth caught it as his lips came down on hers.

He teased her unmercifully, not only with his fingers but his tongue as well until she was on the verge of climax. "Inside me, I want you inside me," she begged.

"No, you will come for me like this, since it is to make up for you having pleasured me," Craven said.

"You had a good reason," she all but cried out when his thumb worked its magic on her pulsating nub.

"As I do now," he said, getting pleasure out of watching her build toward, what he intended to make sure was, more than one climax.

"Please, Craven," she pleaded.

"Later," he said.

"Now," she demanded and her eyes turned wide. "Think of our bairn."

Craven stopped, his own eyes turning wide. "Are you with child?"

She shook her head. "No and I will continue to be barren if you do not come inside me."

He wanted to ignore her words and bring her to pleasure, but their talk of future children, remembering his own siblings and the keep being full of laughter, had him aching to hear the sounds of happy children running through it once again.

Craven yanked her out of the chair and she pushed his plaid aside as he sat her on his lap, piercing her gently with his shaft.

Espy wrapped her arms around his neck and before kissing him, whispered, "Plant a strong, strapping bairn, just like his da, inside me."

He kissed her and in no time they came together in a powerful climax that most certainly took root.

~~~

Early the next morning Craven received an urgent summons from Owen, asking that Craven come with haste. That was where he was on his way now, to MacVarish keep, his wife riding alongside him. She had refused to be left behind, insisting that Owen might need tending, though Craven knew it was an excuse. She was curious as to why Owen summoned her husband with such urgency.

Craven did not mind, though, he always preferred his wife at his side. It was where she belonged.

When they approached the village and Craven caught sight of a troop of about twenty warriors camped on the outskirts of the village, he signaled his warriors with an abrupt shake of his hand. Some of his warriors broke off and rode toward the troop and took up guard around them.

"Something is wrong?' Espy asked.

"A precaution," Craven said but felt uneasy. "You will remain by my side at all times while we are here."

Espy nodded and as they rode through the village, it became even more apparent that something had happened. The people mumbled and turned worried eyes on Craven. Something was wrong. Dreadfully wrong.

Owen MacVarish looked much better, though he was a bit pale when Espy and Craven entered the Great Hall. He did not wait for Craven to reach him, he hurried to his side.

Owen grabbed Craven's arm. "I do not believe he tells me the truth and I do not know what to do. Documents have already been signed, but now…" Owen shook his head. "This cannot be happening. It cannot be happening."

"The old chieftain is having a difficult time accepting the truth."

Craven and Espy turned to a man who had entered the Great Hall. He stood more than a head less than Craven, his body slim, his features pronounced, similar to that of the physician MacPeters. His dark hair matched his dark eyes and his green and yellow plaid, and white linen shirt wore no grime. And he held a rolled parchment in his hand.

"Who are you?" Craven demanded.

"I am Penley, husband of Owen MacVarish's niece Aubrey and heir to the Clan MacVarish and all its holdings."

Espy stared at the man, thinking she had not heard him correctly. He was claiming to be Aubrey's husband. That could not be possible and she shook her head along with Owen, who appeared perplexed himself.

Not so Craven.

"What proof do you have of this?" Craven demanded, trying to contain the anger that had surged in him upon hearing the man claim Aubrey had been his wife. It was not something he would believe. It was not something he wanted to believe.

Penley raised his hand, waving the rolled parchment he held in it. "I went to fetch this to prove to Owen that I speak the truth. Aubrey was my wife and since he claimed Aubrey his heir to the Clan MacVarish that would leave me heir when Owen passes."

Craven held his hand out to Penley, forcing the man to come to him and give him the proof.

Penley pasted a forced smile on his face and approached Craven, handing him the parchment. "You will see it is a valid document, signed and a proper seal affixed."

Craven pulled the tie from around the parchment and rolled it out. His eyes narrowed as he said, "What is this?"

"My apologies, but the young scribe wrote it in Latin," Penley said with a smug smile.

"That presents no problem," Espy said, leaning over her husband's arm to glance at the document. "I love reading Latin. It is such an old and beautiful language."

Craven stopped a smile from springing to his face. His wife was a wonder and he was so very proud of her.

"This does say you wed Aubrey before the eyes of God and man a year prior to when Craven and Aubrey wed." She did not mention the seal was official, her husband would see that for himself.

Craven shoved the document back at Penley. "If she was your wife why would she leave you and why did it take you so long to come for her?"

"I was called away, a matter I had to deal with for the Crown. It took longer than I expected and when I returned Aubrey was gone. There were matters to settle at home before I could begin my search for her. At first, I thought she took up residence at an abbey. Not finding her there, I continued on here, having recalled her telling me of her uncle Owen, her mother's brother." He bowed his head slightly. "It broke my heart to learn of her passing, though it was nothing of the shock I felt of learning she had wed another. Of course, it was an invalid marriage, since she was not free to wed."

"Owen will require more proof than the document alone," Craven said and Owen nodded, confirming Craven's demand. "You will need to produce the person who signed your document so that he may give us his word."

Anger flared in Penley's eyes. "The document should be sufficient proof."

"A document has already been signed granting me the Clan MacVarish and all its holdings. I will not see that nullified without proof positive of what you claim," Craven warned. "Since you made mention of attending to the matter for the Crown, I am sure someone there would agree that until solid proof is produced this matter cannot be settled. Though, perhaps I should ask my friend *Warrick* to speak to his friends at court."

Espy could have sworn she felt a shiver of fear run through the room at the mention of Warrick's name and she believed it even more so when she saw how badly Penley paled.

"I will send a missive immediately with your demand," Penley said, "though I plan on remaining here until he arrives to protect what is rightfully mine."

"I have given you no permission to camp on my property," Craven said.

"I am sure Owen would not mind me staying here until this matter is settled," Penley said with a nod to the old man.

"It is not for Owen to decide," Craven said. "Did you not hear me? The Clan MacVarish and all its holdings have been granted to me. It is mine. You are on my land."

Penley looked as if someone had just lanced him with a sword he appeared so shocked. He turned to Owen, though he was unable to speak.

"It is as Lord Craven says. He is now chieftain of the Clan MacVarish, all belongs to him," Owen confirmed. "You will need to seek permission from him to remain here or anything to do with this matter."

Penley found his voice, though an angry tremor ran through it when he spoke. "I request permission to remain here while this matter is being reviewed."

"I will not give you permission to remain here," Craven said and raised his hands to silence Penley when he went to protest. "You and your men will camp on the outskirts of the MacCara village where my warriors will keep watch over you."

"We are prisoners?' Penley asked insulted.

"Only if you give me reason," Craven warned.

"I have no fight with you, Lord Craven," Penley said.

"You would be wise to keep it that way," Craven urged. "Ready your men to leave, while I speak privately with Owen."

Anger shot like arrows from Penley's eyes and he kept his lips clamped tightly shut as he acquiesced with a nod and turned to stomp out of the Great Hall.

"This cannot be true," Owen said. "Aubrey was a kind and trustworthy woman. She would have never wed you if she had been wed to another."

Craven wanted to believe that. He did not want to think that his marriage to Aubrey had been nothing more than a lie. That she had not been the woman he believed her to be.

It was Espy who spoke up in defense of Aubrey. "Of course, he lies. Aubrey was a kind soul. She never would have married that fool, let alone wed another when she was not free to do so. He lies that is all there is too it," she said as if settling the matter there and then.

Owen smiled. "Now I know why Aubrey liked and admired you so much, but then my Aubrey knew a good and kind person when she met them."

"Of course she did, that was why she never wed that fool and it is why she wed Craven."

Owen looked to Craven, a tear in his eye, though a smile on his face. "You are a lucky man to have had two kind wives." He laughed softly. "Most men cannot even find one."

"I am grateful every day for the time I got to have Aubrey in my life and for fate bringing me Espy." Craven smiled as Espy slipped into his arm that he stretched out to hook around her waist. She always drifted into his arms easily and eagerly and he loved having her there.

"I am glad you are not leaving Penley here. I do not trust him," Owen said.

"Neither do I," Craven said. "He will not be going anywhere without my permission."

Owen bid Craven and Espy good-bye once outside the keep, thanking Craven profusely for all he had done for him. Owen's relief had already spread through the clan or perhaps it was seeing that Craven's warriors were escorting Penley's troop away that had the villagers sending smiles and nods to Craven and at Espy as they took their leave.

Craven kept himself and Espy a distance behind his warriors who followed behind Penley and his troop with six of his warriors followed behind the two of them.

"May I ask you a question?" Espy asked cautiously.

Craven turned to her surprised by the hesitation in her voice. "Need I remind you that you may ask me anything?"

"It is an intimate question concerning you and Aubrey."

"I said anything and I meant it," he assured her.

"Was Aubrey a virgin?"

"Aye, there was blood on the bedding. I remember Aubrey blushing because I had returned to our bedchamber unexpectedly and the servant lasses were removing the bedding to wash and they were giggling at the sight of the blood."

"If that is so then—"

"Then Penley's marriage, if there was one, was never consummated and is invalid," Craven finished, "though I would have no proof of it."

"You are an honorable man and your word respected. Besides, Aubrey got pregnant shortly after you wed, not so with Penley, and why would that be? They either were never husband and wife or he never consummated the marriage, invalidating it."

"You truly are a wonder, wife," Craven said, amazed at her intelligence and her resolve to help him prove Penley wrong.

"I love you too," she said and leaned over to kiss him.

Craven quickly grabbed her waist before she toppled off Trumble, though the horse seemed to adjust as if attempting to keep her from falling as well. He kissed her with haste, then reluctantly eased her back safely in her saddle. Later they would have time alone and he looked forward to it.

"There is something else I took note of," Espy said and Craven listened intently. "Owen said *he lies*, referring to Penley, and it reminded me of what Ober had said with his last breath... *lies*. I wonder if Penley killed Ober."

Chapter Thirty-one

Espy woke with a start as if someone had shouted in her head to wake up and when she did, she realized right away she was not in her husband's arms, which was where she was every night. She was alone. She sat up quickly to glance around the room and saw him standing naked next to the fireplace, his back to her.

The fire's light flickered over his body, highlighting his broad shoulders, taut backside, and muscled legs. His arm was draped over the corner of the roughhewn mantel and his head was bent slightly.

Espy did not hesitate, she scurried out of bed and went to him, pressing her naked body against his as she slipped her arms around him, not that she could fit them all the way around him, but it did not matter. Her intention was to hug him, let him know that no matter what troubled him she was there for him. He was not alone.

A smile tempted Craven, though it did not reach his face, when he felt his wife's breasts press against his naked back and when her arms wrapped around him and gave him a comforting squeeze, his heart melted. He took hold of her arm and eased her around him to hug her against him with his one arm.

She laid her head on his chest and they remained like that for a few moments until Espy pressed a kiss to his chest and looked up at him. "Something troubles you." She had been waiting for this, had expected it when they had retired for the evening, but it was not talk he had been interested in when the door to their bedchamber had closed. They had made love slowly, enjoying each other, touching and kissing, stroking the intimate places that always brought them so much pleasure. Sleep had claimed them after that and now Craven's thoughts, she knew he had tried so hard to ignore, poked at him.

"Tell me," she urged when he did not respond.

He remained stubborn. "It is nothing."

"Something woke you," Espy insisted, "as it woke me."

Still he remained silent.

"Penley tells you lies," Espy said, hoping her words would nudge him enough to talk and just when the silence hung so heavy, she feared she had failed... he spoke.

"What of Aubrey? Did she lie as well?"

"Aubrey loved you," Espy said.

He shook his head and turned his gaze to the flames. "How can I ever be sure of that? How can I not help but wonder if our marriage meant nothing to her?"

Espy's hand cupped her husband's strong jaw and turned his head, forcing him to look at her. "Aubrey loved you."

"Your words do not make it so."

"But her words do."

His arm came off the mantel, his hand taking hold of her wrist and tugging it away from his face. "What are you saying?"

"There is something I should have told you sooner, but I feared you would not believe me. I only hope you believe me now. Aubrey realized she was dying before I refused to admit it. She told me to tell you that she loved you that you made her the happiest she had ever been."

Craven let go of her and stepped away, turning his back on her. "You are just saying that to ease my troubled thoughts."

Espy did not want to tell him this part, it would hurt him, but it also might heal him. "She struggled desperately to speak her last words. '*Craven, you have a huge heart share it.*'"

Craven turned around so fast that Espy stepped back startled. His hand shot out, grabbing her arm. "Aubrey only said that to me when we were alone."

"Then you know the words were her own. You know that she loved you and nothing, no one, can take that away from you... unless you let them. As for me, I am so very grateful to Aubrey, for she freed the beast to love."

Craven pulled her against him. "Aubrey opened my heart to love, but you freed the beast to love." He lowered his lips to hers and kissed her gently, then rested his brow to hers. "I love you, Espy, now and always. You are forever mine."

Espy threw her arms around his neck and kissed him as if sealing his words forever with her lips. It was hours later before they both fell asleep in each other's arms.

~~~

Espy stood outside the healing cottage, enjoying the beautiful day. The sun was still shining and the scent of spring was blooming in the air. She had seen two people for minor ailments earlier and none since then. It made her feel good to know that none were in dire need of her. There were three births expected at the end of spring and three more in late summer. She hoped to soon be counting herself among the women who would give birth in winter, but time had yet to tell.

Her thoughts turned to Penley and how increasingly annoying he had become in the three days since his arrival. He did nothing but complain about how inhospitably he was being treated and that he had the right to remain at the MacVarish keep since it would be his one day.

Espy had told her husband that she was relieved that he had told Penley he could not stay at the MacVarish keep, since she feared he would have found a way to see Owen dead. Craven had confessed he thought the same himself. She only wished there was a way to get rid of the irritating man sooner.

Espy's face brightened and her heart skipped a beat when she caught sight of her husband headed her way. It was not only his fine features or the strength of him that melted her heart when she looked upon him, but how he let her know in words and deeds how much he loved her.

"Tula said that you sent her off for the day since there were few who needed tending, the sure indication of a skilled healer," Craven said as he came to a stop in front of her and bent down to give her a quick kiss. When he lifted his head, he smiled broadly. "I have news."

"Penley is leaving," she said, excitement stirring her words.

"My thoughts as well," he said, "but sadly no. I received a missive confirming what you and Innis had told me that Samuel MacBarnes died when you said he did. I wanted that proof so that no one could deny it."

Espy smiled softly. He was making sure she was safe form any accusations anyone might make and she loved him all the more for it. "It pleases me that there is proof and no one can say otherwise."

Craven placed his hands at his wife's waist and gave it a loving squeeze. Since no one needs you, I thought perhaps you would like to visit with your grandmother today. I am going to see Roark and I can see you safely to your grandmother's and retrieve you on my way back."

Espy scrunched her brow. "What takes you to see Roark?"

"Nothing in particular. I want him to know that I am keeping a close watch on him."

"Perhaps you should have him and some of his men come to the keep one day. One look at them and the black robes they wear, might have Penley thinking differently, perhaps even taking his leave." When she caught his grin, she laughed and playfully poked him in the chest. "That was your intention all along."

"I have given it thought," he confessed.

"I think it is a very good thought and you should go see to it immediately while I visit with Cyra, and perhaps Innis would like to go as well."

"He has already left. I believe he has visited with Cyra almost every day since meeting her," Craven said with a chuckle.

"Well he did come to learn from her," Espy reminded, then chuckled herself. "He does seem besotted."

They were about to walk off when one of Craven's warriors approached in quick strides.

"What is it, Stuart?" Craven asked in haste, seeing the worried look in the young warrior's eyes.

"It is Netty, my lord. She is in pain, but the bairn is not due for several weeks yet."

"I will be right along, go to your wife," Espy said and Stuart bobbed his head to them both and hurried off. She turned to her husband with a sigh. "Go and tell my grandmother I will visit with her soon. I will see you when you return."

She went to kiss his cheek and Craven scooped her around the waist with his arm and lifted her off the ground to plant a hungry kiss on her lips. He ended the kiss abruptly, leaving her breathless and confused.

"I will finish that later, wife," he said and walked off.

Espy smiled and pressed her fingers to her lips, plumped from his ravaging kiss and was eager for later to get here sooner. She jumped when she recalled Netty and hurried to collect what she needed, then hurried off.

It did not take long to determine that Netty and Stuart's bairn was not arriving early, but just to be safe, she told

Netty not to do anything too strenuous and too rest when she could until the bairn finally did decide to arrive.

Espy returned to the healing cottage to take advantage of the beautiful day and work in the garden. She stopped a moment when she thought she heard someone call her name, not hearing anything, she turned to reach for the hoe when she heard it again, her name being carried softly on the light breeze. She recognized the voice. She looked around casually and returned a wave to two women a short distance away. When they were out of sight and before anyone else came into view, she hurried behind the healing cottage.

Once there, she stepped into the woods and called out softly, "Adara."

The young woman appeared from behind a thick tree trunk, looking much too pale. She hurried to her side and with an arm around Adara, she helped her to the cottage. She had her stretch out on the narrow bed and quickly put a hand to her brow to check for fever. There was none.

"Are you in any pain?" Espy asked, pulling a chair beside the bed to sit.

Adara shook her head and turned her head away from Espy.

Espy placed a gentle hand on Adara's arm and she jumped, but she did not yank it away. "Let me and my husband help you." Adara's eyes turned wide and she looked ready to spring off the bed and run, but Espy kept a firm hand on her. "You cannot keep running. Whoever hunts you will eventually find you. You will be safe here under Craven's protection."

"Never safe," she whispered.

Espy shook her head. "That is not true. Craven will keep you safe. I have told him about you." She had to keep a firmer hold on Adara when she heard that. "He has agreed to help you. He even told me he would make certain you are not returned to Warrick's dungeon."

"Truly?" she asked hesitantly.

"Aye," Espy confirmed. "Craven will protect you and you will have the safety of the clan around you. You will finally have a home and need not fear anymore."

Adara's stomach gurgled.

"Have you eaten today?" Espy asked concerned.

Adara shook her head.

"I am going to feed you and then we will go to the keep and I will show you where you will stay until this is settled and a cottage can be found for you. Later when Craven returns, you can talk with him."

Espy was relieved when Adara nodded, and she got busy fixing a hot broth for the young woman along with a chamomile brew. She wanted to ask Adara if she knew anything about the man who brought her to Warrick's dungeon, but she worried she would frighten her away if she knew the man had been here and had been murdered. It would be better if she waited to discuss all that with Adara until Craven returned.

Adara just finished the broth and the brew when Espy heard Tass shout her name. She hurried outside, closing the door behind her.

"It is Owen, an accident," Tass said.

"Can you send word to Craven and get warriors to escort me to MacVarish keep?" she asked.

"A messenger is already on his way to Craven and warriors will be ready soon to escort you," Tass said.

"Let me get my things," Espy said and returned inside the cottage to a frightened Adara. "I will take you to the keep and leave you there where you will be safe."

Adara shook her head. "I go with you."

Espy knew Adara well enough to know she would not stay with strangers. She felt safe with Espy and that was where she would stay or else Espy chanced her running away again.

"I stay with you," Adara said again, ringing her hands together.

Espy cupped her hands around Adara's small ones. "You stay with me. We will ride Trumble together." She was surprised to see Adara smile, then she recalled how much she had enjoyed the tales about Trumble.

Adara stayed close to her side when they left the cottage.

It was not shock that had Tass and six warriors staring at Adara or the fact that they were surprised when Espy explained that Adara was an old friend who had arrived for a visit, an unlikely tale if she ever heard one. No, it was Adara's beauty, her soft smile, she rarely wore, but then she was looking at Trumble, that had their mouths hanging agape.

Adara rode with Espy on Trumble and it seemed to calm her. She was surprised to see that Penley and a few of his warriors were not at the camp when they passed it, but then Craven could not keep them prisoners. They were free to leave if they wished, but where had Penley gone?

Espy felt a sudden chill and would be glad when her husband returned and met them at the MacVarish keep. She did not trust Penley.

Lies.

Ober's last word rang in her head like a tolling bell. She had felt his last word had been one of warning. Did that mean that someone he had trusted betrayed him and what he sought in the end was revenge... *lies.* Ober warned of lies and Espy intended to take his warning seriously.

Adara kept at Espy's side when they entered the keep and she stayed to the shadows when they entered Owen's bedchamber, as if she preferred to disappear.

Owen was sitting up in bed, his head resting against a pillow, and his eyes closed when Espy approached and saw that his foot rested on a pillow and that his ankle was swollen badly and had turned purple.

"An unfortunate accident."

Espy turned to see his eyes open.

"It is quite painful to even try to attempt to walk on it."

"I can only imagine," Espy said. "At least there are no bones protruding from the skin, though a bone may be broken inside. I am going to make a comfrey poultice for it, which will need to be applied fresh three times a day and you will have to stay off it for some time, so whatever is going on inside the ankle can heal. Rest, while I go fix the poultice."

Owen titled his head to the side, looking past her at the shadows that stirred. "Have you brought someone with you?"

"A friend," Espy said.

Owen smiled. "Anyone who is a friend of yours certainly is a friend of mine and welcome in my home."

"Adara," Espy called out, hoping the young woman would not be too frightened to step forward. "Come and meet Owen. He is a good and kind man." When Adara did not seem as if she would respond, Espy looked to Owen. "She is shy."

"You are safe here. No one will harm you," Owen offered.

His words or perhaps it was he was his gentle and encouraging tone that had Adara emerge slowly from the shadows and take tentative steps toward Espy. When she reached the bed side, she pushed the hood to her cloak off her head.

Owen gasped and all color drained from his face. "Oh my God, Faline!" Tears sprang to his eyes. "You are the exact image of my sister."

Chapter Thirty-two

"You have her dark blue eyes like the sky before a storm and your hair is touched by the sun with a trace of fire, a fire she had in her soul for adventure. You are even petite like her. It is as if I am looking upon my sister, you are the perfect image of her," Owen said, a tear running down the corner of his one eye. "Did my sister give birth to another child after she left here?"

Adara shook her head. "I have no family."

"You do now," Espy said, stepping beside her. "You are part of the Clan MacCara. You are family."

"Do you remember your sister Aubrey?" Owen asked.

"I have no sister," Adara said.

"You must be my sister's child. You are the image of her. It is as if she lives again through you," Owen insisted.

Espy could see that Adara was ready to flee and she did not want that. She was still pale and she was sure the young woman needed rest and sleep, having been running and hiding since last she had seen her.

"Rest, Owen," Espy said. "Adara will help me with the poultice and we can talk about this later."

"Aye, we will talk, for this young woman is of my blood and my clan and my land will go to her."

His words echoed through Espy's head and pieces began to fall into place. It was a perfect reason to want Adara dead. The only heir left to the Clan MacVarish. She could not wait until Craven arrived to tell him. He would want even more to protect Adara when he learned she was Aubrey's sister. It would make sense. A younger child with no memory of her parents, perhaps separated from her sister when she was young. It would do Craven's heart good to protect Adara. It would be like saving Aubrey.

Adara once again followed close to Espy until they entered the kitchen. There were far too many people there. People Adara did not know. Did not trust. She got Adara busy helping her make the poultice, keeping her hands and mind occupied, until more people crowded the room. Espy could see that Adara would run if she did not get her out of there soon. She instructed one of the servants on how to finish the poultice and how to apply it to Owen's ankle, then she took Adara outside.

The sky had turned bleak, the sun having vanished along with the pleasant day. She took her far enough away from the kitchen for her to feel comfortable. She wished Craven was there. She needed to tend Owen, but she also needed to see Adara kept safe.

"We should not stay out here long," Espy said, feeling unnerved by the quiet woods a short walk from them, though Adara looked at the dense forest with eagerness. It had turned into a place of safety for her and she looked ready to escape to it once again. "It is not safe for us here alone. We will return to Owen's bedchamber and wait for my husband to arrive," Espy said, hoping to encourage Adara and ease her worries.

For a moment, Adara appeared as if she could not decide, her eyes intent on the woods, then to Espy's relief, she nodded.

They turned to walk back to the kitchen when without warning hands came down on their mouths and arms wrapped tightly around their waists to drag them away into the woods.

Instinct had both women fighting, but it was futile, they could not break free.

The hands continued to hold them strong, forcing them along in the woods. If only her mouth was not covered, Espy could whistle for Trumble. He would come and help them.

After what seemed a distance the warriors who held them shoved them loose and Espy tried to catch Adara before she tumbled to the ground, but she could not stop herself from falling to the ground as well. She landed beside Adara and they both scurried to their feet, their arms locking tightly around each other.

"It was sheer accident or perhaps my good luck that the fool Ober came across you here," Penley said, a sneer twisting his lips. "He recognized you from Warrick's dungeon and thought that Adara might come to you for help. He was here to do away with my fool cousin who thought himself a physician and who I had no doubt would eventually spill the truth to Craven. I knew you had to have something to do with Adara's escape. I had it all planned and you ruined everything. You had to free her. You could not let it be."

"I do not know you," Adara said, as if trying to make sense of what was happening.

"You do not remember me," Penley said, "but I remembered being told of you. You were barely two years when your mum landed on my aunt's doorstep. She was ill and had no place to go. Her husband had died. She asked my uncle to take you to her brother. That he would give him a generous reward for bringing his niece safely to her. She told him and my aunt all about the Clan MacVarish and when last she had seen her brother.

"My aunt was not a trusting soul and did not believe her and either did my uncle. Neither wanted another mouth to feed, but there was no one who would take you. You became Adara. Oddly enough, or perhaps it was a stroke of luck, my aunt and uncle's only child was named Aubrey and my aunt wanted no confusion. It took until you were four to find a family who would take you. I learned all this upon a visit to my aunt and uncle several years after you were gone. My uncle was dead and my aunt close to it. My cousin was the only one left and one night she told me the story about you. She thought perhaps that we could find you and return you home, make up for what her mum should have done. She tempted me with the possibility of a reward, claiming she wanted none of it. But then she was always too kind for her own good. I, however, realized there was so much more to gain than just the reward, so I devised a plan."

"You had your cousin take Aubrey's identity," Espy said as more pieces fell into place. "How did you get her to agree?"

"I threatened her life in unspeakable ways unless she obeyed me. The mistake I made was that I believed her as weak as my aunt. She married that hulking beast to best me and get MacVarish land for herself."

"The mistake you made," Espy corrected, "was underestimating Aubrey's caring heart that had her falling in love and marrying a man who would protect her and one you could not frighten."

Penley sneered at the thought. "She was a fool if she thought to betray me. I followed her every move and when she got pregnant I adjusted my plan, which turned out to be so much better, for it meant I would not have to suffer Aubrey as my wife until I could have done away with her." He waved his hand. "Enough of this. You both need to die."

"The woman and Ober worked with you?" Espy asked, wanting to keep him talking, wanting time for someone to find them, preferably her husband. He would be close by now, at least she hoped he was.

"She worked with Ober, I had no use for her, and they are both where I intended them to be once I no longer needed them... dead."

Espy shook her head. "Why go after Adara when she does not even know you, know any of what had happened when she was a mere bairn?"

"One thing I learned is that you never leave anything behind that may return to haunt you one day. Adara would always be there lurking, the last piece of truth that could be found and could have destroyed everything I gained."

"In the end, it destroyed you anyway," Espy said. "You think my husband will not find out? That he will not come after you?"

"He will not find out. Your bodies will never be found. He will always wonder and he will retreat into grief once again and I will find a way to get his clan and his land. It all truly worked out even better than I had planned."

He caught Espy unaware as he lunged toward Adara, his dagger drawn, and instinct had her jumping in front of the young woman.

The pain struck her fast, her eyes turning wide as she realized the dagger had pierced her side. She rushed her hand there and her warm blood spilled through her fingers. She tried to stay on her feet, but her strength was fading. She crumpled to the ground, feeling Adara, trying to ease her fall. She tried to speak, warn her to run when a tremendous roar ripped through the air.

Only a beast could make such a terrifying sound and as she collapsed to the ground and descended into darkness, her husband's name spilled in a whisper from her lips, "*Craven.*"

Craven and Roark's warriors were on Penley's men before they could move and with power born of fury Craven unleashed the beast, flew off his horse, and descended on Penley.

Shock froze Penley and too late he raised his arm to ward off Craven.

Craven grabbed it and gave it a quick twist, the born snapping for all to hear as Penley let out a horrific cry of pain.

"I am going to tear you apart limb from limb," Craven threatened.

Penley was fighting the pain as he cried out, "Aye, tear me apart like the beast you are as your wife lays dying."

Craven looked to where Epsy lay lifeless, Adara's small hand covered in blood where it lay pressed against Espy's wound. He let out another roar that rumbled like thunder across the land, then with vicious ease, broke nearly every one of Penley's limbs, leaving the man useless to defend himself. Craven extended no mercy when Penley begged for it as he lie at Craven's feet a broken mess. Without a word, Craven viciously snapped Penley's neck and let his body fall in a heap to the ground, stepping over it as he ran to his wife.

He yelled for someone to get Cyra, fear gripping him as he looked at Adara's hand covered in blood as she tried to stop Espy's blood from flowing out of her.

Craven refused to wait, refused to let death win. He would fight it as Espy did, fight for her. He lifted her in his arms and rushed through the woods to the MacVarish keep and up the stairs to a bedchamber. He laid her on the bed and hunched down beside it, taking hold of her hand that was covered with blood. More blood spilled out of her side and all he could think about was the day Aubrey had died and the blood that surrounded her.

"Do not leave me, Espy. I love you. I cannot lose you. Please fight to live, Cyra is coming. She will help you."

"No time."

He almost did not hear her and he was elated when her eyes drifted open, though she was pale, much too pale.

"No time," she struggled to say. "Stop the bleeding now." She groaned. "Sear the wound." She groaned again. "Now... or I will die."

Adara had followed behind Craven and heard Espy's plea. "Hurry," she urged Craven and began tearing Espy's blouse away from the wound.

Craven was quick to hand her his dagger so that she could cut the blouse away, then he took his sword and stuck it into the flames in the fireplace and left it there to return and help Adara.

"Now, Craven, now," Espy said her breathing so shallow she could barely be heard.

Craven grabbed his sword, the blade burning hot and he did not hesitate, he laid it upon the wound and Espy screamed out and descended into darkness once more.

~~~

Espy fought to open her eyes, to escape the heavy fog that seemed to have hold of her. There then there was the pain, the endless pain, though it had eased some of late. She finally managed to get one eye opened and when she saw her husband slumped, asleep in a chair beside her bed, her other eye popped open. Everything came rushing back to her.

"Craven," she said her hoarse voice barely getting his name out, though it was enough to wake him. The shock on his face brought a smile to hers and with effort she reached her hand out to him.

Craven took hold of her hand that she struggled to offer him and leaned down and kissed it. "I was so frightened I would lose you."

She went to speak and coughed, then groaned from the pain in her side.

Craven immediately grabbed a tankard from the bedside table and gently lifted her head to bring the tankard to her lips.

Espy drank gratefully from it.

"It is a brew your grandmother has been giving you." He was pleased to see her smile again after she finished drinking.

"You seared the wound," Espy managed to say, recalling the last memory she had before darkness claimed her.

Craven took her hand again in both of his. "I have done many difficult things in my life, but they were nothing compared to placing my scorching blade to your flesh."

"You saved my life."

"So Cyra and Innis both told me."

"Adara, Penley—"

"Do not worry, Adara is safe and Penley is where he deserves to be... dead."

"Has Adara told you all of it?" Espy asked, her eyes growing heavy and fighting to keep them open.

"We can talk of all that another time. You need to rest, sleep, and heal," he said, seeing her fight to remain awake. He leaned over and kissed her brow. "I will be here when you wake."

His words soothed her as did his tender kiss and she surrendered to sleep, knowing it was best for her.

Espy woke again to find her husband right where he had said he would be and Cyra sat beside him in another chair.

Craven's hand immediately took hold of hers.

"You do much better, Espy," her grandmother assured her. "I am proud of you. As soon as I learned that you told Craven to sear the wound, I knew what had happened. You felt the blade slip through you smoothly and realized it had not hit anything vital, so you wisely told your husband to sear the wound closed so you would not bleed to death, the wise healer that you are."

Craven cringed at the thought of the blade slipping through her flesh and he wanted to kill Penley all over again.

Espy nodded, smiled, and squeezed her husband's hand. "It was the only way, and I knew you would see to tending me after that."

"Innis, Tula, and Adara has helped as well," Cyra said. "All are concerned about you and those at the MacCara keep cannot wait for you to return home."

"How long have I been here at the MacVarish keep?"

"Three days," Craven said, "and you will be staying here until your grandmother says it is all right for you to return home."

"As long as you are with me, husband, it does not matter where I am," Espy said.

"I am not going anywhere. You will get sick of me soon enough."

"Never," she said and her stomach gurgled.

"You are hungry," Cyra said, a grin spreading across her face. "That is good news."

"It is?" Craven asked anxiously.

Cyra nodded. "Very good news. It means the wound is healing well. I will go get some food for you, granddaughter." She stood and leaned over Espy to kiss her brow. "You put a fear in me, but you will do well now."

"Aye, I will, *Seanmhair*," Espy said just the touch of her grandmother's loving hands was all the healing she needed.

"I believe the woman would have given her life for you if she could have," Craven said with admiration for Cyra. "I am relieved that she will be here to tend you when you give birth to our many bairns."

"Many?" she said with a soft smile.

"Aye, many, for I will not be able to keep my hands off you." He kissed her hand he held. "It is an incentive for you to get well."

"I will have a speedy recovery knowing that," she said with a laugh then winced.

"I have caused you pain," he said, guilt stabbing at him.

"A pleasant pain, and one fair less painful than before," she assured him.

Seeing how alert she was, fatigue not haunting her, he asked, "Tell me about Penley. Adara could only say so much. I think she fears me."

"She does not trust easily, especially men and from

what Penley told us, no one wanted her after her mum died and she was passed on to whoever would take her." She squeezed her husband's hand. "She is part of our family now."

"That she is," Craven confirmed.

Espy shared with her husband all that Penley had told her.

"I am sorry that Aubrey did not confide this to me," Craven said upon, hearing it.

"I believe she was too frightened at first and then—"

"Aubrey believed I could keep her safe."

"You would have if she had told you about Penley, but fear often causes us to do foolish things. Or perhaps Aubrey felt as if she were protecting you, keeping you safe from her deranged cousin. We will never know, and I believe Aubrey would be pleased that Adara finally found her way home."

Craven nodded. "Owen wants me to oversee his clan and land, and turn it all over to Adara when she finds a husband of her choosing."

"That will be a long time coming. Adara trusts no man."

"Hopefully, time will heal her wounds and until then I will make sure she is kept safe," Craven said.

"I told her you would do just that," Espy said with pride in a man that was no beast but a loving soul.

"Did Penley say anything about the true physician, Edward MacPeters?" Craven asked.

"No, but I would assume that Penley hired a few men to attack MacPeters group, kill him and all those with him so no witness was left and instill his cousin in MacPeters place. He had said his cousin fancied himself a physician and with him having mentioned Samuel MacBarnes, I would think that he had had some dealings with physicians. Though, I suspect it was Penley who had given him the pouch with the deadly mix to give to Aubrey. He had mentioned that his plan had changed once she wed you and for the better for him, he had claimed."

"I am glad I got to kill him, got to avenge Aubrey's death, take revenge what he had done to Adara, and what he did to you. I only wish I could have made him suffer more."

Espy slipped her hand out of his and rested it against his cheek. "It is done and over with. You know the truth and now Aubrey —"

Craven kissed the palm of her hand. "Can rest in peace because I can finally let her go."

Chapter Thirty-three

Thunder and lightning played in the sky like two irate bairns. Rain would fall soon and soak the land, turning it a deeper green and flowers were already sprinkling it with their vibrant colors. Espy took cautious steps to the keep. It had been several weeks since Penley had run his dagger through her and while she was feeling much better and her wound had healed nicely, she knew it would be wise to be cautious, especially since she realized... she smiled and hugged herself as she walked.

She was with child and could not be happier, and she was eager to share the thrilling news with Craven.

All had been quiet since the mystery of Aubrey's death had finally been laid to rest. Adara was doing well, visiting with Owen and getting to know him. He wanted her to live there with him, at her home, but she was not comfortable with that yet. Craven had settled her in a small cottage near the healing cottage. It was tucked away from the others and she found it quite to her liking. She would help at the healing cottage every now and then, but mostly she kept to herself.

Craven had also spoken to Roark about Adara and asked to settle any debt she owed so that she would be free of worry from Warrick. Roark had left with his men, Warrick having summoned him home and he had given his word to Craven that he would discuss the matter with Warrick.

Her smile grew as she thought about her grandmother and Innis. She was thrilled that her grandmother had found love after all these years alone. Cyra laughed at herself, telling Espy that she was like a young besotted woman in love and it was a glorious feeling. Innis treated her wonderfully and the two could not be happier.

"That is a beautiful smile, wife. What makes you so happy?" Craven asked as he approached her, spreading his arms wide.

"You," she said and hurried into his welcoming arms.

"I am glad to hear that or I would have been jealous elsewise." He kissed her gently. "I came to fetch you before the storm strikes." He glanced up at the angry sky as lightning flashed. "Come, we need to get inside." The first splatter of rain hit Espy's cheek and Craven scooped her up and hurried to the keep.

Once inside, Espy whispered, "I think I need a nap... will you join me?"

Craven's response was to rush up the stairs and to their bedchamber.

They made love slow and lazy as the thunderstorm pounded outside and when they rested in each other's arms, Espy took her husband's hand and laid it on her stomach.

"He will be big and strong like his da." She was surprised when she got silence from him, then suddenly he sat up, scooped her up in his arms, and placed her on his lap.

"You carry our bairn?" he asked as if he could not quite believe it.

"Aye, I do," she said with a smile.

His hand went to rest on her scar the searing had left. "He was not hurt?"

Espy shook her head. "No, the injury was nowhere near where he is tucked safely away." She kissed his lips gently. "The beast battled death for me and our bairn and won. I love you more than words can say. My heart is yours and always will be."

A low growl rumbled in Craven's chest as he whispered, "Aye, your heart is mine, you are mine, and I will love you even when there is no breath left in me and far beyond that. You are my life, Espy. We will share laughter, tears, love and sorrow together… always together."

As he pressed his lips to hers, Espy heard her grandmother's words whisper in her head.

Go home to where your heart is.

She was home… she was finally home.

Titles by Donna Fletcher

Highland Warriors Trilogy
To Love A Highlander
Embraced By A Highlander
Highlander The Demon Lord

The Pict King Series
The King's Executioner
The King's Warrior
The King and His Queen

Macinnes Sisters Trilogy
The Highlander's Stolen Heart
Highlander's Rebellious Love
Highlander: The Dark Dragon

Cree & Dawn Series
Highlander Unchained/Forbidden Highlander
Highlander's Captive
My Highlander

Cree & Dawn Short Stories
Highlander's True Love
Highlander's Promise
Highlander's Winter Tale
Highlander's Rescue

Warrior King Series
Bound To A Warrior
Loved By A Warrior
A Warrior's Promise
Wed To A Highland Warrior

Sinclare Brothers' Series

Return of the Rogue
Under the Highlander's Spell
The Angel & The Highlander
Highlander's Forbidden Bride

The Irish Devil
Irish Hope

Isle of Lies
Love Me Forever

For a complete list of Donna's titles, visit her website.
www.donnafletcher.com

About the author

It was her love of reading and daydreaming that started USA Today bestselling author Donna Fletcher's writing career. Besides gobbling up books, her mom generously bought for her, she spent a good portion of her time lost in daydreams that took her on grand adventures. She met heroes and villains, and heroines that, while usually in danger, always found the strength and courage to prevail. She traveled all over the world and through time in her dreams. Some places and times fascinated her more than others and she would rush to the library (no Internet at that time) and read all she could about that particular period and place. After a while, she simply could not ignore all the adventures swirling around in her head. She had no choice but to bring them more vividly to life, and so she started writing.

Donna continues to daydream, characters popping in and out of her head wherever she goes and filling her with tales that keeps her writing schedule on overload. You can learn more about her on her website.

Donna enjoys living on the beautiful Jersey shore surrounded by family and friends and a cat who thinks she's a princess, but what cat doesn't, and a dog who bows to the princess's demands.

Made in the USA
Middletown, DE
17 September 2025